THE
WHITE
FORTRESS

THE
WHITE
FORTRESS

TALES OF THE LAWLESS LAND: BOOK III

BOYD ✝ BETH
MORRISON

An Aries Book

9 7 5 3 1 2 4 6 8

A catalogue record for this book is available from the British Library.

ISBN (HB): 9781035902095
ISBN (E): 9781035902064

Cover images: Maxim Obsidianbone
Cover design: Simon Michele | Head of Zeus

Map design: Jeff Edwards

Typeset by Siliconchips Services Ltd UK

Printed and bound in Great Britain by
CPI Group (UK) Ltd, Croydon CR0 4YY

Head of Zeus Ltd
First Floor East
5–8 Hardwick Street
London ECIR 4RG

WWW.HEADOFZEUS.COM

For our dad, who would have loved that we became novelists.

The Eastern Mediterranean 1351

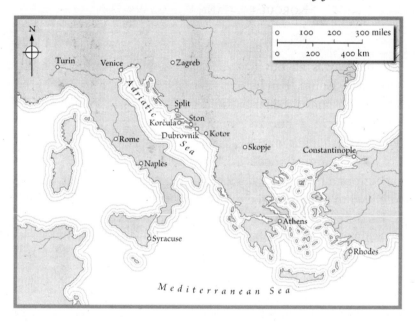

Prologue

The battle was all but lost, but he knew the captain wouldn't surrender. Ennio, barely out of boyhood, watched with both admiration and disbelief as the legendary explorer Marco Polo, resplendent in a fine red tunic and a neatly trimmed beard, continued to bark orders to the crew. Although the warship Polo had commissioned with his family's money was forced to run aground on a rock off Korčula Island, it was obvious that he intended to fight until the very last moment.

Ennio didn't really understand the reason Venice was at war with Genoa or why the two city-states had sent their fleets to battle off the coast of Dalmatia, although he knew it had something to do with trade and money. But when his stern and brutish father had secured a position for him to serve on Marco Polo's ship, he'd gratefully thrown himself into the opportunity to escape his home.

The only other sailor on the *Scopritore* close to Ennio's age was Aurelio, also from Venice. Though they were the same height, Aurelio was more muscular, with a fresh scar on his cheek from an encounter with an older sailor he had laughed at when they were departing Venice.

They loaded another ball of wood chips and straw held together by pitch into the iron launcher of the still-functioning trebuchet mounted on the stern of the ship. Then Ennio and Aurelio stepped back to let the pitchman smear the ball with tar.

"Can't *Milione* see the battle is lost?" Aurelio complained quietly, using the nickname Venetians bestowed on Polo after he'd returned from Cathay and reported that the wealth of Kublai Khan could be counted in the millions.

"Captain Polo knows what he's doing," Ennio replied.

"Then why have we crashed into this shoal?"

"He might be planning to draw them in."

Aurelio shook his head as the tarball was set on fire. "Look around, you fool. We'll be taken prisoner for sure if the *Scopritore* doesn't sink first."

Ennio had to admit that possibility, no matter how much he believed in his master. Most of the Venetian ships had been sunk already, either from the efficient ramming techniques of the Genoans or from the fires set by blazing arrows and tarballs tossed by enemy catapults. Polo's was one of the few left. Still, he wasn't going down without a fight.

From his position at the stern bulwark, the majestic Polo dropped his raised arm and cried, "Loose!"

The trebuchet's rope was released, and the mechanism wound around, flinging the flaming tarball toward one of the approaching warships. It slammed into the mainsail, setting the canvas aflame.

Ennio leaped in exultation. "You see?" he said, slapping Aurelio on the shoulder. "We still have a chance."

Aurelio pointed at the two other ships closing on them. "You're a simpleton if you believe that. We have to surrender or die."

Polo ordered the trebuchet to be reset and another tarball to be loaded. But for the first time, Ennio saw gloom on the famed explorer's face, and he understood why. The enemy ships would be upon them before the trebuchet could launch again. Aurelio was right. They would either be captured or annihilated.

The captain locked eyes with Ennio, who was transfixed by the sudden connection. *Milione* picked up the satchel by his side and dashed across the aftcastle to pull both Ennio and Aurelio aside by their tunics. Despite his earlier bluster, Aurelio was now quaking at being directly addressed by the great man.

"I have a mission for you two," Polo said quickly. "It's risky, but you have the best chance to evade these Genoese swine."

"We are ready to obey, captain," Ennio said. Aurelio simply nodded, his twitchy right eye betraying his fear at what their dangerous task might be.

Polo lifted a satchel and held it out to Ennio, who took it from him.

"These are the writings of my travels to Cathay and back," he said. "The Genoans may destroy these volumes if they capture me, and my decades abroad will count for nothing. I'm trusting you to keep them safe. If you can, return them to my family in Venice."

Ennio held the precious satchel close to his chest, but when he pressed it against him, something didn't feel right. He'd never held a book before, but there only seemed to be one object inside the bag even though *Milione* indicated there should be more than one. Ennio opened it and peeked inside. He saw a single manuscript about the size of a thick slice of bread tightly sealed by clasps.

"Captain," he said, "I see only one book."

Polo scowled and ripped the satchel from him, cursing when he confirmed Ennio's count.

"That useless barnacle brought me only one of them." He thrust the bag into Aurelio's arms. "You. Take that and make the dinghy ready. Ennio, you know where my cabin is. Run there and get the other book." He turned to look at the Genoese ships racing toward them, then back at Ennio. "You still have time. Go!"

"Yes, captain!" Ennio raced for the door under the aftcastle. Polo's cramped cabin was down a short corridor.

He burst through and frantically searched for the book. He took a moment to look through the lone porthole and saw the Genoese warship looming large. Soldiers were massed on the deck, their swords and pikes at the ready to board. If he were still on the *Scopritore* when they arrived, he would certainly be caught. He couldn't let *Milione* down.

The small desk was covered with maps and drawings, but

there was no book. The trunk by the bed was closed, but the lock was open. Ennio ripped the lid open and started tossing out everything in the chest. Clothes, knives, waxed bag, silverware, a fragile-looking white container wrapped in cloth and painted with a long sinuous blue dragon. He even found several gold coins, and although it felt like stealing, he shoved the coins into the waxed bag to take with him since he would need funds to make it back to Venice and complete his mission. To bless his journey, he also took a small reliquary pendant with an image of Saint Blaise, putting it into the bag. Everything seemed to be in the room except a manuscript.

He lay down on the deck to look at the floor, but nothing. He couldn't go back to the captain empty-handed to ask where to find it. There simply wasn't time.

He sat on the bed, dejected, but a lump in the straw pallet underneath him got his attention. He stood and wrenched the mattress up, letting out a triumphant yell when he saw what he'd come for. The second book looked identical to the other, clasped tightly to protect the contents. He and Aurelio just had to get the manuscripts back to Venice so that the story of *Milione*'s incredible travels would be saved for history.

Ennio stuffed the manuscript into the waxed bag and slung it over his shoulder. He ran out and back onto the deck, sprinting for the bow where he'd seen the dinghy being lowered into the water. He was momentarily jolted off his feet as the Genoese ship rammed into the *Scopritore*. As he stood back up, soldiers from the enemy ship swarmed over the bulwarks. The Venetian sailors raced to meet them in hand-to-hand combat.

It wouldn't be long until the ship and everyone on board was taken. He made it to the bulwark of the ship and peered over the side, expecting to see Aurelio waiting for him below with the other precious manuscript.

He gasped when he saw Aurelio already rowing the dinghy away toward the shore of Korčula Island through the wooden remnants of other ships that had already been destroyed.

"Aurelio, come back!" Ennio cried out.

"You must be mad!" Aurelio shouted back as he pulled on the oars as hard as he could.

Ennio was so angry at the traitor that he could spit. "You filthy worm-head! I hope you rot!"

Aurelio ignored him and kept rowing. Ennio whirled around and spotted Marco Polo swinging his sword valiantly, but a Genoese soldier tackled him from behind, sending him to the deck. Three more men jumped on him, and the four hauled him to his feet, restraining the captain as they shouted in victory.

Polo looked around until he saw Ennio. He tilted his head toward the sea, indicating that Ennio should get to safety any way he could. Ennio nodded, bringing a satisfied look to Polo's face.

Bolstered by reinforcements from a second ship that had run up against the *Scopritore*, the Genoese soldiers were making quick work of the rest of the crew. Ennio had only moments until the entire deck was overrun.

He secured the bag in his grasp, took a deep breath, and leaped over the side of the ship. His stomach lurched as he fell, and he closed his eyes as his feet hit the water. He plunged down into the sea and kicked as hard as he could to get back to the surface.

His head came up and he took a huge breath. Thankfully, growing up in Venice he'd learned to swim at an early age, and even with the bag weighing him down, he was able to stay afloat. He saw a wooden plank not far away and paddled over to it, lifted the waxed bag onto it, and used the plank to keep his head above water.

He rotated until he was facing Korčula Island, intending to follow Aurelio that way, but he saw his betrayer rowing madly, his face etched in terror. Another rowboat with four Genoese sailors was in close pursuit.

Aurelio reached the shore safely and scrambled out of the water as soon as the dinghy was beached. He ran up the rocky shore with the satchel in his hands and disappeared into the thick woods.

Ennio couldn't follow him with those enemy sailors in the way. His only other choice was to swim for the opposite side of the narrow strait. If he could get there without being seen, the Genoans might not even know he'd escaped.

With his heart pounding and only the top of his head sticking out above the water's surface, he pushed the plank ahead of him as he kicked. The distance he had to go was forbidding, but he couldn't give up now.

Captain Marco Polo was counting on him to make it.

THE LURE

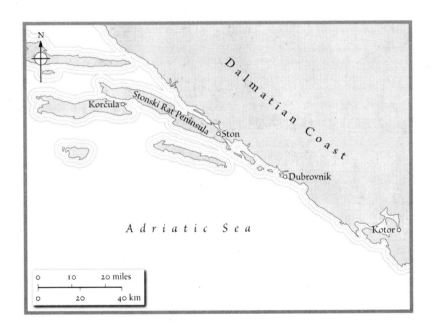

October, 1351

THE MEDITERRANEAN SEA

Willa, ginger root in hand, came up onto the *Viandante*'s deck to look for her husband. It was still strange to call Gerard that, and stranger still to think of herself as his wife. They'd been married for only a week, five days of which had been spent at sea. Although various adventures had forced them to pass themselves off as husband and wife as they'd traveled across Europe in the past months, she could now officially call herself Lady Fox. To be wedded to a knight was a far cry from her life as a lady's maid back in England.

The Venetian ship they had boarded in Lindos on the island of Rhodes was bound for the bustling port city of Dubrovnik, where they would be easily able to transfer to one heading to France, their ultimate destination. Their voyage was now stalled, however, so that the crew could make repairs to the mast before a squall arrived. They were currently anchored along the western coast of Albania, and the captain assured them that they would be underway as soon as the storm passed.

Willa found Gerard amidships, and her heart skipped a beat seeing him bathed in the few rays of the morning sun that peeked through the looming clouds. He was taller than any other man on the ship and far more handsome, and the memory of their wedding night together made her giddy. His shoulder-length brown hair danced in the breeze, and he stroked his full beard as the man beside him spoke.

Petar was a squat man bulging with muscles built from hard

manual labor. Tufts of thick hair poked out from the top of his tunic, and his skin was baked brown and leathery from days spent in the hot Mediterranean sun. A strong brow and nose canted to the right from some old injury made him look like a mauler instead of the thoughtful and kind man he was.

Gerard and Petar were using their common tongue of Italian. Although it was tiring to constantly speak in a foreign tongue, Willa was at least comfortable with the language after their weeks spent on the Italian peninsula. Petar had explained that, since most of the Dalmatian coast was part of the Venetian Republic, many of the residents spoke Italian in addition to their native Croatian dialect.

Fox spotted her and breathed a sigh of relief.

"Where did you find it?" he asked as he took the ginger root and began chewing on a morsel.

"It was in Zephyr's saddlebags, just where I told you it would be." It had actually been in the bags of her own horse, Comis, but she wasn't going to tell him she'd been wrong after insisting so vehemently where he should look.

"I'm sorry I've used up so much of your medicinal treasure," Petar said. "But I will say that it has made the return voyage from Rhodes much more pleasant on the open waters. The longest I'd been at sea before now was the two-day journey it takes to travel from my home in Ston to Dubrovnik."

The open sea didn't agree with Gerard's stomach either, so he'd secured a large amount of ginger before they'd departed. When he'd seen how green Petar had been during rough swells, he'd offered to share it with the Croatian. Together they'd gone through so much of it that Willa would have to trade for a fresh supply in Dubrovnik.

"Does Jelena need any?" Willa asked, gesturing toward Petar's wife, who was standing on the forecastle at the bow, alone, a simple cloak wrapped around her.

"She doesn't suffer from seasickness," Petar said.

"Neither does Willa," Gerard said. "It's quite annoying."

"We could ride on horseback to France from Dubrovnik, if you prefer," Willa said.

"Actually, you can't," Petar said. "The Dalmatian coast is much like this." He gestured up at the mountains rising nearly straight out of the sea. "Although Dubrovnik oversees Ston, you can only get between the two by a rough footpath, which is why we usually go by boat. You'd have to find a way inland and travel north through Bosnia, which I wouldn't recommend since the Serbian Empire and the Kingdom of Hungary are fighting over it."

Willa wondered if Petar's current journey had to do with the trouble that he and his wife claimed they were in. Despite her efforts to get them to open up on the voyage, it seemed they were unwilling to share their problems with people they hardly knew.

Jelena was especially anxious, often staring out at the sea as she was now, her lips moving in a silent prayer as she fondled a small reliquary tied around her neck by a leather cord.

"Is she all right?" Willa asked Petar.

Petar shrugged. "I doubt it. Only the Lord can help us now." He nodded at the two of them and went through the door to go below deck.

"Shall we take our morning practice while the ship isn't moving?" Gerard asked.

"You set up the targets," she said. "I'll be back in a moment."

Willa went up to Jelena, who barely acknowledged her presence. Instead of asking her directly about her problems, Willa reached into the neck of her own kirtle and drew out a pendant.

"I noticed your beautiful reliquary," she said. "I have one as well."

She showed Jelena the enameled case adorned with gems.

"It's lovely," Jelena said. "Is it something from your patron saint?"

"Yes. Saint Isabella. It contains a lock of the saint's hair and was given to me by my... friend. Her name was Isabel."

"Did you lose her to the Pestilence?"

It was a likely question since the Great Mortality had wiped out vast swaths of the European populace in the previous five years.

Willa nodded. "I miss her." She couldn't very well say that she was a former lady's maid and that her mistress had been killed in an escape from the brutal lord she was set to marry, much less that Willa had taken her lady's identity for a time.

"Thankfully, my hometown of Ston was spared the worst of it." Jelena hesitated for a moment, then proudly held up her reliquary for Willa to see. "This was given to me by my father. It holds a fingerbone of our town's patron, Saint Blaise."

The outside of the slim gilded wood case had an image of the saint standing, his hand raised in a blessing. Jelena opened it, and on the inside, a sliver of bone was nestled beneath rock crystal, while the lid opposite had a tiny painting of Saint Blaise reaching out to a child held by a kneeling mother.

"That's an image of the saint curing a child who was choking on a fish bone. Saint Blaise was martyred by the Romans soon after."

"I'm sure this comforts you in your troubles," Willa said.

"I thought it would guide us, but..." She trailed off, as if completing the sentence would extinguish all her hope.

"Perhaps my husband and I can help you."

"Yes, your offer was kind, and still is." She paused as if she might finally reveal the issue at hand, then said, "Our problem is too great for any single person to solve, and I wouldn't want you to interrupt your journey for a lost cause."

"You might be surprised to hear the ordeals we've overcome already."

"I'm sorry, but you can't help us. It was wrong for me to burden you with our troubles in the first place. Please, leave me in peace."

She began to cry quietly and turned back to looking out at the sea. Willa saw that it was fruitless to continue pestering her, so she left as she'd been asked.

When she returned to Gerard amidships, he had completed setting up the two hay bales marked with red painted circles.

"Anything?" he asked, glancing at Jelena.

Willa shook her head. "She's frightened of something, but she won't say what. Did you have any luck with Petar?"

"He was grateful for the ginger, but I think he doesn't trust me since I mentioned that we came most recently from Venice."

"But he knows you're English?"

Gerard nodded. "And partly French. I told him about my mother."

"Not the whole story, I hope." About his mother's abduction, how she was forced to bear a child and died during his half-brother's birth, about the resulting confrontation that led to Gerard's unjust excommunication. His alienation from the Church had taken its toll on both of them.

He chuckled mirthlessly. "He wouldn't believe me if I told him. We're just going to have to accept that we can't help everyone we meet, especially if they don't want it."

He picked up two bows and handed one to Willa. While his was a horseman's recurved bow brought back from the Crusades, hers was beautifully inlaid with a pattern of leaves made from ebony wood and ivory. It was one of the few remaining artifacts from the Templar treasure they'd discovered. She could barely comprehend all the fantastical adventures she'd already had in the short time she'd known Gerard. Having him encourage her to shoot with the bow was just another facet of her new life as his wife, and she needed the practice since she was still getting used to its weight and draw.

"Think you'll hit the target today?" he jested. She could tell he was trying to get her mind off Jelena.

"Perhaps we should raise the stakes," she replied, taking a bag of arrows from him.

"I like that. Say, a piece of gold for the one who gets all their arrows closest to the center of the target?"

"I was thinking of wagering something more intimate, but we can do that."

He flashed a rueful grin at her. Because sleeping quarters for the men and women were divided, they'd been chaste since boarding the crowded ship, which had been a hardship for both of them.

Gerard nodded at the crew, who had stopped working to watch their daily practice, and leaned closer to her, speaking in a low tone. "Ready to perform for our audience?"

"You'd think they'd be over seeing a woman shooting a bow by now."

"I think they're more interested in seeing if you can do it better than I can."

"Then let's find out."

Just like Gerard, Willa plucked three arrows from her bag, holding them between the fingers of her draw hand. Then she focused on her target at the bow end of the ship, propped against the bulwark of the forecastle. Both drew their strings.

"Loose!" Gerard shouted.

Using the technique he had taught her, one from the Holy Land that his father had passed down to him, she nocked the first arrow against the string, drew back, and loosed it at the target. While it was still in flight, she was already pulling back the string to launch the second arrow. Then she launched the third in the same fashion.

She lowered the bow and saw Gerard walking to the target to retrieve his arrows. No matter how fast she was, she couldn't match his speed, despite having hunted rabbits with a bow since she was a girl. Even though she knew Gerard had been practicing for years as a mounted archer, she still couldn't help being envious of his skill.

The crew who had been watching mumbled and shook their heads in wonder at the display from their passengers before going back to work.

Gerard turned when he reached the targets and smiled. It was clear why. Although the grouping of her arrows in the circle was respectable, his arrows were virtually touching each other at the center.

She trudged over to him.

"My gold piece, please," he said.

"Stop your gloating. After all, you only beat a woman." The wager was just for pride, really. They'd acquired enough gold from the Templar treasure to buy an entire estate back in England. The satchel containing the coins was well concealed in their belongings and was actually supplemental to their real valuables, the diamond, ruby, and emerald gems each of them had sewn into their undergarments.

"You mean I barely beat a novice," Gerard said. "You would have been victorious over most men with that grouping."

"I have a good teacher."

"And I have a good student."

"Careful," Willa said, walking closer to him. "This kind of sweet talk might get us into trouble."

"It would be worth it."

Before she could respond, they were interrupted by a crack of splitting wood high above. They looked up to see a sailor who was working on the repairs at the top of the yard. He was struggling to hold on to a damaged spar that threatened to break off. It was supported by a single rope.

The crew below, seeing the danger, scrambled to get out from beneath it. Willa ran aftward as well. She turned her head to ensure that Gerard was with her, but she was stunned to see that he had dropped his bow and was charging up the stairs of the forecastle.

Willa stopped and yelled, "Gerard!" but he was already up the steps and throwing himself at Jelena, who was oblivious to the danger above. With an even bigger crack, the spar finally came loose and swooped down, swinging on the line in an arc toward the bow.

Gerard tried to tackle Jelena to get her out of harm's way, but he was too late.

The spar struck them both, launching them over the side of the ship and into the churning waters of the bay.

 2

Fox burst through the water's surface and gasped for air. His back ached where the wooden spar had struck him, but he was more concerned about finding Jelena. He twisted in a circle until he saw her pop out of the water, flailing and coughing in the choppy sea.

As he swam to her, she caught enough breath to scream. Her words were in Croatian, so he understood none of them, but it looked as if she were having trouble staying afloat. Her sodden cloak and skirts were threatening to drag her under again.

When he reached her, she frantically tried to climb atop him in her panic. Fox deflected her to the side. He turned her around and put his arm around her to support her, untying the cloak from her neck to lessen the weight.

"Jelena, calm down," he said in Italian. "I've got you."

She thrashed for another moment before she realized she wasn't sinking.

"I don't want to die!"

"Can you swim?" he asked her.

"A little."

Although the mid-autumn water was chilly, it was warmer than he expected, so they weren't in immediate danger of freezing to death. He looked up at the ship. Willa was leaning out over the bulwark, but she was way too far above them to reach.

"We're going to lower a rope," she said. "Swim to us."

"You're going to have to help me, Jelena," Fox said, trying to keep a soothing voice despite his own fear that she might pull him down.

She nodded. He paddled awkwardly toward the *Viandante*, but he soon realized that he was being swept past the ship aftward.

"Why are we moving that way?" Jelena asked, the panic rising in her voice again.

"We're caught in a current," he said. He swallowed seawater as he spoke, and the nausea started to return.

He shifted the direction of his paddling to fight the current. Jelena tried kicking to assist him, but her skirt made the effort useless. They were drifting quickly toward the stern.

Fox heard Willa calling to him. Now some sailors had joined her at the bulwark and were dropping a rope over the side. It was only ten feet away, but it might as well have been a mile. By the time the knotted end was in the water, Fox and Jelena were already past it.

"No!" Willa called out. "We need to go farther back or we'll miss them. The stern!"

A hysterical Petar was beside her, attempting to climb over the side of the ship. Fox was thankful that Willa restrained him from jumping overboard. A third person in the water would be a nightmare.

Willa pointed out to Fox the spot where he should go. She was followed by the sailors holding the rope as she walked quickly along the bulwark beside Petar.

"We'll be there!" he yelled up to her. "That way," he said to Jelena.

With all his strength, he kicked toward the ship, but he could see they were coming up fast to the stern. He'd have to time it perfectly to grab the rope. The sailors played it out until it was brushing the wave tops.

The distance to the rope wasn't shrinking fast enough.

"Kick, Jelena!" Fox shouted.

Even with her skirts hampering her, the rapid kicking gave them a small boost. The rope was just a few feet away.

With one last stroke, they closed the distance. Fox stopped paddling long enough to reach out for the rope. His fingers touched the hemp at the same time as an especially large wave made them rise up.

The wave pulled the dangling rope just out of reach. Fox kicked hard, but the current was too strong.

Willa cried out, "Gerard!" But there was no way to reposition the rope in time. They were swept past the stern and out toward open water.

Not far offshore, the storm front was rapidly approaching. The coming rain shower looked like a curtain. If they were still in the water when the squall arrived, Fox knew he and Jelena would be as good as dead.

Willa turned to the captain, who had been in charge of lowering the rope in their attempt to rescue Gerard and Jelena.

"We have to get the *Viandante* after them!" she yelled.

The captain shook his head. "Not with that storm coming."

"Then the rowboat."

He nodded and went to break out the rowboat that was stowed on deck. But Willa realized that would take too long. By the time they had it lowered into the water, Gerard and Jelena would already be lost in the squall.

Gerard was making a valiant effort to stay close to the ship, but it was a lost cause. They were getting smaller with every passing moment.

"We have to do something!" Petar screamed. He desperately picked up a coil of rope and tried to throw it to them, but it got nowhere near them and simply flopped against the side.

He picked it up to try again, but Willa stopped him.

"That will never reach them. The only way to get it to them at this point would be by catapult."

"We have to try! Help me throw it. We might be able to do it together."

Then it struck Willa.

"Not a catapult," she said. "An arrow. Can you tie knots well?"

Petar looked at her in disbelief. "What?"

He was a workman, so she had to assume he could. "Get a long thin rope for me."

"Why?"

She didn't have time to explain. "Just find one."

Willa sprinted amidships to get her bow and arrows. When she returned, Petar had a length of rope no thicker than a finger piled on the deck.

"We need to tie the end of that rope to the arrowhead," Willa said, "but I'm no good with knots."

He immediately saw what she intended. While he quickly wrapped the end of the rope around the tip of the arrow, Willa gauged the wind and distance to the target.

"Gerard!" she cried out. "Be ready!"

"For what?" he shouted back. He was so far away now that she could barely hear him.

She screamed out, "To grab a rope!"

She just hoped it was long enough. They might only get one attempt. Not only that, but she had to shoot it over Gerard's head. If she misjudged the wind, she might hit one of them instead, but it was a risk she would have to take.

Petar cinched the rope tight and handed the arrow to her. She tested the hold, and it seemed sturdy. The extra weight on the tip would change its flight through the air, but she just had to trust that all her recent practice would enable her to make the necessary adjustment.

"Stand back," she said. "Hold the other end of the rope and make sure it doesn't get tangled."

He nodded, taking the end and wrapping it securely around his arm.

She nocked the arrow and pulled back on the string as hard

as she could, angling the bow up to get as much distance as possible.

She loosed the arrow, and it flew in a high arc, playing the rope out behind it.

She couldn't tell if it would land far enough for Gerard to reach, but the direction was perfect.

At least it was until a gust from the approaching storm blew it sideways.

The arrow hit the water a few feet behind Gerard, but off to his right, with the rope trailing behind it. The waves were tossing the buoyant rope back and forth.

Gerard must have understood how important it was to get to it. He let go of Jelena and swam for it.

"What is he doing?" Petar shrieked.

"If he doesn't grab it now," Willa said, her insides roiling, "there'll be no second chance."

Unburdened, Gerard was a strong swimmer. He quickly reached the rope about twenty feet from where it was tied to the arrow and snatched it to him. But now Jelena was floundering behind him.

He put the rope in his teeth, and swam back toward her. But before he could get to her, the rope yanked him backward.

"Play out more," Willa said to Petar.

"There isn't any more."

"That's all there is!" she shouted at Gerard.

He nodded and swam down the length of the rope, racing to get to Jelena before she was no longer in reach.

She was doing her best to swim toward him, but she wasn't nearly the swimmer he was. The current continued to impede her, and she was barely staying afloat.

"Come on," Willa muttered to herself. "You can do it."

At the end of the rope where the arrow was floating, Gerard launched himself as far as he could, but just missed her arm as the rope jerked him back. Jelena went wide-eyed and screamed, and Petar gasped in terror.

However, Gerard did grab hold of something floating in front of her. It was the wooden reliquary around Jelena's neck.

He pulled on it, and Willa prayed that the leather cord wouldn't break. When Gerard had Jelena next to him, he released the reliquary and put his arm around her. Then he twisted the rope around his arm three times to make sure it was a tight hold.

"He did it!" Petar cried out in joy.

"Hurry," Willa said, grabbing the rope. "Pull them to us."

When she realized that the two of them could barely hang on to the end of the rope with the weight of two bodies dragging through the water, she turned her head and shouted at the crew. "Come help us!"

Crewmen who had been preparing to launch the rowboat came running. They grabbed the rope, and strong hands hauled Gerard and Jelena to the ship. The thin line wasn't strong enough to lift them aboard, so once they were beside the *Viandante*, a heavier rope was lowered to them. Gerard tied it around his chest and held Jelena in his arms as the crew pulled them up.

The two of them flopped onto the deck, and the crew cheered in amazement as the pair coughed up water.

Willa kneeled beside Gerard. "Are you all right?"

"Some dry clothes would be nice. That was quick thinking."

"I had a good teacher."

The crewmen backed away and went to restow the rowboat. Gerard rolled over and got to his knees. Petar was cradling the stunned Jelena in his arms. Tears rolled down his cheeks.

Surprisingly, Jelena looked almost serene. She held out her hand to Gerard, who took it in his.

"It's a miracle," she said.

"I think some credit should go to Willa's cleverness and skill," Gerard answered.

Jelena shook her head vehemently. "No. It's just as Saint Blaise foretold in the prophecy."

"Prophecy?" Fox said in confusion.

Petar ignored the comment and turned to his wife. "You think they are the strangers we've been seeking to help us?"

"To help you do what?" Willa asked.

"To rescue our son, Niko," Jelena said. "He has been abducted."

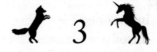

3

DUBROVNIK

Bogun had to admit that his host knew how to serve a fine meal. The roast lamb was served on a silver platter engraved with Vitomir's coat of arms. Bogun could discern the cinnamon, cloves, and black pepper that spiced the meat. It had been weeks since he had been able to indulge in a proper meal. The fish stew, flavored with saffron and onions, was equally good. Occasionally he paused to drink from a gilt flagon filled with a local red wine famed in the area. He made ample use of the ornate salt cellar prominently featured at the center of the table, made of rock crystal carved into the shape of a boat and mounted on a golden pedestal. It was appropriate that the salt trade was going to secure his greatest victory for the Serbian Empire. The only thing to mar the meal was his host.

For this midday dinner, he was alone in the stately home's great hall with the owner, who couldn't seem to stop talking about his possessions. Lord Vitomir, treasurer of Dubrovnik, was eager to show off his collection of valuable artifacts to his guest. He gestured at the great hall's tapestry depicting the Apocalypse, pointing out elements in the meticulously woven scenes as the candlelight glittering off the highlights executed in golden thread.

"You can see the four horsemen – Conquest, War, Famine, and Death – from the Book of Revelation, the Whore of Babylon, the seven-headed dragon…"

"No river of blood?" Bogun said as he dusted his food with the powdery salt. Although the Serbian and Croatian languages were quite similar, he chose to speak in Italian with Vitomir. "Isn't that part of the prophecy?"

Vitomir shifted in his seat as if the subject made him uncomfortable. He unconsciously touched the raised merlot-colored birthmark shaped like an oak leaf that distinguished the left side of his forehead.

"When I commissioned the tapestry, I specifically asked for it to be left out. I avoid the sight of blood if I can help it."

"Then you'd better hope you're not around at the end of time."

"All any of us can do is hope that the Apocalypse awaits a future generation."

"In the meantime, it's good you're adept with numbers. You wouldn't enjoy being a soldier."

Vitomir laughed. "No, I would not."

The city's treasurer was better with accounting than anyone Bogun had ever come across, boosting Dubrovnik's tax proceeds so much that it was now seen as the jewel of the Adriatic. The man could recall long lists of figures and add large numbers in his head, an unusual skill no doubt much prized by Dubrovnik's rector, the Venetian governor who ruled the city. Bogun knew that Vitomir had earned his position by his attention to detail and being a master negotiator who could get the best price for the city's goods, the most valuable being the supply of salt. The rector depended on him to oversee the city's most important income, which was why Vitomir would be an excellent ally.

Unlike the bearded, muscular Bogun, who bore an ugly burn mark around his scarred right ear, Vitomir was an aristocrat, with a slender build and a clean-shaven face. The Croatian was attired in the fine wool robes of a nobleman, while Bogun wore the more simple clothes of a merchant that wouldn't betray his position as a long-time soldier from Kotor in northern Serbia. Although the Venetian Republic and the Serbian Empire were constantly at odds politically, fighting over lands and rights, a brisk trade relationship between the two ensured that his presence in the treasurer's house would not be perceived as anything out of the ordinary.

Taking another bite of the delicious lamb shank, Bogun pointed to the spiraling unicorn horn mounted conspicuously next to the fireplace. He had never seen its like in a private home. He knew Vitomir must have paid an exorbitant amount for such a rarity.

"You certainly enjoy your luxuries."

"What good is having money if you can't take time to appreciate the finer things in life?"

"Very impressive, but I prefer having a plot of land for hunting and providing venison for rich dishes. Which brings us back to my plan." Bogun took a sip of wine and relished the flavor before continuing. "The timing is two weeks."

Vitomir's jaunty mood dissolved.

"I need the money quickly."

"And I will get it for you. It's my good fortune that your reckless investment in those ships with Dubrovnik's income sank along with them in that storm off Sicily. Otherwise, you never would have asked for my help paying back the city's money."

"I need it done sooner. It is only a matter of time before the rector figures out that the excess funds are missing."

"Two weeks is how long it will take to assemble my invasion force. You'll have to delay your rector until then. Once Ston and its salt pans are in my hands, you'll get your money."

"What if it takes longer than you think to conquer the town?"

Bogun eyed him with a deadly gaze. "You said your man in Ston will open the gates for us when we need him to."

"He will."

"Then what's the problem?"

Vitomir opened his mouth but then closed it without saying anything.

"Tell me you have this man under control," Bogun said sharply. "With the garrison there to repel my army, it would take weeks to breach the walls, exposing me to the inevitable counterattack from Venice."

Although the preparation for the invasion was complex, the plan of attack was relatively simple. Once Bogun's force arrived, Vitomir's man inside the walls would operate as a Trojan horse and open the gates in the middle of the night. Bogun would sneak into the town and slay its defenders before they realized what was happening. Then Venice could throw whatever army they wanted at him, but the siege would be fruitless against such a well-defended position. As far as he was concerned, the Venetian Republic could retain its possession of Dubrovnik and everything else along the Dalmatian Coast, but Ston and its valuable salt works would belong to the Serbian Empire.

"You'll have time to prepare for the attack," Vitomir said. "I swear."

"What about this method you've told me about for tripling salt production?" Bogun asked, gesturing to the salt cellar dominating the table. "If I'm going to be taking this risk, I need to prove its worth to Emperor Dušan. His Imperial Highness would never approve of this action in advance, and if I start a war with Venice for nothing, he'll have my head."

"Once we blame the locals for welcoming the Serbs by opening the town gates, the Venetians will lose faith in the rector, and then you and I can split the income from the salt harvest between us."

Bogun gave him a wary look. "That had better be true. I imagine the Doge of Venice wouldn't be kind to a minister who is found to be a traitor."

"I'm a man of my word."

That made Bogun laugh. While the Croatian was intelligent and calculating, he was ruled by nothing more than greed. Bogun would no sooner trust him than he would a dog foaming at the mouth.

"Please continue your meal," Vitomir said, standing.

Bogun didn't mind finishing eating by himself, but the abrupt departure in the middle of dinner was odd.

"Where are you off to?"

"You said you were leaving soon to go back to Kotor for several days. I have my own business to attend to. I will see you out before you depart."

"Don't worry," Bogun said. "I'll return in a week at the latest to conclude our planning."

He had business to take care of back in Kotor, a demonstration that would cement his soldiers' loyalties and ensure no interference from the emperor's bureaucratic functionaries.

Vitomir gave him a thin smile. "I look forward to it."

But it was clear the sentiment was not genuine. Bogun disliked him as well. However, they both needed each other, and that was all that mattered.

Vitomir was glad to be out of Bogun's presence and felt calmer as soon as he exited the room. In Dubrovnik, he was outranked only by Rector Amero, yet with this Serbian warlord he was forced to play the subservient vassal. With thick brows, a full beard, and that vicious burn scar on his neck and ear, Bogun had a formidable build and manner that made him both intimidating and strangely compelling. Despite his resentment at being ordered around like a servant, Vitomir admired how Bogun always seemed in control of himself and the situation. With such fearlessness, Vitomir could easily see why his soldiers would follow him into war.

The Serbian, responsible for a number of important victories over the Bosnians and Hungarians, had a reputation for tactical brilliance and prowess with weaponry, but his renown didn't extend outside of the Serbian Empire, which was why he was able to pass himself off as a trader here in Dubrovnik. Still, Vitomir wanted to conclude this affair as soon as possible. Every meeting with Bogun was a risk, even if the potential benefits were immense.

He certainly didn't regret striking this deal with Bogun. Without it, he would be ruined. He had personally guaranteed a huge investment from Dubrovnik's coffers, one that far exceeded the outlay known and approved by the rector, which funded a shipping fleet intended to make Dubrovnik a rival to Venice's trading power. When it returned with the goods from the eastern Mediterranean, Vitomir would be rich, and Dubrovnik's risky investment would be paid off handsomely.

But then he got the worst news imaginable. The entire fleet was sunk in a storm off Sicily. Only a few survivors brought back word of the disaster. If the rector found out the truth, his position as treasurer would not only be forfeit, but he would also be accused of stealing from the city.

His wife's wealthy family wouldn't come to Vitomir's aid. They had bestowed a generous dowry and would accuse him of squandering it on poor investments instead of merely having bad luck. Bogun was the only person he knew with the financial resources to repay the investment. If he could refill the coffers quickly, he could falsify the accounting ledgers and the rector would never know. This deal with the Devil was the only way out for him.

But it all depended on Bogun successfully capturing Ston. Without that victory, Bogun would withhold the funds he'd promised, and Vitomir could very well be hanged if his role in the attack were exposed.

Trying to match Bogun's sure demeanor, Vitomir had tried to sound more confident about his end of the bargain than he really was. It had been two weeks since Petar and Jelena had disappeared, and Vitomir worried that his plan was going awry. The garrison captain at Ston reported that the couple hadn't returned as expected. Either they had died on the journey back to Ston—though he hadn't heard of the loss of any ships on the regular routes going up the coast from Dubrovnik—or they were carrying out some plan of their own.

Vitomir headed up the stairs to the top floor. There was only one person in the house who might know where Petar and Jelena were, and that was their son.

Niko was being held captive in a small storage room next to the kitchen. It was primarily used for items reserved only for special occasions, such as valuable spices, embroidered linens, gold tureens, pewter platters, and silver candlesticks, so it was the sole room in the house with a lock on the door.

Vitomir took the key from his purse, unlocked the door, and pushed it open. The spice cabinet, bulky cupboards, and shelves stacked with crates and serving dishes took up most of the small room. Beams of light shined through chinks in the shuttered window.

A small skinny boy of no more than eleven years crouched in the far corner next to a waste bucket and a dinner plate licked clean. His hair was cut in a haphazard mess of curls, and he had an upturned nose paired with the full cheeks of a child nearing maturity. Instead of fear, Vitomir saw only curiosity in his lively brown eyes, likely because the boy was visited only twice a day by the guard who brought the food and emptied the bucket. This was the first time Vitomir had come to see him. He closed the door behind him.

They regarded each other for a moment. Vitomir expected pleading or crying, but the boy silently watched him, impassive.

"Are you well fed?" Vitomir finally asked.

"If this is what you feed your pigs," Niko replied with sarcasm, "they must be fat indeed."

"I asked as a courtesy. I know for a fact that you aren't going hungry."

"It's like a feast in here every day."

"You should show some respect to your betters."

"If any appear, I will certainly do so."

Vitomir stalked over to him and hauled him up by his tunic until their faces were almost touching. "You apparently don't realize how dire your situation is, my boy."

"Don't call me that."

Vitomir gave him a hard slap. "I'll call you what I want."

Niko glared at him, his cheek red and his eyes tearing up. "I'm not yours."

"You *are* mine. Your whole town is mine. I am the treasurer for Dubrovnik, and that makes Ston my responsibility."

Vitomir let him go, and Niko slumped to the floor.

"Why am I here?"

"Because I want to ensure your parents' loyalty to me. You'll be free to go once that is demonstrated."

For the first time, Niko's brave façade faltered, and he suddenly looked like the frightened child he was.

"Really? You'll let me go? I can go back to my mother and father?"

Vitomir thought reassurance was the best way to get what he wanted, despite how hollow it might be.

"Of course. I don't want to hurt you. But I do need to know something."

"What?"

"Where are your parents?"

Niko frowned. "Aren't they in Ston?"

"No, they're not. And I'd be aware by now if they were still in Dubrovnik. I have to know where else they could have gone."

"How would I know? I've been in this little room for a week."

"Closer to a fortnight. Do you have family somewhere else?"

Niko shook his head.

"Think, boy. If you hold out on me, I'll make things very difficult for you and your family."

"I swear, I don't know."

Vitomir grabbed him by the wrist and twisted hard. "Tell me."

"I don't know!" the boy screamed in pain. "I don't know!"

He seemed to be truthful. Breaking Niko's arm would only complicate things. Vitomir let him go.

"If anything comes to mind," Vitomir said, "I'll have my cook make you some honeyed apple pottage."

Niko nodded meekly, massaging his wrist.

Vitomir turned to go. But as he opened the door to leave, Niko dived through his legs and out into the corridor.

Vitomir tried to grab him while the boy was still scuttling along the floor, but Niko had the quickness of a cat and sprang to his feet before Vitomir could get a hold of him. The boy dashed to the stairs to make his escape.

"Guards!" Vitomir shouted as he ran in pursuit. "Catch that boy!"

Vitomir was still a vigorous man, but he was no sportsman. He was breathing hard by the time he reached the second floor. Niko was already out of sight down the stairs. Vitomir continued to yell for aid in recapturing him.

As he rounded the corner at the bottom of the steps, he was greeted by the sight of Niko dangling from the hand of Bogun, who was holding up the boy easily with one arm. Niko repeatedly slapped at his arm, but his weak efforts were no match for the muscular Serb.

"Let me go!" Niko cried.

"Is this little one causing you trouble, Lord Vitomir?" Bogun said.

"He's my insurance," Vitomir said between breaths.

"Then you better keep a tighter grip on him."

Guards came running a moment later. Bogun handed Niko to them, who held him tight by both arms.

Trying to recover his composure in front of Bogun, Vitomir commanded, "Take him back to the storage room. Someone is to guard the door at all times when anyone enters."

The guards nodded and hauled Niko away. He didn't bother to struggle, but he stared daggers at Vitomir until he was out of sight.

"I hope you have the rest of your business under better control," Bogun said.

"A temporary problem," Vitomir said with all the certainty he could muster.

Bogun narrowed his eyes. "I don't like problems, no matter how fleeting."

Vitomir thought about the mysterious disappearance of Petar and Jelena.

"Neither do I."

# 4

With the storm passed and the repairs to the ship's yard completed, it didn't take long for the *Viandante* to travel the remainder of the journey. Fox, now dry, stood at the bulwark next to Petar, both of them marveling at the walled city of Dubrovnik in the distance. Although the view was bobbing up and down with the swells, the ginger was keeping his stomach from roiling.

The wealthy Dalmatian trading center perched on a promontory jutting into the Adriatic. Jagged mountains stretched along the coast behind it, providing a natural barrier to inland enemies. Fields took up every spare acre of land between the peaks and the city walls.

Those walls rose eighty feet high in some places, and even higher along the coastline where they arched up to hug the rocky cliffs. Fox had no doubt they would repel any army foolish enough to attack. In a few places, he could make out the red-tile roofs of the larger buildings peeking over the battlements that surrounded the city. High on a seaside outcrop in the distance was a fortress overlooking the northern side of the city.

The harbor itself was unprotected by walls, but it was in the lee of the city, out of the direct wind from the sea. Dozens of boats of all sizes and designs were huddled together at the port, which had a waterfront of docks feeding into a sturdy gate.

"A dire threat to the White Fortress," Petar said in a distant voice. He seemed understandably preoccupied with the danger to his boy.

"The White Fortress," Fox repeated. "Is that what Dubrovnik is called?"

"No, that's something we call my hometown, Ston. It's a little more than a two-day sail from Dubrovnik, which oversees it." He went silent again.

"I'm sorry about your son."

Petar nodded. "Right. Niko. He… he wasn't even supposed to be in Dubrovnik. He came to warn me of the danger I was in."

"He must be very brave."

"More than you know."

"This danger you speak of. Was that why he was abducted?"

"I was naïve. I thought we could outwit Lord Vitomir, but he is too powerful."

"We? You mean you and your wife? And who is this Vitomir?" Fox had asked Jelena to help Willa feed the horses so that he could have this time alone with Petar. With the couple separated, he thought they might be more open to talk.

Petar shook his head. "I mean me and Jelena's older brother Drazhan. We had come to Dubrovnik to inform Rector Amero of a Serbian plot to invade my hometown of Ston. Vitomir is the treasurer of Dubrovnik, and he's betraying his city and the Venetian Republic to help the Serbs do it. He killed Drazhan and took Niko to make me aid his plan."

"This talk of Venetians and Serbians fighting each other over lands along the coast is more confusing than the political intrigues and wars in my own corner of the world," Fox said. "How could your small town be worth the Serbians risking a war with Venice to capture it?"

"The Venetian Republic owns all of the Dalmatian coast, patrolled by its powerful navy, and the republic has a fragile peace with the Serbian Empire, which has been busy fighting the Eastern Roman Empire and Hungarians lately. Serbia sold our town and the peninsula we sit on to Venice eighteen years ago for money to expand their empire, and now Dubrovnik controls it on behalf of the Venetians. I am the harvest master of our salt pans. This year Drazhan discovered a way to treble our salt production.

We call it 'white gold.' The salt harvest provides a third of the income for Dubrovnik. The increased production would make us the most valuable place in the entire Venetian Republic."

Fox didn't know much about salt, but given that it was essential for preserving food like the salted fish that had been the staple of their diet since leaving Rhodes, he could imagine that it was a valuable trade item. Then he suddenly understood.

"Ston is the White Fortress."

"Yes. Although we often refer to our home simply as Ston, we actually live in twin towns, Ston and Mali Ston, separated by a short valley between rugged mountains. Ston is where we harvest the salt, and Mali Ston is the walled town beside our port. We think our walls are strong enough to repel invaders until reinforcements from Dubrovnik arrive, but if someone on the inside were compelled to open the town gate, we would be easily conquered. Then it would be the Venetians who would be hard-pressed to take it back."

"That's why Vitomir took your son, to force you to open the gate for the Serbians."

Petar nodded with a dejected look.

"Lord Vitomir even threatened to have the bishop excommunicate me if I didn't do as he said." The statement caused Petar to shiver in dread. "Taking my child wasn't enough for that monster. Can you imagine how awful it would be to face eternal damnation? My wife wouldn't even be able to talk to me, and I wouldn't want her to. I couldn't risk her even being slightly associated with an excommunicant."

The reminder of his own undeserved sentence to hell made Fox think of the vile church official who had consigned him to that fate. Only proof that the recently deceased Cardinal Molyneux had captured his mother and made her bear his child would convince the pope that the charges against Fox were fabricated.

"Anyone who would do such a thing to an innocent person should be the one spending eternity with the Devil," he said before changing the subject back to their current problem. It was clear that although Fox was asking for Petar's confidence, he would not be able to share his story in turn. "Vitomir must benefit in some way if the Serbians capture Ston."

"He wants nothing more than to be rich. I have to think it's about money."

Petar's troubles were making sense, but there was still one part of the story that puzzled Fox.

"Your wife mentioned a prophecy."

"I've heard that prophecy my whole life," Petar said. "I never thought it had anything to do with me."

"And you think it does now because of your wife's near drowning?"

"Jelena does, certainly. But maybe I'm starting to believe, too." He turned to face Fox, a deadly serious look on his face. "The prophecy is nearly a hundred years old, and it never seemed to be meaningful before now. It was given to Ston's parish priest in a vision. The priest had prayed to our patron Saint Blaise to save him when he was buried in the rubble of an earthquake. At the moment of his salvation, Saint Blaise appeared before him to deliver a prophecy."

Fox had heard about many prophecies, not just the ones written by biblical prophets like Jeremiah and Isaiah. The most impressive was from the sixth-century prophet Merlin who said that two dragons would fight. *The Red Dragon will be overrun by the White One: for Britain's mountains and valleys shall be leveled, and the streams in its valleys shall run with blood.* Merlin had correctly predicted the fall of the Saxons—the red dragon—to be replaced by King Arthur and his knights—the white dragon.

But Fox didn't put much faith in prophecies, relics, and other mystical artifacts. He'd seen them corrupted by greedy and vile men too many times. Still, he recently had personal experience with a relic, a manuscript containing an ancient painting of Mary and the Christ child called the Hodegetria. Willa had certainly believed in its power, and he couldn't deny that they had come through many grueling ordeals with it in their possession. Petar seemed to have a similar strong belief in such portents, so Fox had to hear him out.

"Can you tell me the prophecy?"

"Of course. Every resident of Ston has heard it since we were children, and it's widely known along the Adriatic."

Petar gazed at Dubrovnik as he recited the words, surely thinking about his son.

The lure of precious crystals sparks a dire threat to the White Fortress.

My hand guides strangers from across the sea to provide aid in this time of need.

Hellfire rains down when a sacrifice summons a dragon to destroy any enemy refusing to flee.

A miracle inspires a new leader to show the way to liberation.

The meaning of the prophecy's first line was obvious. According to Petar, the increased production of the salt crystals had lured Serbia into sparking a dire threat against Ston.

But it was the second line that caught Fox's attention.

"You think we're the *'strangers from across the sea'* who are supposed to come to your aid?"

"You already have," Petar said. "Jelena is now convinced, and I'm coming around to her thinking. The fingerbone of Saint Blaise pointed to you when you grabbed the reliquary pendant to save her. You and your wife are meant to be our saviors."

Willa patted her white palfrey, Comis, on the neck as the horse munched on her daily feed. Jelena gently rubbed the muzzle of Zephyr, Gerard's mottled silver Arabian courser. Willa was surprised that the picky stallion didn't seem to mind.

"Zephyr likes you," Willa said. "He doesn't often let strangers get so friendly with him."

"I've always had a way with animals," Jelena said. "Unfortunately, you'll have to stable them outside the city when we get to Dubrovnik."

"Is it too crowded for horses?"

"There are people everywhere. It's the biggest city I've ever seen." Then she shrugged. "It's the *only* city I've ever seen."

"I understand it's an important trading port."

"Petar tells me there are ships from Venice, Constantinople, Alexandria, the Holy Land, and faraway places I can't even pronounce. I couldn't believe how many odd languages I heard when I was there. And the clothes! So many unusual fashions and beautiful colors."

"Is that where your son is being held captive?"

Jelena set her jaw in an apparent attempt to stave off tears.

"He's in the house of a man named Vitomir. He is the treasurer for Dubrovnik, the second most powerful man in the city after the rector who represents Venice."

"Why would he be holding your son?" Willa asked. "For a ransom?"

Jelena regained her composure and responded with a steady voice. "In a way. But it's not money he's after. We have very little."

She went into a story about Vitomir's plan to help the Serbians take over Ston for its valuable salt. Everything the Venetians did depended on the salt trade, from the health of its citizens and the preservation of meat and fish for withstanding sieges, to taxation and the exchange of goods throughout the Mediterranean. Whole kingdoms would grind to a stop without salt. When Jelena was finished, Willa understood why empires would fight over it.

"Although we don't have much money ourselves," Jelena said, "Ston is the key to much of the wealth of Dalmatia. And now thanks to Saint Blaise, you're here to help us. I was almost ready to give up, but when your husband saved my life by grabbing on to the sacred relic, I knew that you were sent to fulfill the prophecy."

She relayed the lines to Willa.

The lure of precious crystals sparks a dire threat to the White Fortress.
My hand guides strangers from across the sea to provide aid in this time of need.

Hellfire rains down when a sacrifice summons a dragon to destroy
any enemy refusing to flee.
A miracle inspires a new leader to show the way to liberation.

When Jelena was done, she went on.

"I had faith in Father Matko's vision. Our salt luring the Serbians into the coming invasion has to be the threat he envisioned. When Niko was taken, I could think of only one possibility for strangers from across the sea to help us. I have a distant cousin in the Knights Hospitaller. We knew they were meeting on Rhodes, so Petar and I traveled there to have an audience and request their aid. But when we arrived, the palace of the grand master was shut to all visitors because of some kind of crisis. The Hospitallers wouldn't let us make our petition because they were convinced spies were trying to get into their palace. Then my cousin was dispatched to try to find the spies, and we didn't know what else to do, so we left. We had lost all hope. But now you and Sir Gerard have saved me. It can only be divine providence that led you to us."

Jelena gripped the pendant tightly in her hand, her mouth moving in a silent prayer. Willa's stomach twisted with guilt, for she knew why Jelena and Petar hadn't been allowed into the palace. When she and Fox had been in pursuit of the lost treasure of the Knights Templar, she had created a disturbance at the Grand Master's Palace, which led to the Hospitallers locking out all visitors for fear of spies coming to attack the knights.

Zephyr whinnied, and Willa turned to see Gerard approaching. Jelena stepped aside, and the horse nuzzled Gerard's hand, chuffing happily.

"I know," he said. "We'll get you off this infernal boat soon." He looked at Jelena. "Your husband would like to talk to you."

Jelena took Willa by the hands and said, "Thank you." She walked to the stairs, leaving Gerard and Willa alone.

"It's my fault," Willa said.

"What is?"

"They were in Rhodes to get help from the Hospitallers. Jelena thought *they* would be the strangers from afar foretold in the prophecy to help them."

"Petar recited it for me."

"When I caused the knights to lock out all visitors, Jelena and Petar couldn't get the aid they were seeking."

"We don't know that the Hospitallers would have helped them. You were only in there because of the plan we both came up with. Besides, if you hadn't caused the palace to be locked down, you would have been killed, and then we never would have been married."

All of the sailors were up on deck, so Gerard took her in his arms and kissed her greedily. She returned the kiss with a passion she didn't know could exist. It took all her will not to bed him down right then and there in the hay beside the horses.

With great reluctance, she extracted herself from his embrace.

"You have no idea how much I want to continue this, but all I can think of is Jelena's sorrow about her son."

"You believe in this prophecy?"

"Don't you?" Willa asked. "You also doubted the Hodegetria at first, but you witnessed its power firsthand. Look at how right this prophecy has been until now."

"And it also talks of hellfire and a dragon."

"Prophecies come true. Hildegard of Bingen predicted that: *The German Empire will be divided. Peace will return to Europe when the white flower takes possession of the throne of France.* She foresaw the reign of Louis IX."

"Saint Louis of France. I forgot how well-read you are."

"Only because I was the maid of a lady who loved books." She took her husband's hands in hers and gave him a pleading look. "Gerard, we have to help them. Even if you don't take it as a true portent, we're the only strangers that might be able to give them aid."

"I'm not sure what we can do," Gerard said. "How can the two of us stop a war?"

"By rescuing their son."

"He's been taken by one of the most powerful men in a city

we've never been to. We know nothing about this region except for what Petar and Jelena have told us. We have just recently learned Italian, and don't speak any Croatian. Besides, we have our own problems to resolve." Gerard looked around to make sure no one was listening. "We're heading back to France to find evidence that will allow us to reverse my excommunication. You convinced me that it would be possible if we didn't give up hope, and I'm eager to continue on that quest, no matter how difficult it will be."

Willa understood his frustration at the delay, but she couldn't stand the thought of abandoning Petar and Jelena to their fate, especially because she felt somewhat responsible for their plight.

"I think this is a test, Gerard," she said, taking his hand. "If we can help them, even if it's in a small way, perhaps it will prove we are worthy of absolution."

Gerard quietly patted Zephyr's neck as he considered her words. Finally, he nodded.

"I suppose you're right that it's our fault that the Hospitallers wouldn't hear them out," he said. "We made an unbreakable vow to each other last week. I intend to honor it until death do us part."

Before this moment, Willa didn't think she could love him more. "Then that means…"

Gerard gave her hand a loving and reassuring squeeze. "You've been wise about a great many things since we met. I can bear a short delay in our travels if it means a better chance at the life we want. Though I may not believe in Petar and Jelena's prophecy, we'll see what we can do to help them get their child back."

5

KOTOR, SERBIAN EMPIRE

Bogun, dressed in his leather cuirass embossed with a Serbian double-headed eagle and buffed boots befitting a commander of soldiers, shook his head in disgust as he watched Emperor Dušan's legate struggle up the 1339 steps to the fortress overlooking Kotor. The sweating man, accompanied by a lone aide, was named Zavida, and he was the personal representative of His Imperial Highness. He wheezed in the midday sun, stopping every few steps to catch his breath. Bogun could taste the bile in his throat knowing that Zavida had achieved such a lofty position by cheating Bogun out of his rightful inheritance.

The climb up the steps was taking much longer than he wanted, but he tried to relish what was to come. He'd returned from Dubrovnik for this very moment, so perhaps it was better not to rush it. Still, Bogun impatiently rapped his hand on the stone parapet of the fortress, which had an unparalleled view for miles around. No fleet could approach without being seen long before it arrived.

The legate's ship was one of a dozen anchored in the harbor, and soon he'd discover the significance of the assembled fleet. Situated on a vast bay that was protected on nearly all sides by mountains, the walled town far below teemed with soldiers brought here for the coming invasion of Ston.

Bogun's lieutenant, Cedozar, joined him at the wall. The man had been at Bogun's side ever since the early days when Bogun had been forced to prove his worth as a soldier to the Serbian Empire. Cedozar stroked his bushy mustache and grimaced.

"It's taking him an eternity to make the climb," Cedozar said.

"It's a disgrace," Bogun said. "He's not worthy to represent our emperor."

"Perhaps I should run down and carry him the rest of the way on my back." He chuckled at his own jest.

"Let him suffer. He might do us a favor and drop dead during the climb."

"We could only be so fortunate." Cedozar cleared his throat. "My lord, the men are ready to hear from you."

Bogun followed him to the opposite side of the wall walk. The twenty top officers in his invasion force were assembled in the fortress's large courtyard below him. They went silent and straightened up as their commander reviewed them. Bogun could sense the admiration and fear that the men felt in equal measure, a balance he was careful to cultivate.

Although Bogun believed Orthodox Serbians were a superior breed to the Catholic Venetians who controlled the Adriatic, they were also a superstitious lot, and he was here to ease their apprehension about the upcoming assault. Bogun needed to buttress their devotion to him, and Legate Zavida was a key element of his plan to rid them of their belief in magical words.

"You men were hand-selected by me because you are the bravest fighters in the empire. You're all versed in the plan for the upcoming mission to assault Ston, and I know you'll perform your duty to Emperor Dušan to the best of your abilities. All I require is that you carry out my orders to the letter. Our success will usher in a new and glorious era for the Serbian Empire, one that will mark the decline of our enemies in Venice."

The men below cheered half-heartedly, and that was the problem.

"Unfortunately," Bogun continued, "I've heard tell that some of you are wary of such a mission. You know the prophecy handed down from their blasphemous priest, and you erringly put stock in it. Cedozar, remind us of it so that we can hear its absurdity."

Cedozar didn't need a scroll to read it. All of them had it memorized.

The lure of precious crystals sparks a dire threat to the White
Fortress.
My hand guides strangers from across the sea to provide aid in this
time of need.
Hellfire rains down when a sacrifice summons a dragon to destroy
any enemy refusing to flee.
A miracle inspires a new leader to show the way to liberation.

Bogun took a moment to let the words sink in. Some of the men, all of whom had fought valiantly in bloody battles, were as white as phantoms.

"Yes," he said finally, "we are lured by the crystals that will provide uncounted funds to expand the empire. The 'White Fortress,' as they call it, is a prize worthy of capture for our emperor. We are protecting him by undertaking this plan without his knowledge, but he will reward us all when we present our victory to him. We are not a threat to Ston, we are a blessing. Ston will thrive once it is again part of the Serbian Empire, so the prophecy has nothing to do with us and our plans."

On cue, Cedozar asked, "But what of these so-called 'strangers,' my lord?"

"No one is coming to save them. My man inside Dubrovnik has assured me of that. After we take the town, we will repel any reinforcements coming from Venice. Once we have it, there will be no getting it back. And it will be the next step in the rise of our glorious empire!"

"And what of the dragon?" called out one of the men below. A few of them mumbled in agreement and nodded their heads. The thought of being burned in hellfire terrified them.

"Have you ever seen a dragon?" Bogun asked.

The man looked down and shook his head.

"Are we also to believe they are protected by griffins, elephants, and unicorns?" Bogun knew that such fantastical creatures haunted their nightmares.

But he could see that they weren't convinced. Being on the wrong end of a prophecy held a firm grip on their minds, and it would take a persuasive demonstration to convince them it was a fraud.

"You all know that our visiting legate is safeguarded by a protective writ signed both by the emperor and the Patriarch of the Serbs promising to rain instant hellfire on any person who so much as touches him, yes?"

The men all nodded. Every citizen knew that killing a legate would instantly bring the wrath of God down on the one who murdered him, which allowed them to travel throughout the empire safely.

"Of course," Bogun went on, "that writ hasn't kept Legates Repoš and Predimir from dying in gruesome ways."

"But those deaths were from bad luck," another man said.

Bogun nodded sagely. Repoš was killed in a housefire, and Predimir died when he drowned in Skopje's Vardar River. Tragic accidents both, or so everyone thought. What nobody knew except for Cedozar was that Bogun was responsible for both deaths, tying Repoš with ropes so he couldn't escape the fire and holding Predimir's head underwater until he floated down the river to be found by two boys playing in the Vardar.

Both killings were deserved retribution for their parts in stealing Ston and the entire Stonski Rat peninsula from Bogun's family—the inheritance that was owed to him—and selling it to the hated Venetians. Although some of the resulting money went to pay for campaigns to expand the Serbian Empire, much of the wealth went to fund the legates' lavish lifestyles.

With Repoš and Predimir dead, Zavida was the only one of the three legates left.

Bogun heard the legate panting as he entered the fortress. "I will soon prove to you that prophecies, witchcraft, and curses are nothing to fear."

Zavida walked into the courtyard, waving his heavy robes to cool himself. Bogun signaled to him from the parapet.

"My lord, please come join us up here."

Zavida frowned at the stairs leading up to the wall and held up a finger. After he'd caught his breath, he plodded up the steps.

When he was positioned beside Bogun, he gasped, "You should have held your place at my side during the climb. Do not forget who I am or what is due to someone in my position. Now may I know why I've been asked to make this infernal trek?"

"Don't you enjoy the view?"

"It is not worth jeopardizing my health. I only came because you insisted it was important that I be here."

"And that it is. Do you see those ships below you?"

Zavida leaned over so he could see the harbor, but Bogun could tell he was wary of getting too close to the vertiginous height of the wall overlooking the cliff. The harbor was almost a thousand feet below them, but the immediate drop from the wall was a hundred feet. The aide also stayed a respectful distance away.

"I see many ships," the legate said, "and I saw many soldiers. But what I do not see is a proclamation from our emperor to you authorizing the kind of military action this suggests."

"That's because I don't have one."

"Then can you explain why it looks like you're preparing for war?"

"I can. I'm going to take Ston by force."

Zavida peered at Bogun, first confused by his ridiculous statement, then shocked when Bogun betrayed no sign that he was jesting.

"Are you mad?" the legate cried out. "His Imperial Highness would never approve such an act of aggression against Venice. It would put us in a state of war, a war that we would be hard-pressed to win."

"Only because of weak-willed advisers such as yourself."

Zavida scoffed at him. "Are you still angry about the peninsula being sold to the Venetians? That was years ago. You know that was for the good of the Serbian Empire."

"I know it was for the good of you. And you had no trouble convincing His Imperial Highness to give away the land that had been promised to my family. Years go by at a crawl when you've been wronged and are looking for justice."

Finally Zavida took notice of Bogun's tense stance. The legate's face didn't reveal any fear, but he clasped his hands together so tightly that his knuckles were bone white.

"You are well aware that I am a direct representative to His Imperial Highness, Emperor Dušan. It's as if he were standing in front of you himself. I am untouchable."

"That is what we are all told," Bogun said. "Shall we test that thought?"

"I don't know what you think..." was all Zavida could say before Bogun grabbed him by the collar of his robe and dragged him toward the brink of the parapet.

"Unhand me immediately!" the legate shrieked. "I cannot be harmed!"

Zavida's aide took a half-hearted step toward them, but a scowl from Bogun halted him in his tracks.

Bogun stopped when his toes were touching the edge. A great drop yawned below them.

"It *has* been years," he said, pulling Zavida toward him so that the adviser was only inches away, the man's sickly sweet breath a stench that made him want to gag. "And the passage of time only makes this moment that much more satisfying."

With a flick of his wrists, Bogun sent Zavida sailing over the side, his scream echoing across the valley until a crunch far beneath ended it. The only other sound was the surprised cries of a few of the soldiers.

Bogun could see the body sprawled across the rocks at an unnatural angle. He took a deep breath, reveling in a sight that he had been dreaming of since the day he'd been betrayed.

He turned to the aide, who stared at him with a slack jaw and horrified eyes.

"Please don't throw me down there," the aide begged.

"I can't," Bogun replied. The aide was momentarily relieved until he saw Bogun draw his dagger. "You have to pay for pushing your master off the wall."

The aide was so petrified that Bogun was able to bury the knife in his heart before he could even think of retreating. He collapsed to the ground, and Bogun wiped his dagger clean on the man's cloak before he resheathed it.

Then he turned back to his men. They watched him with expectant looks of horror, as if he'd be struck down by a bolt of lightning from the clear blue sky.

Bogun waited. He wouldn't reveal to the men peering at him that a sliver of doubt churned his insides, the same doubt he'd experienced after killing Repoš and Predimir.

But nothing happened. Just as he thought, the curse had no power.

He remained alive and well. The Lord favored his rightful destiny.

"Now do you see?" he said, raising his hands over his head. "God is with us. Just as the protection of this repulsive man was a false divination, so is Ston's ridiculous prophecy."

When the men saw that no punishment was forthcoming, they began to nod and smile. Zavida had been notorious for fattening his own coffers at the expense of soldiers' welfare, so no love was lost at his death. These men had been specifically chosen because they were all true believers dedicated to the rise of the Serbian Empire like Bogun was.

"Now," he said, his voice rising in exhortation, "who is with me? Who will join me and taste the glory of our inevitable triumph?"

This time the men cheered uproariously. As long as he was their leader, he had them. Nothing would stop him from conquering Ston and regaining what was rightfully his.

6

DUBROVNIK

When the *Viandante* docked at the city's port, Willa went for a ride on Comis along with Gerard atop Zephyr. The horses gamboled about like playful foals after being confined on the long trip from Rhodes, and Willa laughed at their giddiness. Even Gerard was smiling, obviously relieved to be back on dry land, especially because his ginger supply was gone.

Once they'd tired out the horses, they found a stable outside Dubrovnik's walls since the city was far too crowded for horses to be of use. They secured their most valuable items in the lockbox provided by the stable, then went into the city to rendezvous with Petar and Jelena. Willa and Gerard agreed that the least they could do was put all four of them up in a tavern. Thanks to their share of the Templar treasure, the cost at the inn was a trifle.

They entered through the city's northern gate and immediately found themselves walking down the Stradun, Dubrovnik's main thoroughfare. As Jelena had mentioned, the wide street teemed with residents mingling with visitors from all over the world. Willa found herself constantly turning to take in the amazing variety of languages, cultures, and clothing styles that swirled around her. She gawked at a man in a long flowing robe with full sleeves, red shoes, and a strange peaked head-covering.

"Where do you think he's from?" she asked Gerard quietly in English.

"I think I remember seeing an outfit like that in Venice. Constantinople, perhaps? The *Viandante*'s captain told me that

Dubrovnik is a central trading city connecting Europe to the East, and many of those goods flow through the Eastern Roman Empire."

"I've visited so much of the world already, and this is just a reminder of how much I have left to see." Growing up as a lady's maid, Willa didn't think she'd ever leave the county of Kent, much less travel all the way to an exotic city like Dubrovnik and encounter travelers from Constantinople.

"Hopefully we won't be staying long," Gerard said. "We'll help Petar and Jelena get their son back and then continue on our way to France."

They hadn't mentioned their own troubles to the couple, especially Gerard's excommunication, which would make Petar and Jelena recoil in horror. It seemed unlikely that the couple would associate with them even if they believed the truth that he had been unfairly sentenced. They had to return to France to uncover the evidence that would absolve him and allow his lands and title to be granted back to him.

"I do feel awful that we ruined their chances of getting aid from the Knights Hospitaller," Willa said. "However, I'm beginning to agree with you about not being able to help them on our own. We should go to the rector and see if we can reason with him."

Gerard shook his head. "Petar and Jelena may trust strangers from a foreign land, but there's no chance the rector would believe a knight from England. Even if he did listen to me, which I think unlikely, the first thing he'd do is ask Vitomir whether I was telling the truth. Vitomir would lie, and then Niko would be dead. We have to find some other way to help them."

"What about sneaking into Vitomir's house and taking Niko out with you? Jelena said her cousin works for him, so she could provide us information about where the boy is."

"I've thought about that. Getting into Vitomir's house is the hardest part. Apparently, it's well protected. Then I'd have to escape from the house undetected with a young boy in tow, and we'd have to exit the city before Vitomir knows Niko's gone. The treasurer is quite powerful in this city, and there are only four gates to close if he realizes his captive is gone. It's too risky."

"Then what should we tell them?"

Gerard shrugged. "That we've got some ideas we can't reveal yet."

"But we don't."

"We just need more information. Perhaps. We'll think of something."

Willa spotted the couple coming toward them from a side street. Jelena gave a shy wave. Petar looked relieved as he shook Gerard's hand.

"I wasn't quite convinced we'd ever see you again," he said.

"I didn't have any doubts," Jelena said, taking Willa's hands. "You were sent to us by God."

"We'll do what we can," was all Willa felt she could say.

"I thought you might have trouble spotting us," Gerard said.

Petar surveyed the crowd, then pointedly looked up at Gerard's unusual height. "You stand out."

"Were you able to find a tavern?"

"Two rooms just as you requested. We can't thank you enough for paying for our lodging."

"Our pleasure," Willa said. "It's the least we could do." *Which might end up being all we can do*, she thought.

They continued down the Stradun. Vendors were set up in arched doorways, but only one half of each door was fully open from top to bottom. On the other half, the bottom part was a wall waist high, and many of the shops used the ledge to show off their wares and conduct business from inside to any passersby. Willa had never seen such a thing.

Jelena must have noticed her confused look. "Is something wrong?"

"Those doorways are unusual."

"They are?"

"We don't have anything like them in England."

Petar and Jelena exchanged a surprised look.

"They're very common in our region," Petar said. "They're called knee doors."

"See?" Jelena added, pointing out the corner of the wall. "It looks like a leg bent at the knee seen from the side."

The two of them seemed proud of being able to describe something new to their visitors. They led Willa and Gerard down the Stradun to the main cathedral, showing off the city as if they'd built it themselves. Petar explained that, although Ston was their hometown, Dubrovnik was their capital, even if they were all under the rule of the Venetian Republic.

Petar leaned close and said in a hushed tone, "There is even talk that Dubrovnik could be its own republic someday, but to do that, the city will need sources of funding. Ston could be a large part of it."

He guided them to a steep set of stairs leading up to the area of town closest to the seawall.

"This is where all of the richest citizens live," Jelena said. "The sea breeze keeps the homes cool in the hot summers."

Petar stopped them as they came to a corner. "Jelena and I can't go any further without the risk of being seen by Lord Vitomir. His home is the grand one flying the Venetian banner on the doorway."

"The red field with the image of golden winged lion," Gerard said to a nodding Petar. Willa and Gerard knew it well from their time in Venice. "We'll take a look and see if we can discover anything of use."

"We are to meet my cousin Zrinka here," Jelena said. "I originally came with Petar to Dubrovnik so I could convince her to leave the employ of such a beast, but now I'm glad she is still a servant there. She'll be able to tell us what we need to know about his house."

"We'll be back soon," Gerard said, holding out his arm for Willa. She took it and they strolled around the corner.

She could smell the faint scent of seawater, a relief from most cities she'd visited, which were often redolent with the stench of manure deposited on the streets. But other than a few donkey carts, she'd seen no animals leave their dung, and human waste seemed to be disposed of less publicly than in London or Paris.

"There it is," Gerard said, nodding at a huge townhouse nearly abutting the defensive wall dividing the city from the sea behind it. The building was four stories tall and twice as wide as any of the other houses. "It looks as if there is some kind of rear courtyard separating it from the wall."

Two guards were posted at the front door where the banner was draped. Willa and Gerard acknowledged them pleasantly and kept walking without stopping. Gerard was expert at pretending to talk to her while he was actually examining as much of the house as he could.

Once they were out of earshot of the guards, she said, "I suppose there is no easy way to sneak into the house."

Gerard shook his head casually. "Those guards may not be standing there at night, but surely there will be some inside. And we don't even know where this boy is being kept."

They walked to the next street and noticed a building that was a burned-out hulk with a caved-in roof. Gerard looked back toward Vitomir's house then up at the destroyed four-story home.

"Wait here."

"Why?" Willa asked, though she thought she knew the answer.

"I'm going inside. I might get a better look at Vitomir's house from up there."

"I'll go with you."

"It could be treacherous in there."

"That's why I wear boots under my skirts."

He squinted at her. "You're going to follow me no matter what I say."

Willa smiled. "*You* can follow *me*."

She hiked up her kirtle and went through the front door that was ajar. The dim interior had been stripped of anything valuable so that it held little more than dirty cloths and rat droppings.

The stairs were still intact, although the wood was rotting in places. Willa climbed the steps, careful to watch out for any loose boards that could trip her.

"I wonder why they didn't rebuild this house," she said.

"The Pestilence," Gerard answered. It was the one word that explained much in the world since the terrible calamity that struck Europe just a few years before. And he was likely right. Whoever owned this house might have perished as the last members of their family after the disease had already taken the rest of them. And because lawyers were no less susceptible to the Pestilence than anyone else, the courts were years behind in processing all the wills and figuring out the rightful inheritors of property.

When they reached the top floor, they had to climb over charred timbers that had held up the ceramic roof tiles now scattered across the floor. It was clear that a fire in the kitchen had been the original cause of the house's ruin, exactly the reason for the stoves and ovens to be located on the top floor instead of underneath the sleeping chambers. They reached the rear of the home and leaned out a hole that once was a window. They had an excellent view of Vitomir's house not far away.

The city's wall overlooking the Adriatic stood only ten feet away from the window, with a small overgrown garden below. Willa could make out a single guard patrolling one section of the wall. In some places, the battlements were wide enough only for two men to walk abreast while they looked out over the crenellations. But behind Vitomir's home, the wall widened, allowing enough room for an entire squad of men to be posted. Another guard emerged from a tiny weather-protected guard post farther along. Iron sconces were set into the wall at regular intervals for holding torches at night.

Gerard studied Vitomir's house from this angle.

"What do you see?" Willa asked him.

He pointed at the gap between Vitomir's house and the city wall, which was three times the width of the gap where they were standing. A rope holding up drying linens extended from one of the sconces on the city wall and disappeared from view toward his house.

"He must have a large yard or patio below, but those brick

walls closing it off at the sides prevent us from seeing it from the outside." Under his breath, he murmured, "It's possible."

Willa recognized the flash of inspiration in his eyes. "You have an idea for how to get Niko out without being seen."

"Perhaps. We need to know more first. *You* follow *me* now."

He led her back downstairs and out onto the street. By the time they made their way back to Jelena and Petar, the Croatians had been joined by a third person, a thin woman Jelena's age.

"Good, you've returned," Jelena said. "Zrinka can't stay long or she will be missed." Then she switched to Croatian instead of Italian. Only about half the people Willa had encountered so far could speak in the language of their Venetian rulers.

Zrinka eyed them carefully, then spoke in rapid Croatian to Jelena, who wiped away a tear before turning to Willa and Gerard.

"She said that Niko is being held on the top floor next to the kitchen in a storage room. It's locked at all times."

"Is the door to the room under guard?" Gerard asked.

When Jelena translated, Zrinka shook her head.

"Is Vitomir home now?"

This time Zrinka answered in a rush of words. Jelena's expression grew concerned, and Petar ran his hand through his thick hair at the news.

"What did she say?" Willa asked.

"Lord Vitomir is preparing to leave Dubrovnik."

"For how long?" Gerard asked.

"Only a few days. But she overheard where he is going and why. That is the problem."

Willa frowned at Gerard. He looked just as confused as she was.

"What is the problem?" she said.

Petar responded. "Vitomir is going to a town called Korčula for the All Hallows' Eve celebration. A wealthy merchant there has offered to sell him a manuscript."

"What does that have to do with us?" Gerard asked.

"It contains special instructions from Cathay for how to work salt pans. Jelena's brother Drazhan told me that's how he was able to demonstrate a threefold increase in production, but I have never seen this book."

"And you're certain it's the same book?" Willa asked.

Jelena translated the question, and Zrinka nodded vigorously. She looked at them and recited the name.

"Marco Polo."

Gerard glanced at Willa with a dubious look, saying, "Marco Polo? Not long ago, we were talking about his famous journey to the East. What could a Venetian merchant have to do with salt production in Ston?"

"And why would the book about his travels be so valuable?" she asked them. "I've read it, and I don't remember anything about salt harvesting methods."

"That's not the same book," Jelena said. "The one you've read was written by an author of romances named Rustichello from stories that were told to him by Polo while they were captive in a Genoan prison. Polo had been captured by the Genoans at the battle of Korčula, an island just up the coast from Ston. The book that Vitomir wants was written in Polo's own hand during his travels, not after. It belonged to my father Ennio, who later became governor of Ston. Papa was from Venice and served on Polo's ship, but he escaped the battle and stayed in Ston when he fell in love with our mother. He felt so guilty for not returning the book to Venice as he'd been commanded by Polo during the battle that he only told Drazhan about it on his deathbed earlier this year."

"That is quite a story. But you don't have this book?" Gerard asked.

Petar shook his head. "Drazhan died before he could show me where he hid it. It might be lost forever."

"Then how could Vitomir be purchasing it?"

"Drazhan told us that Ennio claimed there is a second book," Petar said. "Jelena's father was very sick at the end and it was hard for him to speak, but Drazhan thought he was trying to say that it was a copy given to a man named Aurelio. It appears he still lives in Korčula. If Vitomir gets the codex in his possession, he may decide that he no longer needs me once the Serbs conquer the town. Jelena and I have another child back in Ston. I fear Vitomir will bring in his own people to harvest the salt and execute my whole family. With that book in his hands, he might let the entire town be slaughtered."

7

Vitomir hurried toward the gate near Dubrovnik's harbor, eager to get on the ship to Korčula. His guard and the attendants carrying his things scurried along behind him. If they didn't leave within the next hour or so, they'd risk sailing the last part of the voyage during the night. Vitomir didn't relish traveling by sea in the dark.

The thought of obtaining Marco Polo's original codex necessitated his haste. Of course, the Venetian's travels were famous throughout Europe thanks to the book recounting his journey, including the lavish illuminated copy Vitomir had in his own house, but those writings were all second hand.

The manuscript that Vitomir was on his way to purchase was composed by Polo *during* his twenty-four-year journey to Cathay. The fool who intended to sell it had no idea how valuable it was or the importance of the details it contained, and Vitomir had to take it off his hands before he figured it out.

When Drazhan had originally told Vitomir of the Polo book nearly a year ago after his father Ennio had died, he hadn't really believed the Ston saltman. Drazhan had a reputation for making up stories, mostly to make himself look good, rather than actually doing anything useful. Vitomir knew that it was only his father's position as the town's governor that ensured him a job in the salt trade, but now that the old man was dead, the townspeople were dreading the thought of Drazhan taking charge. The only one who didn't seem to know how unfit he was for the job was Drazhan himself, so Vitomir humored him and delayed announcing a new town leader, telling Drazhan that if the harvesting process worked as described, he would name him governor.

To Vitomir's shock, just a month ago Drazhan provided proof of his increased salt production method. When he showed off the mounds of additional salt, Vitomir had had his men search Drazhan's house for the manuscript. When Drazhan found out about the unsuccessful search, he claimed he'd destroyed his copy. Vitomir hadn't thought the saltman was smart enough to realize he might try to get the book for himself. And according to Drazhan, the only other one had been taken back to Venice long ago with a boy named Aurelio.

But Drazhan wouldn't have revealed that if he'd known that Aurelio had never left Korčula and was now a rich trader there, a man whom Vitomir had dealt with on several occasions. When Vitomir had sent an inquiry about the manuscript, Aurelio had apologized for the delayed reply after a trip to Split and said that he'd be happy to sell it. Now that Drazhan was dead, buying the other existing copy of Polo's codex would allow Vitomir to possess the secrets about salt production that would make him rich.

As he and his guard passed through the gate, he could see the ship he'd hired for the journey tied up at the dock.

"Lord Vitomir!" someone behind them cried out.

This was the reason he'd wanted to leave quickly. He feared a citizen had spotted him and was intercepting him to curry favor or ask for something. He sighed and turned, ready to brush him off with a few curt pleasantries.

But he frowned when he saw a young clerk rushing toward him. Vitomir recognized him as a minor official from the rector's palace.

He was out of breath when he came to an abrupt stop and bowed his head.

"What is it, Braslav?" Vitomir said, taking no trouble to hide his annoyance at being delayed. "I'm departing for a short voyage and my ship is waiting."

"I beg your pardon, Lord Vitomir, but Rector Amero has asked for you to meet with him."

"The rector is here?" Vitomir said, surprised. He was expecting his superior to be in Venice for another few weeks.

Braslav nodded. "He arrived yesterday evening. He got word you were leaving and wants to speak to you before you go."

Vitomir had no desire for an audience with the rector, but he bit his tongue. He couldn't refuse the meeting.

He spoke to his guard. "Load everything onto the ship and have the captain ready to sail as soon as I'm aboard."

When the guard nodded, Vitomir brusquely waved his hand at Braslav. "Lead the way. Quick step."

They marched back across the gate and through the maze of streets until they emerged into the main square at the southern end of the Stradun. They continued on past the newly built church dedicated to the city's patron Saint Blaise, which had been erected in just three years in the hope that the saint would protect the city from any return of the dreaded Pestilence. Beyond the church was the stately rector's palace. The stone structure was the most opulent building in Dubrovnik, with lavish reception rooms on the ground floor surrounding an open central courtyard, offices and the rector's personal chambers on the floor above, and a third-story loggia for looking out on the citizens.

Vitomir planned to live there when he was made rector once the current rector was deposed by Venice for losing the valuable salt pans at Ston. Then he'd be able to blame his predecessor for the unfortunate investments he'd made. He would be the first non-Venetian rector, but given how valuable his services would be in making the city wealthy, he believed the doge would make him a Venetian citizen and endow him with the position.

Braslav led him past the guards at the front entrance and up the stairs to the third level.

"We're not meeting in his chambers?" Vitomir asked.

"The weather is so pleasant that the rector is conducting his business outside today."

They wound their way up to the top floor and out onto the loggia, an open-air covered gallery with arched colonnades holding up a roof that blocked the region's powerful sun rays. The afternoon air had a touch of warm breeze.

Rector Amero, a wrinkled man almost twice Vitomir's age, worked at a portable desk on his lap. The rector was poring over a sheaf of documents as Vitomir came to a stop before him.

"Your Eminence," Braslav announced, "Lord Vitomir."

The rector held up a finger and didn't look up from his reading. Vitomir didn't dare take a seat until he had been offered. All he could do was stew as the rector ignored him.

After an interminable silence, Rector Amero finally looked up. He smiled blandly at his visitor.

"Oh, Vitomir, I was so engrossed with this edict from the doge that I didn't notice you there." He pointed at the chair opposite him. "Sit. That's all, Braslav."

The clerk bowed and left. Vitomir had to clench his jaw tightly to conceal his fury. He knew very well that the rector's slight had been purposeful.

"How may I help you, Your Eminence?" Vitomir asked. "I was at the harbor preparing to depart."

The rector sat back and nodded. "Yes, your excursion to Korčula. Is your wife going with you?"

"No, she is at our estate in the hills with the children." His was a marriage of convenience and money. He felt no love for his plain wife and saw her as little as possible, especially with the current business he had to conclude. When he did need companionship, he could easily procure it in Dubrovnik.

"I hope all is well with your two girls," the rector said with a too-casual tone. Pointing out the painful truth that Vitomir didn't yet have a son was one way for his superior to needle him.

"Your Eminence, I don't mean to be abrupt, but I do need to depart soon if I am to make it to Korčula by nightfall."

"Are you partaking in the city's All Hallows' Eve festivities?"

"Nothing so exciting. I have a matter to attend to there."

The rector turned to look out at the high fortress atop the outcropping overlooking the sea to the north of the city.

"Does this have anything to do with the business you conducted at Fort Lovrijenac while I was gone?"

Vitomir sat up straighter. "You know about that?"

"Not as much as I should."

So the rector thankfully didn't know the details of the trap he'd set for Petar and Drazhan. Vitomir waved his hand as if it were trivial, but his innards were roiling.

"That was an unfortunate affair with one of our more rebellious citizens. I needed to make an example of him or he might have inspired more unruly behavior."

"And he was from Ston?"

"It is under control."

Rector Amero peered at him for a moment, then nodded. "As treasurer, running Ston profitably is part of your responsibility. But running all of Dubrovnik is mine. That's why you're here."

Vitomir feigned surprise. "I don't understand." Though he feared he did. He had invested far more money than the rector approved.

"I think you do, Vitomir. I gave you permission to expand your financial responsibilities to foreign trade, including a new fleet that would bring untold riches to Dubrovnik. The first payment on the city's investment has come due, but my clerk informed me that the funds have not yet been received. You're here to tell me why."

Vitomir had to keep his knees locked so that their trembling didn't betray his unease.

"I've gotten word that the fleet has been delayed in Sicily. Storms wrecked part of the port at Syracuse, so the lading of most of the cargo had to be postponed until repairs could be made."

"When you convinced me to loan you money from the treasury for this investment, you assured me that the return would make us all rich."

"And it will. I just need more time."

The rector glowered at him. "How much more?"

"A few weeks at the most." He had hoped to have the whole

business with Ston concluded before the rector returned from Venice.

He absorbed his superior's gaze for what seemed like an eternity. Then the rector smiled.

"I suppose I can wait that long."

Vitomir let out a breath of relief. He rose out of his seat. "I appreciate your understanding, Rector Amero."

"I am in a forgiving mood today. But failure to repay debts is a serious crime. I won't always be so understanding."

He got the message that the rector was hammering into him, although the rector had no idea that his crime went far beyond a late payment. "Nor should you be."

Rector Amero turned back to the items on his desk and began reading his missives.

"Have a safe voyage to Korčula," he said without looking up.

The dismissal was as abrupt as it was insulting. As he walked back down the loggia, Vitomir knew he was treading very dangerous ground. If he failed to repay the investment the rector knew about, he'd be lucky to lose only his position, home, and money, but given the true extent of the losses, he would likely lose his head.

Before he exited into the stairway, he took a last look at Fort Lovrijenac, the edifice standing on the headland protecting the northern approach to Dubrovnik. If the rector ever found out what had really occurred there just a fortnight ago, he might as well measure out his own coffin.

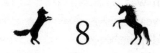

8

Two weeks ago—October, 1351

DUBROVNIK

Vitomir had chosen Fort Lovrijenac for this meeting because of its isolation. In times of war, the fortress would be stocked with a full garrison, but today only his men occupied it. Constructed with three levels of stone terraces on a promontory overlooking the northern side of Dubrovnik, the impregnable bastion was built hundreds of years before to guard the city against a Venetian invasion. It was ironic that the Venetians now used it to protect their possession of Dubrovnik.

He thought about the inscription carved above the door leading into the fortress: *Non Bene Pro Toto Libertas Venditur Auro.*
Freedom cannot be sold for all the gold in the world.

How naïve the people of Dubrovnik were. Everything had a price, including freedom. Otherwise, they would not be under the rule of Venice at that very moment.

Peering through an arrow slit in the fort's wall, Vitomir could see Petar and Jelena climbing the steep set of stairs up to the only gate. With them was Jelena's older brother Drazhan, a wild-eyed man with frazzled hair and a long beard to match. He gesticulated maniacally as he spoke. No wonder he had never married or fathered any children. Fortunately, the man's antics seemed to be distracting all three of them. None of them looked in the least wary.

Vitomir watched with satisfaction. The weasel had actually come. His deception had worked to perfection.

After Vitomir's attempt to steal Polo's book and his subsequent demand that Drazhan open the Ston's gates or face his wrath, he feared that Drazhan was only humoring him and might betray him to the rector, revealing the whole plot to take the town. So to test the saltman, he'd quietly sent word to Ston that this would be the time and place where the rector would be taking his monthly public audience. They would have no idea that the rector was actually in Venice. He couldn't be sure that Drazhan would take the bait, but if he did, Vitomir would be able to intercept him and teach him an important lesson in keeping one's bargain.

With a small retinue of loyal guards at Vitomir's command in the otherwise empty stronghold, Fort Lovrijenac was a suitable location for his trap.

Through the arrow slit, he could make out the conversation of his three prey as they approached.

"Jelena will have to wait outside the fort, of course," Drazhan said. "This is man's business."

"I wish you had waited in the city," Petar said.

Jelena scrunched her face at him. "I'm very capable of making this climb, even if I'm not allowed in for the audience."

"You know very well that my sister is as stubborn as an ornery goat," Drazhan said, which drew a slap on the arm from Jelena.

They came to a stop just under Vitomir and around the corner from the guards standing at the front gate.

"Do you know what you are going to tell the rector?" Jelena asked.

"It's simple," Petar said. "That Lord Vitomir plans to aid the Serbs in taking Ston."

"I'm still worried that it's a terrible accusation to make without evidence."

"He wouldn't believe either of us alone," Drazhan said, "but together I think we can make our case." His expression became somber. "I'm sorry I've gotten us into this. If I hadn't been so blinded by my own ambition, I never would have approached him to make the bargain to become governor."

"You've done something stupid," Petar said. "We're beyond that now."

"But you have to believe me that I had no idea of his plans to invade Ston when I struck that bargain. Will you forgive me, Jelena?"

"Of course, I do," she said, rubbing his shoulder in a motherly fashion. "That doesn't mean I don't consider you a fool as well. Most sisters would have disowned you for trying to overtake her husband's position in managing the salt works."

"I had a moment of weakness."

"I'm well aware of how weak you are," she said with a smile. "Which is why I forgive you."

"And I forgive you since you came to me after Lord Vitomir made his demand of you," Petar said.

"I may be craven, greedy, and difficult," Drazhan said, "but I'm also loyal to Ston. When he changed our agreement to make me open the gates to invaders from Serbia, I had no choice but to accept it or he would have had me slain on the spot. I couldn't very well go to the head of the Ston garrison and tell him that Lord Vitomir was plotting against the town. The captain would have gone straight to Vitomir."

"Then let's convince the rector of Lord Vitomir's betrayal."

Petar kissed Jelena on the forehead, and the two men walked to the entrance. Situated out of sight, Vitomir couldn't see them enter. He nodded for his guards to go out and ensnare them.

Shouting and indignant protestations rang through the vaulted arches as the two men were hauled into the main courtyard as instructed. Vitomir let the clamor go on for a few moments, and then emerged from his hidden position.

The blood drained from Drazhan and Petar's faces at the sight of him.

To one of the guards, he said, "Her, too."

"Where is the rector?" Drazhan demanded.

"He's not coming," Petar answered. "Can't you see that?"

"You're obviously the smarter of the two of you," Vitomir said.

Jelena was dragged into their midst as well. The guard threw her into the arms of Petar, who embraced her protectively.

"I'm sorry you've been drawn into this, Jelena," he said, then turned to Vitomir. "This doesn't concern her."

"On the contrary. It concerns your whole family."

"What are you going to do to us?" Jelena asked.

"You are to remain silent. You should have stayed in Ston with your children where you belong." Pointing at Drazhan, he added, "And you should have stayed there to do my bidding."

Drazhan stammered, "We... we weren't going to—"

"Weren't going to accuse me of high treason to Rector Amero? Is that what you were about to say?"

The weasel collected himself and thrust out his jaw. "We weren't going to leave out how you plan to sell out Dubrovnik's greatest asset to the Serbs."

"It's you who were selling out your own sister's husband."

"That was a mistake."

Vitomir circled them. "Was it? Your proposal seemed reasonable to me. In exchange for tripling the salt production, I make you master of the salt harvesters and governor of the town. I didn't believe it at first, that you discovered your process thanks to a book by Marco Polo, but the evidence of your increased haul was persuasive."

"He didn't know you would use his method to sell us to our enemies." Petar addressed the guards directly. "Do you men realize that your patron is planning to betray your homeland to the Serbs?"

"I can answer for them," Vitomir said. "They do, and they will profit handsomely from the bargain. You will, too."

"And if we won't help you?" Drazhan asked. "Petar and I are the only ones who know the process for trebling the salt harvest."

Petar frowned at Drazhan.

Vitomir grinned. "Is that so?"

"Even if you knew the instructions from Polo's book," Drazhan said, looking at Petar, "whose secret I have no doubt is protected by Blaise, you need an experienced salt harvester to understand it. Without us, your promises to the Serbs will go unfulfilled."

"You make a good point," Vitomir said. "However, I don't need both of you."

Although he found these kinds of displays vulgar and distasteful, he needed to show his guards that he was decisive. He also needed to convince the remaining man from Ston what was at stake in order to enact the next part of his plan. Vitomir nodded, and his bodyguard drew a dagger to slice Drazhan's throat. Vitomir despised the sight of blood, so he turned before he could see the results. He heard Drazhan's shriek cut short as Jelena screamed. A final gurgling cough preceded the thump of Drazhan's body hitting the stone.

After a few moments, Vitomir's guard came over and nodded that it was all right for him to turn around. Drazhan's corpse was covered as he'd ordered. No blood was visible.

Petar held Jelena close as he stared wide-eyed at the still form of his dead brother-in-law.

"I do need *you*," Vitomir said to Petar. "Not just for the salt harvest, but also to open the gates to Ston when the Serbs arrive. Otherwise, the garrison stationed there will be a stubborn force to conquer."

Petar nodded. "Of course. I'll help you."

"No, you won't. You're smarter than your brother-in-law, so I know you'll tell me what I want to hear now, and then you'll try to figure out some way to disobey me when the time comes. But what if I had your son?"

Jelena's head snapped up. "Emerik?"

Vitomir shook his head. "Your other son. Niko." They looked both confused and terrified as he turned to the guard standing farther down the colonnade. The guard stepped around the pillar, removing the hand that had been covering the mouth of the boy he'd been holding.

"Bring him here."

"Mama!" the boy cried out as he struggled in attempt to free himself. "Papa!"

Both of them stared in shock at Niko, followed by Jelena's cry, "My baby!"

The guard brought the child to a stop next to Vitomir. Niko bit the guard's hand and got a slap across the face in exchange.

"He's a spirited one," Vitomir said. "It seems Niko overheard something he shouldn't have when I was back in Ston after making my bargain with Drazhan."

"I heard him talking about killing the weasel if he came to Dubrovnik," Niko explained to his parents. "I thought I'd get in trouble for snooping if I told you. I didn't know he was talking about Uncle Drazhan until Nonna told me that's what she'd heard Lord Vitomir call him once. I thought he'd hurt you both."

"Isn't this brave?" Vitomir said to Petar. "The lad came to warn you of what I was planning, but fortunately I was able to catch him first."

"Are you all right?" Petar asked gently. "Niko?"

Niko stared at the motionless covered shape until his father repeated the question.

"I'm sorry I couldn't get to you before Lord Vitomir found me," Niko said.

"How did you get here?" Jelena asked.

"I stowed away on a ship bound for Dubrovnik. I didn't know what else to do. I had to save you."

"And you have," Vitomir said to the boy. "You will save him yet again." He turned to Petar. "Your son's surprising appearance gave me a new idea. I will keep him in the safety of my home until Ston is in the Serbians' hands. If you do as I command and open the town gates for them, little Niko here will be returned to you unharmed. If you don't..." He gestured to Drazhan's corpse.

"No!" Jelena cried. Petar shushed her.

"We'll do as you ask," he said.

"I'm glad we have an agreement. I hope you understand that any further attempt to go to the rector will not only be fruitless, but unwise. Now, you may leave while I have my men clean up this mess. I promise your brother will get a proper burial."

Petar seemed to appreciate the gravity of the situation, grudgingly dragging Jelena away from her dead brother and her captive child. Niko's shouts for his mother didn't help calm things down, so Vitomir motioned for the guard to silence the boy again. A second hard slap stopped his cries.

Vitomir couldn't help thinking that all of this would have been so much easier if he'd had Marco Polo's codex in his hands.

9

October, 1351

Korčula

Fox hadn't been eager to get back on a ship so soon, but he had realized that getting the Marco Polo codex before Vitomir did would give them bargaining leverage they might be able to exchange for Niko. Petar also mentioned that Drazhan believed the manuscript held the instructions for building a powerful weapon that might be used to defend Ston with fire.

Fox chafed at this additional delay, and he could hardly believe that he was wrapped up in a plot involving the treasurer of Dubrovnik, Marco Polo, and the Serbian Empire, but he had promised Willa to help free the child. Hopefully this small side trip would solve that problem and then they would be free to go on their way.

At least Fox's stomach was settled from the ginger they'd bought. Now that they were in the narrow strait between Korčula Island and the Stonski Rat peninsula, the calm waters minimized the ship's pitching and rolling. Willa stood beside him at the bulwark as their vessel maneuvered to dock. To eliminate the chances of Petar and Jelena being seen by Vitomir and ruining their attempt to obtain the book, Fox had convinced them to stay behind. Because he wouldn't have been allowed to carry his sword through the streets, particularly during a holy celebration like All Hallows' Eve, he allowed Petar to hold it as a symbol promising their return. Besides, the Croatian couple wouldn't have been much help since they had never visited Korčula, either. Fox and

Willa had already come up with a plan together that should allow them to make use of being strangers.

Korčula was a compact but formidable stronghold. Red-tile roofs and a central church steeple rose above stout torch-dotted walls that bordered the port docks and surrounded the town. With the sun setting behind the island, the heavily forested hills were already cloaked in shadows.

"It looks like a smaller version of Dubrovnik," Willa said.

"The smaller size should make it easier to find Aurelio's home." Apparently, he was a wealthy trader in the city.

"Finding it won't matter if Lord Vitomir has already purchased the book."

"According to Petar, the book isn't really Aurelio's to sell. In any case, we'll get it one way or another."

"You mean steal it."

Fox shrugged. "If we have to. Then we go on our way."

"Even if we haven't solved Petar and Jelena's problem?"

"We're two foreigners going up against a powerful man in a city we barely know, to prevent a war between a republic and an empire. If we accomplish this task tonight, don't you think we've earned our chance to move on?"

Willa tilted her head and pursed her lips as she regarded him.

"I think you're trying to convince yourself, not me. But I know you well enough at this point that this won't be something you can simply let go. Not until Niko is back in his parents' arms."

Willa had seen through him as usual. He did feel a sense of duty to come to their aid. His chest tightened as he thought about Petar and Jelena's predicament, the agony they were going through not knowing if they'd see Niko again.

"You're right," he growled. "Again. Vitomir abducted their child. Even though I've never met this foul man, I know him. I know his type. He thinks he's untouchable. It does burn me to think of him getting away with it. But let's concentrate on this task and then we'll decide what's next."

She nodded in understanding of his veiled reference to the abduction of his own mother when he was a child himself. That terrible event had influenced his guiding principles. If he could spare another family the same pain of a child being separated from his parents, she knew that he would do whatever it took to make that happen, no matter what hesitation he might express.

When the ship was tied up, Fox and Willa disembarked, winding through the busy dockworkers and joining the horde of visitors entering the town for the evening's festivities. Fox kept his eyes moving to see if he could spot Vitomir. Petar had told him that the Dubrovnik treasurer would be easily recognizable from the red-wine-colored birthmark on his forehead.

The crowd bunched up near the gate as those arriving by ship entered the city. He felt someone bump into him, and he immediately looked down to see the flash of a small blade slicing through the cord of the purse he was carrying around his waist.

He'd been anticipating this possibility. Cutpurses were attracted to large events where people carrying substantial amounts of money were distracted, drinking, or simply unwary. They targeted the most crowded places like this and used the expected jostling to relieve visitors of their belongings. Always visitors, never locals. He should know. He himself had made use of these facts for his own benefit on past occasions. So as soon as they disembarked from the ship, he'd attached a bulging purse temptingly to his side. He was the only one who knew that it was stuffed not with money, but with hay.

Fox's hand shot out to grab the wrist of the offender, expecting a quick young man who could duck away with the prize before the victim realized they'd been robbed. But he was surprised to see that the thief was a cherubic girl only a few years younger than Willa. Her clothes made her look like a plain maiden carrying out her chores, and she had a tattered satchel slung over her shoulder.

He squeezed her arm until she dropped the knife. Willa stooped to pick it up along with the bait purse as Fox dragged the girl aside until they found a place where they could be alone.

The girl, who hadn't made a sound, glared at him.

"You speak Italian?" Fox asked.

The twitch in her eyes told him that she did.

"You were smart not to squawk," he said. "I'm sure Korčula has harsh punishment for thieves. You wouldn't want to lose that hand."

"They don't much care what happens to newcomers," she spat back. "And I've never been caught."

"You just were," Willa said, which drew a look of contempt and frustration.

"Don't feel too badly," Fox said. "You're not the first cutpurse I've snared." In other cities, he'd snagged cutpurses and relieved them of their ill-gotten bounty when he'd needed funds. "But you need to work on your technique."

"As soon as I caught the purse, I could tell that there were no coins inside," the girl said. "You tricked me."

Willa looked at Fox. "She's smart. I think she can help us."

While Fox gripped her hands, Willa opened the girl's satchel. She removed two purses that had previously been stolen.

"You haven't been doing this long, have you?" Fox said. "You need to empty the purses and throw them away. You don't want them on you if you ever do get caught."

"Again," Willa added. "What's your name?"

"Are you taking me to the *berrovieri*?"

Fox knew the term was the Italian equivalent of the local guards responsible for keeping order.

"Not at all," he said. "We need your help."

The girl eyed them suspiciously, but she understood that she was in no position to refuse.

"I'm Magda. What do you want me do?"

"Nothing much. You know an old man named Aurelio?"

Magda made a face and spat on the ground. "He's a rotten, no-good, pig-loving louse."

"So you do," Willa said. "Good. You're going to take us to his house."

"And then you'll give me my money back?"

"It's not your money," Fox said, emptying the contents of the thieved purses into his real purse concealed safely under his tunic. "But seeing as how we'll never find the owners, I suppose we can return it to you. After we've done our business in Korčula, you'll get your pickings returned to you."

"That way, you'll keep our interest in Aurelio quiet while we're here," Willa said.

Magda peered at them while she considered their offer before reluctantly nodding her head.

She led them back to the gate into Korčula. The city inside had been transformed for the All Hallows' Eve celebration. Torches sprinkled through the narrow streets lit the colorful banners that stretched from house to house. Music played from all directions, and revelers who were dressed in costumes and masks drank, danced, and laughed as they caroused through the town. Some appeared to have animal heads—deer, dogs, and rabbits—while others had exaggerated features such as oversized noses, or unlikely brightly colored faces with huge eyes. Whatever their disguise, they could engage in raucous behavior under the very eyes of righteous neighbors and zealous officials of the church without worry of discovery.

Fox and Willa followed Magda up what appeared to be the main street until they reached a square in the center of town. The festival was at its height in this area, a party celebrating a successful harvest and thanking the saints blessing the city. Tavern owners had set up barrels outside their establishments for ease of purchase by patrons. On one side of the square, a platform had been built as an outdoor theater, where an audience watched raptly as a woman dressed as Saint Catherine was being dragged toward a huge wooden wheel. Fox wished he could stay to see how the play portrayed God's miraculous destruction of the torture device.

Nearer to them, a group of children clustered around a miniature playhouse to see a performance enacted by marionettes. He could see a jointed wooden figure of Saint George held up by strings valiantly striking down a dragon made from thin sticks of wood covered with linen. Its wings and mouth were cleverly made of separate pieces manipulated by an operator who remained out of sight standing behind a curtain. The children cried out in glee as the dragon faltered and died. Just then, a parade of colorfully dressed men on stilts began to cross the square, drawing a line of riotous revelers after them. It seemed the entire town was out and about, determined to make the most of the celebration.

Leaving the festivities behind, they turned down an empty side street. The streets were so narrow that Fox could have stretched out his arms and almost touched the front walls of opposite dwellings. They had made their way along the serpentine street and passed one cross street when Magda stopped and pointed at a luxurious townhouse. Although other townhouses abutted it on either side, like all the houses in Korčula, its unusual width indicated its wealthy owner.

"He lives there," she said.

"What does he look like?" Willa asked.

"You'll know soon, I suppose. He always comes out to join the evening prayers at vespers. The hypocrite."

"It sounds like you know him well," Fox said.

"He bankrupted my uncle, who took care of me and my brothers after my parents died in the Great Mortality."

The Pestilence was a scourge on many families. Fox's own father died in the Great Mortality that swept across Europe.

"You should go back to your uncle," he said.

"I can't," she said. "When Aurelio drove him to ruin, he left to find work in Dubrovnik. Two months later, I got word that he was killed in a tavern brawl. He was always prone to drink. Now I'm the one looking after myself and my brothers."

The story didn't sound false to Fox. Although the tone had been flat, the eyes couldn't lie. Hers were haunted by the tragedies she had suffered. He had been wavering about returning her ill-gotten gains at the end of the night, but it was clear she needed every bit of it for her and her brothers to survive.

And he certainly had no qualms about taking the book from Aurelio any way he could before Vitomir laid hands on it.

The front door of the townhouse opened, and the three of them ducked into the shadows further along the curved street. The look of raw hatred on Magda's face should have scorched the person who exited. Fox had been expecting a toad of a man, but Aurelio was quite handsome, with hair grayed at the temples and a jaunty pointed beard marred only by a thin scar on his cheek. He swished opulent green robes around him as he closed the door and locked it with a key.

His hands were empty, and he didn't carry a satchel, which made it likely that Marco Polo's manuscript was somewhere inside. The dark house looked untended, which gave Fox an idea.

"Follow him," he said to Willa. "See if he makes contact with Vitomir. And take Magda with you."

"If he does?" Willa asked.

"Send her back to find me."

"Where are you going?"

Fox took the lock-picking tools out of the small pouch in his sleeve where he always kept them.

"In search of Marco Polo."

10

Aurelio sauntered toward the central square where the celebration was well under way, with no idea that he was being followed. Willa couldn't help but feel sorry for the young girl at her side. If not for different circumstances, it could easily be her in Magda's place, scratching out a meager existence by stealing from those who had more. She admired Magda for doing what she could to help her brothers.

The Bible said, "Thou shalt not steal," but weren't she and Gerard doing the same thing for a good cause? She had killed as well—another violation of the Ten Commandments—but she'd done it to save a life. Her experiences over the past six months had convinced her that there were no absolutes.

That was why just two weeks ago she had married a man excommunicated by the Church. She knew in her heart that it was an unjust sentence, carried out by a corrupt cardinal, and she had faith that someday it would be expunged. Her good deeds with Gerard in facing up against evil were tests of their devotion and worth. There was no doubt in her mind that their continued efforts to help people like Petar and Jelena would be rewarded by the Lord.

Now it seemed as if Magda was yet another one of the endless downtrodden in need of their help.

"Where do you live?" Willa asked, keeping an eye out for Vitomir while also holding Aurelio in her sight thirty yards ahead.

"In a hut outside the city walls," Magda said. "There are many empty ones because of the Great Mortality."

Willa eyed the girl, who seemed in good health despite her situation.

"You don't seem hungry."

"Ships come through here all the time with rich traders, and I'm good at what I do. Your husband was the first person who's ever caught me."

"He's good at what *he* does."

"Can he teach me how to be better?"

"Isn't there something else you'd rather do?"

Magda laughed at that. "What? We no longer have a family business, and no connections to help my brothers get taken on as apprentices. Should we buy a ship and sail away? With what money?"

"What about trading? You said many ships come through here."

"I have nothing to trade, and I doubt any man would trade with a lowly girl like me."

That was too true. Willa had become a savvy trader herself, but she often was not taken seriously unless Gerard was with her. However, there was another way.

"You could trade with women," she said to Magda. "Surely there are some husbands who died in the Pestilence and left their businesses with their wives."

Magda nodded warily. "Yes. But what have I got that they would want?"

Willa looked around to make sure they weren't being observed, then reached into her bodice and withdrew a small pouch. She opened it for Magda and motioned for her to take a sniff.

Magda smelled it, then raised an eyebrow. "Is that pepper?"

"You have a good nose."

"My father used to have me grind it and put it in our stew on special occasions."

"It's worth a knight's wages for a week. I've learned that carrying around spices is easier than hauling gold coins, and almost as easy to trade if you know how to sell them. With this, you can trade for other goods, and eventually, set up your own livelihood."

She pressed the pouch into Magda's hand. The girl stared at her, wide-eyed.

"You're giving it to me?"

"Consider it a payment for your help."

"But I tried to steal from you."

"Aurelio stole your life from you. Has he been punished?"

"Not likely."

"If it weren't for coming across Gerard, I might be like you. Probably much worse off. I want to do what I can for you."

Willa guessed this forlorn girl hadn't been shown much kindness in recent years, for tears welled in her eyes at the gesture.

"Thank you, my lady."

"You can thank me by keeping your hands for more legitimate pursuits after tonight."

"I'll try."

Ahead of them, Aurelio raised his arm and waved to someone ahead of him. Willa followed his gaze.

A man accompanied by a guard strode toward him and took Aurelio's arm in greeting. Even from this distance, the wine-colored birthmark on his forehead was visible.

It was Vitomir.

The music and frivolity surrounding Vitomir was off-putting. He preferred his entertainment in the form of good food, wine, and women. He'd suffered this meeting place only because Aurelio had requested it, and the man had what he badly needed. It was just his poor luck that he'd arrived on the holiday. It was hard to hear anything above the din of the townspeople, and they had to pick their way carefully as the celebrants drunkenly wove from one place to another to gawk at yet another spectacle.

"It is a pleasure to meet you, my lord," Aurelio said, narrowly avoiding two boys chasing each other with wooden sticks crudely carved into makeshift swords.

Vitomir had to restrain the urge to go directly to business. He knew all too well that any offense could sour the bargain.

"You're looking well now that you are back from your visit to Split, Master Aurelio." He did look surprisingly fit for a man in his sixties. His reputation as an astute trader and businessman preceded him. "I hope I'm not distracting you much from the festivities."

Aurelio waved his hand dismissively at the revelers around them.

"The commoners need their fun once in a while or they become difficult. Much easier to keep them in their place when they've had a chance to forget their worries for a night."

Vitomir didn't mention that Aurelio was also a commoner, just a rich one.

"I'm so glad you contacted me and allowed me to meet with you to talk about our mutual interest."

Aurelio beamed at him. "When I returned home to find your inquiry about a book by Marco Polo, I assumed you were hoping to find an edition of the travels we all know so well from Rustichello."

Vitomir's back went rigid. Had he misunderstood what he was getting?

"Is that what you are trying to sell me?"

"Not at all. I wish I had one. By all accounts, it is a gripping piece of literature, telling of dog-headed men, fabulous gems, unicorns, deserts, and fantastical cities stretching as far as the eye can see."

"Yes, it's quite exciting," Vitomir said. "I have an illuminated copy of those tales read aloud at dinners when I am hosting guests. Many of the goods that come through Dubrovnik started far to the east, and my guests enjoy hearing of the place of their origins during feasts."

"Now that is the type of celebration I would love to attend."

The Venetian native was obviously fishing for an invitation, one Vitomir had no intention of fulfilling.

"Then we shall have to have you come to my home the next time you are in Dubrovnik."

"I would be honored and delighted. Our business tonight has more benefits than I expected."

"Then you do have what I want?"

"I believe I do. Have you brought the sum I named?"

Vitomir hoisted a pouch of gold out of his sack and let Aurelio peek inside.

"You drive a hard bargain," Vitomir said, "but I am willing to pay the price for what I want." Aurelio's demands had been outrageous, but Vitomir had no time for endless haggling.

"If I had known how valuable it was, I would have tried selling it long ago."

"It has value only to me."

Aurelio smiled at the generous payment and tried to take the pouch, which Vitomir held back.

"The book?"

"It's not here. We'll conclude our business at my house." He glanced at the guard. "Your man is welcome to join us."

Although Vitomir felt safe enough in his home city to walk about alone, he wouldn't go anywhere without a guard in an unfamiliar town, especially while carrying a bag full of gold. Besides, he had to ensure that he wasn't cheated.

"Thank you," he said as they began to walk to the edge of the square. "But you're certain you have what I've been looking for?"

"Absolutely. You want a book written in Marco Polo's own hand. That is what I own."

"And how do you know for sure that is what you've got?"

Aurelio smiled even wider, and Vitomir's heart pounded as he listened to the Venetian's next words.

"Because I knew the great man. The book was given to me by Marco Polo himself."

11

While Fox was picking the lock on Aurelio's door, he had to pause several times when celebrants passed by to head for the festival. Finally, he got enough time alone to open the door. He ducked inside and locked it behind him.

The house was lit by candles, which implied he wouldn't be by himself for long. No one left such expensive candles burning if they were going to be away for an extended period. He would have to search quickly.

He contemplated where Aurelio would keep the book. The two likeliest choices were his private sleeping quarters and the solar where he relaxed and conducted his personal business.

If the three-story home were designed as he expected, the kitchen and servants' quarters would be on the top floor, with Aurelio's personal chamber and the solar on the second floor.

The entire first floor consisted of the main hall, and a table was already set with platters of fruit, cheese, and bread, a pitcher of wine, and two sets of plates and goblets. Clearly, Aurelio was returning soon to entertain while his servants were romping with the rest of the city.

Fox took the stairs two at a time to the second floor. The first room he found was Aurelio's chamber. A large bed was topped with a wooden frame from which hung embroidered curtains to keep in the heat, an armoire stood against the wall, and a trunk sat at the foot of the bed.

Fox threw open the armoire and rummaged through the shelves of clothes. No book.

The trunk was next. Fox lifted the lid to see piles of bed linens inside. A quick search turned up nothing.

After checking beneath the pillows, mattress, and bed, Fox was satisfied that Marco Polo's codex was stored somewhere else. He left the chamber and went to the second-floor solar at the front of the house.

The solar had a small curtained alcove for the window overlooking the street below and was sparsely appointed with a wooden bench covered in velvet with a carved wooden front, two chairs on either side of a table, and a shelf holding five books, all with simple brown leather bindings sealed by clasps.

Fox rushed over to them and cracked open the first one. Instead of a narrative written in Italian, the parchment pages had a series of notations with numbers beside them. Wool, silk, and linen were listed down the page with columns for quantities and prices paid in Venetian ducats.

It was a ledger for Aurelio's trading business, with each page denoting the week and year. The other books were most likely the same, but Fox had to check them anyway. He opened and replaced them as fast as he could, knowing his time was running out. As he suspected, they were all the same, ten years of records for the deals Aurelio had made.

Aurelio hadn't had a satchel with him, so Fox didn't think the businessman left the house with the book. It had to be here somewhere. He threw aside the curtain, but all it revealed was a small stone ledge and the shuttered window.

He turned and scanned the room for any other hiding place. The table had no drawers, and there was no trunk. As he walked toward the door intending to continue his search on the third floor, his eye caught a glint under the bench through the openwork carving, just at the correct angle to reflect the dim candlelight in the room.

He moved the bench to the side to find an iron lockbox anchored to the wall by a thick chain. Fox felt a thrill down his spine at locating his target.

He kneeled before it and took out his lock picks. It was a more complicated lock than the front door had been, but Fox knew he could open it.

He'd only been working at it for a few moments when he heard a sound from outside. Singing. A woman's voice, high and sweet, rang out with a French ballad, one he had sung himself many times when he was bored during long rides.

It was Willa. She was warning him. Someone was coming.

The urge to work faster made his hand fumble the pick, and it fell to the floor. At the same time, a key rattled in the door downstairs.

Fox grabbed the pick and attempted to get the lockbox open in time to escape, but it seemed to mock him by refusing to open.

Now he could hear voices down on the first floor, and they were getting louder. He rushed to get the lockbox open, but he was out of time. Boots reached the second floor.

Fox quietly replaced the bench and dashed over to the curtained alcove. He climbed onto the ledge and swiped the drapes back together just as the door opened. Through a small slit in the curtains, he could see Aurelio smoothly push the door closed then move the bench so that he could get at the lockbox. He quickly took the key from around his neck, opened the box, and removed a book that looked very much like the ones on his shelf.

He placed the book on the table, closed the lockbox, and reset the bench. Then he opened the door to let in his visitor.

A richly dressed nobleman with a red birthmark on his forehead swept into the room.

"Lord Vitomir, would you care to take a seat?" Aurelio said.

Vitomir looked at his huge guard standing in the doorway, armed with a long dagger.

"Wait out there."

The guard nodded and closed the door. Vitomir lowered himself into the chair, and Aurelio took the seat on the other side of the table. He slid the book across to Vitomir.

"I believe this is what you've come for."

Vitomir picked up the book and opened it to the first page. He read out loud.

"Here begins the account of Marco Polo in the year of our Lord 1271. I leave the Most Serene Republic of Venice accompanied by my esteemed father Niccolò and my uncle Maffeo on our journey to the Levant, Armenia, and the land of the Tartars, to fulfill a solemn vow to bring to the Great Khan oil from the lamp that burns above the sepulcher of our Lord Jesus Christ in Jerusalem." Vitomir looked up. "This does not sound anything like the beginning of the well-known travels that I have read."

Aurelio shifted uncomfortably in his chair. "Because it was written during his trek. I assure you it is authentic."

"And how can I be certain?"

"As I told you, I received this book from the hands of Marco Polo himself."

Aurelio then went on to tell a story about a sea battle off Korčula Island between the Venetians and Genoese. Fox had heard of this battle because it was supposedly where Marco Polo had been captured and taken to prison in Genoa.

In this telling, however, Aurelio made no mention of Jelena's father Ennio and the manuscript entrusted to him.

"Why didn't you return this book to Marco Polo's family in Venice?" Vitomir asked.

"There was a reason I joined the fleet. I had nothing back in Venice, and I found the opportunities better here." He spread his arms, indicating the house. "As you can see, I have done well for myself."

Vitomir turned the book over in his hands. "You could have forged this."

"I only found out about your desire for this book last week. How would I have produced this work so quickly? And although I speak Italian, I could never compose a manuscript in the language. You can see from just the first page that it must be the work of Marco Polo himself."

Fox briefly considered springing from his hiding place and taking the book from their hands. Even armed with just his dagger, he could easily best these two preening jays. The guard outside the door would serve a greater challenge because of his size and dagger, but Fox gave himself a respectable chance against him.

But he couldn't risk this encounter turning deadly. Vitomir might have left orders to execute Niko if he didn't return. And getting out of Korčula alive with the book might prove to be a problem.

Fox stayed still.

"You have a point," Vitomir conceded after examining the book. "This does look genuine."

That brought a smile to Aurelio's face. "You'll see that there are detailed drawings and maps that he has included. I couldn't possibly have drawn all that with such precision. I don't even understand what most of them are supposed to represent. You have in your hands the only book of its kind."

Vitomir flipped through the manuscript, stopping several times to peruse what was on the page. When he finally closed the book, he seemed satisfied.

"I believe you."

Aurelio let out a sigh of relief. "Then it is yours for the price we agreed on."

Vitomir removed a pouch from his purse and upended it on the table, spilling out gold ducats. Aurelio swept the princely sum into his palm and put them back into the pouch.

"It is a pleasure to do business with you, my lord." He hesitated before speaking further. "Now that our bargain is complete, may I ask what your interest is in this book? If you are a collector of Signore Polo's works, perhaps I could help you find more of them."

"My interest is none of your concern," Vitomir snapped, sitting forward to make his point. "And if anyone learns of this bargain, I assure *you* that I will return with a squad of guards to cut your throat and hang your body in Korčula's main square. Am I understood?"

For the first time, Aurelio's pleasant demeanor disappeared, along with all of the blood in his cheeks. He nodded vehemently.

Vitomir smiled. "Good. I know you will be a loyal trader

with Dubrovnik in the future. I wouldn't want to have to restrict transactions between our cities as I have done with others."

"You have a faithful servant here, Lord Vitomir. I'll make sure our dealings will be mutually beneficial."

"I'm glad to hear that."

Aurelio stood, clutching the pouch of gold to his chest. "Now that we are finished here, perhaps you would join me for some refreshments, and I would also be honored to host you as a guest in my home for as long as you wish."

"I am not staying here overnight, but the ship's captain said we cannot sail until the moon rises, so I suppose a late supper would be welcome."

Aurelio walked around him and opened the door. "Please see yourself to the hall and pour some wine. I apologize for the absence of my servants, but I felt sure you would want to conduct your business in absolute privacy, so I dismissed them to the holiday celebrations. I will join you momentarily."

Vitomir placed the book in his satchel and walked out. Aurelio watched until Vitomir and his guard were tramping down the stairs. He rapidly placed the pouch with the gold coins in the lockbox and put everything back before leaving.

When he was sure he was alone, Fox climbed out of the alcove, furious that he had come so close to getting the Marco Polo codex and failing. But all was not lost. There was still time to acquire it before Vitomir returned to his ship. And the remaining books on the shelf gave him an idea. He plucked one and tucked it in his belt.

Fox couldn't go down the stairs and risk being seen from the main hall. He'd have to go out the window and drop to the street below.

First, however, he would relieve Aurelio of the undeserved gold he'd received.

12

Willa was relieved to know her warning had worked when she and Magda had seen Gerard climb down from the window of Aurelio's house. At first she thought he had retrieved the book they had come for, but he explained what happened inside. He told them they had to put a new plan into action while Vitomir was taking his meal.

When Magda heard Gerard's proposal that would in some small part humiliate Aurelio, she told them to acquire a mask and robes for Willa before she dashed away. While Gerard kept an eye on the house from down the street, Willa did as instructed and purchased a mask and robe from a reveler all too eager to take her silver. She quickly pulled the robe on over her kirtle.

Then they waited for Magda to come back. Crucially, Gerard could take no part in the plan to steal the book. Willa convinced him that any man approaching Vitomir, especially a tall and imposing stranger, would instantly raise the suspicions of his guard and make it impossible to take the manuscript without Vitomir knowing. She and Magda would have to do this on their own.

By the time Magda returned at a run, she was breathless. "It is set," she said.

"What is?" Gerard asked.

"I will switch the books as you wanted. Give me that."

She took the book that Gerard had stolen from Aurelio's house and hid it under her cloak. She focused on Willa.

"All you need to do is give me a few moments of distraction."

"What should I do?" Willa asked.

"Pretend you're interested in Vitomir's guard. Take his eyes from his lord long enough for me to work."

Gerard's eyes threatened to jump from his sockets. "And how will she do that?"

"It won't be difficult. She has a beautiful figure to use."

"That I know," he said with a scowl. "I won't allow it."

"Do you want the book or not?" Magda asked, obviously amused by his affront.

Willa put her hand on his arm. "I promise that I will be thinking of you the entire time."

"That does not make me feel any better about this."

"If it gets out of hand, you can come to my rescue."

He glowered at her and then Magda before saying, "I won't be more than a few steps away. What will you be doing? Vitomir might notice his guard being distracted."

"I have a plan," Magda said. "Better that it be a surprise. I don't want Willa to unknowingly warn him."

Fox was going to object when Willa said, "Trust her. I do."

Magda guided them to the main square where the festival had reached its apex of music, frivolity, and drunken carousing. Gerard did his best to retreat to the edge of the piazza, but Willa saw his progress impeded by several women trying to get him to join their celebration. Instead, he took up a position along the wall, his hands at his sides, his eyes locked on Willa.

"They'll have to come through here to get back to the ship," Magda said, pointing at an archway. "I'll stand over there. When I nod at you, that is when you should distract the guard. Do you understand?"

Willa nodded. "I have an idea of what to do."

Magda smiled. "I thought you would. You have secrets, don't you?"

"More than you can imagine." Willa put on her mask and tied the cord around her head.

"If only I had time to hear them," Magda said.

She scurried away, leaving Willa to pretend to be one of the locals rejoicing in thanks for the autumn's bountiful harvest. Her mask was that of a white cat, complete with ears and black spots around the holes for the eyes. She tugged at the front of her kirtle and the chemise beneath so that the neckline was lower than anything she would normally have worn. All the while she kept switching her view between Magda's alert attention, the street where Vitomir would appear, and Gerard—who looked decidedly displeased waiting to the side.

It was Magda who spotted Vitomir coming. She tilted her head to alert Willa. Vitomir was marching into the crowd behind his guard, who was parting the sea of people to make way for him.

Willa waited as they approached. When they reached the center of the square, Magda nodded, and Willa made her way toward the guard. As she walked, she girded herself to do what was needed.

Watching Willa strut toward the guard, swaying her hips as she walked, Fox's stomach roiled as if he were on a rocking ship. He wasn't concerned about her safety as much as he was jealous of her even pretending to give attention to another man. He squeezed his fingernails into his palms to keep himself from rushing over and throwing himself in her path. Still, if it went too far and Willa did find herself in jeopardy, he wouldn't hesitate to slay the guard with his bare hands.

Magda looked like a wolf circling her prey. She edged around until she was behind Vitomir. But her task wouldn't be as easy as cutting loose the strap of Vitomir's satchel over his shoulder. He would raise an immediate alarm if his satchel were stolen, so she had to make him think the book wasn't taken. It was a much higher level of difficulty, and Fox honestly didn't know if she was up to it.

Then several things happened all at once. If he hadn't been paying close attention, he would never have noticed what was actually going on.

Willa threw herself at the guard as if she were consumed with drink and lusting after him. He attempted to swat her away, but she wrapped her arms tightly around his neck and nestled into his chest, which practically sent Fox into a fit. He forced his feet to stay firmly planted, lest he ruin the plan.

At nearly the same instant, two boys approached Vitomir and pushed platters with honeyed pastries at his waist, causing him to throw his hands up. When they cajoled him to purchase some, Vitomir refused, but the boys wouldn't take no for an answer and jostled him even harder. The guard had his hands full trying to dislodge Willa, so he had no idea his master was being accosted. Vitomir looked annoyed that his guard was otherwise occupied when he needed him.

While all of this was going on, Magda skillfully stole up behind Vitomir, slipped Aurelio's book into his satchel, and removed the Marco Polo book at the same time. The difference in weight couldn't have lasted for more than several eye blinks, and Vitomir didn't so much as flinch at the contact.

When she was away with the book, she raised her hand, which seemed to be a signal. The two boys immediately disengaged and melted into the crowd. Willa released her grip and staggered backward, leaving a clear path for the guard to continue making a corridor for Vitomir. The two men exited the square without a pause.

Fox rejoined Magda and Willa on the other side of the square and went down a side street just in case Vitomir discovered the missing book.

"Are you all right?" Fox asked Willa.

"It was more unpleasant than you could know," Willa replied. "The guard smelled like he'd been baked in a sweat oven."

"Good."

That prompted a smirk from her before she turned to Magda. "Did you get it?"

The girl pulled the book from under her cloak and gave it to Fox. He opened it and in the dim light spilling from the square, he saw the words that Vitomir had read.

Here begins the account of Marco Polo in the year of our Lord 1271.
He felt a sense of awe at holding a codex that the great
Polo had written himself. He closed the book and tucked it under
his arm as the two boys ran up to them, their platters discarded
somewhere. They chattered in excited Croatian to Magda.

"These are my brothers," she said. "Mislav and Lovro. They are
learning my trade."

"Quite well," Fox said.

"You've kept your part of the bargain," Willa said. "Now we'll
keep ours."

She nodded at Fox, who took the pouch from his own purse
and handed it to Magda.

"Look inside," he said.

When she did, her eyes goggled at the sight of the gold coins.

"The gold is compliments of Aurelio," Fox added.

"Remember what I told you about trading," Willa said. "That
should be enough to get you started."

Magda's lips quivered as she nodded and closed the pouch
tightly in her hand. She threw her arms around Willa.

"Thank you, my lady. You don't know how this changes
everything for us."

"In fact, I hope I do."

Magda nodded in thanks to Fox, and she and her brothers
dashed down the street and out of sight.

"Do you think they'll be all right?" she asked Fox, taking his
hand.

"She seems almost as smart as you are, which means she likely
will be."

Willa's compassion for the girl and her brothers made Fox's
chest ache from love and pride. He certainly believed she would
have made a kind and caring nun, as she had once intended, but
he was happy she hadn't gone down that path. In fact, it was time
that they remembered they were a newly married couple.

"Let's find a tavern for the night," he said. "Then we'll get the
first ship we can back to Dubrovnik so we can give this to Petar
and Jelena."

They began walking back to the square. "You want some privacy to read through that book and see what is so important about it?" He smiled at her with a lustful grin. "Not one page."

With the moon fully risen, Vitomir gave the captain the order to set sail as soon as he was back on the ship. Despite Aurelio's offer of a warm bed for the evening, he was glad to be departing with his prize.

Now that he had Marco Polo's book in his hands, Petar was useful only for allowing Bogun and his men to conquer Ston in one swift strike. Then he could eliminate the troublesome saltman and monopolize the salt trade throughout the Adriatic coast and beyond.

As they prepared to shove off, Vitomir went to his tiny cabin and lit a candle. He wanted to see if he could spot the page with the valuable information he needed. He'd search the drawings first to see if he could find one that would lead him to the right section of text. If he couldn't recognize anything that looked like salt pans, he'd just have to read the whole thing.

He flipped it open to the first page and sucked in a breath when he saw what was written there. Instead of Marco Polo's words, crude markings denoting products, quantities, and prices ran down the parchment.

He threw the book across the cabin. Then he realized what must have happened, where the switch had taken place. He picked it up and yanked open the door, screamed for his guard. The man came running.

"Yes, my lord?"

"Tell the captain to cease his departure," Vitomir snarled. "We're going back to Aurelio's house this instant and find out how he switched books on me while I was eating. And I don't care if you have to pull his arms off to do it."

 13

DUBROVNIK

Church bells rang throughout the city for evening vesper services, but Bogun would not be attending. He had more important business to conduct. Being back in Dalmatia put him on edge, especially because he had to walk around the city without his sword to fit in with his disguise as a trader. Only venturing into Venice itself would feel worse.

But this final expedition was necessary. His men were assembled, his supplies would allow him to endure a long siege from the Venetians once he conquered Ston, and his ships were ready to sail. The last piece of the puzzle was to find a local guide familiar with the Stonski Rat peninsula.

"I don't understand why your own sailors can't help you," Vitomir said as they approached the warehouse that was under construction near the port. He seemed to be in a foul mood, with dark rings under his eyes.

"Serbian sailors don't know that region of the Dalmatian coast well enough. It's been almost two decades since the peninsula was under our purview. I need someone who can guide us to a cove where not only can we come ashore safely, but that also allows us a relatively easy march to Ston."

"If you sailed into Mali Ston, it would be a short walk for your men."

Bogun rolled his eyes at the simplistic suggestion. Dubrovnik's treasurer was a master of coin, but apparently he had no tactical sense.

"If we sailed into Mali Ston, the soldiers in the garrison would see us coming from miles away and shore up their defenses."

"But my man will open the gate—"

"And how will he do that if the defenders are on alert? In order for us to slaughter the garrison in their sleep, your man will have to open the gate in the middle of the night so that my squad can enter the town before anyone knows that they're there. Then the rest of my force can reinforce the town, ready to withstand any assault Venice can muster."

It was a foolproof plan as long as Vitomir pulled off his end of the bargain.

"How many men do you have under your command?" Vitomir asked.

"More than one hundred fifty."

"Surely that's enough men to take the town even if you have to make a frontal assault. The garrison numbers less than twenty guards."

Bogun stopped and pulled Vitomir aside so that he was only inches from his face.

"You are not a soldier, are you?"

"I've read the *Romance of Troy*."

Bogun's lip curled in unconcealed disdain. "That account is not exactly a treatise on war tactics. Let me educate you. A walled city can be easily held by a handful of men even against a force that outnumbers it ten to one. All they have to do is defend the few places where we attempt to climb over, having used crossbowmen to decimate my army long before we even reach the wall. A siege of that type could last for months—time I will not have. Do you think Venice would hesitate to send a vast army to wipe us out as soon as they learned Ston was under attack?"

Vitomir shook his head. "You would have two weeks at most."

"And the emperor will not support us with further troops, not unless we already have Ston under our control. So. At the next full moon, will your man be there to let us in after compline or not?"

Bogun got the strained nod he expected.

"Good. Then we need to make landfall far enough from the

town that we won't be detected. Which is why I need your help finding a guide. You said you had two potential choices."

"Yes. The one we're meeting now is a young mate on a trading ship that frequently carries salt from Ston. Currently he's working as a laborer while his ship is under repair."

"And the other?"

"An old man who used to collect oysters on Stonski Rat. He's blind in one eye now, but I think he'd get the job done."

"And they'll do this for a price?"

"In my experience," Vitomir said, "the right amount of money will overcome any misgivings. But better to meet somewhere we won't be seen." He stifled a yawn.

"Do you find this discussion boring?" Bogun asked.

Vitomir shook his head. "My apologies. I didn't get much sleep last night. My business in Korčula was tiring, and the journey back took longer than I expected."

"What was your business there?"

He hesitated before speaking, which made Bogun think he was devising a lie.

"I went to acquire a valuable ledger. It turns out I was lured into a deception."

"So you didn't get the ledger?"

"Unfortunately, no. But I dealt conclusively with the man who cheated me."

So he killed the man, Bogun understood him to mean. Or more likely, Vitomir had the man killed. He knew Vitomir was curiously averse to the sight of blood. Bogun harbored no such cowardly squeamishness.

"Are you up for this meeting?"

"Of course," Vitomir said. "The sooner it's done, the better. I asked him to stay after the others have gone home so we can have some privacy."

They continued on, passing fishermen who reeked of the day's catch as they exited the port after their work at sea. A long fortified seawall protected the port, whose narrow entry was guarded by a rounded tower. A series of large warehouses lined the quay, ready to receive and exchange the trade items that made Dubrovnik famous. Their destination was a half-built warehouse where the last of the construction workers were leaving for their evening tankards of ale. The sun had already descended below the city walls and twilight would fall shortly, perfect for a clandestine meeting. They waited outside until they were alone so that no one would see them go inside.

They went through the doorless entrance and were immediately plunged into shadowy gloom. Most of the walls were complete, but the roof was still under construction. Only a portion of the wooden frame high above was in place. Scaffolding with stacks of stones lined the far wall that still had the top story left to finish.

A lone man sat on the scaffold, drinking from a bladder. He was shirtless and covered in dust and sweat. Muscles rippled as he tilted the waterskin back, revealing scars on his arms and a nose broken and knitted together badly at the bridge.

When he saw his visitors walking toward him, he put the waterskin down and hopped off the scaffold, throwing a tunic over his head. He swaggered over, towering half a head over Bogun.

"Ulfo," Vitomir said, "this is the trader I was telling you about."

Ulfo looked Bogun up and down. "Does he have a name?"

Bogun avoided the question. "I'm told you have knowledge about the Stonski Rat peninsula."

"Some."

"Enough to guide me to a landing place within five walking miles from Ston?"

The ship's mate narrowed his eyes and tilted his head as if he were examining Bogun more closely.

"What is it?" Bogun asked.

Ulfo paused, then said, "What will I get?"

"You'll get what we agreed to," Vitomir said.

"This journey will take me from my ship for an extended time. How can I be sure I'll have work on it when I return?"

"I guarantee that you will have employment after you've assisted him. You know from my position in the city that I can make good on my promise."

"And all I have to do is be a guide?"

"Timing is everything," Bogun said. "You must be ready to sail within the week. You'll be back in a month at most."

"Your Croatian accent is good," Ulfo said, "but you're not from here."

"My mother was Serbian. Is that a problem for you?"

"If you cross my palm with silver, I won't have a problem."

"And I won't have a problem as long as you carry out my orders to the letter."

"Excellent," Vitomir said. "Then it's settled."

But then Bogun saw Ulfo's expression change. He couldn't hide his look of recognition.

Bogun sighed when he realized that their meeting had come to naught.

"Where?" he asked.

Ulfo shook his head. "What do you mean?"

"Where was it you saw me?"

Vitomir's eyes flicked between them. "What is going on?"

"Ulfo here knows who I am. I'm guessing I was involved in some event in his life, and I doubt it was a pleasant one."

Ulfo looked at Vitomir with fiery eyes and snarled, "He's Bogun, a Serbian murderer. He's the man who burned down my village when I was a boy. His men raped my mother before killing her and my father."

"I'm surprised you survived," Bogun said.

"Only because I hid in an empty barrel until you left. I got the barest glimpse of you, but you said nearly the same thing to one of your men all those years ago. 'Carry out my orders to the letter.' I thought I recognized your voice, but I wasn't sure until you said those words." He turned to Vitomir. "We should take him to the rector."

Vitomir shook his head. "I'm afraid that won't happen."

Ulfo's mouth dropped open. "You knew?"

"Not about that or I would never have come to you. But I know the kind of man he is."

"You sicken me." Ulfo's fists balled into two boulders. "I was too small to fight then. Not anymore."

Bogun noted a flash of fear on Vitomir's face as the treasurer quickly stepped back, not wanting to get involved in the violence to come.

Ulfo was larger and younger, but Bogun had skill and experience on his side. The ship's mate had no idea what a deadly mistake he was making.

As Ulfo put up his club-like fists, Bogun briefly considered using his dagger to end this quickly, but a laborer with stab wounds was not the scene he wanted to leave behind.

They circled each other before Ulfo lunged with his first blow, a strike that Bogun easily dodged. The brawler had power, but he used so much strength that he might as well have announced exactly what he was going to do. Bogun could anticipate his every motion.

Still, this was good practice. He hadn't had a proper fight in weeks.

The next time Ulfo struck, Bogun backhanded him across the face just to get his attention. The slap had the intended effect, infuriating the young fighter. He lashed out with another jab, and Bogun spun around and elbowed him in the gut.

Ulfo was more resilient than he expected and recovered quickly enough to grab for Bogun's neck. A squeeze from those massive hands might do some damage, but Bogun latched onto Ulfo's thumb and snapped it downward, breaking it with a satisfying crack.

Ulfo screamed, which Bogun put a stop to with ferocious punch to the throat. The ship's mate wobbled and gasped for breath as he pawed at his ruined neck.

It was time to end this. Bogun came to his side and struck a mighty kick to the side of Ulfo's knee. It bent at an unnatural angle, and he went down writhing in agony.

Bogun was pleased to see Vitomir watching with wide eyes at how easily he'd bested this young giant.

"We can't leave him here like that," Vitomir croaked out.

"Of course not. Stand back."

Bogun went over to the nearby scaffolding and gauged the height of the stones perched on top. They would do.

He drew his dagger and sawed at the rope securing the structure to the wall. When they were free, he pushed against the scaffolding.

Ulfo realized what was happening and scrambled to crawl away on his one good leg, but he was too late. The scaffolding came crashing down on top of him, crushing him beneath the limestone blocks destined to complete the final story of the building. His legs shuddered for a moment before going limp.

Bogun replaced the dagger and brushed off his hands as if he were done with a fine day's work.

"We should go," he said to Vitomir, who ripped his eyes away from Ulfo's broken body as blood pooled on the ground. "We don't want to be found at the scene of this tragic accident."

Vitomir nodded as they hurried out. Once they were in the open air and away from any connection to Ulfo's death, Bogun said, "Now, I trust we won't have this kind of problem with your one-eyed oysterman."

14

The smoky tavern served a simple meal of wine and fish stew, but Willa thought it might be the tastiest food she'd ever eaten. The whitefish was fresh off the boat, and the salt from Ston gave the dish a flavor that made her mouth water every time she raised the spoon. At the same time, she would have traded it in an instant for her mother's cheese and mutton pie. She loved experiencing all the new foods during their travels, but it seemed so long since she had had a taste of home.

She sat in an out-of-the-way corner with Gerard, Petar, and Jelena, who were also savoring their supper, momentarily quieting the discussion about Marco Polo's book, which lay on the table. The tavern was packed with laborers, so the cacophony masked their conversation from anyone attempting to overhear it.

"Are you sure there isn't anything about salt in there?" said a disappointed Petar.

Gerard drained the last of his stew before setting down the bowl.

"I read the book cover to cover on our way back from Korčula. My understanding of Italian is good enough to know that Polo didn't mention anything about salt. Nor was there a fantastical weapon that shoots flames."

"Then how could my brother's hidden copy tell him how to increase salt production?" Jelena asked.

"Because we don't think what Drazhan had was a copy," Willa said. "This book seems to be the first of two volumes."

Petar frowned. "How could you know that?"

"From the dates," Gerard said. "Polo was meticulous about dating his entries. The last one is from 1282. That's only about halfway through his travels."

Willa nodded. "He returned to Venice in 1295. I remember that from Rustichello's account."

Disgusted by what he'd heard, Petar leaned back and pounded the table. "Then this was all for nothing. And we still have no way of freeing Ni— Niko."

"But we do appreciate your efforts," Jelena added quickly.

Petar's expression softened. "Of course. I didn't mean to blame you."

"Not at all," Willa said. "You must be under unimaginable strain about him."

Jelena glanced at her husband before saying, "We're petrified about what might happen to him."

"I promise we'll do everything we can to get him out," Gerard said.

After discovering that the book wouldn't be valuable enough to warrant the release of Niko, he and Willa had agreed that their efforts to help Petar and Jelena were incomplete. Now they would have to take a bigger risk to get the couple's son back. This time it had been Willa who had reservations about the scheme since Gerard would be in the greatest peril, but he'd convinced her it was the only way to save the child and earn the Lord's favor. She had known that he wouldn't be able to abandon this Croatian family in need, but she hadn't counted on it putting her husband in such danger.

"I don't think the book is worthless," Gerard continued. "In fact, I believe it can help with our plan tomorrow."

"How?" Petar asked.

"Vitomir wants it badly," Willa said. "That gives Jelena a perfect reason to talk to him."

"Are you sure he will leave the rector's palace at the hour of sext tomorrow?" Gerard asked.

Petar nodded. "Zrinka said he always returns to his house for midday dinner. I watched today, and he took the fastest route."

"No guard was with him? Even with the Hungarians furious at him?"

"No. He considers himself untouchable when he's in Dubrovnik."

According to Petar, Vitomir had banned all trade with Hungary over a grave insult. The official story was that they had denigrated the rector of Dubrovnik while Vitomir was visiting their court on a diplomatic mission, but there were rumors that the insult had been about Vitomir himself since he was the one who'd insisted on the ban. Given what she'd heard about his inflated sense of self-importance, Willa thought the rumor much more likely to be the reason.

"Then he won't be expecting an attack," Gerard said, "and everyone can blame it on the Hungarians."

"Do you really think this will work?" Jelena asked. "It's quite bold to carry out an attack like this in broad daylight."

"It's our only chance to get him alone," Willa said. "That's why you need to pull him into a quiet alley. He seems to have a low opinion of women, so he won't suspect anything if you are alone."

"I've never done anything like this. But if it helps free Niko, I will."

"I think you're more than capable," Willa said.

"You don't seem worried about this."

Of course, Willa dreaded all the ways this plan could go wrong, but she couldn't let on about her apprehensions to Jelena. She put on a brave face.

"Gerard has worked this all out. I'm sure it will turn out just the way we want."

"It's getting late," Gerard said, "but we'll go over it again in the morning. If there is any problem, we can always put it off for another day."

"We can't afford to wait long," Petar said. "Zrinka said Bogun is back in town. She overheard them talking about ships that would land within the next two weeks. It must be when they're planning to attack Ston."

"I worry about Zrinka as well," Jelena said. "I fear what could happen to her if Vitomir learns that she has been spying for us."

"You said she's from Ston," Willa said. "Could she return there with us?"

"I think she might be happy to do that. She's mentioned several times how she was sorry she ever left."

"Then we'll all go there together when this is over."

Jelena nodded. "You're a good person. Both of you are."

"And you, too. I admire anyone who would go to such lengths to protect their town."

"I don't mean to sound ungrateful," Petar said, "but why are you doing all this for us? You've only known us for a week."

Willa looked at Gerard. She knew they were both thinking about the train of events that had brought them here. From his unjust excommunication to their adventures in Rhodes that had led to the gates of the Knights Hospitaller's palace being closed against the Croatian couple. But they couldn't tell Petar and Jelena any of the story for fear that their assistance would be rejected. To knowingly associate with those who had been excommunicated would be a heretical crime against the Church.

"We've been where you are now," Gerard said. "We know how hopeless it can feel when you're at the mercy of those who abuse their power in this world. If we can help you find justice, perhaps we'll earn it for ourselves."

That seemed to satisfy Petar. "I won't ask what your own tragedies have been. I will just say thank you."

"You're both a blessing," Jelena said as they stood to go, then repeated a line from the prophecy. "*My hand guides strangers from across the sea to provide aid in this time of need.* I thank the Lord that you have been guided to us."

They said their goodnights and retired to their individual rooms, a luxury when most boarders would be sleeping all together on rushes in the main hall once the tables had been cleared.

After the door was closed, Gerard said, "Do you really think Jelena will be able to carry out her part?"

"She's a mother," Willa said. "Her child is in danger."

"I wasn't questioning her determination, but her ability."

"I told her exactly what we needed, and she came back not long after with the pig's blood and the bladders. She's nervous—who wouldn't be in her situation?—but she has a good head on her shoulders. She'll be ready. What about Petar?"

"I had to argue with Petar this afternoon for a good while. He wanted to be the one on the attack, but I made him realize that he had a vital role to play. Are you sure you want to do this?"

"I love playing dress-up. But I was going to ask you the same thing."

"If I could think of a better plan, I would have. This is the best option we have for getting Niko out of that house and back to his parents."

"As long as it's not a 'sacrifice.'"

She had memorized the prophecy, so she recited it again for him.

> The lure of precious crystals sparks a dire threat to the White Fortress.
> My hand guides strangers from across the sea to provide aid in this time of need.
> Hellfire rains down when a sacrifice summons a dragon to destroy any enemy refusing to flee.
> A miracle inspires a new leader to show the way to liberation.

"Believe me," Gerard said, "if I could summon a dragon to rain hellfire on this enemy, the plan would be completely different."

Willa had her own misgivings about this scheme, but she trusted Gerard's judgment. She caressed his cheek.

"I know you meant what you said to Jelena and Petar. About earning justice for us."

Gerard took off his cotte and sat on the bed of straw to remove his boots. Willa's heart stirred at seeing his muscles strain against the fabric of his tunic.

"If I'd told them about my excommunication, they would have fled. We can't be certain we'll ever get the evidence that we'll need for my absolution by the Church, but you're the one who taught me not to give up hope. If we can help commoners like Jelena and Petar resist powerful men like Vitomir and Bogun, it will show that evil doesn't always flourish, even when the odds are in its favor. Then I can believe I'll regain my good name and that we'll be able return to England with honor. But if we leave them now in this dire predicament, I wouldn't be worthy of redemption."

"I'm glad that you've come to see it my way," Willa said playfully as she ran her fingers through his hair. "I think you'll find that it's just easier to agree with me."

Gerard pulled her down onto his lap.

"You're probably right, but we're both agreed about getting back to our own problems after this interlude."

"And what plans do you have for us once we're living in Caldecott Mote?" she whispered. She had never seen Gerard's family estate back in Oakhurst, but she hoped to settle there with him someday.

"It will need work after being left unoccupied for all these years," he said, kissing her neck deliciously. "And of course we'll have to expect the blessing of children. Four would be nice."

"All boys?"

"At least one boy. I don't think I could stand to be outnumbered five to one in my own household."

Willa smiled and ran her hand down his chest and stomach. "And when do you think we'll begin having this family?"

"That will be up to providence," Gerard said, his eyes wild with lust as he took her down to the bed and began to unlace her kirtle. "But in the meantime I will certainly revel in the trying."

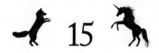 15

The last person Vitomir expected to see on his walk back from the rector's palace to his home for midday dinner was Jelena. As he entered the crowded square near the church of Saint Blaise, she stepped out of a side street. He was shocked to see her nervously clutching a book in her hands. It looked just like the Marco Polo codex that Aurelio had showed him.

He was utterly confused. How could this peasant possibly have come across it? And where the devil had she been for the past weeks?

She came to a stop out of arm's reach, a mask of anxiety on her face.

"Lord Vitomir, I need to speak to you."

"Then speak."

"Not here. My husband doesn't know I'm talking to you. He thinks I'm somewhere else."

She glanced at the wide staircase in the distance that narrowed at the summit and was topped by a stone balcony behind it. Vitomir could make out Petar standing at the top, but he was looking in another direction.

If she hadn't been carrying the book, he might have dismissed her. After all, what could a woman say to him that would be of value?

"We must hurry," she said. "Before he sees me." She moved toward the side street from which she'd emerged.

The manuscript provided enough of a lure for Vitomir to

follow her. After all, what threat could she pose when he knew her husband to be elsewhere? They went down the narrow street until they were out of Petar's sight. The din from the crowd was muffled now that they were alone. She remained a wary distance from him.

He nodded at the book. "What is that you're holding?"

"Before we talk, I want to know how Niko is faring."

"He's well fed, though perhaps a bit bored in his room."

Jelena's eyes glistened with tears. "Can you tell him that I love him and think about him every day?"

Vitomir waved off this emotional display. "Why am I speaking to you?"

She held the book to her chest. "I think you want this book."

"Why would you think that?"

"Because it was written by Marco Polo."

His breath seized for a moment. Could this really be the copy that was stolen from him in Korčula?

"Show it to me."

She shook her head and took a step back. "How do I know you won't just take it?"

"You question my honor?"

"You had my brother killed in front of me."

He narrowed his eyes at her. "Read from it."

"I can't read."

"Then I don't believe you."

He turned to leave but stopped when she said, "Petar hired a cutpurse to take it from you."

Vitomir whipped around. "What did you say?"

"It was in Korčula's central square. Boys distracted you while the thief made the switch. Petar forced me to throw myself at your guard."

Now he recalled. The celebration. The children thrusting their pastries at him. The lascivious woman climbing all over his guard. It hadn't been Aurelio who'd tricked him. No wonder he hadn't confessed before his death, despite what Vitomir would have thought was adequate persuasion.

Blood boiling, Vitomir took a step toward her. "That is my rightful property."

"I'll give it to you for Niko."

"You simple witch. You'll give it to me because it's mine. I bought it."

He rushed toward her to snatch it from her hands, his fury so overwhelming that he didn't register the large, bearded man charging at him with a drawn sword. The stranger raised it and cried out, "*Attento!*"

Terror seized Vitomir, and he shrank from the attack, throwing his arms in front of his face in what would surely be a useless gesture. His insides liquified at the knowledge he was about to die.

But instead of striking him, the bearded man clasped onto his cloak and tossed him to the ground as easily as if he'd been a child.

Vitomir fell on his backside, only to see a wicked blade slicing down towards his neck. At first he was confused, but then realized it was wielded by a second man he hadn't even seen, a frightful vision dressed in a hooded cloak and mask.

The deadly steel was stopped inches from his throat, prevented from beheading him only by the intervening sword of the bearded stranger.

The bearded man wasn't an attacker but a savior.

Jelena shrieked in fear and fled back into the square with Marco Polo's book.

The savior pushed the attacker's sword away and kicked out, but the blow was expertly dodged. Another swing of the sword sliced the savior's arm. He cried out in anger and grabbed it. Blood oozed between his fingers.

Vitomir was frozen in shock, the sight of the blood curdling his stomach. He wanted to scramble to his feet and flee as Jelena had, but his legs were paralyzed.

The would-be killer swung wildly and gave his savior an opening. He thrust forward, catching the attacker on the side. The strike cut through the cloak and blood quickly soaked the fabric.

The attacker howled in pain and staggered backward. It wasn't a lethal strike, but a wound that would hobble anyone.

"*Ennek még nincs vége!*" the man cursed in a high-pitched scream, then turned and ran, ducking around the nearest corner and out of sight.

His savior, clutching his arm, didn't give chase. The whole attack took mere moments. The duration was so short that it hadn't attracted any attention from people in the nearby square.

The stranger wiped clean his sword, which Vitomir recognized as a rare Damascus steel blade from the unique swirled pattern. After sheathing it, the savior bent down and held his hand out to Vitomir, who took it with a trembling hand. He'd never before been so close to death.

"You're safe for now," the man said in his English-accented Italian. "I'm Gerard Fox."

Vitomir got to his feet on shaky legs, averting his eyes from Fox's bloody arm.

"My thanks to you, Sir Gerard." Although Fox hadn't mentioned a knighthood, his manner of dress and his prowess with the unusual sword made it a logical assumption. "My name is Lord Vitomir, treasurer for Dubrovnik."

"With such a position, why don't you have a guard with you?"

"I never thought it necessary to have an escort in the city center, but I can assure you I will from now on."

"The murderer may return with comrades. Can I take you somewhere more secure?"

"My home. It's a short walk from here."

"Lead the way, my lord."

Fox kept close as they walked toward the square to the west. Vitomir glanced at the steep outdoor stairway far in front of them. Petar angrily stared at him with Jelena at his side before he grabbed her arm and hurried them out of sight.

Vitomir had briefly considered that it was Petar in the mask, but he couldn't possibly have made it all the way to street level and then back up to top of those steps in that short amount of time. Besides, now that he thought about it, the man who'd tried to kill him was shorter and slighter of build.

"Do you think the attacker was after you or the woman you

were speaking to?" Fox asked as he kept turning his head to look for any signs that they were being followed. He gripped his arm where the sword had slashed him.

"He must have been there for me." Vitomir said nothing more about the woman, and Fox didn't inquire.

"Why do you think that?"

"The man spoke in Hungarian before he ran off. He said, '*Ennek még nincs vége.*' It means 'This isn't over.'"

"Then it's good we are moving to safer ground. Is Venice or Dubrovnik at war with the Kingdom of Hungary?"

Vitomir shook his head. "I banned all trade with Hungary because they insulted our rector. They must have thought that sending a murderer for me would change their fortunes."

In reality, at a dinner held for him during a diplomatic mission to the Hungarian court, the assembled courtiers consumed gallons of wine and drunkenly began making jests about Vitomir marrying a Venetian to secure his position, as if he had not earned his place as treasurer. Given his precarious position as a guest in their hall, he hadn't dared storm out in anger, pretending to take their jibes in good humor. But the hearty guffaws at his supposed subservience to a woman still rang in his ears. As soon as he'd returned to Dubrovnik, he'd invented the story of the insult to the rector and cut off all trade with Hungary.

Apparently they were furious enough to kill over it.

"I will have our forces track down this killer."

"If they can find him. Surely he's long gone by now."

"He might be easy to find. Thanks to you, he's injured. So are you."

"It's nothing," Fox said. "Just a scrape. I've had far worse."

"Then you've been in battle?"

"Many times. I was with King Edward's army during the invasion of France. It's where I received my knighthood."

"No wonder you fought off that man so easily."

They mounted the stairs where Petar had been watching them. Vitomir was as wary as Fox.

"I shouldn't have let him draw blood," Fox said.

"Still, you came to my aid and were wounded in the process. It was a brave thing to do. I will be forever grateful to you for saving my life."

"It's part of my oath as a knight to help those in need."

"May I ask why you are in Dubrovnik, Sir Gerard?"

"I am the second son, so my brother inherited the family estate. Once my service to the king's army concluded, I struck out to find my fortune on the road as a man-at-arms. Through a long and boring series of events, I found myself on a ship to Dubrovnik."

Given what was about to transpire with Bogun, Vitomir could use another guard, especially one so expert in battle.

"And are you still seeking employment?" Vitomir asked.

Fox looked at him with surprise. "Are you offering me a position?"

"I am always in need of skilled fighters like you, and you've proven yourself quite worthy. I have room at my home for you to stay, if you are looking for lodging."

"That's generous of you, Lord Vitomir. I don't know how long I will stay, but while I am here, I accept your offer."

"Good." He gestured to the four-story building close to the Dubrovnik city walls. "This is my home."

They entered an antechamber where Vitomir's steward rushed to them, taking his cloak.

"Call the captain of my guard at once," he commanded, and the steward scurried away. Vitomir led Fox into the main hall decorated with a series of tapestries depicting scenes from the Apocalypse. Elsewhere in the room, a couple of servants were laying wood in the enormous fireplace while others were busy around a series of trestle tables setting up for the midday meal.

"Are you hungry, Sir Gerard?"

"I would be most grateful for a meal, but first I'd request some privacy to tend to my wound."

"We have a healer in the house who can look at that."

"That is much appreciated, but I'd rather treat it myself." When Vitomir looked at him oddly, Fox added, "Although I'm sure yours is first-rate, I've had some poor experiences with healers in the past."

Vitomir nodded. "I understand. I admit I share your wariness. I'll have my steward take you someplace private."

Before the steward returned, Bogun entered the hall. If he weren't dressed in trader's clothing, his formidable build and purposeful soldier's gait could have signified him as the captain of the guard.

"Ah, Master Bogun," Vitomir said. "I'm glad you're here. I wish to present my savior, Sir Gerard Fox."

Bogun raised one of his thick brows and looked Fox up and down as if he were sizing up either a potential ally or enemy.

"My pleasure, Master Bogun," Fox said.

"Bogun is from Kotor in Serbia. He is my guest while he is in Dubrovnik to negotiate our salt trade for the next year."

"Your trade?" Fox asked. "I thought Venice and Serbia were not friendly."

Bogun replied in gravelly Italian. "Your accent is strange. Where do you hail from?"

"England," Vitomir said. "Sir Gerard saved my life from a robber just this day. He has agreed to be a man-at-arms for me."

Bogun's eyes bored into Fox. "Is that right?"

"As for our business," Vitomir continued, "you likely don't know that salt is one of Dubrovnik's main exports, collected from the pans at Ston. It provides more than a third of our city's income, which is my responsibility. Whatever rivalry we have with Serbia is outweighed by their need for salt and our need for gold."

Fox nodded. "As I will be providing security for you from this point on, I would like to hear more about this trade at dinner. Perhaps it will shed light on your attacker. Before that, however, I would like to dress my wound so that I may be at full capacity."

"Certainly. The steward entered the hall with another strapping man. It was the guard Fox had seen with Vitomir in Korčula. After the introductions were made, the steward guided Fox away. Bogun never took his gaze from Fox as they exited.

"Is something bothering you?" Vitomir asked him.

"I'm curious about your lucky escape," Bogun said. "Tell me exactly what happened."

As Fox climbed the stairs with the steward, he said, "My good man, I require some herbs to soothe my wound." He nodded to his bloody hand, which continued to clutch his arm. "Would it be possible for you to take me to the kitchen so that I may choose them before I attend to the wound?"

"Of course, my lord. It's on the top floor."

When they reached the fourth floor, Fox saw a door with a lock clasped to the handle. Normally it would simply be a storage room for food and cooking supplies. For it to be locked meant that there was something valuable inside.

Fox made no indication of his interest in the locked door as he was led into the kitchen. Cooks were hard at work baking bread, stirring stews, and gutting fish brought in daily by the local netting fleet. The steward explained Fox's need to the cook while Fox took in the layout of the room, particularly the window looking out on the city wall. Clothes were draped on a drying line outside. The cook led him to an array of fresh herbs, and he made a show of selecting several, along with a mortar and pestle to grind them. Fox requested a private space so he could dress the wound, and the steward obligingly carried the materials, gesturing for Fox to accompany him to a small chamber just across from the kitchen. He left briefly to bring in a basin with some water and a cloth for Fox to clean himself, then closed the door behind him when he left.

Now that he was alone, Fox removed his tunic, revealing a lamb's bladder strapped to his arm. Dried pig's blood was caked on its opening from when he'd squeezed out its contents after the sword strike. He untied it and wiped the blood from his unblemished skin with the damp cloth.

He went to the window and scanned the streets outside. There was Willa standing at the next corner.

He waved the bloody cloth until she spotted him. She shook her head in equally visible relief and worry upon the visual confirmation that the attack had gone exactly as planned.

Fox was in.

THE THREAT

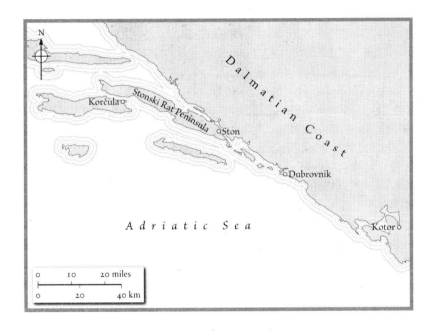

16

Once Willa saw that Gerard was safely inside Vitomir's house, she drew a little comfort from the thought that if his plan had gone this well so far, the rest of it would, too. She gave a gentle wave to him, and he smiled before leaving the window. As she withdrew to meet with Jelena, she tucked away the reassuring image of her confident husband.

Jelena was waiting down the stairs and around the corner. She still looked stunned from her role in the fake attack on Vitomir. In her arms was the cloak Willa had been wearing, wrapped around the mask, gloves, and bloody pouch of pig's blood. The leather armor that had protected Willa's side from Gerard's sword was still strapped to her waist under her robes.

Petar had already gone to hide the sword and acquire what they would need for the next part of the plan.

"Did it work?" Jelena said, chewing on a fingernail as they started walking back to the tavern.

Willa nodded. "He's inside the house and knows where Niko is being held captive."

"You're sure?"

"He gave me the signal that the plan should go forward as we designed it."

"As *you and Gerard* designed it. I've never met a woman who was so good at planning a fight."

"You did well yourself," Willa said. "We never could have made it work if you hadn't drawn him onto that quiet street."

"I was so scared when I saw you coming at Lord Vitomir. I could have sworn you really were a murderer trying to kill him."

"It seems we fooled him, too, or he wouldn't have invited Gerard back to his house."

A gloomy look crossed Jelena's face. "I hope Lord Vitomir was telling the truth about Niko."

Willa put her hand on Jelena's shoulder. "I'm sure he's fine. Vitomir still needs Petar to harvest the salt for him after Ston is conquered."

Willa didn't know if that was true, but she couldn't put doubts into Jelena's head that this would all be for naught. If Niko was still alive in Vitomir's house, she had to believe that Gerard would get him out safely.

When they reached the tavern, Willa went to her room, taking the clothing from Jelena. She would have to find a way to dispose of it all later. She took off the constricting leather armor and saw the spatter of blood on it that she'd rinse off when she had time.

An inspection showed how good Gerard's aim had been. Her sword had been dulled because she'd been so worried about hurting him if she hit him by accident. He only had to squeeze out his pouch to make it look as if she'd hit him on the arm.

But Gerard couldn't blunt the exquisitely sharpened blade of his sword called Legend, so he had to be much more careful about where he hit her. The small cut on the leather armor showed a mark of the steel edge's impact after it had sliced through the pouch. It had helped that they'd practiced the moves two dozen times before staging the actual attack.

Once she was back in her kirtle, she knocked on the door of Jelena's room. She called her in, where Petar was waiting with a somber expression.

"Is something wrong?" Willa asked. "Were you unable to get the plank?"

He shook his head. "I got just what you and Gerard suggested. Twelve feet long. Wide enough to walk on."

The plank was a key part of Gerard's plan to escape from Vitomir's house with Niko. They couldn't come down the main stairs without being seen by the guards. Even if they somehow made it out the front of the house, which was highly unlikely, Vitomir could order the immediate closure of all four gates out of the city. The two of them would be trapped in Dubrovnik with the city guards searching for them until they were recaptured. Gerard would be executed for his efforts.

Instead, they would escape from the top floor of Vitomir's home and out onto the city wall, waiting until the night guard was far away on his patrol just before daybreak. It would be a short run along the wall walk to the house with the burnt roof that was unoccupied and under construction. Willa, Petar, and Jelena would extend the plank to the wall for Gerard and Niko to come across into the house to complete the escape. The five of them would be through Dubrovnik's city gate at first light when it was opened for the day, long before Niko would be reported missing.

Zrinka had given them all the information they needed. She hadn't been able to see her young cousin for fear of revealing herself, but she was glad to depart the house for the last time. She was waiting for them with the horses at the stables outside the walls where they would meet her as soon as Niko was free to go to Ston.

"Where is the plank now?" Willa asked.

"I have it stowed for later tonight. No one will take it."

"Then what's the problem?"

"I got the plank near the port where the refuse lumber is taken to be sold for firewood. There were two carters there unloading rotten wood from their donkey cart. I overheard them say it was a long walk back up to the house where they'd gotten it."

Willa could feel an itch at the back of her mind that he was about to tell her something troubling.

"He asked them which house it was," Jelena said.

"It's from the burnt house," Willa said. "Isn't it?"

Petar nodded. "I asked them what part of house the wood was from. They didn't know. They were just paid to haul it away. I'm not a joiner, but it looked like floorboards to me."

"Perhaps it's just wood from the roof," Jelena said hopefully.

"Or it could be from the floor on the top story," Petar said. "If it's been taken out, we won't be able to get up there to extend the plank for Niko's escape. The longer they run along the wall, even at that time of day, the more likely is that they'll be stopped by one of the guards."

"We need to find out before we go in there tonight," Willa said.

"We should call off the plan and start over," Jelena said.

"No. I don't want Gerard in that house any longer than he has to be. Besides, I don't know how I'd get a message to him. Zrinka has already left. As far as Gerard knows, we'll be there for him by the time he leaves in the morning."

Petar sat on the bed, put his face in his hands, and groaned, "How could I have let this happen?"

Jelena took a seat next to him and took his hands down. "What are you talking about, my love? You've done everything you can to get our child back."

"I shouldn't have let Niko be taken in the first place. I shouldn't have let your brother be killed. Ston will be conquered. Because of me."

"This is not your fault. You know how headstrong our child is. And it's Vitomir who killed Drazhan."

Willa had experienced that kind of failure, too, so she had suffered the same sharp pang of guilt in her stomach that he must have felt now. She understood his feelings of guilt, but she also knew that wallowing in it wouldn't help them at the moment.

"Petar, Jelena is right. You went all the way to Rhodes to help your town and find a way to get your son back. And you found us. Gerard and I want to help you, but you need to find the strength to help *us*. Jelena and I alone won't be able to push that plank out for Gerard and Niko. We need you."

He took a breath and rose resolutely to his feet.

"Yes. Please excuse my weakness. I will fight for Niko and our home."

"Good," Willa said.

Jelena stood. "But we still don't know if the plan will work."

"True. We need to know if we can use that house. I'll go and find out exactly what they are doing."

"You?" Petar said. "Why not me?"

"Because the house is too close to Vitomir's," Willa said. "We can't risk you being seen in that vicinity in broad daylight."

"She can do it," Jelena said. "You should have seen her attack Lord Vitomir earlier. She was incredible. I was quite in awe."

Willa could feel her cheeks flush from the praise. "Stay here. I'll be back soon. Hopefully, it will be nothing that affects our plans."

"You are a good woman, Willa," Petar said.

"And you're a good man."

With that, she left and headed out of the tavern back the way she'd just come. It didn't take long to reach the house with the burnt roof. Carters were loading a pile of rotted wooden boards into a cart.

Grunting and hammering was audible from the interior. The carters were distracted with their labor and the door to the house was open, so she slipped inside.

It didn't take long to see the problem they would face. It wasn't the top floor that was being removed.

A group of workers swarmed over the staircase, tearing it out one step at a time. Thanks to the light streaming in from above, it was clear they'd already taken out the flights to the third and fourth level.

One of the workmen looked up and saw Willa gaping at the sight. He called out to her in harsh Croatian. He walked over to her, pointing his hammer at the door.

Willa spoke back in Italian. "My mistress asked me to come check on your progress."

Now that the worker thought he was speaking to a representative of his employer's wife, he suddenly adopted a fawning tone and switched to broken Italian. "We finish taking stairs today. They all no good." He picked up one of the boards and showed her the rot. "Water from open roof. We build more tomorrow. Maybe one week, we finish."

She nodded, her mind reeling at the implications of what she was seeing. "Thank you. I'll let her know."

As she went out the door, Willa's mind raced with how they were going to get up those four stories in complete darkness and then back down with no stairs but with a child in tow, and all before daybreak.

17

In appreciation for saving his life, Vitomir sat Fox at the head table beside Bogun, while around the rest of the hall guards and attendants not tasked with serving the meal sat at trestle tables on benches. The Serbian sampled the hearty fare of fish, mutton, bread, and apples like a connoisseur of fine food while Vitomir proudly expounded on his collection of art, including a selection of illuminated manuscripts. Even though Fox's mind was on the escape he had planned for the wee hours of the morning, he made a show of rapt attention.

"And in your honor, Sir Gerard," Vitomir said, "we will have a reading from Marco Polo's travels after the evening meal tonight."

"You have a book of his?" Fox asked with genuine intrigue.

"Made in Venice by the finest craftsmen. The colorful illustrations are magnificent. As a knight, I think you will especially enjoy the image of a battle waged from the backs of elephants and another where men with only one eye in the center of their heads fight dragons."

Fox had seen such images in Marco Polo's account before, so he knew it was the Rustichello version. "I look forward to it."

"Tell us, Sir Gerard," Bogun said, "what you were doing when you so kindly came to Lord Vitomir's rescue?" His tone wasn't simply curious, but brusque and probing.

"I suppose it was just good fortune, really," Fox answered as he chewed a bite of his mutton shank. "I only arrived in Dubrovnik today from Venice hoping to find work as a man-at-arms."

"And now you have found it. That is good fortune indeed. For both you and our host."

"And the woman Lord Vitomir was speaking to. She could have been killed as well."

Bogun's eyes flicked to Vitomir, who avoided his gaze. "Then your presence was even more fortuitous." He downed his goblet of wine and poured another. "You do know that men aren't allowed to be openly armed in the city. It's also good fortune that Lord Vitomir didn't report your violation."

Fox smiled. "I was carrying Legend on my back with my satchel. When I spotted the killer who attacked Lord Vitomir, I was able to unsheathe it quickly enough to come to his defense."

"Legend is a name you've given to your sword?" Vitomir asked.

"It's a family treasure passed down to me by my father. His grandfather acquired it in the Holy Land."

"It's quite remarkable."

"May I see this famous sword?" Bogun asked.

His interest in weaponry was unusual for a trader, which only further strengthened Fox's suspicion that he wasn't actually who he said he was.

Fox pushed his stool back and retrieved Legend from where he'd stowed his things nearby. He stood and unsheathed it to show them the patterned blade that was a byproduct of the mysterious Damascus process for forging the steel. It gave the weapon a keen edge that never dulled.

Bogun stood to inspect it more closely. Then he held out his hand.

"Do you mind if I hold it?"

Vitomir looked on expectantly. Fox was loath to let anyone else touch his sword, but as a guest in the house and a new hire, he felt obliged to honor the request.

He reluctantly handed it to Bogun, who weighed it in his hand, then stepped back and took several expert swipes and jabs with it. Fox didn't know any traders who could handle a weapon so deftly.

Bogun smiled and gave it back. Fox forced himself not to snatch it away.

He resheathed Legend and said, "You handle a sword well."

"Travel with valuable goods can be dangerous, so I've taken the trouble to learn some basic defense."

The way he'd brandished the sword, it was obvious he had used one more than just occasionally. But Fox merely nodded and took his seat to finish his meal. Bogun sat down again as well.

"And now you're involved in the salt trade, Master Bogun?" Fox said. "I don't know much about salt. Where does it come from?"

"Oh, I merely ensure the Serbian Empire has the supply it needs. Lord Vitomir knows much more about the source of it."

The deflection was clever. Bogun was clearly a quick thinker, something Fox would have to keep in mind.

"Most of Dubrovnik's salt comes from a town called Ston further up the coast," Vitomir said. "There are vast salt pans where it's harvested."

"What is a salt pan?"

"They're flat tidal areas that are filled with seawater. When the sun burns off the water, the salt comes out in huge quantities."

"These salt pans must be quite valuable."

"Why do you think the Hungarians are so furious with him?" Bogun said. "Their loss is our gain."

"We in Dubrovnik are well aware of the value of salt. Have you heard the local fable about the king and his daughters?" Vitomir asked.

Fox shook his head.

"A king has three lovely daughters and no sons. He is forced to leave his kingdom to one of them, but he wants to leave it to the daughter who is most worthy. So he gives them a test of their devotion to him. In turn, he asks each to describe the depth of their love for their father."

"He's leaving his kingdom to his daughter?" Bogun scoffed.

Vitomir laughed uproariously. "I did say this was a fable."

"How does salt come into this story?" Fox asked.

"Well," Vitomir continued, "the oldest daughter proclaims that she loves her father more than all the gold in the world. The middle daughter goes even farther, saying that she loves him more than any quantity of diamonds and rubies."

"And the third daughter?" Fox asked.

Vitomir gave a crooked grin. "She tells him that she loves him more than salt. Upon hearing this, the king is furious at being compared to such a lowly product. He might have forgiven sugar or saffron, but salt is a true insult. He banishes her from the kingdom."

"Serves her right," Bogun said.

"Years pass, and the salt mines in the king's realm are running dry, causing his subjects to fall ill with all sorts of maladies. He has no choice but to make peace with his rival in the next kingdom to get their salt, and he is treated there to a feast far more lavish than this one. All of the food looks superb, and the other guests rave about their meals, but the king can barely choke down his food because it's so flavorless. He demands to meet the cook who has spoiled his celebration, and the daughter he had banished emerges. She tells him that she didn't let a grain of salt touch his food so that he would know how important the spice is to his life. He immediately begs her forgiveness and welcomes her back to his kingdom to become his heir."

"I have to admit," Fox said, "I've had plenty of saltless food in my time, and it's quite inedible. And I've seen horses that couldn't get salt wither and perish."

Vitomir nodded. "So you see why the salt trade is my chief responsibility as treasurer of Dubrovnik."

"Enough about salt," Bogun said with a wave of his hand. "Lord Vitomir tells me you served in the English army. I suppose you faced battles against the French."

"You know of the war?"

"Of course I've heard tell of it by travelers, although it's difficult to get much information this far away. I do know that the English invaded Normandy five years ago with a large army and routed the French knights. Even here we have heard of the famous Battle of Crécy."

A bolt of lightning flew down Fox's spine at Crécy's mention. That day was a pivotal moment in his life, for his older brother died in the battle, leaving Fox as the only surviving son to inherit the estate. That single event started him on the path that had led him to this very room.

But he wasn't going to share any of that with Bogun and Vitomir.

"The French cavalry got mired in the mud," Fox said, omitting his role as a mounted archer and the details of his role in the battle. "It was a one-sided victory for us."

Bogun eyed him, waiting for more. When Fox didn't go on, he said, "That's it? I was expecting tales of you wading through soldiers, hacking them down right and left or slicing through mounted knights with a single mighty blow from your treasured sword."

Fox shrugged and told the truth. "The battle was won by the longbow archers."

That got a chuff from Bogun. "You may be a fine swordsman, but you need to practice your storytelling."

"I'm sure there's more to it," Vitomir said, "and we will have plenty of time to hear about his further adventures later." He pushed back his chair and stood. "I have to get back to the rector's palace. Sir Gerard will accompany me."

"I need a word with you before you go," Bogun said.

Fox took his things and stood. "I will go find the privy and stow my things."

"The steward will show you where," Vitomir said.

Fox nodded and followed the steward through the hall toward the back of the house. Before they turned the corner to head toward the latrine out in the garden, Fox took a last look at Bogun who was chatting quietly with Vitomir as the rest of the servants began clearing the hall of food and furniture. Bogun glanced at him once with a wary eye.

Everything Fox had heard convinced him of one thing—Bogun had to be the one Vitomir was in league with, the commander who would lead the army to attack Ston.

Bogun watched Vitomir's new man-at-arms leave and couldn't shake the sense that something was off about him.

"Are you sure you trust this man?" he asked Vitomir quietly.

Vitomir frowned at him. "Why shouldn't I? He saved my life."

"Did he?"

"You weren't there. That Hungarian would have slaughtered me if it hadn't been for Sir Gerard."

"You're sure it was the Hungarians who tried to kill you?"

"I heard him say 'This isn't over' in Hungarian. Who else would try to kill me?"

"Perhaps this salt harvester whose son you're holding?"

Vitomir shook his head. "Not possible. I saw him only moments before and after at a spot a great distance from where we were. Besides, the man who attacked me was shorter. Why are you asking these questions?"

"It seems odd to me that this Englishman simply happened to be right by you when you were attacked."

"And thank the Lord he was."

"You've never seen him before?"

"No. Have you?"

"No. But he seems to be a curious man."

"And I'm curious about him. His travels must have given him many stories that I'd like to hear. Although, you're right about one thing. By the way he bested my attacker so quickly, he's obviously an expert fighter, but his skills as a raconteur leave something to be desired."

Bogun considered the situation for another moment, but he could not think of a reason to object to Fox guarding Vitomir.

"And this woman Fox spoke of?" Bogun asked.

The question appeared to catch Vitomir off guard. He brushed it off with a shrug.

"Just a resident asking me about some tedious business of hers. I really didn't hear much before the attack."

Now it was Vitomir who was being evasive. Bogun had to be wary of everyone, it seemed.

"We are still on schedule for our plans, yes?" he asked.

Vitomir straightened up. "Of course."

"That's good. Because if I don't capture Ston, Emperor Dušan won't show me any mercy for an embarrassing failure that was undertaken without his knowledge. But before he executes me, I'll make sure you share my fate."

Vitomir swallowed hard. "We won't fail."

Bogun would succeed at his quest or die trying, because he wouldn't go through another humiliation like the one he remembered so well from all those years ago when his family's lands were so brazenly torn away from him.

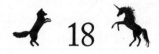 18

Eighteen years ago—June, 1333

KOTOR, SERBIAN KINGDOM

Bogun spurred his horse toward the town's southern gate, a smile on his face and a freshly killed deer slung across the front of his saddle. The midday bells for sext were ringing as if to announce his arrival from the successful hunt, an accolade that wouldn't have surprised him. Even at this young age, his skill with the crossbow was renowned throughout this region.

Cedozar rode beside him and pointed to the ship that had arrived the day before with the king's three legates. "They're likely already at the feast."

The thought of aggravating those pompous functionaries gave Bogun a warm feeling. They had no idea what a real soldier could do for the Serbian Kingdom. "I've been waiting for this day all my life. Let them stew."

"They're certainly drawing out this announcement that you're getting the Stonski Rat peninsula."

Cedozar had been Bogun's manservant and friend since they were young boys, so he knew well that the peninsula had been promised to their family for years. But the presentation was always put off on one pretext or another. There was always one more task to be completed, one more test of loyalty for his father to be proven worthy. The old man had been a fool, driving himself harder and harder, sure that his efforts would be rewarded. At least his death, when he was killed in a battle that had resulted in significant gains, would be seen as the ultimate service to the kingdom and the peninsula given to his son in thanks as his legacy.

"What else do they have to do but make their pronouncements into a dramatic social event where they can reveal the details of the arrangement? I may have to play along with this formality, but I'll do it at my pace. We waited long enough and now they can wait. This ceremony should never have taken this long to happen, but once the pronouncement is made, you and I will drink until morning in celebration."

"Will we move there right away?" Cedozar asked.

"I have to begin building my family's castle, don't I?"

"Do you have a site chosen yet?"

Bogun shook his head. "I don't remember enough about Ston from that one visit we made with my father all those years ago."

"I don't, either. We hadn't even really learned to ride by then."

"But I intend to make it the grandest castle on the Dalmatian coast thanks to the salt trade I'll build."

They rode through the town gates and handed off the horses and the deer carcass to the waiting attendant. After washing up and changing into their ceremonial attire, they made a grand entrance into the town governor's house.

With the town and its huge fort serving as a military outpost of the Serbian Kingdom, the feast attendees were a mix of high-ranking officers and town dignitaries, all of them milling about with goblets of wine. The three legates—Zavida, Repoš, and Predimir—were gathered at the table of honor, raised on a dais at the front of the great hall. The three had generous bellies and flabby jowls, showing off how well fed they were at the king's court. The royal guards that had traveled with them stood rigidly against the walls.

Zavida, the king's most senior representative, spotted Bogun and waved him over with an exasperated sigh.

"There you are. What has taken you so long to get here?"

"My prey was elusive today," Bogun answered, "but I chased it down."

Zavida, who seemed to assume the guise of an unwanted counselor, shook his head in disappointment, as if hunting were a boyish occupation. "Such useless entertainments. You're a man now, and you should learn how to be a worthy Serbian."

Bogun had to swallow the bile rising in his throat. He just had to get past this formality, and then he could take possession of the peninsula and forget what it had cost to get there.

"I hope to be taught by your example."

"Don't be smart. Well, I suppose we can begin now." Zavida clapped his hands, indicating that everyone should take their seats and the food should be served.

Heaping platters of roasted venison, baked fish, bread, glazed carrots, and a wealth of other dishes specially prepared for the occasion were brought out. After much raucous celebration, the meal concluded, and Zavida rose to address the guests.

Bogun sat up straighter as he anticipated the news that the legates had come so far to deliver.

"My comrades and I are most grateful for the gracious welcome and this wonderful feast. You honor us with your generosity."

Bogun recited the required obeisance with as much courtesy as he could muster. "It is we who are honored by your visit. To receive three such esteemed guests is a true privilege. Please convey our most humble devotion to His Highness when you return to Skopje." Only the last part had meaning for Bogun, who was a true servant of the kingdom.

Zavida bowed ever so slightly in response. Bogun wanted to retch.

"And now," Zavida said with outstretched hands, "we have come to relate the best of news to you in person. As you know, our glorious Serbian Kingdom has been at war with the Eastern Roman Empire and the Hungarians for years. Our victories, while impressive and resounding, have come at a great cost. King Dušan has glorious plans for Serbia, conquering the barbarians of neighboring lands to form a majestic new empire so deserved by the fearlessness and faith of God's chosen people, the Serbs. This ambitious plan will require sacrifice from all of his worthy subjects." He unrolled a parchment scroll. "Therefore, in his great wisdom, His Highness Dušan the Mighty has made the decision to sell the Stonski Rat peninsula to the Venetian Republic. I will now read the—"

Shocked, Bogun leaped out of his chair, shouting, "This is outrageous! I will not listen to this filth."

He charged forward, but Cedozar held him back from attacking Zavida.

"My good boy," the oily legate said, "this is a chance for you to prove your loyalty as a Serb, a worthy son of your steadfast father."

"That land was promised to my family! We have paid for it over and over, not our enemies, the Venetians! It is my birthright."

"This is what the king has decided. Who are you to argue with it?"

Bogun pointed a finger at Zavida and his two comrades. "You have done this. All of you!"

"I don't know what you mean," Zavida said, making a show of confusion to his fellow legates.

"Oh, yes, you do. How much have you profited from this transaction?"

"How dare you accuse us of such impropriety!"

Bogun shook off Cedozar's grip, stalked over to Zavida, and snatched the scroll from his hand.

"Here is what I think of your bargain."

He spat on the document, drawing a collective gasp from the audience. Then, white hot with fury, he put his hand to the dagger on his belt.

"You'll pay for this," he snarled at Zavida.

The king's guards unsheathed their swords and advanced on him, but before he could draw his blade, Cedozar pinned his arms to his sides.

"We are going," Cedozar said into his ear. "Now!"

"I won't forget this!" Bogun screamed as his friend dragged him away.

Only when they were out of the hall did Cedozar release him.

"Why did you do that?" Bogun demanded.

"Because they would have killed you the moment you pulled out your knife. I could see what you were planning to do before you knew it yourself."

"That would have been better than living with this shame."

"You aren't in your right mind now."

"I'll kill all of them."

"How? With that display in there, the legates will certainly report your behavior to the king. We are both pariahs now. We have to leave Kotor."

Bogun took a few breaths and felt his boiling blood begin to simmer down. Cedozar was right. Bogun was already beginning to think more clearly.

And he knew what he had to do.

He gripped Cedozar's hand. "I'm honored by your company. You'll continue by my side?"

Cedozar nodded and doubled the grip with his other hand. "To the end, my lord."

"Then help me in my quest. We are outcasts now, but I will prove my worth to Serbia. In battle. In deed. My victories will be so great that the king will be forced to welcome me back with open arms."

"And then?"

Bogun's lip curled in anticipation of the great personal crusade that was to come. Despite the day's vile humiliation, he vowed that Ston and the Stonski Rat peninsula would nevertheless be his someday.

"Then I will take what is rightfully mine, and I will revel in it."

 19

November, 1351

Fox stayed still for a good long while after the bells for matins rang in the middle of the night. He wasn't an honored guest like Bogun, who had his own room. Instead, he was bedding down on rushes in the main hall with the servants. Still, he didn't sleep much. He'd been waiting for the hour before lauds, which would be when the kitchen staff would rise to begin baking the daily bread.

With the bells long quieted, he got to his feet and collected his things in silence. Several people sleeping in the hall were snoring loudly, but he carried his boots to be as quiet as possible sneaking out of the room and up the staircase.

Once he had Petar and Jelena's son, he wouldn't be coming back down this way. The front door was barred with two guards sleeping beside it. He'd never get it open without making considerable noise. They'd be caught before they got to the next street.

Once he was up the stairs to the top floor, Fox put his boots back on and strapped Legend around his waist. Something caught his ear, so he paused for a few moments to listen. However, it didn't sound as if anyone were following him, so he walked down the corridor past the kitchen to the storage room where Niko was being held captive. Using the banked kitchen fire, he lit the rushlight he'd brought with him for illumination.

He drew the lockpick tools from his sleeve and was about to start in on the lock when that same sound intruded again. This time it was much closer. It was as if stone were scraping on stone.

It seemed to be coming from the kitchen.

Worried that one of the bakers had come up early to begin his tasks, he tiptoed to the kitchen and peered around the corner. The room was dark and empty.

But there was the sound again. It wasn't the scurrying of rat claws searching for morsels that fell from the ovens. This noise was coming from inside the kitchen wall.

When it happened again, he localized it to a patch of wall separating the kitchen from the storage room. Another scrape made him realize it was along the floor.

Fox bent down and was stunned to see a stone pushing out from the wall bit by bit. The large limestone block was now three-quarters of the way out, progressing an inch at a time.

He propped the rushlight in an iron pot and waited, impressed by what was happening. It took a little while for the stone to come completely out of the wall. Once it was free, two small hands curled around the edge and kept pushing until there was ample space for a child to wriggle through. Just as Petar and Jelena had described him, he was a thin boy with scraggly hair.

The moment he was fully out, Fox dashed forward and grabbed him from behind, wrapping his hand around his mouth to keep him quiet. The boy thrashed, wiggling to free himself and even trying to bite Fox's fingers.

"Be still, Niko," Fox said in Italian, keeping his voice low. "I'm not going to hurt you. I'm here to get you out of here. Do you understand? If so, nod your head."

Instead of complying, Niko stomped on Fox's boot. It was a surprisingly painful blow for someone so small.

Fox winced and gripped him even more tightly.

"Use your head, boy. If I were with Vitomir, I wouldn't be here by myself in the middle of the night, would I? I'm helping your mother and father. Now, do you want to get out of here?"

Fox prepared himself for another fight, but Niko finally nodded.

"Good. I'm going to take my hand away from your mouth. But know that if you scream, you will be caught again and I will be killed. Is that what you want?"

Niko shook his head. Fox slowly removed his hand, ready to clamp it around Niko's mouth again if he took a breath to cry out. "Thank you. This will all go well if you just cooperate."

"You have a funny accent," Niko said.

"My name is Gerard. I'm a knight from England."

"What does that mean?"

"England is the name of my country. It's far away."

He eyed him dubiously. "How do I know you're telling the truth?"

"I thought you might need to be convinced, so I asked your mother to give me a message for you. Something Lord Vitomir wouldn't know."

"That shouldn't be hard to think of. He's a fool."

"She said, 'Although this trial has made you a man, you will always be my little honey playing with *bubica*. Please do what Gerard says, and I will see you soon.'"

Fox could feel the boy immediately relax in his arms. Niko sniffled, then shook his head clear.

"What does *bubica* mean?" Fox asked.

"It means little bug. It's what I called a dog that I liked in Ston when I was little. It means that I have to trust you, Sir Gerard."

Fox slowly released him. Niko didn't try to run.

"I don't have to like it, though," he went on. "You ruined my only chance to escape. I've been planning it for weeks."

Fox pushed the stone back into the wall. "No, I kept you from getting captured again."

"Nobody but you knows that I removed the mortar from around this stone."

"A remarkable feat. How did you do that?"

"With this." Niko held up a thin skewer used to truss birds. "I found it behind a crate in the storage room. Sharp enough to scrape, but too small to use as a weapon. They said there will be a feast tomorrow, so I knew I had to get out before lauds. That's when the cooks will come in to start the meal. They would have noticed the missing mortar when they took out the gilt tableware from the storage room to use at dinner."

"And what was your plan once you were out of your cell?" Fox asked as he pushed the loosened stone back into place.

Niko shrugged. "I'm sure I would have found a way out of the house."

"Or you would have been discovered by the first sleeping guard you stumbled over."

"You have a better plan? Hide me under your tunic as you sneak me out?"

"You're a smart lad, aren't you?"

"Smarter than Lord Vitomir. Maybe smarter than you."

"I meant that you're..." Fox didn't know the Italian word for 'mouthy.' "You don't have much respect for your elders, do you, boy?"

"Stop calling me 'boy.' My name is Niko."

"Look, Niko, we just need to get out of here, and then you can talk back to your parents all you want. In the meantime, you should follow what your mother said and do what I tell you."

"I think you added that."

Despite his insolence, he was a smart child. Fox did indeed add that bit. He thought it would help keep the boy in line, a challenge he had underestimated.

"Come with me," Fox said, grabbing the rushlight in one hand and Niko's arm in the other. He led them out of the kitchen and back to the storage room door.

"Aren't we going down the stairs?" Niko asked.

Fox gave the light to Niko and took out his lock picks again. "No, we're going back in the storage room."

"What kind of stupid plan is that? They'll catch us when they bring me my morning water and bread."

"No, they won't, because we won't be there."

"You're making no sense. Are you the best my mother and father could find to rescue me?"

"Believe me, I'm beginning to think this was a mistake, too."

Fox had the lock opened in moments. Niko looked decidedly unimpressed.

"You do know the only other way out of this room is through a shuttered window over a four-story drop to the garden below."

Fox shook his head. "I'm truly amazed that your parents want you back so badly."

He opened the door and ushered the reluctant boy inside. Despite talking back, Niko was holding the light at exactly the right angle for whatever Fox needed. Maybe the boy would turn out to be an asset for what was to come, if he could stop talking long enough to hear the plan. Fox latched the door behind him.

"Well, this is brilliant," Niko said. "We're back in the room I just escaped."

"We can talk more easily in here without being heard. If you'll shut your mouth for a few moments to let me explain, I'll tell you how we'll get out."

"You mean, get out *again*." Niko crossed his arms. "I can't wait to hear it."

Fox rolled his eyes. This was going to be an ordeal.

"First, tell me. How good are you at climbing?"

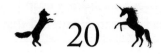

20

Standing on the second level of the burned-out house, Willa steadied the plank from below and Petar held it from above while Jelena climbed up the pieces of wood they had nailed into every foot of its length. The makeshift ladder was working as they'd planned, but the climb was taking longer than they had expected because it was so unsteady. It had repeatedly slipped out when they started to climb, and it took them a while to figure out how to wedge it effectively. The bells for lauds had rung long ago, and dawn would be breaking soon.

"You're doing well, Jelena," Willa said, hoping to prod her to go faster. Although Willa had tried to talk her into staying on the first floor, Jelena had insisted on joining them to help Niko get to safety, but she was moving very tentatively.

As soon as Jelena was at the third floor, Petar helped her up and over. She caught her breath, then held on to the board with him for Willa's climb.

She hiked up her skirt and pulled herself up by the handholds one by one, careful to make sure her feet were secure before reaching for the next rung. She got into a rhythm and reached the third floor quickly.

"I wish I were as agile as you are," Jelena said.

"I've had practice," Willa replied, without saying that the other time she had made a climb like this was when she was scaling a scaffold in Florence's Duomo while she and Gerard were fleeing for their lives.

"One more floor to go," Petar said, hauling up the board with the rope he'd tied to a hole drilled into the plank. The rope was long enough that they could use it to climb quickly all the way down to ground level when they had Fox and Niko with them.

Once he had the plank up, they placed it for the climb to the top floor, wedging it into a crack in the wood flooring. While Willa and Jelena held on to the bottom, Petar put the torch that was their sole source of illumination into his mouth and began to climb, the coil of rope slung over his shoulder.

When he reached the top, they repeated the steps they'd used on the other floors, with Jelena going second and Willa taking up the rear.

Everything went smoothly until Willa was nearing the top of the board. Whether it was how she was putting her weight on the plank or that the grips of Jelena and Petar had shifted, the bottom of the board slipped out of the groove it had been anchored in. The plank slid backward, and Willa could feel that it was only moments from falling away.

She sped up her climb and reached out for Petar's hand just as the plank slammed downward. An inadvertent squeal escaped her as Petar held on to her wrist. She was dangling over the opening in the stairwell and watched the board tumble down the opening where the stairs had been with a horrific clamor. It finally came to rest on the first floor.

Willa was hanging more than thirty feet above the ground. A fall from this height would be crippling, if not fatal. She scrambled to grab hold of the wooden floor above her with her free hand, but it was too far. Petar couldn't reach out with his other hand because as the coil slipped off his shoulder, he was able to catch the end of the rope in the hand that wasn't holding her.

"Jelena, help me," he growled through gritted teeth.

Jelena had been simply watching with her hand over her mouth to keep from crying out and adding to the noise that might already have been noticed by someone.

"Jelena, I need your hand." Willa, still breathing hard, said it as calmly as possible to snap the woman out of her paralysis. "You can do this."

Jelena nodded and bent down, lowering her trembling hand to Willa.

Willa took it and the two of them pulled her up until she could lift a leg over the side and roll onto the top floor. She came to rest on her back and took a few breaths to compose herself after her near brush with death.

She sat up and took stock. She was unhurt, but her arms ached from pulling herself up. In the silence, she heard the footfalls of boots approaching.

"What are we…" Petar began before she put up her hand to quiet him. She motioned for them to get down, extinguished the torch with a cloth, and crawled over to the window.

She raised her head until just her eyes peeked over the sill. It was difficult to make out the torches burning along the wall, and in the darkness it took her a moment to figure out why.

A dense early morning fog had rolled in. It seemed to come in waves, for she could see the torches flicker into view and then out again.

Another torch bobbed up and down along the wall, accompanied by the slap of leather boot soles on the stone. A guard must have heard the ruckus from the falling board and was coming to investigate.

He came to a stop not more than ten feet away across the gap between the city wall and the window. Even though they were now bathed in gloom inside the house, she ducked down on the small chance she could be seen through the fog.

She crawled to Jelena and Petar and gave the briefest hiss to keep them from speaking, but they must have also heard the guard coming and could see the glint of the torch through the window.

After a few moments, Willa heard the guard mutter something to himself and start walking again at a calm saunter. She waited until the footfalls were inaudible before talking.

"I don't think he saw us."

"Thank goodness you put out the torch," Jelena said.

"That just shows we need to wait until the last moment to extend the plank to the wall. We shouldn't do it until we see Gerard and Niko coming toward us."

"But we don't have the plank," Petar said, lighting the torch again. "I just tried pulling it up with the rope, but it's stuck. It must be caught on something below."

Willa peered down through the empty stairwell, but the torchlight didn't penetrate all the way to the bottom.

"We'll have to climb down and free it."

"And do the climb all over?" Jelena said. "I don't know if I could do that again."

"Our plan was to tie the rope up here to lower ourselves down once we had Gerard and Niko," Willa said. She looked around and saw a joist that would serve as an anchor. "Here. We'll use this."

Being from a seaside town where shipping by boat was common, Petar was an expert at tying knots, so he had it secure in no time. "I'll go down on my own. It'll be faster, and I can lift the board myself."

Willa grudgingly agreed to stay with Jelena. He was by far the strongest of them, but she could still help haul up the rope.

Jelena put her hand on Petar's face. "Be careful."

Petar took her hand in his own and kissed it. "I'll be right back."

He lowered himself over the side while Jelena held out the torch over him to give him as much light as possible while he descended hand over hand. Willa stood with the rope in her hand to steady it, although she couldn't help but feel that time was slipping away from them.

She looked up through the open roof that had been burned away. Willa couldn't tell if her eyes were playing tricks on her, but it seemed like the sky was no longer pitch-black. The stars were disappearing.

The sun was starting to rise.

 21

Despite the comfortable straw bed, Bogun had been struggling to sleep all night. Something about the Englishman who had shown up out of nowhere to rescue Vitomir bothered him, but no matter how much he turned it over in his head, he couldn't figure out why Gerard Fox's appearance made him suspicious.

Was it simply the coincidence? Certainly, it was possible the Hungarians had sent someone to kill Vitomir. Bogun couldn't blame them. If Vitomir had shut down all trade with Serbia, he might have considered doing the same thing.

But the fact that an armed soldier just happened to be walking along that same narrow street was fortunate indeed. And from the way the cowardly Vitomir had described the event, the attempted murder seemed half-hearted. If Bogun had planned it, he would have sent enough men to assure that the job was done.

Bogun couldn't lie there any longer. He got out of bed and walked to the window. He could just discern through the gathering fog that the barest lightening of the sky had begun. Soon the bells for the hour of prime would ring.

Once the day had started, Bogun would corner Fox again and ask him some more pointed questions about the route he had taken and how he had arrived in Dubrovnik.

What did Fox say exactly? He was a second son, a former soldier, a landless mercenary traveling around looking for work. Bogun had never met an Englishman before, and it seemed odd for him to have ended up in just the right place at the right time to save Vitomir's life.

But perhaps that was simply fortune smiling again on the Croatian treasurer. It fit the charmed life he led. A wife who brought him wealth, a position that conferred power on him, even his birthmark enhanced his status rather than detracting from it. It made him recognizable to everyone in the city.

Everyone, that was, except for the stranger from a faraway land. So why was he on that particular out-of-the-way street when the attack had occurred? Another question for Fox.

Bogun didn't like coincidences, not when so much was at stake for him. Only the good fortune of coming across this wandering knight had saved Vitomir. A well-planned strike should have left him dead on the ground. Bogun was surprised his attacker would have made such a risky move and yet was so incompetent.

Surely the killer would have waited until Vitomir was alone to launch his assault, although perhaps a single woman didn't seem to add much of a threat. But Vitomir normally traversed crowded streets from the rector's palace to his home. He shouldn't have been so isolated.

Then Bogun understood what was nagging at him. Fox had hinted that it looked as if Vitomir knew the woman. He would expect the treasurer of Dubrovnik to speak to many men in the course of his duties, but why would a woman want to speak with him? And even odder, why would Vitomir speak to *her*? From what Bogun had observed, Vitomir had no time for women unless they were servicing him in some way.

Vitomir had brushed her off as a woman with tedious business, implying that she had accosted him during his walk. But if that were true, Vitomir would have dismissed her as he made his way home, likely not even breaking stride as he waved her away. She would have had to approach him in the middle of a busy street.

But he had stopped to speak with her. He had made a point of talking to her *alone*.

Bogun felt his heart racing as he realized the most important question that he had not pressed before. How had Vitomir ended up in that isolated alley?

Bogun quickly dressed, threw on his boots, and armed himself with the sword he always traveled with but kept hidden in his trunk. He raced out of the room and down the corridor to Vitomir's chamber.

Without knocking, he flung the door open and barged in. Vitomir, who had been sound asleep, sat bolt upright in bed at the commotion. He rubbed his eyes and squinted at Bogun in the darkness.

"What the devil are you doing in my room?" he demanded.

Bogun walked straight over to his bed, his sword pointed at his host.

"Tell me immediately," he snapped as he stared down the blade. "Who was the woman you were speaking to when you were attacked?"

Vitomir gulped as he eyed the sharp point of the weapon. Bogun wouldn't hesitate to use it if he didn't get an answer.

"Jelena. From Ston."

Bogun shook his head in disgust. "The mother of the boy you have in your custody?"

"She said she had some information for me."

"What kind of information?"

"A book. Marco Polo wrote it. It has the secret to increasing salt production."

So that was how Vitomir had promised to treble the salt harvest, although it sounded like his ability to guarantee that was in doubt.

Now the question he'd come to ask. "Did you suggest that you speak in private or did she?"

Vitomir considered that for only a moment. "She did."

"So she guided you to where you talked."

"Yes, but what of it?"

Vitomir really was ignorant about attack strategy.

"Don't you see, you fool? She took you there so that you could be attacked."

"By the Hungarians? Why would she be helping them? Do you think they are trying to take Ston from us?"

"I don't think you were attacked by a Hungarian at all."

"I heard him speak in Hungarian."

"It must have been a comrade who could speak the language or learned those few words to trick you. They wanted you to believe that lie."

Vitomir rubbed his temples as he tried to wake himself up. "Then I don't understand. Why go to all that trouble?"

"Think about it. You invited a complete stranger into your home because of that attack."

"Sir Gerard? But he saved my life. He was injured in the process."

"Did you see the injury?" Although Bogun knew the answer. Vitomir couldn't stand the sight of blood.

"Well, no," Vitomir said. "He treated it himself."

"I think this entire affair was a ruse."

Even in the dimness, Bogun could see Vitomir's expression as the truth dawned on him.

"You believe he's here for the child? But why would an English knight be helping some peasants from a remote Dalmatian town he's probably never even seen?"

"He's a mercenary, is he not? You said the salt harvest was extraordinary this year. Perhaps they promised to pay him."

Vitomir leaped out of bed and threw on his clothes. "I will see that he is hanged in the main square for his deception. No one does this to me."

"He already has."

"We'll get him while he sleeps."

"We need to be careful. He's a clever man to have gotten this far. Gather your guards. Quietly. We'll have them in place to apprehend him before he knows we're there. Hopefully we can catch him while he's still sleeping."

Vitomir nodded. Together they went down the corridor to where the captain of his guard and his top lieutenants slept. They woke the men, and Vitomir explained what they needed to do.

When the guards were ready, Vitomir and Bogun led them down the stairs as silently as they could. From what Bogun recalled, Fox had chosen to sleep in the main hall near the stairway.

When they reached the bottom of the stairs, Bogun took one of the torches from the guards and rushed over to the spot where Fox had been lying, his sword drawn and ready to strike if the Englishman resisted.

But when he got there, all he saw were the rushes he'd been sleeping upon.

"Where is he?" Vitomir cried out, rousing the rest of the people sleeping in the hall. They groggily arose, grumbling about what was going on until they saw Vitomir and went quiet.

Bogun called to the guards by the door at the other end.

"Is the front door still barred?" he shouted.

They didn't answer until Vitomir repeated the question. They confirmed that the door's bar was still in place. Fox couldn't have gone out that way, even if he'd done it quietly. He would have had no way of putting the bar back in its cradle.

"Then where the devil is he?" Vitomir snapped, looking around for any sign of him.

But Bogun knew. He sprinted for the stairs.

"Come with me!" he yelled over his shoulder. "He's gone to rescue your captive."

 22

With the sun just about to rise, the bells for prime would ring at any moment. Fox listened at the door of the storage room but heard nothing except the bakers making the morning bread.

"Do you understand what to do?" he asked Niko.

The boy nodded and rubbed his hands together. "I can do this."

"Then it's time."

Before he could move, Fox heard heavy footfalls crashing up the stairway. Angry shouts and clangs of steel roared toward them. Guards would be charging into the storage room at any moment.

But the locking mechanism was on the outside. He had no way of barring it since the door opened out into the corridor.

Fox looked around for anything to keep it from being yanked open. A heavy paddle with a long iron handle for getting bread out of the oven was propped against the wall. He picked it up and skewered the handle through the thick iron door ring so that the flat paddle was pinned against the door frame.

The moment it was in place, Fox heard shouting on the other side. He recognized the voices.

"Get it open!" Bogun commanded.

"I have the key!" Vitomir replied as he inserted it.

It rattled in the lock, a useless gesture since Fox couldn't have locked it from this side. The door creaked as someone on the other side pulled at the opposing ring. The paddle and its handle didn't yield, and the riveted iron ring in the door would be impossible to dislodge.

"It's stuck!" Vitomir said.

"He's in there," Bogun said. "Sir Gerard, come out now and we won't hurt you."

That was an absurd lie. Fox had no doubt he would either be cut down the moment the door was opened or he would be tortured to get information about why he was there.

"I have your word?" Fox asked.

Niko opened his mouth to speak, but Fox clamped his hand over it.

"Of course," Vitomir answered.

"All right. I jammed the door on this side. It'll take some time for me to get it open."

He pulled Niko to the other end of the room and put his finger to his lips before removing his hand.

"What are you doing?" Niko whispered.

"Buying us some time."

At that moment, the bells for prime began to chime throughout the city. With the ringing masking any other sounds, Fox took the opportunity to pry open the shutters that had been barring the window, which was barely big enough for Fox to fit through, just as Zrinka had warned them. A fog drifted in through the opening, intermittently obscuring the view of the wall outside.

Niko looked at him as if he were crazy. "We can't possibly reach that wall from here!"

Fox looked out the window to the left. There was his escape route.

A rope was slung between two pulleys, one lashed by a chain to a stone outcropping beside the house's kitchen window, the opposite end chained to an iron torch sconce on the city wall. The rope was strung around the pulleys so that clothes, rugs, and tapestries could be hung on it to dry. The pulleys allowed the rope to be moved back and forth the twenty feet from the house to the wall, stopping when the single knot tying it together reached a pulley.

Fox had seen the rope when he'd been up in the burned-out house down the street. His intrusion into the kitchen the day before to get herbs gave him a view confirming that it was next to the kitchen window.

It would have been easy to grab on to the rope from there. But from this window, the rope was two arm lengths away. If they were to reach it, they'd have to jump the gap to snag on to it.

Fox looked down and saw the privy and garden below. Stones covered the cesspit next to the privy to reduce the odors arising from it. Even in the unlikely chance it weren't fatal, a fall from this height would break bones.

"He's not coming out," Vitomir said loudly.

Guards started slamming into the door. The frame was sturdy, but Fox didn't know how long it would hold.

"Get an axe," Bogun ordered.

One of the men with them went running. It would be only a matter of time until they broke in.

Fox climbed up onto the sill. He leaned down and held out his hand.

"Quick. While they can't hear what we're doing."

It wouldn't be long before one of them figured out what he and Niko were doing and opened the window shutters in the kitchen to intercept them.

The boy grabbed at his knees as if he were reaching to pull up his hose, then shook his head momentarily before taking Fox's hand. Fox hauled the boy up.

"Get on my back."

"Why?"

"We have to jump. It's too far to reach."

"Then throw me," Niko said. "I can catch on."

"I'm not taking that chance."

"I can do it."

"We don't have time to argue."

"I'm not climbing onto you."

"Then you can stay here," Fox said. "Because I'm going."

Niko scowled at him. "What a gentleman you are. All right."

While Fox balanced himself on the sill, Niko scrambled onto his back and wrapped his arms around Fox's neck.

Niko's leg kicked the sheath for Legend. "This would be easier if you left your sword behind."

"I'd sooner leave *you* behind."

With Niko's weight balanced precariously on his back, Fox stood up on the sill gingerly, holding on to the top of the window frame, which was even with his chest. The fog let up briefly, giving a clear view of the rope going over to the wall.

"Are you sure that rope is strong enough to hold us?" Niko asked.

"It has to be," Fox answered more confidently than he felt.

An axe started hacking away at the door. Fox got into a position to leap but his boot slipped on the stone sill. Niko yelped, and Fox caught himself before they tumbled to the ground below.

"We're all right," he said. He hesitated as he tried to position himself for the best possible angle for the jump. He'd only get one chance. A miss would be deadly for them both.

"What's going on in there?" Bogun called out. "Do I feel a breeze under the door?"

"The window is open," Vitomir replied. "But they can't scale down the wall. They wouldn't be able to get out of the garden anyway."

The axe kept chopping, and Fox heard the frame give way. The door flew open with a bang.

"Go! Go!" Niko yelled in his ear.

As men rushed into the storage room, Fox flexed his legs and propelled himself into the air.

 23

Bogun watched in astonishment as Fox leaped out of the window with the boy clinging to his back. Surely the man hadn't planned this entire scheme simply to kill them both.

"Is he mad?" Vitomir exclaimed as they both rushed to the window.

When they peered out, they could see Fox hanging on by one hand to a rope slung between the house and the city wall. He flailed until he could grab it with the other hand, then began to pull himself hand over hand toward the wall.

"That's the drying line," Vitomir blurted.

"Come," Bogun yelled, and ran out of the storage room into the kitchen.

Vitomir, close behind him, shouted, "Everyone out!" The bakers scurried away.

Bogun banged open the shutters and saw that the loop of rope ended at a pulley lashed right next to the window. Thanks to the pulley, the rope could be moved back and forth to bring in the dry clothes and hang the wet clothes.

Fox and Niko were already halfway across with the Englishman dangling from the rope. Bogun raised his sword to cut the line, but Vitomir yanked his arm down.

"No, we need him!"

"Fox?"

"The boy. He's our way to capture Ston."

Despite Bogun's annoyance, the Croatian was right. They needed Niko so that Petar would open the town gates for them.

He sheathed his sword and began pulling on the rope. All of the progress that Fox had made was reversed in a flash. Bogun didn't stop until the single knot in the rope got stuck in the pulley at the other end.

Now Fox was just a few feet away. Bogun leaned out the window to grab Niko, but they were just out of arm's reach.

"We'll kill you for this," Bogun told him.

"I know," was Fox's terse reply before he proceeded forward again.

"Order one of your men after them," Bogun said to Vitomir.

Vitomir looked dubiously at the rope. "Will it hold?" Bogun didn't think the man cared about his guard's safety. He was more worried about his captive dying.

"We have to find out. Do you want them to get away?"

Vitomir shook his head. He turned to the leanest guard and pointed out the window.

"Get out there and bring the boy back here."

The guard hesitated as if he were considering disobeying the order. Vitomir shoved him toward the window.

"Either go out that window or go out the front door feet first."

The guard swallowed and nodded. He climbed onto the sill and gingerly grasped the rope. Bogun watched the chain and pulley as he settled his weight onto it slowly.

"Hurry up!" Vitomir shouted.

When the man was fully hanging by two hands, he sighed with relief, nodded, and began climbing hand over hand across the rope.

Since he was unencumbered, he made fast time catching up with Fox, who was slowed down by the weight of the boy.

When the guard got within reach, Fox lashed out with his leg, but the guard swatted it aside, causing Fox's grip to loosen. Fox took a moment to steady himself while the guard closed the distance.

The man snagged Niko's leg and pulled, trying to dislodge the boy, but Niko kicked out, his shoe catching the guard in the chin.

"You little monster," the guard yelled as he released his grip with one hand. He tried to grab the boy again, but Fox removed one of his hands from the rope and punched the guard in the face.

"I can't hold you and fight," Fox said. "Climb the rest of the way."

Niko scrambled up Fox's shoulders and pulled himself along the rope until he could wrap his legs around it, hanging from it like squirrel. He began shimmying toward the wall while Fox and the guard traded jabs with the spare hand that was not holding each of them up.

"He's getting away!" Vitomir cried.

"Then have your men intercept him before he can get off the wall," Bogun replied.

"The stairs up to the wall are blocked by the city guard. I'll have to go with them to authorize their access. Stay here in case they try to come back."

Vitomir and the guards raced out of the room, leaving Bogun alone.

"Kill him," he shouted to the guard. "We don't need him alive. Just the boy."

The guard nodded and drew his dagger. He thrust it at Fox's face, but the Englishman caught his wrist when the point was mere inches from his eye.

They struggled like that for a moment, and it looked as if the knife might plunge right into Fox's brain. But slowly the guard's wrist was turned as Fox applied pressure with his fingers. The guard screamed in pain, but he didn't let go of the dagger.

That was a mistake.

Having gained the leverage, Fox yanked the guard's hand around and forced the guard to stab himself in the shoulder of the arm hanging on to the rope. The wound didn't look deep, but it was enough to force the guard to let go of the rope.

He cried out as he fell four stories to the ground below. He smashed through the roof of the privy, his neck snapping awkwardly before he disappeared into the latrine.

Fox, who was panting hard, latched on to the rope with both

hands again. He raised his eyebrows at Bogun as if to say, "Is that the best effort you have?" Then he began climbing toward the wall again.

Bogun shook his head in disgust. "The Devil take it, I suppose I have to do this myself."

He hopped up onto the sill, held the rope until his feet were dangling over the garden below, and began going hand over hand as fast as he could. He swore under his breath on all that was holy that Fox would not live to see the end of the day.

 24

Willa wasn't sure she had drawn a single breath as she'd watched Gerard fighting that guard whilst holding on to the rope with only one hand. Thankfully, with all that was going on, the guard hadn't noticed her at the window. It was only after the guard dropped out of sight and Gerard kept climbing toward the wall that she inhaled a deep lungful of relief.

She felt a hand gripping her arm and finally noticed that Jelena had her fingers clenched on like a vise, her eyes on Niko. Her son was contorting himself so that he could climb up the pulley chain to the torch sconce.

He latched on to the iron fitting and pulled himself up, throwing his leg over the stone wall. When he was safely crouching on the parapet, Jelena released Willa's arm.

She seemed both elated and panicked at seeing her child so close, yet still so far away. It looked like she might call out to Niko to reassure him, so Willa pulled her down and put her hand on her mouth.

"We must stay quiet. We can't let anyone know we're here."

Jelena nodded in frustration, so Willa removed her hand. Still, she could sympathize with the mother's instinct. She wanted to yell out to Gerard that they were set to receive him, but he had to trust that they were going to be there for him.

At that moment, Petar at last finished pulling up the plank from the lower level. When it was secured on the floor, he lay back drenched in sweat.

"Niko is there," Jelena said to him. "We have to put the plank out."

The comment seemed to energize the weary Petar, and he leaped to his feet, picking up one end of the plank to prop it on the windowsill so they could slide it across the ten feet to the city wall. Willa put her hand up to stop him.

"Not yet," she said.

"But we need to have it out there so they can come across," Jelena protested.

"If we put it out too soon, one of the wall guards might see it."

Petar nodded. "Jelena, she's right. It will take just a few heartbeats to push it across when they are getting near. Besides, it's heavier than I was expecting. We might need Sir Gerard to catch onto the end of it from his side."

Willa watched Gerard nearing the city wall. A second man was quickly following him on the rope when disaster occurred. The end of the rope connected to the house fell, either snapped or cut.

Both Gerard and the second man dropped out of sight. Willa had to stifle a scream. But it was Niko who gave her hope.

The boy bent down and held out his hand. The pulley chain was still taut, as if it were holding a great weight.

Then a hand appeared. Gerard hauled himself up the rope hand over hand. He waved off Niko, likely worried he would pull the small boy down if he took the proffered hand.

Instead, he carefully grabbed onto the pulley chain. He was still only partway up when a city guard ran toward Gerard along the wall walk past the burned-out house.

Willa didn't know if she should yell to warn Gerard and give away their position, but the guard did it for her, yelling something in Croatian.

Niko's head swiveled around, and he got to his feet. He went across the wide terrace so that he was next to the parapet overlooking the ocean. The guard didn't realize the boy was distracting him from Gerard climbing up.

The guard shouted at him, and Niko replied calmly, his eyes

firmly fixed on the guard and not on Gerard, who was now silently raising his foot onto the wall.

"What are they saying?" Willa asked.

Petar translated. "He's saying, 'What are you doing here?' Niko says, 'I got lost.' 'You got lost? How did you get on to the wall?' 'I'm a good climber.' 'Nobody is that good.' 'He is.'"

Niko had taken so much of the guard's attention that he only noticed that he was in peril when Gerard was already on his feet and charging toward him. Gerard kneed the man in the groin. When the guard doubled over in pain, Gerard brought his elbow down on the man's head. He went limp. Gerard took the guard's sword and threw it over the parapet so that it would fall safely to the sea far below.

But now it was Gerard who was distracted, so he didn't see the danger coming.

This time Willa didn't stay quiet. She rose to her feet and cried out.

"Gerard! Behind you!"

Fox was so surprised by Willa's call that he turned to see where she was instead of heeding her caution. She was right where she was supposed to be, standing in the window beside Jelena and Petar.

Then he turned further and saw why she was calling to him.

When Bogun had gotten out onto the rope and began climbing across, the attachment at the house finally gave way. The rope had let loose and they both were slammed into the city wall. Fox was closer, so he didn't hit as hard, but Bogun had crashed into it at a high speed.

Fox had seen him still holding on, but it looked like the wind had been knocked out of him. After carrying Niko and fighting with the guard while clinging to the rope with just the fingers on one hand, Fox had been getting dangerously close to losing his grip from exhaustion.

He paid no more attention to Bogun and focused solely on getting to the top of the rope, which was precariously holding by just the knot stuck in the pulley mechanism. He paid no mind at all to Bogun's similar troubles.

When Fox had reached the top, the city guard accosting Niko on the terrace had taken the rest of his attention. The smart little lad had used his wits again to take the guard away from him. When he got to his feet, he used the last of his strength to knock out the guard and toss his sword into the Adriatic. The man was just doing his job, so Fox refrained from killing him.

When Willa called her warning, Bogun was still pulling himself up. But the Serbian wasn't waiting to make his move. A dagger was in his hand, balanced like he was preparing to throw it.

"Get behind me!" Fox shouted to Niko.

With a practiced motion, Bogun flicked the knife.

Because of the awkward throwing angle, the velocity of the knife hadn't been high and the aim was low, but it was enough that the tip sank into Fox's thigh. It hurt like a demon, but he didn't cry out.

The leg gave way, and he went to one knee to pull it out.

"No!" Niko yelped, gaping at the dagger embedded in his rescuer's leg.

"Go!" Fox said through clenched teeth as he yanked the knife out. Blood seeped from the wound, but it wasn't gushing, so he didn't think it was mortal.

"But you're hurt."

"Just go! Your parents are there."

He nodded to the window where Petar and Jelena were waving for Niko to run to them.

The boy followed his command and went off running, but Bogun was quicker. He rolled up on to the wall and took off after him. Fox gave chase, but his bad leg slowed him down.

Bogun caught up to Niko as the wall walk narrowed and lifted the skinny child up by the back of his tunic. But he didn't bother to draw his sword. He spun around and held the boy over the edge of the parapet, dangling him eighty feet above the rocks and water below.

"Stay where you are," Bogun demanded. "Or I'll drop him. You can believe that promise."

Fox had already drawn Legend and was preparing to slice Bogun in two, but he halted when he understood that Bogun's threat was not idle.

Bogun nodded at the sword. "Put that down."

Instead of dropping it to the stones, Fox resheathed Legend and put up his hands.

"I said to put it down," Bogun repeated.

"I don't want it to get dirty. What shall we do now?"

Bogun looked around until he saw something that caught his eye.

"We'll wait for them."

Through the veils of fog that had parted for a moment, Fox saw Vitomir and his personal guards in the distance at the bottom of the long stairway that allowed them to access the city wall walk.

Fox guessed at how much time he had before he was surrounded by Vitomir's guards and all his chances were gone. It wasn't long. He had to make his move before then.

He was still calculating what that would be when it was Niko who took the initiative. He grabbed on to Bogun's arm, but he was far too weak to wrestle loose from his hold.

So the boy opened his mouth and bit down hard on Bogun's hand. Bogun angrily cried out in pain and released Niko's tunic, but he also drew his arm back.

The motion caused Niko to lose his grip on Bogun's arm. Fox rushed forward, but he was too far away.

Niko fell over the parapet and out of sight.

# 25

Ignoring the screams that came from a house behind him, Bogun was determined to take advantage of Fox's shock at losing the child. Blood coursed from the edge of his palm where Niko had bitten him. Not a deep wound, but it stung as he drew the sword from his scabbard.

Fox snatched his own sword out of its sheath and rushed toward him, hobbling on his injured leg. He went for a killing blow by raising the weapon above his head and bringing it down with a furious cry.

Although Bogun was able to block the strike, the immense power of it sent him careening backward. He was an experienced fighter, but Fox lived up to Vitomir's opinion of his skills as a swordsman. It was clear he had underestimated the Englishman from the very beginning.

"You have failed in your task, Sir Gerard," he said, regaining his footing while parrying several more slashes. "The boy is dead. Leave with your head while you still have it."

Fox paused to catch his breath and said, "Not until I have yours."

Then he launched himself again, swinging the sword with angry slices that Bogun strained to fight off. But the Englishman was favoring his wounded leg, which gave Bogun an increasing edge.

All he had to do was wait for his moment.

He finally got it when Fox braced himself for a thrust intended to skewer Bogun through the belly. Bogun feinted to one side, then dodged to the other. The unusual sword barely missed impaling him.

At the same time, he kicked out and slammed his heel into the fresh dagger injury on Fox's thigh. The English knight screamed in fury and pain. He tumbled to the ground holding his leg.

But before Bogun could follow through, Fox expertly rolled and came up onto his good leg, the toe on his other barely scraping the stones as he balanced himself.

"Try that again," Fox said through gritted teeth.

Bogun smiled. "Do you think I'm not fighting fairly?"

"This isn't a battle of honor. You're a murderer."

"The boy is the one who caused himself to fall. He made me let go."

Which was true, but Bogun was only upset that the leverage over the child's father was now gone. They circled each other looking for an opening to strike.

"How did his parents pay you to do this?" Bogun asked. "With salt?"

"You're stalling."

Bogun could indeed wait for Vitomir's guards to get there and assist him, but he'd rather finish this fight himself.

"Not at all. I just thought you might volunteer information before I kill you."

"Why?"

Bogun shrugged. "Although I figured out your ruse, I don't really know you."

"I know you. Men like you. Ambition, greed, power. That's all you want."

"You know nothing about me. Do your worst."

Fox threw himself at Bogun, bashing him with a flurry of sword strikes that drove Bogun back toward the outer parapet of the wall. Bogun caught the wrist of Fox's sword hand, and Fox did the same to him.

But despite his injured leg, Fox had the advantage as he bent Bogun backward over the edge.

That's when he heard the cry. They both did.

They turned their heads and saw Niko ten feet below the lip of the wall, hanging by his fingertips from the branch of a scraggly tree growing from the side of the sheer cliff. The fog hugging the sea disguised the horrors that awaited him below if he fell.

"Help me!" the boy screamed. "I'm slipping!"

Fox was so astonished to see Niko alive that he momentarily lost his focus on Bogun. The Serbian kneed him in the leg, and the explosion of pain sent him staggering backward.

"This is fortunate," Bogun said. "I get to kill you, and we get the boy back."

Fox didn't have any more time to squander. Vitomir and his guards were approaching rapidly, so he had to dispatch Bogun with haste.

He charged the Serbian, using his sword to distract from his real aim. He cut a swath that was countered by Bogun's sword, but his actual plan worked. He jammed his shoulder into Bogun's stomach, and ignoring the agony in his thigh, lifted the Serbian off his feet and drove him backward along the terrace.

When he reached the long series of steps down where the wall walk followed the lay of the rocky outcropping down, Fox tossed Bogun onto the stairs. The Serbian went somersaulting down, coming to rest at the bottom, motionless.

Fox would have loved to finish him off, but the sound of Niko's cries were growing more panicked by the moment. He could also hear the desperate cry of his parents from the house opposite.

He went over to the drying line that had come loose from Vitomir's house, cut the knot with Legend before he sheathed it, then hauled in the length of rope. When he had it all gathered, he ran to the outer wall and dropped it down beside Niko.

"Grab on!" he yelled.

Niko gingerly reached out to get it, but he immediately held on to the tree branch again.

"I can't!"

"You can do it!" Fox angled the rope even closer to him. "You'll be all right."

"You promise?"

"I swear to the Lord. I won't let you go."

The boy reached out and grasped the rope.

"Do you have a good grip?" Fox asked.

Niko nodded, so Fox began to raise him. His injured leg was barking at him, but his good leg held strong.

"You're doing well, Niko," he said, trying to keep a calm voice through gritted teeth.

"I'm scared."

"No need for that. I've almost got you."

He heard Willa calling out to him from behind in the same urgent tone she'd used before. Fox stopped pulling to see what the danger was.

Not one danger. Two.

Vitomir and his guards were racing toward him from the right. But it was what he saw on the left that was the true cause for alarm.

Bogun lurched to the top of the steps, his face bruised and battered, pure hatred in his eyes.

26

Petar and Jelena had been hysterical when they'd watched Niko drop from the hand of the man who'd been holding him, who had to be Bogun from Zrinka's description of the burn scar on his ear and neck. But when Willa had seen Gerard get the rope and lower it over the side of the city wall, she'd convinced them that Niko was still alive.

She'd hoped it wouldn't take long for Gerard to pull the boy up, so they were pushing the plank out to span the gap between the wall and the burned-out house in anticipation of them coming across.

It was going to be close with Vitomir and his guards rushing toward them. The plank was heavy and awkward, and without Gerard there to support it from the other end, they were struggling to push it out all the way without letting it fall to the garden far below.

The situation took a turn for the worse when Bogun lumbered into view from where the wall descended along the cliff. He had a murderous look in his eye.

"Gerard!" Willa called out. "He's back!"

Gerard had been so intent on hauling up the rope that he wasn't able to see the threat. She whistled sharply, and this time he turned to look at her.

She pointed toward Bogun, who was now charging at him. Gerard frantically tried to pull Niko up before he could get there since he had no way to defend himself with his hands occupied.

Bogun lowered his shoulder just as Niko rose into view. His face was scraped from the fall, but otherwise he looked unhurt.

"My baby!" Jelena screamed.

Just as Gerard lifted him up on to the parapet, Bogun rammed his shoulder into Gerard. The three of them vaulted onto the narrow parapet, Gerard with one hand gripping Niko and the other holding on to Bogun's tunic. All of them were precariously balanced on the edge.

"No!" Vitomir shouted as he raced toward them with his men.

"Hurry!" Petar yelled as they struggled to get the plank in place. "I can help them."

Bogun punched at Gerard's wounded leg, but that didn't make him release his grip, so the Serbian started slamming his fist into Gerard's face.

Willa knew her husband was tough, but she didn't know how much more punishment he could take.

Then Bogun switched to digging his thumb into Gerard's shoulder. She could see the intense pain and determination on Gerard's face. He was holding on with every fiber of strength he had.

Finally, the plank settled onto the wall opposite them. It wasn't a sturdy placement, but it was good enough.

Petar leaped onto the sill and walked across urgently but carefully.

He was only halfway across when Gerard at last couldn't hold on anymore. He gave a sorrowful look at Willa and shook his head.

"Don't!" was all she could scream.

Bogun's repeated punching must have been too much for Gerard's aching arm. His hand slipped off Bogun's tunic, and with a shove from the Serbian, Gerard and Niko tumbled off the parapet.

"No!" Jelena and Petar shrieked in one voice.

Willa could only stare, frozen in shock, her voice caught in her throat at the horror of watching them fall. She remembered well

seeing the rocky cliffs as they had sailed into Dubrovnik's harbor.
A fall from that height onto the crags below would surely be fatal.

"What have you done?" Vitomir cried out.

Bogun peered over the side and shouted back. "They're gone!"

At those words, it felt as if a lance had pierced Willa's heart. It
was a catastrophe worse than she'd ever known. Her new husband,
the man she was supposed to spend the rest of her life with, had
been ripped from her. The impact of losing him sent bolts of cold
lightning shooting through her, causing her insides to burn like
molten iron until the pain was too much to bear, and she let out
a primal scream.

"Gerard!"

The tortured wail made Vitomir whip around. Beyond Bogun, he
was surprised to see the boy's father Petar standing motionless on
a wooden plank suspended between the city wall and the burned-
out house of his neighbor. They must have devised this all well
in advance and planned to escape that way. The Ston man's wife
Jelena was wailing in the window, while a beautiful blonde woman
stood beside her dumbfounded.

"Get him!" he shouted to his men, and two guards raced to the
plank Petar was perched upon.

"We need to go!" the unidentified woman yelled through her
sobs. "Now!"

Petar finally came to his senses and turned to head back to the
house, teetering along the board.

As he reached the house, two guards leaped onto the plank.
They moved rapidly along the board, but as Petar jumped off
it, the unknown woman pushed the end of the plank sideways
with all her might.

The board dropped, along with the guards who were navigating
it. Their screams were short-lived, punctuated by two thumps as
they hit the ground below.

Jelena was still keening at the window, but the other woman shook her into action. The three of them disappeared from sight, no doubt realizing that Vitomir would capture and kill all three of them now that he'd lost his leverage with Niko's plunge to the sea.

He pointed to his remaining guards. "The city gates are open by now. Half of you try to intercept them and the others split up and go to each gate. Stop those three if they try to leave the city."

The guards sprinted away while Vitomir strode up to Bogun, who was breathing hard as he casually sat on the parapet as if he were enjoying the light of the sunrise filtering through the fog.

"Are you mad?" Vitomir barked at him. "You could have saved them both."

"Sir Gerard would have pulled me down with him."

From what Vitomir had seen, that was a lie. Bogun didn't look as if he'd been in any danger of falling.

Vitomir leaned out over the parapet and looked straight down. Other than a scraggly tree, there was nothing but a straight drop to the fog far below.

He was stunned at Bogun's sheer recklessness. If the Serbian had simply waited for his guards to arrive, they would have easily overpowered Fox and gotten Niko back for their ransom. Now their bodies were feeding the fish of the Adriatic.

"Could they be caught on the rocks?" he wondered.

"Possible, but unlikely," Bogun said. "The tide will carry them out to open water unless we go look for their bodies."

"Why would we do that?"

"To confirm they're dead. If nothing else, I'd like to get that beautiful sword he carried. Send a boat out there to retrieve them."

"In this fog?"

"It will lift by noon."

Vitomir shrugged. "All right, as you wish. But I suppose we will have to put off the attack on Ston now."

"We will put off nothing."

"But my hostage is gone. Thanks to you. We must cancel our plans."

Bogun straightened up. He looked terrifying with bruised forehead and sweat pouring down his brow. The expression on his face sent a chill into Vitomir's stomach. He suppressed a shiver of fear.

With a finger jabbing Vitomir's chest, Bogun snarled at him.

"This is your fault. All of it. If it weren't for your stupidity, Sir Gerard would never have been in the house. I don't care what you have to do, but you're going to make good on your promise to me. In two weeks' time, Ston and the entire Stonski Rat peninsula will be mine."

THE STRANGERS

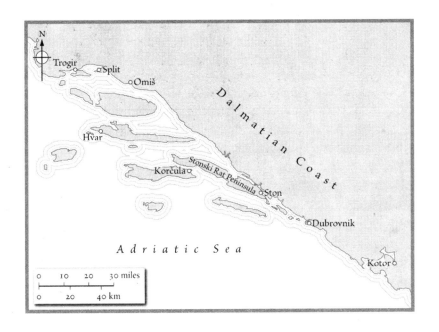

27

As the mid-morning sun burned off the fog, Willa was so numb with shock that she could barely feel her fingers gripping the sides of the boat. She just couldn't believe that Gerard was dead. Although Petar and Jelena seemed convinced of the fact that their child was gone, Willa knew she would never give up hope until she saw her husband's body with her own eyes. At the very least, she wanted to recover his corpse, so she and Petar had paid to borrow a small rowboat to scour the rocky coastline for Gerard and Niko.

Jelena had been so inconsolable that Petar could barely drag her out of the Dubrovnik gates in time to avoid Vitomir's guards from locking them down. She couldn't bear the possibility of seeing her lifeless child floating in the water, so they left her behind with the horses. Zrinka was there to comfort her during their absence. If they were able to collect the bodies, they'd sling them over the saddles and walk them back to Ston—only a single day's sailing by boat if they didn't circumnavigate the Stonski Rat peninsula to Mali Ston, but a two-day journey on horseback—rather than trying to find a boat big enough for Zephyr and Comis.

Petar pulled on the oars as they headed out of the small cove on the north side of the city, far from the busy port. Willa sat at the prow, her eyes scanning the water for any sign of something in the water. Both of them had hoods concealing their faces from the walls above, just in case Vitomir and his people were still searching for them.

Willa dreaded the possibility of seeing Gerard's dead body, but she feared even more never knowing what had happened to him. She focused intently on the rippling surface for any sign of him or Niko, hoping against hope that they would somehow find the two both still alive.

"The tide has been going out since this morning," Petar said, his tone grim. "They could be miles out to sea by now."

"We have to try," Willa replied without turning.

"I agree. But I don't want you to get your hopes up."

Other than a couple of masts on the horizon and a few fishing vessels closer to shore, the lonely expanse of blue was daunting. Petar was distressingly correct. Unless the bodies had washed up on the rocks, the chances of finding them were tiny.

Willa's frustration boiled over.

"The plan should have worked," she said. "If it hadn't been for that man Bogun, he and Niko would have made it."

"That has to be who will be invading Ston in two weeks' time. He and Vitomir were probably conspiring against us the whole time."

"He moved like a soldier," Willa said, remembering his skilled fighting style. "Otherwise, Gerard would have made quick work of him."

"Even with a leg wound?" Petar asked dubiously.

"Gerard is…" she couldn't force herself to use the past tense "…is an expert swordsman. I've seen him defeat some of the best." A duel to the death that she'd witnessed him win was a prime example.

"Then why couldn't he save my child?"

"He did what he could. You saw him."

"He should have tied off the rope so Niko could climb up. Perhaps my baby would still be alive."

Petar's complaint was too much, and Willa turned to snap at him. "My husband died trying to save him. He could have let Niko go, but he didn't, and now we're rowing around looking for their corpses." Her chest heaved, but yet again she fought the urge to cry.

Petar stared at her with an expression of remorse that almost broke her. He bit his lip and nodded.

"I should have done what Vitomir bade me to do. If I had followed his orders, Jelena wouldn't be mourning another lost child."

"You've lost other children?"

Petar nodded solemnly. "Three. Two in childbirth and one to disease. We have one son left: Emerik."

"I'm so sorry."

"And now we've lost a fourth. Because of my stupidity."

"You weren't stupid. You were forced into an impossible choice. And none of this was your fault. It was Vitomir and Bogun's. You did what you had to so you could save Niko and your town."

"I suppose I should be grateful to you and Sir Gerard. You both did far more than we could have expected."

For the first time, Willa began to doubt whether they had done the right thing in helping Petar and Jelena. Despite their good intentions and careful planning, the end result was devastating for all of them. Willa knew that part of her despair was based on a feeling of guilt that she had talked Gerard into all of this. And now he was gone. If she and Gerard had simply stayed out of their business, both he and Niko might be alive right now.

But where would that have left Petar? To get Niko back, he would have had to open his town gates to an invading force, and who knew what the Serbians planned to do with the people who lived there once they had conquered them. They might end up as little more than slaves for their occupiers. She knew that Gerard would rather risk his life than leave them undefended.

Willa didn't want to think about what her own future held. She could survive for a time with the money she had, but a single woman alone with no family, property, or station did not have many prospects in this world. All of a sudden, she felt very far from home. She was tired of speaking foreign languages all the time, eating strange food, and sleeping on the road. She just wanted to be back in England, where everything was familiar. On the road with Gerard, she had shared a sense of adventure with him. Now that he was gone, she felt isolated and so alone.

The situation was anguishing for both of them, and they fell silent again. Her regrets were for herself—a bride and possibly a widow within just a few weeks. Willa instead tried to focus on her task, her eyes roaming the stony base of the city walls.

With the exception of a few sheer cliff faces, most of the shoreline was a jumble of jagged rocks that would be deadly to land on. If that had been Gerard and Niko's fate, Willa could only hope that the end had been swift.

She kept scanning all around her when something caught her eye, a shape bobbing in the water. It was just a hump lying on the surface, but it was no fish. She pointed for Petar to change course.

"Over there."

"What is it?" he asked as he came about.

"I can't tell."

He rowed faster. Willa swallowed hard at the thought of what they might find. As they neared it, she leaned out over the bow. When she finally recognized what she was looking at, she was both profoundly disappointed and at the same time relieved.

"It's just a log."

Despite her pronouncement, Petar kept rowing, and the boat knocked into it. He leaned over the side to look at it. He cursed in Croatian before switching back to Italian.

"That storm we had last week must have washed some dead trunks into the water."

"Let's keep looking."

Petar headed back toward the cliffs under the walls. As they came farther around, Willa could see another larger boat hugging the coast a hundred yards away. Four men were aboard it, and they seemed to be searching the shoreline as well.

She looked up and saw Vitomir and Bogun atop the wall pointing down at something almost directly under them. One of the men in the boat crouched over the side and lifted an object out of the water. When he held it aloft, Willa felt her breath seize in her throat.

It was Gerard's cloak. A huge hole was ripped through the center.

Willa couldn't help standing to get a better look to see if they found anything else.

"Careful," Petar warned.

"That's Gerard's."

"Sit down before you swamp us!"

But as she shook her head in disbelief, the breeze blew the hood from her head. Before she could snatch it back, her golden curls must have caught the morning sun.

Bogun and Vitomir noticed. Her hair color was uncommon in this part of the world. Both of them pointed at the tiny rowboat and began yelling at the guards holding the cloak. They shouted back, confused, but it wouldn't be long before they understood that they were supposed to take off in pursuit.

Willa sat back down and turned to Petar.

"Hurry! Get us back to shore."

"But our search…"

"Is over. They'll come after us now that they know we are still here."

He quickly turned the rowboat and used muscles honed from daily labor to pull powerful strokes. By the time the guards on the boat got the message, Willa and Petar already had an insurmountable lead.

"They might catch us onshore," Petar wheezed between pulls.

Willa shook her head. "They don't have Zephyr and Comis. We'll be long gone toward Ston before they land."

But her heart threatened to burst at that, for she also knew that they couldn't come back to look again.

Niko and Gerard were truly gone.

 28

Vitomir had watched in impotent frustration as his men failed to catch up with Petar and the unknown woman in his company before they went out of sight around the far end of the city wall. He and Bogun waited there for the results of the chase, but he was disappointed to see his head guard Kulin striding toward them alone, the sodden cloak in his hands.

"They got away?" Vitomir asked, although he knew the answer.

"Yes, my lord," Kulin replied. "They were long gone when we made it into the cove. We found a peasant who said they rode away on horseback."

"Did he see where they went?" Bogun demanded.

Kulin looked at Vitomir, who nodded for him to respond.

"Toward the mountains. That's all we know."

"The entire coastline is made up of mountains," Bogun said, exasperated.

"Shall we prepare a chase, my lord?"

"There's no point," Vitomir said, pointing to the tattered cloak in Kulin's hands. "Their son is dead, along with that Englishman."

"You didn't see their bodies?" Bogun asked.

Kulin shook his head. "There was no sign of the corpses. They must have been washed out to sea before the fog lifted."

"I told you they were dead," Vitomir said, indicating the torn mantle as he waved his hand for Kulin to leave them.

Bogun angrily snatched it away and tossed the evidence of his failure over the wall.

"Along with your leverage. You need to pull the garrison out of Ston."

Vitomir laughed at the absurd suggestion. When he saw that Bogun was serious, he lost his humor.

"Do you realize what that would look like to the rector? How could I possibly explain such an action?"

"My attack force is already on the way. I'm going to rendezvous with them in three days."

"At which time you'll need to turn around and go back to Kotor so we can develop a new plan."

"And if I do that, you won't be able to refund the Dubrovnik treasury and your deceit will be revealed. You'll lose your position and be ruined." Bogun nodded to the nearby house. "Where do you think you'll live in that case? If the rector doesn't just execute you outright."

Vitomir glowered at him. But there was apparently no argument that would get Bogun to call off his assault. He was just angry because the Serbian was right. The rector had made it painfully clear that he expected full repayment of the city's investment in the immediate future. They were both committed no matter what.

"If only that defect in the Mali Ston wall hadn't been repaired," he said.

"What defect?"

"A terrible storm undermined part of the wall, creating a channel underneath. They wanted to tear down the whole section of wall to rebuild it. I told them to fill it in with rocks."

"Can it be accessed without being seen?" Bogun asked.

Vitomir shook his head. "I don't see how. The garrison patrolling the wall would see anyone digging into it. There must be another way."

After a moment's consideration, Bogun said, "Does Petar have any other children?"

"Niko has a younger brother, Emerik. But that boy is back in Ston."

"Which is where we have to assume Petar is going."

"We don't know that. He and his wife have been missing for weeks. Apparently, they were even in Korčula while I was there."

The memory of the Marco Polo codex being stolen from him during that city's All Hallows' Eve celebration continued to sting.

"That was because you had Niko captive. Obviously, they went looking for help from someone and found it in the likes of Sir Gerard."

"Whom you killed."

"He died because of his weakness for that little hedgehog. And now they still have assistance from that blonde woman in the boat."

Vitomir scoffed at the thought of a woman being any use in their plight. "If a knight couldn't save them, you think that spindly young thing will make a difference?"

"But now we've lost our hostage to get Petar to open the Ston gates for us."

"We could try to take his other son for the ransom of opening the gates."

Bogun narrowed his eyes. "You're quite certain Petar has *another* son?"

"His mother confirmed it," Vitomir said.

"And how would we snatch him away without alerting the garrison there of the abduction?"

"I could send one of my guards to do it."

"You've been to Ston with your guards. They would be recognized by the garrison soldiers and by Petar. They would stop the guard from taking him, and then they'd surely believe Petar's tale of your treachery if he goes back to Ston and is bold enough to tell them about it."

"What about Cedozar? Petar hasn't seen him."

Bogun shook his head as if he were disappointed.

"An unknown Serbian walking into Ston would be even more suspicious. We're going to use my plan. We'll remove the soldiers in the Ston garrison and replace them with my men."

Vitomir stifled a shudder at that. Ordering the men to abandon Ston would be a huge risk for him.

"We can't do that."

"Of course we can. Cedozar will go with you into the town. It should have been our plan from the beginning, but I indulged your concerns about staying out of this directly. No more."

Vitomir gasped. "You're not suggesting I go with you?"

"How else are we going to make the entire garrison abandon their posts? They'll listen to Lord Vitomir."

"But they'll report to the rector that I withdrew them as soon as they return to Dubrovnik."

Bogun tilted his head at Vitomir as though he just wasn't understanding.

"What makes you think I'd let them get back to Dubrovnik?"

29

MALI STON, DALMATIA

With the horses riding fast on the few sections of flat ground, the trek from Dubrovnik took only a day and a half. Zephyr had accepted Willa as his rider, with Zrinka behind her, but he was more difficult to control without Gerard on his back. Comis was a more forgiving horse, so Petar had ridden on her with Jelena. The ride had largely been a silent one. Petar and Jelena both seemed to dread the return home without their child, and Willa barely noticed the dramatic scenery around her, so preoccupied was she in thinking of her own loss. It seemed at least one of them was crying at any given point the entire way. Only Zrinka seemed eager to return to Ston, although she too mourned the death of her young cousin and stayed respectfully silent.

They emerged from the coastal forest to see a walled town sitting on the coast of a wide bay where a couple of fishing boats and a larger shipping vessel were anchored. The sight of the town roused Willa from her grief. After coming from the bustling city of Dubrovnik, its diminutive size of fewer than two hundred inhabitants was startling given its disproportionately stout defenses.

A single dock jutted out into the water. A ridge soared high above the town. To the west was a dirt track that led into a narrow valley through two forested mountains. A lone donkey cart trudged along the path.

Strangely, a wall five times the height of a man in places snaked up the mountain and over the ridge out of sight. It seemed to guard nothing, and Willa couldn't fathom the purpose of it.

She didn't see any sign of the famous salt pans that everyone coveted.

Two soldiers stood on the wall above the open gates with pikes in their hands. Another strolled along the battlements munching on a hunk of bread. None of them seemed the least bit wary of potential enemies.

"I can understand why Bogun wouldn't want to attack Ston in a frontal assault," Willa said.

"That's not Ston," Petar said, his first words since they'd left Dubrovnik that didn't involve food or directions. "It's Mali Ston."

"Mali Ston?" This was the first time Willa had heard the term.

"We sometimes refer to this entire area as Ston, but it's actually made up of two towns, Ston and Mali Ston, which means Little Ston. Mali Ston is where the salt traders, fishermen, oystermen, and soldiers in the garrison live because of its deep harbor. Ston is on the other side of that ridge. That's where we live along with the other salt harvesters. It's also where the church of Saint Blaise is."

"How far is it?"

Petar pointed at the dirt path through the valley. "It's just a short walk through there."

Jelena tapped her husband on the shoulder with a worried look on her face. "Do you think Emerik will remember me?"

Petar patted her hand. "Of course, he will, my love. We haven't been gone so long as that."

"I was afraid I was beginning to forget what he looks like." She turned to Willa. "I've never been away from him for more than a day, and now he's all I have left."

Willa felt a sharp pang in her chest as she tried to remember her own dearly departed parents' faces. Although she could recall the warm feeling of their presence, their images were blank.

Could she lose Gerard's, too? Except for venturing off the trail last night to weep alone until she could weep no more, she'd had no chance to properly mourn him. Now the thought of his beautiful face vanishing forever threatened to bring back her tears. Although Jelena and Petar had each other and their son, Willa had no one, a terrible reality. She tamped her loneliness down as best she could and forced a smile for Jelena.

"I'm sure he'll be so happy for your return," she said. "Who is he staying with?"

"My mother. She's the town's best seamstress, and a healer too."

Petar frowned. "I didn't think about it until now. Not only does she not know about her grandchild's fate, but she also hasn't yet heard about your brother's death."

Jelena's breath caught. "You're right. The news will crush her."

"Just focus on what you still have to protect," Willa said. "If the townspeople know what an awful tragedy your family has suffered, perhaps it will prepare them for the coming fight."

She supposed she had to prepare herself for the battle as well. Willa still didn't know what she was going to do now that Gerard was gone, but at least she'd help the last two people she could count as friends. The rest of her life seemed like a gaping maw of emptiness, so frightening that her mind turned back to the immediate future, something she could still contribute to.

"What is that wall over the mountain defending against?" she asked to distract them and herself.

"It connects Mali Ston to Ston. Eventually Ston will have a wall around it as well, but it is under construction and won't be completed for some time. That valley between Ston and Mali Ston is the only way onto Stonski Rat by land. Any invasion force would have to take Mali Ston before conquering the rest of the peninsula."

"And what about from the sea?"

"The peninsula stretches like a long finger to the north, so it takes time to sail around it. The Venetian patrols would spot a large invasion force before they could make landfall at Mali Ston. The coast southwest of Ston is very rugged but exposed, and any fleet would be easily seen coming into Ston's bay."

"Then I don't see how Bogun can hope to invade."

"He'd be foolish to do so, now," Jelena said. "But I hope he does. I'd kill him myself for what he did to Niko."

"I also think he and Vitomir have to give up," Petar said. "They no longer have my child to hold over me."

"Men like that don't give up so easily," Willa warned. "We have to assume they will come no matter what."

"Then the garrison at Mali Ston will repel them."

"How many soldiers?"

"Twelve when I left. I'm told that's enough atop the walls to defend the town from even a large force and hold off a siege until reinforcements arrived."

"Unless the gate is opened for them."

"I won't do that now. Not with our child gone."

"How can you be sure they won't give up?" Jelena asked.

"Because men like that won't stop until they get what they want," Willa answered. "I've seen their kind up close. It's the way of this world."

When they reached the gate at Mali Ston, one of the guards above nodded at Petar and spoke to him in Croatian. Willa had learned a little of the language in her time with the couple, but not enough to understand the rapid dialogue.

Jelena said something in a worried voice. Petar spat out a curse and turned Comis around.

"What is it?" Willa asked.

"Jelena's mother is staying at our house in Ston," Petar said, "even though we told her to remain here in Mali Ston."

"She wanted the comfort of our bigger home while we were gone," Jelena said.

Zrinka dismounted and bade her a muted thanks for bringing her home before going through Mali Ston's gate. The three of them took off at a canter along the path through the valley. Trees on either side shrouded the track, deepening the shadow cast by the mountain. The wall on the ridge above them paralleled their ride the entire way, an excellent way to observe anyone traversing the road.

They slowed as they emerged from the valley, a vast pond becoming visible. It was divided into sections by low stone walls, the water as still as a mirror reflecting the afternoon sun. A huge stone building sat at its edge.

"Those are the salt pans," Petar said. "They're fallow for the winter." He pointed at the stone building. "That's where we store the harvested salt to keep it out of the rain until we take it to Mali Ston for shipping."

Now that the mountain was no longer shielding her view, Willa could see the town of Ston, a neatly organized group of red-roofed buildings beside a compact church. The beginnings of a protective wall were taking shape along Ston's border, but it was obviously years from completion.

They rounded the unfinished wall into the narrow streets of the town, with Petar leading the way. Even before they stopped in front of a neat but rustic two-story wooden house in the center of town, he was calling out. "Emerik! Marija!"

As soon as the horses halted, Petar and Jelena leaped down. They ran into the house, and almost instantly came back out. Both of them were babbling in Croatian, but Willa could tell they were terrified that they couldn't find their son or Jelena's mother.

Some of the townsfolk came running at the commotion. An older woman who had to be Marija, her hair streaked with gray and carrying a bolt of linen cloth, dashed around the corner and dropped it with a cry of happiness to envelop Jelena with a great embrace. Jelena wriggled out of it and implored her mother with a question. The only word Willa could make out was "Emerik."

Marija shook her head and looked around, which sent Jelena into a panic. Petar tried to calm her, but Jelena was hysterical.

She shrieked Emerik's name in agony, and Willa feared the worst.

But Jelena's voice turned to a delightful shout of elation when a boy of no more than seven years ran toward them from behind a building, a huge smile on his face. Jelena sprinted to him and swept him up in her arms.

"Emerik, Emerik," she repeated as if to soothe herself.

Petar went over and rubbed the boy's head in relief.

Willa dismounted and allowed herself some joy at the lovely reunion. At last there was something to celebrate.

Petar introduced Willa to Jelena's mother, who was looking at the stranger dubiously.

"Willa is a friend," he said in Italian. "She lost so much trying to help us."

"Help you in what way?" Marija said in a melodious but puzzled voice, obviously speaking the same language for their visitor's benefit. "Where is Drazhan? Where is Nika?"

Willa stayed silent. She knew she had to let Petar and Jelena deliver the terrible news.

Marija must have sensed the tension. "What happened to her?" she demanded. "Tell me."

Willa was suddenly confused and asked Petar, "Her? Does she mean me?"

Petar shook his head and looked at Jelena, who nodded as if she were allowing him to say something he'd been holding back.

"It's time you knew," Petar said solemnly. "I'm sorry we kept it from you, but we didn't know if you and Sir Gerard would help us if you learned the truth. Her name was actually Nika, not Niko, and she wasn't a boy. She was a girl."

30

The Adriatic Sea

Nika wound her way through the hold of the Venetian trading ship cradling a cup of water and a loaf of moldy bread. Several of the crew watched her curiously as she shuffled by, but they said nothing while they chewed on their own midday meals. So far, she didn't think anyone suspected she was actually a girl.

Keeping up her disguise as a boy on the ship only presented a problem when she had to relieve herself, so she ate and drank as little as she could during the voyage. After being plucked out of the water far from the Dubrovnik walls, she'd kept up the deception she'd used ever since cutting off her hair so that she could sneak away from Ston in an attempt to warn her father that he was entering a trap laid by Vitomir. Boys could get away with that kind of thing, but girls couldn't, so she'd taken the name Niko instead of Nika. When Vitomir had caught her trying to find her father, she'd continued the lie. She was just glad that her parents went along with it.

She made it to the opposite end of the hold and kneeled beside Gerard Fox. For two days he'd been in and out of consciousness from hitting his head when they'd plummeted off the wall and crashed into the sea.

They'd been able to stay afloat long enough to latch on to a stray log, but Gerard had barely been able to hang on as they were swept out to sea. Nika hadn't dared call for help, knowing that Bogun had been watching for them from above the fog bank. It was better to chance the open sea than Bogun's wrath.

She tipped the crude clay cup of water so that it trickled through Gerard's lips. He swallowed some of it, then coughed. The action must have finally woken him, for he sat bolt upright and grabbed Nika's tunic, pulling her close to him with a confused look.

"It's me—Niko," she said anxiously.

His expression softened when he recognized her, and he let go. "Where am I?"

"A Venetian trading ship. They found us far from the coast and hauled us aboard."

Suddenly, he patted the deck around him. "Legend," he said, almost in a panic.

"What?"

"My sword."

Nika pointed behind him. He looked vastly relieved when he saw his weapon lying against the bulkhead.

"Your sword has a name?"

"It was my father's sword, and his father's before that."

"It's quite pretty." When he raised an eyebrow, she added, "You've been out for a while, and I was bored."

"How long has it been?" he asked.

"Two days. Your leg is healing well. I wrapped it with cloth."

He flexed it and winced, then turned to inspect it and nodded appreciatively when he was done.

"Fine work."

"Some of the crew helped me. They put a poultice on it to keep it from spoiling."

"I'm surprised they took us aboard."

"They think you're rich because of your sword. They want a reward for finding you."

"They'll get one. But we can't be going to Dubrovnik or we would have been there already."

"They offered to take us back, but I told them we wouldn't be welcomed there. They seemed happy not to have to turn around. They were heading toward Split, so I said that was where we were from."

"We?"

"I told them that you're my father. We fell overboard from another passing ship, in case they ask you."

"What else did you tell them?"

"That you're a knight, and I'm all that you have left after the Pestilence killed our family."

"I suppose that's believable. Anything else?"

"Like what?"

Gerard gave her a cock-eyed grin. "Like the fact that you're really a girl?"

Nika stopped breathing for a moment. She quickly looked behind her to see if anyone was listening, but no one was close enough to hear.

"Why would you say something mad like that?"

"Oh, you were very convincing. I'm not surprised that you fooled Vitomir. And your parents continued the masquerade well. But you gave yourself away."

Nika jutted out her chin, unwilling to admit it just yet. "What do you mean?"

"When we were escaping from the storage room back at Vitomir's house. You were getting up onto the windowsill, and without thinking, you reached down to lift up your skirt. You tried to cover up the mistake, but I noticed. That's what girls do when they're climbing, not boys. Plus, you confirmed it when just called my sword 'pretty,' not something a boy would usually say."

Not many men would have spotted the errors, so she was both appalled and impressed that her secret was revealed.

"You can't tell anyone."

"I wouldn't dream of it. Is Niko really your name?"

"Nika is my actual name. You should still call me Niko."

"All right, Niko. But why pretend to be a boy in the first place?"

"Lord Vitomir came to visit Ston late in the summer. I was playing near the house where he was staying. He didn't see me when he was talking to his guard. He said that Lovrijenac was where he'd execute the weasel and any other traitors. I didn't know what he meant, and I didn't say anything to my father because I thought I'd get in trouble for listening to him when

I shouldn't have. But after my parents and uncle Drazhan left for Dubrovnik, my grandmother told me that they were meeting with the rector at Fort Lovrijenac. She also told me that she heard Lord Vitomir call my uncle a weasel."

Gerard nodded. "And you were worried that they were walking into a trap."

"I had to do something. My grandmother would never let me go, so I cut off my hair, stole a boy's clothes, and stowed away on a ship that I knew was going to Dubrovnik. I tried to warn my parents, but I was caught by Lord Vitomir before I could get to them." Her lips quivered. "They killed my uncle right in front of us."

Gerard said nothing, so she wiped her face.

"I wish I could kill Vitomir."

"No, you don't."

"How do you know?"

"Because I've killed," Gerard said. "It's not something I'd wish on anybody."

"You think I can't do it because I'm a girl?"

"Keep your voice down." He appraised her for a moment. "You've already done a lot, so maybe you could. But you don't want to. It's hard on the soul."

"I don't care. Vitomir deserves it."

"That I agree with. Anyone who abducts a child is pig offal in my view."

She suddenly had a better thought. "Will you kill him?"

"I'm more intent on getting you home to your parents. I'm hoping that's where my wife is. No doubt they all think we're dead."

"You're married?"

He showed her the ring that he extracted from a hidden pouch in his tunic, pointing to the engraving on the inside.

She couldn't read, although she wanted to someday. "What does that say?" she asked as he put it back on.

"*Ubi amor ibi fides.* It's Latin for: 'Where there is love, there is faith.'"

"And you think your wife is in Ston? Why?"

"Willa was the woman in the window with your mother and father when I was fighting Bogun. She's smart, so I have faith that she followed our escape plan from Dubrovnik with your parents before Vitomir could capture them. Where else would they go but your parents' home? As soon as we reach Split, we'll hire a ship to take us back to Ston."

"What about the Serbians? The invasion?"

"You know about that?"

"I heard Lord Vitomir say that he is making my father open the gates for them."

"He won't now."

"So Ston is safe?"

Gerard shook his head. "Bogun and Vitomir seem committed to this course. If I were them, I'd find some reason to remove the garrison from Ston."

"If that happens, Ston will be defenseless."

"That's why we need to get back there."

She raised her eyebrows in doubt. "You can defend Ston by yourself?"

"Willa is good with a bow."

"Good enough to fend off an army?"

"I'll teach your townspeople to fight."

"They're salt harvesters and fishermen and farmers." Nika's heart hammered with terror. "They'll all be killed. My family will be killed."

"You'd be surprised what people can learn when they need to."

Nika slapped her hand on the floorboards. "No!" Then she lowered her voice. "We need to find men who will fight for us. Ston is rich. We can pay."

"You're suggesting I hire mercenaries?"

"What are those?"

"Men who will fight for money."

Nika lit up. "Yes, get mercenaries to defend Ston."

"If Bogun is a good strategist, and I think he is, he'll be

attacking in the coming weeks, so I think we need to get back as soon as we can."

"Then we must get to work as soon as we arrive in Split."

Gerard chuckled at that. "So you're going to help me in this search?"

"Are you saying I can't because I'm a girl?"

"Because you're a child."

"If you don't help me, I'll do it myself."

"I really think you'd try." He tilted his head at her. "Are all children like you?"

"You don't know what children are like?"

"I haven't been around one in years."

"I can tell. You're the only man who talks to me like I'm not one."

"And the experience is exhausting."

Nika stood and put her hands on her hips. "Are you going to help us or not?"

"I've already *been* helping you, if you hadn't noticed."

"My town needs these mercenaries."

Gerard put up his hands in defeat. "You win. I'll find some mercenaries for you. Let's just hope they don't kill *you* first."

31

DUBROVNIK

Bogun climbed the ladder from the rowboat up to the deck of the ship newly anchored in the city's harbor. Cedozar knew better than to offer a hand to help him over the bulwark. Bogun hopped onto the deck to face a reedy man with a thick beard.

"You're Miloš?" Bogun said without preamble. Cedozar's message had told him that a legate of the emperor had forced his way on to the ship before it left Kotor.

The stick-thin man huffed, "*Lord* Miloš to you. You must be Bogun."

"Why are you on this ship?"

"You have no right to question me. I am the one to ask such things of you."

Bogun glared at Cedozar. "You couldn't keep him off?"

"He was very insistent," Cedozar replied. "He likes to throw his weight around. What there is of it."

Miloš's face turned scarlet at that. "How dare you neglect to show me the proper respect. I am a representative of Emperor Dušan himself."

"You're right," Bogun said. "Come. Let us have a refreshment while we talk, and I will answer all your questions."

Cedozar led them to the aftcastle where he had three stools and wooden tankards of ale brought for them. When they were seated, Bogun gulped half his cup and swung his arm at Dubrovnik. "This is why we're here."

Miloš frowned at the walled city. He hadn't touched his drink. "What the devil are you talking about?"

"You were going to ask what I'm doing here, weren't you?"

"I arrived in Kotor to find sailing vessels loading up with soldiers. Not warships, mind you. Which seemed very odd to me given that we'd had no word from Lord Zavida since he was sent to you. So I ordered Cedozar to bring me to you."

"I told him that Zavida never got there," Cedozar said. "He must have encountered some delay along the way to us."

Bogun nodded. "Or some unfortunate accident, perhaps. Travel can be quite dangerous these days with bandits and marauders."

"Lord Zavida is protected by his position," Miloš said. "Everyone in the Serbian Empire knows that. No one would dare attack him."

"I hope you're right. It would be terrible if anything happened to him."

"Someone will know what became of him. What I want to know is why you are in Dubrovnik."

"Why shouldn't I be?"

"What I mean is, why are you here with a ship full of soldiers? The emperor has given no orders for any kind of assault or raid against the Venetian Republic."

"This city is the jewel of the Dalmatian Coast. Don't you think the emperor would enjoy having it as part of his empire?"

Miloš scoffed. "You think you're going to take Dubrovnik with one ship of men?"

"I have five ships. More than one hundred and fifty men in all."

The legate's eyes bugged out at that. "Are you mad? You could not conquer this city with fifteen thousand men. Its walls are invulnerable."

Cedozar laughed. "Do you really think we are planning to attack Dubrovnik?"

"Your thinking is limited," Bogun said, "though I'm not surprised."

"Then what are you doing here?"

Bogun leaned over to Cedozar. "Do you think we should tell him?"

Cedozar shrugged. "Why not? We're all serving the empire, aren't we?"

Miloš slammed his goblet to the deck. "Tell me what, you fools?"

"We're going to take Ston, Mali Ston, and the Stonski Rat peninsula for the glory of the Serbian Empire."

The legate gaped, his eyes flicking from one to the other.

"You really are mad. The emperor would have told me if he were planning an invasion."

"The emperor doesn't know about it," Bogun said.

"Yet," Cedozar added.

"You're invading Ston without an order from His Imperial Highness?"

Bogun leaned forward until he was only a few finger widths from Miloš's face. "What do you think Dubrovnik runs on?"

"I don't understand."

"You fail to surprise us again," Cedozar said.

"Money," Bogun said. "They need it to pay their soldiers, to bring in food, to maintain their thick walls. And where does much of that money come from?"

"How should I know?"

Bogun sighed at his stupidity. How this man got so high in the emperor's court eluded him.

"Salt. The sale, trade, and taxes on it pay for everything. Without salt, Dubrovnik would be starved of resources. If we capture Ston, we would control the entire salt trade along the Dalmatian coast and procure a valuable new source of income for the Serbian Empire. Dubrovnik would fall into our arms."

"But the Venetians!" Miloš sputtered. "They bought it by contract from His Imperial Highness."

"The emperor was tricked into selling my birthright."

"The Venetians would go to war to get it back."

"Let them. Once we have taken the fortress at Mali Ston, it would be impossible for them to reclaim it, especially once we are reinforced by Emperor Dušan's army."

"How can you possibly do this if it is as well protected as you say?"

"That is none of your concern."

"His Imperial Highness will never approve of this."

"Which is why I didn't tell him what I was planning. But once he learns that the brave soldiers from his outpost in Kotor have achieved a great victory, I have no doubt he will send his army to protect his new treasure."

Miloš leaped to his feet. "I will inform the emperor of what you're planning, and we'll see if he is so understanding of your venture."

Cedozar stood and grabbed him by the arms. "Who says we're sending you back to him?"

"Take your filthy hands off me!"

Bogun slowly got to his feet. "He's right, Cedozar. Let him go."

Cedozar immediately freed him.

"This is an outrage. Take me back to Kotor at once."

Bogun shook his head. "I need this ship. We'll put you off down the coast with your attendant and a donkey. It will be up to you how to get back to Skopje."

"That could take me weeks," Miloš protested.

"Try not to take that long," Cedozar said. "We'll need those reinforcements."

Miloš looked at them both as if they were crazy and was met with icy stares. When he saw that they weren't bluffing, he stalked away.

When he was out of earshot, Cedozar said, "Do you really think letting him go is wise?"

"He is nothing. The emperor will have to hear about our conquest one way or another. Might as well let him do our work for us. He won't get back to the capital in time to stop us."

"And what about Emperor Dušan? Will he come to our aid, do you think?"

"Everything depends on Vitomir removing the garrison at Mali Ston," Bogun said. "Because if we don't follow through and capture those salt pans, we might as well never return home."

32

STON

On the third day after Gerard and Nika plunged off the wall in Dubrovnik, Willa entered Ston's church to attend the traditional Mass for the dead. It was the first time she had participated in a Mass since she'd married an excommunicant, which had made her a heretic as well. According to Church law, she should not take part in the ceremony, but she couldn't explain that to her hosts. They would banish her if they knew the truth.

"Are you certain you don't want our priest to name Sir Gerard during the Mass?" Jelena asked her as they made their way to the front of the nave. Petar and Jelena's mother were holding Emerik's hands in front of them.

"I don't believe he's dead," Willa answered. She wouldn't give up hope for a miracle, not yet. But if he were really dead, she couldn't bear the thought of him spending an eternity in Hell. That was the punishment for an unrepentant heretic, and even if it was an unjust excommunication, she feared the Church's ruling would nevertheless determine his everlasting fate.

"You mustn't torture yourself with such thoughts," Jelena said. "I know my Nika is with our Lord in Paradise. I'll miss her always, but I know I will see her again when I join her at God's feet."

Willa envied Jelena's certainty that Nika was living in Heaven. Although her tears were no less frequent, her miserable grief was leavened by a loving memory and warm belief in Nika's peaceful rest.

"I have to believe that God has other plans for us," she said. "I can't bear the thought that he was taken away from me so soon after we married."

They stopped before the altar, and Jelena took her hands. "We can't understand His plans. But it seems that they fulfilled the prophecy, as much as we didn't want them to."

Willa shook her head as she recalled the prophecy Jelena and the rest of the Ston residents took as gospel.

"Hellfire rains down when a sacrifice summons a dragon to destroy any enemy refusing to flee? We haven't seen a dragon."

"Not yet," Jelena said.

Willa's experience with the Hodegetria, the painting of Mary and the baby Jesus that she had successfully safeguarded in the past, convinced Willa that this prophecy could be real as well. But she didn't see how it could possibly be fulfilled, and she didn't like to think that she and Gerard had come all this way for him to be the sacrifice the prophecy spoke of.

"It wasn't a sacrifice," she said.

"But it was. He was holding Nika, trying to save her. If he hadn't done that, Bogun couldn't have pushed him off the wall."

Something about her argument seemed wrong, but Willa didn't have time to counter it, for the Mass began. The priest recited the Latin prayers for the dead, naming Nika and Jelena's brother Drazhan but leaving out Gerard as she had asked. Marija wept, Petar struggled to keep a stoic expression, and Emerik didn't seem to understand what was happening. Jelena clasped Willa's hand tightly, but Willa refused to cry now because deep down she believed Gerard was still alive. She'd seen him survive ordeals that would have killed any other man. Their life together was not over. It couldn't be.

When the Mass was finished, the two parents greeted the other townsfolk and accepted their condolences. Before leaving, Zrinka gave a big hug to Jelena, who translated Zrinka's blessing and thanks to Willa for helping return her home to Ston.

After they were all gone, Jelena removed the reliquary from around her neck and laid it on the altar as an offering in exchange for the priest to say a daily prayer for Nika's soul. He took it to place it in the church's treasury and left Willa alone with Jelena and her family.

"Our friends have prepared a meal so that we may mourn the dead and remember them," Petar said.

"We should help them get ready," Marija said.

Jelena shook her head. "Willa and I would like to stay a while. We'll join you a little later."

Petar nodded, for he knew the real reason Jelena wanted to stay behind.

"Come, Emerik," he said, putting his arm around the boy. "I brought you something from a far-off island called Rhodes."

The three of them exited the church, leaving Willa and Jelena as its only remaining occupants.

"I'm sorry you have to delay your meal," Willa said.

"This is the only time we can be sure we won't be interrupted. Do you really think we'll find Marco Polo's book in here?"

"Drazhan would have hidden it somewhere dry, so it wouldn't be buried in the ground or a tree stump. You told me that you think your brother was trying to give you and Petar a clue in front of Vitomir when he said that Blaise would protect it. And we know it's not in his house or Vitomir would have it already. Since this is the Church of Saint Blaise, it must be in here somewhere."

"I don't know where," Jelena said. "Certainly not in the floor. It's nothing but dirt."

"There's got to be a secret panel or loose stone in the building."

"It seems as if you've done this before."

"I have, in a cathedral far bigger than this."

Willa remembered a similar search in Siena's massive main cathedral, which would have taken days to comb through. Ston's more modest church was still large enough to take considerable time to scour.

Willa showed Jelena how to check for openings or loose stones, then set her off on the north side of the church while Willa took the south side. The hiding place wouldn't be out of reach or require a stool or ladder to get to. Drazhan would have wanted to be able to remove it and replace it quickly without being seen.

Willa ran her hands over the smooth stones of the walls and pillars, but they were all firmly attached. Nothing seemed out of place or unusual. She was methodical in her search, and several glances over at Jelena confirmed that she was being equally thorough.

The two of them reached opposing sides of the altar at the same time. Willa was about to continue her examination onto the altar, but Jelena stopped her.

"My brother may have been a liar and a trusting fool, but he was also a devout parishioner. He would never have hidden something on the altar."

Willa conceded her point, but only because she also thought it would be too likely that the priest would discover such a hiding place.

"Let's go back the way we came to make sure we didn't miss anything," Willa said. "I'll take your side and you take mine."

They repeated the search, but again without any luck. They met at the church's front doors. Jelena looked as frustrated as Willa felt.

"We need that book," Willa said. "Petar seemed to be convinced that Drazhan found a powerful weapon described by Marco Polo. It might be our only chance of successfully defending Ston."

Jelena shrugged. "If Saint Blaise is protecting the book, it has to be in here."

What she said struck Willa wrong. "Didn't you say that Drazhan told you Blaise was protecting the book?"

"Yes."

"Did he say Blaise or Saint Blaise?"

Jelena cocked her head in thought. "You're right. Drazhan said that the book is 'protected by Blaise.'"

"Don't you think it's odd he wouldn't say 'Saint Blaise'?"

"I suppose. What do you think it means?"

"I don't know. Is there anything else in Ston related to Blaise? Is there a person named Blaise, or perhaps it's a place name?"

Jelena's eyes suddenly went wide. "Blaise and Lazarus."

"Who are they?"

"All of our harvest pans except one, Mundo, are named for saints like Anthony, Balthazar, and Francis. Blaise and Lazarus are the granite-lined pans for producing our highest quality salt."

"Drazhan couldn't possibly have hidden the book out there, exposed to the weather."

"I know my brother," Jelena said. "He was a saltman above all. I don't know how, but the answer to his riddle must be out there in the pans."

33

SPLIT, DALMATIA

Fox had heard from the sailors that the city of Split dwelt inside the walls of an ancient palace built by a Roman emperor named Diocletian, but he didn't quite believe it until he saw the central square with its Roman pillars and the octagonal cathedral built out of a mausoleum for the emperor himself. A massive bell tower soared above, displaying the wealth of this trading city.

Like Dubrovnik, Split was populated by a wide array of people from all over the Mediterranean and beyond. It was as good a place as any to find mercenaries to help their cause in defending Ston from Bogun.

Fox was trailed by Nika as he walked through the paved streets. He stopped outside the door of the fifth tavern they'd been to since arriving in the city. He adjusted Legend, which was sheathed and wrapped in a cloth that was strapped to his back. The local law didn't allow him to wear it on his waist and walk around armed with a weapon of war. It was cloaked under the new mantle he'd purchased to replace the one he'd lost in the Adriatic.

He didn't know how much longer they could do this search without any success, and he wondered how he would break the news to Nika.

"What's the matter?" she asked.

"What we've been doing hasn't been working," Fox said.

"Maybe we need to offer more money."

"That doesn't seem to be the problem. No one is interested in the words of an Englishman and his Croatian page."

To keep up the fiction that Nika was a boy, they'd settled on calling her his page. While he was attempting to recruit mercenaries to aid him in the defense of Ston, he would have rather left her somewhere else instead of taking her into taverns with him. But there was nowhere to leave her safely by herself, and he didn't speak Croatian, so he took advantage of her skills as an interpreter.

"You swore that we would find men-at-arms to protect Ston."

"I can't force them to join us. Even mentioning that we'd be fighting Bogun and the Serbs hasn't convinced them to defend their land from invaders. In fact, it might be scaring them off."

"That's because you make the situation sound hopeless," Nika said.

"They deserve to know what they'll be up against."

"You think it will be a massacre."

"If I did, I would have gotten on the next ship out of Split and evacuated Ston as soon as we arrived there."

"We'd never abandon our homes, no matter the chances."

"You're probably right. But I would have tried to convince them if I thought that was their best hope. If we can't recruit anyone to come with us, that may be the only choice."

Nika took his hand and tugged on it. "Please. Let's try two or three more taverns. I'm sure we'll find someone to help us."

Surprisingly, she wasn't whining like he thought a child would. She sounded much older than her years.

"All right. Do you have any new ideas for what would persuade them to come with us?"

"Tell them the rector of Dubrovnik will grant them lands of their own."

Fox frowned at her suggestion to lie. "I can't promise them something I have no power to deliver."

"You really are a knight, aren't you? My grandfather Ennio told me stories about Sir Lancelot and the knights of the Round Table. You take vows to be good and just."

"We do, although not all knights live up to those vows.

However, I take them seriously. I don't have much more than my honor right now. We'll try more money."

Nika frowned at that. "I guess we'll do it your way."

Fox pushed open the door of the tavern and led her into the smoky room, dimly lit by cresset lamps. A dozen men sat at tables drinking ale and slurping from bowls of pottage.

Fox went over to the only man wearing an apron.

"Are you the proprietor?" he asked in Italian. Nika translated it into Croatian for him.

The man looked him up and down before nodding.

"I have business for a man-at-arms. Are there any here who might be looking for work?"

The tavern keeper raised an eyebrow but said nothing. Fox could have made an announcement to the whole room, but he was trying to keep his interests quiet.

He pressed a coin into the tavern keeper's palm. The man nodded to a table where a man was sitting alone.

Fox gave his thanks and went over to the table. The man looked up from his food. He was about Fox's age, with a flat nose, hairy forearms, and the scarred hands of a brawler.

He spoke in Croatian, and Nika translated.

"What's this about?"

"Are you looking for work as a mercenary?" Fox asked.

"Who wants to know?" was his reply.

"My name is Gerard. This is my page Niko. We are on our way to Ston, and we have need of strong men to defend the town from enemies."

"What enemies?"

"A group of Serbians led by a man named Bogun."

The mention of the name sparked something. "I know of him. Not interested."

"You haven't heard the price for your services."

"Not interested, Venetian."

"I'm not Venetian. I'm English."

"I don't care."

Fox took a sizeable ruby from his purse. "You'll get this for your troubles if you come with us."

The mercenary squinted at them.

He said something derisive.

"He thinks it's a piece of glass," Nika said.

Fox wasn't surprised. He'd met the same doubts in the other taverns. He replaced the gem and took out a gold Venetian ducat, one of the twenty he'd acquired from a gem trader earlier that day.

"You'll get one of these to wield your sword."

The man held out his hand for it, but Fox just held it close to him so he could inspect it. The man thought for a moment before responding, and Nika answered without translating. They went back and forth several times. Then the mercenary stood up and nodded.

"What did he say?" Fox asked.

"He said he'd join us."

"And what was all that you were talking about with him?"

"I said that you would give him the money now."

The mercenary was holding out his hand. Fox couldn't believe Nika had told him that.

"I'm not going to pay him now."

"Why not?"

"Because he'll take the money and leave."

"But he promised he'd come."

"You're too trusting."

Nika seemed genuinely surprised. "You mean, he would lie about that?"

The Croatian thrust his hand out further and spoke in an insistent tone.

"Tell him you misspoke," Fox said. "He gets paid when he does the job."

Nika reluctantly translated, causing the man to yell at them.

Three men at a nearby table jumped to their feet.

"What did he say now?"

A voice behind them said in accented Italian, "He wants all of your gold."

Fox took a glance over his shoulder and saw a man with a strong chin and a thin mustache. He had the erect bearing of a nobleman, and the cloak and tunic he wore were made of rich cloth. As a knight himself, Fox could recognize another when he met one.

"It's *my* gold. Not his."

The stranger grinned wryly. His eyes darted amongst the men arrayed against Fox. "He says it was offered to him."

"It wasn't my offer," Fox replied. "My page spoke out of turn."

"You're the Englishman looking for men to fight against Bogun?"

"Yes. How do you know that?"

"Word gets around. I've been looking for you. My name is Cristoval."

The Croatian, who'd been watching this exchange, dropped his hand and walked around the table.

Cristoval spoke in Croatian, but the mercenary apparently didn't like what he said. Flatnose launched himself at Fox, who dodged the fist and slammed his elbow onto the back of the man's head as he flew past.

One of the other three men grabbed Nika. She kicked him in the nethers, causing him to cry out and double over in agony, which made the other two rush Fox. He kneed one in the stomach, but the other was able to wrap his arm around Fox's neck. He flipped the man over his head, bringing him down on the table with enough force to splinter it.

He heard a noise behind him and turned just in time to see the mercenary he'd been negotiating with. The man dropped the dagger he was aiming at Fox's back as Cristoval used his fist to land a crushing blow across the man's temple.

The four men were laid out, either unconscious or groaning in pain.

"We should go," Cristoval said, switching to Italian.

"I think you're right," Fox said, grabbing Nika by the arm. "Come on, page."

When they were outside, Cristoval led them through the

streets until they were far from the tavern. He came to a stop in the square beside the soaring bell tower.

"Thank you for your aid, Cristoval," Fox said. "Although I noted that you waited until we had dispatched those men."

"I had to see if you were a serious fighter."

"Sir Gerard is a knight," Nika said.

"I can see he has the skills of one," Cristoval said. "Perhaps you have a chance of helping me."

"We help *you*?" Fox said.

"You said you were looking for allies to fight against the Serbians and against one man in particular."

"Bogun."

Cristoval's lips curled into a sneer at the name. "You're sure he will be at this coming battle?"

Fox remembered Bogun's palpable desire for conquest when he mentioned Ston.

"I'm sure of it."

"Good. I'm going with you."

"You don't look like a mercenary," Fox said. "Why would you do this?"

"For the oldest reason," Cristoval answered, his eyes glittering with barely restrained fury. "Revenge."

34

Nine months ago—March, 1351

BOSNIA

Despite the heavy snowfall the week before, the warm March sun had melted enough to make the ride over the pass easier than Cristoval had been expecting. The mountain range that towered over them gleamed white with the remnants of the storm, and the melted runoff was feeding the rushing river beside the road.

Cristoval rode next to his brother Lorenzo. Neither of them had been so cold in their lives. Their home in the southern Spanish city of Córdoba rarely felt the touch of snow, even in the depths of winter.

"I hope this is the last we see of snow for a long time," Cristoval said. He was wearing a broad-brimmed pilgrim's hat pinned with a badge from Santiago de Compostela, their first stop on this journey to the Holy Land.

"It's just another of God's tests on this pilgrimage," came Lorenzo's infuriatingly cheerful reply. He was dressed in a long brown robe with a hood to protect him from the wind. He wasn't able to keep his tonsure as clean-shaven as usual in the months they had been traveling, but at the moment his hair was still shorter on top than along the sides. "Any pain and suffering we experience reminds us of the sacrifice our Lord willingly took on for our salvation. If God didn't test us, this pilgrimage would be in vain."

"Can't he just test *you*?" Cristoval said.

Lorenzo gave him a crooked smile. "Because I'm a priest and you're a lowly knight?"

"'Lowly'? You should be glad to have me along. Who else would you complain to about your saddle?"

"I can't very well pray to the Lord about my aching rump. It wouldn't be proper."

"So *I* get to hear about it instead."

"I'm not a horseman like you are. I've spent more time in the saddle the last few weeks than I did my entire life before that."

"So you should be used to it by..." Their bickering was interrupted when an unusual sight caught Cristoval's eye. "What is happening here?"

Smoke rose above the hillock ahead of them, black and thick. It was far too much to be coming from a hearth or even a pile of hay, though not enough to be from a forest fire.

When they reached the top of the hill, he could see the wooden roof of a church burning ferociously. It was in the center of a small town nestled in a valley of verdant fields. None of the other buildings had caught fire. Cristoval couldn't make out movement in the village or hear any commotion from the residents.

The odd situation bothered him. He pulled his horse to a stop, and Lorenzo did the same.

"We should turn around," Cristoval said.

"No, we should help these people."

"Something isn't right here."

Lorenzo frowned at him. "What wouldn't be right is abandoning people in need. We should embrace acts of charity as part of the journey. Isn't that why we're on this pilgrimage?"

"That's why *you're* on this pilgrimage. I'm here because our sister insisted that I come along to protect you, and I don't like the look of this."

"Why?"

Cristoval couldn't quite tell him. "It's too quiet."

"Perhaps we can't hear them from here. As a disciple of the Lord, it is my responsibility to help those who are troubled."

"And my responsibility is to you."

"Although I'm appalled by your lack of compassion for those less fortunate, I'm touched by your concern for me."

Cristoval shook his head ruefully. "My concern is for my backside should anything happen to you. Madelena would lash me to ribbons if you came back with so much as a scratch."

Lorenzo smiled at him. "I do enjoy that a big, strong knight like you still fears our dear sister."

"Then you don't remember that time you stole her platter of honeyed cakes from the kitchen. I don't think you sat down for a week."

That got a laugh out of Lorenzo. "I was young and selfish back then. I hope I've grown out of it."

"You're doing God's work," Cristoval said with a solemn glance. "We're all proud of who you've become."

"I know you are," Lorenzo replied. He nodded at the village. "You know I must help them. Or rather, *we* must."

Cristoval sighed. "All right. But stay by me."

They trotted down into the valley and entered the town. The smell of charred wood was strong, but another scent was more disturbing. The village reeked of burning flesh.

They had passed several buildings before Cristoval spotted the first dead body.

It lay sprawled on the ground, blood pooled beside it. The man's torso had been slashed across the stomach. Cristoval easily recognized the work of a sword.

They passed another building and were met with the horrific sight of at least a dozen other corpses—men, women, and children who had all been cut down as they fled from some kind of terror. Such an attack sadly wasn't uncommon in a village like this one unprotected by walls, but they hadn't seen any evidence of violence in the other towns they had recently passed through.

"We must leave," he said. "Now."

Lorenzo was agape at the carnage around him. He hadn't been exposed to battle as Cristoval had.

"But we don't know if there are still people left alive who might need help. And it's a long way back to the next road," Lorenzo countered. "It'll take us another week to find a new path."

"Then that's what it takes," Cristoval said. "These bodies are fresh. It looks like the entire town was slaughtered. These murders happened in the past few hours. Whoever did it will be nearby. We don't want to continue on and cross them."

Lorenzo nodded. "Perhaps you're right." Then his head snapped around. "Did you hear that?"

At first Cristoval didn't know what he meant, then he heard it, too. It was the faint sob of a woman crying.

Before Cristoval could stop his brother, Lorenzo kicked his horse and cantered toward the sound, with Cristoval following behind. Lorenzo stopped beside a house and jumped off his horse. The sound had ceased, but Lorenzo circled around and pointed behind it. Whoever had been crying was there.

Cristoval put up his hand to make his brother wait. He dismounted and drew his sword, going around the other side.

He edged around the corner, and the wide, reddened eyes of a young woman stared up at him in abject fear. She scrambled away from him, right into Lorenzo's arms. She struggled furiously and then abruptly stopped when she looked at who had caught her.

"Pilgrim?" she asked in the Italian they had learned a bit of while crossing from France to Dalmatia.

"That's right," Lorenzo said slowly and deliberately. "We're pilgrims. And I'm a priest. From Spain. You have nothing to fear from us. Cristoval, sheathe your sword, for goodness' sake. You're scaring her."

Cristoval put his sword back in its scabbard. "Who are you?"

"Hicela. Pilgrim also." She pointed at herself and then Cristoval's hat. "I see Santiago de Compostela. I from Split." Apparently, her Italian wasn't much better than theirs, something they'd found with many Croatians. Thankfully, Italian and Spanish were close enough to understand these simple words.

"What happened in this town?"

"Bad men. Serbians. Fighting. Kill all people. We travel through."

"Who travels through?"

"We pilgrims too. Bad men burn the church. All dead but my husband Ivanis. My child Dmitar."

"Where are they?" Lorenzo asked.

"Place where make flour." Hicela pointed toward the other side of town.

"She must mean that there is a mill," Cristoval said.

"Yes, mill. They hide in mill when fighting happen. Bad men were there."

"We have to find them," Lorenzo said.

"If they're even still alive," Cristoval said.

"Yes, I saw them," the woman eagerly said. "We separated during attack."

Lorenzo stared with beseeching eyes at Cristoval, who sighed and said, "All right. But only if you stay here with Hicela and the horses. And try to stay hidden. If you run into any trouble, I want you to ride out of here as fast as you can."

"We won't leave you behind," Lorenzo protested.

"You have to protect her, don't you?" Cristoval cared much more about the safety of his brother than this stranger, but he couldn't say that to either of them.

Lorenzo considered his point and then grudgingly nodded that he would do as Cristoval bade him to. "Take care."

"Always."

Cristoval left them and made his way toward the still-burning church, looking back to make sure Lorenzo and Hicela stayed with the horses. Soon he was out of sight of them.

The church wasn't in the center of town, but actually near the eastern edge. The roof had collapsed along with part of the stone wall. When he passed the front door that had crumbled from the heat, one look inside was enough to turn his stomach.

Most of the village's inhabitants had likely retreated to the sanctuary of the church when the attack had started, but the raiders hadn't treated it as such. They had barred the door from the outside and thrown torches onto the roof to incinerate those within. Some of the torches that had rolled off were still burning in the dirt where they'd landed.

Cristoval crept past the church and finally saw the mill beside the stream, where the paddles dipping into the water would drive the millstone inside. Adjoining it was a granary where the grain and milled flour would be stored for the winter.

He crouched down when he saw movement on the other side of the granary. No one had spotted him, so he dashed to a hidden position where he could watch.

Two large oxen-drawn wagons were partially piled with sacks of flour. Twelve men were emptying the granary. Grain and flour dust wafted out of the door and around them as they loaded their bounty.

That's why they had slaughtered an entire town. Just to steal their flour. Cristoval had heard that there was disputed Bosnian territory between the Kingdom of Hungary and the Serbian Empire, but he thought the fighting was farther to the south. Perhaps these Serbians wanted to render this town worthless to both the Bosnians and Hungarians. He had no doubt they planned to burn down the mill and granary as soon as they had taken what they'd come for.

Perhaps he'd help them.

If Hicela's husband and son were really in the mill, they were likely too scared to attempt to leave for fear of being caught by the Serbians. Cristoval needed a distraction. And he had just the thing.

He stealthily raced back to the church and picked up one of the burning torches. Then he went to the opposite side of the granary from where the doors were. He heaved the torch onto the roof.

Without waiting to see that it had caught fire, he made his way to the outer wall of the mill. He held there until he heard one of the Serbians raise his voice in alarm. All of them rushed to either find water to put out the fire or hurriedly remove as much of the remaining flour as they could.

While they were occupied, Cristoval stole into the mill. The brake on the millstone had come loose, so it was grinding away, the noise covering his footsteps.

"Ivanis," he hissed. "Dmitar."

He went around the grinding millstone and stopped in his

tracks when he saw two feet pointing straight up. When he came around further, his heart sank at what he found.

It was a man wearing a pilgrim's hat like his. His throat had been cut. The Serbians must have found him hiding in here.

"Ivanis," Cristoval said at seeing the dead body. But he didn't see the boy's corpse. "Where is Dmitar?" he wondered aloud.

At the name, a pile of hay in one corner stirred. Cristoval went over to it and reached in. He pulled out a boy of no more than six years of age. The boy was about to shriek, but Cristoval put his hand over the child's mouth.

"I am Cristoval. Your mother is here."

The boy stared at him wide-eyed and uncomprehending. Perhaps he didn't speak Italian.

"Your mama. Hicela."

The boy's expression softened at his mother's name. Cristoval motioned that he would take the boy to her and for him to keep his mouth closed. Dmitar nodded.

It was easier to carry the child, so Cristoval swept him up in the crook of his arm and went back to the door. He peeked out, but the men were still preoccupied with the fire progressing across the granary roof. He took the chance to sneak out and go back the way he'd come.

He'd only gotten halfway to the church when he saw a terrible sight.

A brutish-looking Serbian was forcing Lorenzo at sword-point to lead their horses and Hicela back toward the granary along the swollen stream. He stopped when he saw Cristoval holding Dmitar.

"Cedozar," the Serbian yelled, followed by something in his native language.

"I'm sorry, Cristoval," Lorenzo said. "He surprised us."

Cristoval set down Dmitar, who ran to his mother.

"You speak Italian?" the Serbian asked.

Cristoval nodded. "Who are you?"

"I am Bogun. When I found these two and the horses, I knew there must be someone else. Is that all?"

"My brother and I have another twenty men here."

Bogun tilted his head in amusement. "Twenty men with a couple of pilgrims? You are a bad liar. And I can't have anyone left to say what happened here."

He raised his sword to cut down Hicela and the boy, but Lorenzo foolishly stepped in the way. He tried to grab Bogun's hands, but he was no fighter. The Serbian easily shrugged him off.

By this time Cristoval had drawn his sword and was rushing to defend his brother, but he was already too late. Bogun's blade thrust into Lorenzo's stomach, and he collapsed to the ground as soon as it was withdrawn.

"No!" Cristoval screamed.

He charged at Bogun with a fury he'd never known. He brought his sword down on the Serbian, who parried it deftly. He smiled, obviously relishing the thought of a challenge fighting a real soldier instead of murdering a group of innocent townspeople.

"I'll kill…" was all Cristoval could get out before a tremendous explosion rent the air.

The stone granary blew apart as the dust erupted in a fireball, sending stone shards and wooden pieces in all directions, taking half of the mill with it.

Bogun was tossed backward into the stream. Cristoval was hit in the head by a jagged stone and tumbled along the ground until he came to rest face down. He shook his head and looked up.

The granary was a blazing inferno. Half of Bogun's men had been torn to shreds, while others ran around trying to extinguish their burning clothes.

Cristoval had no idea what had caused such a huge blast, but it didn't matter. His head ached, and he couldn't see out of one eye because of the blood coursing down his brow. But he had to find Lorenzo.

He staggered to his feet and walked on trembling legs over to where Lorenzo lay. Hicela was cradling Dmitar beside him. They looked stunned by the explosion, but neither of them seemed to be hurt.

Cristoval kneeled next to his brother, who looked up at him

with serene eyes. The wound in his stomach was deep. It had to be mortal.

Cristoval took his hand. "Lorenzo, I..." He trailed off, not knowing what to say.

"Get Hicela and Dmitar to safety," Lorenzo said, blood bubbling from his lips as he spoke. "To Split."

"You're going to be right there with me."

"No, I won't. I know that. It's all right. This is why the Lord sent me on this pilgrimage. To save them. Do this for me. A sacred vow."

Cristoval nodded. "I swear it." Then he forced a smile. "Madelena will be furious."

"Tell her..." Lorenzo's words were interrupted by his chest shuddering. He breathed in once more, then let it out.

He was gone.

Cristoval shook his head, the sorrow so all-consuming that it took him a moment to notice Hicela shaking his shoulder.

That's when he also perceived the rumbling noise coming from the mountain where she was pointing.

At first he couldn't understand what he was seeing. It was like an enormous white cloth was rolling toward the town at great speed. Suddenly, he saw the leading edge hit some evergreen trees, and they collapsed, disappearing in the blink of an eye. Then, he realized what it was. He had never seen one before, but he had heard of such things. Large masses of snow had broken free and were carrying everything in their path. In a very short time, the village would be buried. Cristoval had just moments to think.

Several thoughts shot like lightning through his mind. They had to go. Now. He couldn't leave his brother's body behind, but he didn't have time to take him. He had to fulfill his last promise to Lorenzo. He had to get Hicela and Dmitar to safety.

The churning snow was racing down the slope, likely dislodged by the noise of the explosion. Cristoval had no time to waste.

He threw them both onto the saddle of Lorenzo's horse despite her protestations about Ivanis. Cristoval didn't have time to tell her that he was already dead. He leaped onto his own steed, and not knowing if she was a horsewoman at all, took their horse's reins in his hand and kicked his horse into a gallop. The two horses took off, sprinting through the town.

They reached the edge and began racing up the hillock just as the snow reached the village. Cristoval sneaked a look behind and saw the buildings swallowed by the white mist preceding the rushing snow.

He brought them to a stop at the top of the hillock. The mist slowly faded away, revealing an utterly changed landscape. The only sound was Hicela's sobs as she hugged her son.

Only the roofs of most buildings were now visible, the broken snow and ice blocks piled up around some and inside others. The church fire was finally extinguished, and so was the fire at the granary.

On the other side of town at the edge of snow's extent, he saw a lone figure kneeling by the stream. He reached in and pulled a man out of the water. Bogun climbed out, sopping wet.

He shook himself off and looked in Cristoval's direction, shaking his fist. They had horses as well, but Cristoval wasn't worried about a pursuit, no matter how much he wished they would. There was no way for a horse to cross that field of tumbled snow and ice to reach them.

He wanted to kill Bogun right here and now for what he'd done to Lorenzo, but that would have to wait until he fulfilled his oath to return Hicela and Dmitar to Split. Then he would stay in Dalmatia until he fulfilled an oath he made to himself—find Bogun and make him pay for what he'd done.

Cristoval wouldn't return to Spain until he could tell his sister that justice for their brother had been served.

35

November, 1351

STON

While Jelena looked after her son, Willa rode Zephyr out to the salt pans with Petar atop Comis. She knew Gerard's horse wasn't aware of his fate, but the stallion nevertheless seemed more agitated than usual, so she thought getting him some time with his familiar saddle on would calm him down. Or maybe it was just for her, to have a connection with Gerard.

She pushed those thoughts away to focus on the riddle at hand. Jelena's brother Drazhan slyly implied that the key to finding the hidden Marco Polo codex lay in the protection of Blaise. Not Saint Blaise. Petar agreed that it might have something to do with the salt pan named for the saint, so they were going to inspect it for any clues they might find.

The salt pans stretched far out in a series of rectangles, with earthen berms separating each one. Her quick count tallied up more than fifty of them. The closest ones were empty of water, the bottoms made of granite instead of clay.

"Jelena said the pans have names," Willa said as she dismounted beside a stone marker that read "SS. Blaise & Lazarus."

Petar nodded and got out of Comis's saddle. "We always call them Blaise and Lazarus without referring to them as saints. That had to be what Drazhan was telling me back in Dubrovnik. Only us salt harvesters would know that." He sneezed and wiped his nose with a kerchief.

"God bless you," Willa said reflexively. Even since the Great Mortality, people were wary of any kind of sickness and a prayer after a sneeze to invoke divine protection against disease became all too common. "Are you all right?"

He nodded and waved his hands as the horses went off to graze in a nearby field.

"It's nothing," he said with a sniffle, his voice hoarse and hollow from a stuffed nose. "The recent travel and sea breezes must have gotten to me."

"Yes, I'm surprised I haven't gotten sick with all our recent adventures." She turned her attention back to the matter at hand. "Why are the pans named after saints?"

"So we can tell each other which ones we'll be filling or emptying. It's nice to think of the saints blessing our work, but we refer to them by their first names as a shorthand. It makes them seem almost like friends. Most of our salt is coarse, but the Blaise and Lazarus pools are where we gather our finest and most expensive salt. It's fitting since Saint Blaise is the town's patron. The flakes from that pan are as soft and light as snow." He said it with obvious pride.

Willa inspected the stone marker, but there were no indentations where a book might be hidden. She gestured to the salt pan, and Petar nodded his permission for her to step onto the granite. A few paces out, she stopped and turned in all directions. There didn't seem anywhere a book could be stored safely out of the weather.

"You've looked in his house again for it?" she asked him.

"Yes, at midday while you and Jelena were searching the church. As I thought, it wasn't there. He probably feared Vitomir would find it there, so he chose another hiding place."

"How do you harvest the salt?" Given that Drazhan was a saltman himself, the answer had to be out here somewhere. Perhaps learning about the process would guide them to the hiding place.

Petar pointed the farthest pans, the ones that were closest to the sea.

"At the end of spring, when it's starting to get warm and sunny, we drain all the pans. Then we flood the outermost ones.

After the sun has baked the water, it gets saltier. We allow that water to flow into the next set of pans to repeat the task, getting saltier each time it floods into a new pan. By the point it reaches the named pans, the salt begins to form at the bottom of the pool."

"That's how you get the fine salt in the Blaise and Lazarus pans?"

He shook his head. "Because of the granite, that salt floats to the top and we use skimmers to collect it."

"You said the Marco Polo book showed Drazhan how to treble salt production. How?"

"I don't know exactly. I didn't believe that he could do it. None of us did. We've been harvesting salt the same way for generations and saw no reason to believe that it could be improved. But he was insistent that he be allowed to try, so we gave him a tiny pan at the very end. I didn't pay attention to what he did—now I wish I had, of course—but it was something about the timing of the flooding and the depth of the water."

"Show me."

She whistled loudly, and Zephyr and Comis came running from the field.

"That's quite a trick," Petar said as the horses came to a stop beside them.

"Gerard taught it to me." The memory of the Italian horse race where she'd first used it gave her a fleeting moment of joy.

She and Petar walked the horses to the end of the pans where a small one set apart from the others had been formed. Again, there didn't seem to be any way to store a book.

"I don't understand why he mentioned Blaise," Petar said. "As you can see, his tiny pan is nowhere near it."

"What happens to the salt once you collect it?"

"We shovel it across the pan into large piles, then we load it all into carts."

"Then you take it to Mali Ston for shipping?"

Petar pointed at a large stone building in the distance near the farthest pan. It was two stories tall and the length of a cathedral. A ramp led up to the second level.

"We take it all there for storage. You have no idea how much salt we collect. Thousands and thousands of pounds. The harvest has to be done quickly so that we can get the salt out of the weather for it to dry out. We roll the carts up that ramp and then dump it over the side, where it settles into huge piles. Then we collect only what we plan to load onto ships and use donkey carts to tote it to Mali Ston."

A dry salt house would be exactly the type of place where Drazhan would keep the book.

"Let's go see if we can find anything there," Willa said.

They walked the horses along the berms until they reached the salt house. After tying them up, Petar led her up the ramp. He unlatched the door and went inside.

Dim light filtered through a smattering of openings at the roof edge. The interior was framed up to a point at the ceiling and supported by joists. The center of the second level was wide enough for the carts that were lined up for winter storage. On either side the space was open. She leaned over and saw a sea of white beneath her.

The wealth of Ston was piled high below, twice the height of a man. It was more salt than she had ever seen, nearly a year's worth of harvesting. It had to be worth a fortune.

"Why are the carts up here?" she asked.

Petar went to one of the carts and flicked a latch on the side, opening a large gap.

"We would never be able to pile the salt as high as we do without bringing the carts up here. Once we fill them, we roll them in here, open the sides, and the salt rains down onto the piles below."

"Is there any rhyme or reason to it?"

He nodded. "We always harvest in the same order. That way we know which piles come from which pan."

"And the Blaise salt?"

He waved his hand. "This way."

He walked to the far end of the salt house. It was a loft packed with canvas sacks.

"This is the Blaise and Lazarus salt," he said. "It's too fine to dump it into piles. We keep it here until it comes time to ship."

"Would he put the book in one of the bags?"

"No, he couldn't be sure that it would be safe. It might get carried out at any time."

"Then let's look around. There must be some other clue."

Petar took one side of the loft, and she took the other. The joists were too solid to hide something within.

They'd been searching fruitlessly for a long time when Petar called to her. "I've found something."

Willa raced over to him. He was pointing to a letter B carved into one of the joists.

"I've never seen this before."

"B for Blaise," Willa said. "That must be it." Next to it, a crude but recognizably carved finger pointed down. She had seen such manicules in manuscripts, where something especially important in the text was being pointed out.

They pushed and pulled on pieces of wood. Nothing happened until Willa dislodged one slightly. She moved it further and realized it was a false joist that had been placed in front of the actual one.

With another push, cloth was revealed. She tugged on it and felt the unmistakable shape and texture of a book underneath. She removed it from its hiding place and unwrapped it.

"I've got it!" she claimed triumphantly.

As Petar watched, she unwrapped the cloth. There was the codex, bound in leather. She opened it to the first page, but the light was too dim to read the lettering.

They went back outside, where Willa could see now that it was written in the same Italian script as the book they'd retrieved in Korčula.

The first page began, "*On the blessed day of the Feast of Saint Mark in the year of our Lord 1293.*"

"Is it the same?" Petar asked.

Willa flipped through the pages. As a book enthusiast, she'd studied the other volume extensively. Immediately, she saw that the information was different in this codex.

"No, this must be a second volume," she said excitedly. "That's why we didn't find the salt information in the one we already have. The one we took in Korčula ended in 1292, and this one begins in April of 1293. This is what we've been looking for!"

She couldn't wait to show it to…

Willa had to hold back sudden tears when she realized that she couldn't share this find with Gerard. She fought back the urge to cry. She wondered if she would get excited by anything ever again without her first impulse being to share it with her beloved husband. She could so clearly see in her mind the look of pleasure and pride that would light up his face. But they had found this book for a reason, so she had to concentrate on her task. Maybe it would help her forget her pain, even for a short time.

She turned the pages quickly past words and drawings until she saw the familiar grid layout of the salt pans and the word "*sale.*" Italian for salt.

"Here are the instructions Drazhan used."

Petar put his hands together in prayer. "Thank the Lord."

She kept going, looking for anything that might look like a weapon that could help them against Bogun.

Her search stopped when she saw the drawing of an arrow. But this one was unusual. On it was mounted a device of some kind. It looked as if flames were coming out of it. The second drawing showed the arrow hitting a group of warriors and the entire device seemed to shatter, throwing some of the men into the air.

Petar frowned at it. "What is that?"

Willa shook her head. "I don't know. It looks like it's a flaming arrow, but one that explodes when it hits its target."

"What is it called?"

She leaned in closer and saw the word. "It says *rocchetto*. I don't know that word. What does that mean?"

Petar thought about it. "I believe it's a tool for spinning wool. It does resemble a distaff, with the yarn wound at one end forming a kind of bulb and a thin stick at the other."

Rocchetto. Like most Italian words, taking the final vowel off would transform it to a word in English.

Willa would call it a rocket.

36

Split

Even after Fox explained what they could expect in defending Ston against Bogun and his army, Cristoval had insisted on coming with Fox and Nika. He was willing to do anything he could to get justice for his brother's death. Despite their bond against a common enemy, Fox still thought it was prudent to continue Nika's disguise.

Cristoval's story about his murdered brother struck close to Fox's soul because he'd lost his own brother James at the Battle of Crécy. Although Fox couldn't help but have doubts about the Spaniard, especially because Cristoval had sought them out instead of the other way around, his tale had a ring of truth in how accurately he'd described Bogun. Even though Fox and Nika had only been searching for a short time, they hadn't had even a single bite among all the taverns they had approached. In fact, what they had gotten was outright hostility. Fox was also feeling increasingly urgent about getting to Ston, not only to let Willa and Nika's parents know they were alive, but also because he felt Bogun's noose was tightening with every day that passed. They had no choice but to accept Cristoval's help.

While Cristoval went to secure a spot on a ship for their travel, Fox waited with Nika in the small room Cristoval was letting from a wine merchant. The two of them had nothing to do but stare at the decorative alcoves carved into the Roman walls that were once part of Diocletian's palace.

Fox had wanted to go with him, but Cristoval said it would

be faster for him to work alone. He was reluctant to let Cristoval out of his sight, but given the antagonistic reaction Fox had been receiving, he'd grudgingly admitted that Cristoval would have a better chance of working his connections by himself. But it sent a tingle of suspicion up his spine. It did seem convenient that he was looking for men to fight against Bogun, and one found him instead.

"Why do we have to go to Trogir?" Nika asked as she played with a golden ducat that Fox had given to amuse her. She was spinning it on the table to see how long it would stay upright on its edge.

"I may know a mercenary there."

"How could you know anyone in Trogir? I thought you'd never been to Dalmatia before."

"Before I came here, I was sailing on a ship with a captain named Giovanni. It was a long trip, so we had plenty of time to talk. Since he was living in Venice, our conversation came around to Marco Polo, who was from there. He mentioned that he once had a crew member named Tino, whose father claimed to be one of the workers on Marco Polo's Venetian palazzo. I know my wife would say it was fate that the first people we meet here also have a connection to the great man. Giovanni mentioned that Tino was a good fighter and a skilled repairman on the ship, but he didn't want to spend his life at sea."

"So you think he's still there?"

"Giovanni said he dropped him off in Trogir just a few months ago to work at the fortress as a man-at-arms. It's a short sail over there from here. If we can't find him quickly, we'll move on."

"Then we need to go now."

"Cristoval will come back as soon as he finds a ship for us."

Nika must have sensed something in his tone.

"You don't trust him?"

"Trust is earned, not given."

"Even though he saved you at the tavern?"

Fox scowled at her as he massaged the healing leg wound that still ached thanks to Bogun.

"He didn't save me. He assisted me."

Nika snickered. "He assisted in keeping you from being stabbed in the back."

Fox grudgingly conceded her point. "Then he's half-earned it."

"What about that story he told you?"

"It sounded reasonable enough. But people don't always reveal the whole truth. For example, we haven't told Cristoval that you're a girl." Fox also thought about hiding his own problem as an excommunicant from Nika and her parents.

Nika came and sat next to him, looking up at him with the eyes of a fawn and taking his hand. "Sir Gerard, I trust you. You've earned it."

Fox was so surprised by her heartfelt candor that he was momentarily at a loss for words. He simply squeezed her hand, smiled at her, and nodded.

Footsteps approached the door, so Fox let go of Nika's hand and stood as Cristoval entered the room. He raised an eyebrow at them.

"Is everything all right?"

"We're just eager to go," Fox said.

"Did you find a ship?" Nika asked as she got to her feet.

Cristoval nodded. "It's a Croatian trading vessel out of Dubrovnik. The captain has agreed to take us to Trogir before heading toward Ston for the fee we agreed on. They're ready to sail when we are."

Nika clapped her hands.

"Then let's go," Fox said.

After Cristoval gathered the few belongings he'd left with them, the three of them went down the stairs and out onto the narrow street.

"You didn't tell me why you're in Dalmatia," Cristoval said as they walked.

Fox considered how much he could say without raising the specter of his banishment from the Church. A lie was better than the truth.

"Like you, my wife and I were on pilgrimage."

"To the Holy Land?"

"Eventually."

"How long have you been wedded?"

His tone sounded conversational, but Fox understood that the questions were a test. Cristoval didn't trust him so much, either.

"A short time. We're going to pray for a large family."

Cristoval nodded in approval. "But your journey was interrupted by the troubles of this boy's family?"

"My name is Niko," Nika said. "And I'm right here."

"Does he always talk like this?" Cristoval asked with a raised eyebrow.

"He grows on you."

"Sir Gerard said Tino in Trogir will join us," Nika cut in. "Do you know anyone who could help us?"

"Niko is quite curious, no?" Cristoval said.

"He's like no boy I've ever met," Fox said, winking at Nika on his other side.

"I wanted to make sure we had transportation before mentioning it, but I do know a man in Hvar who might come with us. He's a Serbian who also hates Bogun. We agreed to seek each other out if one of us ever discovered a way to find him."

"Seems like Bogun has made himself quite a number of enemies. Is Hvar far from here?" Fox asked.

"It's on the way from Trogir to Ston."

They went down some stairs into a dark underground bazaar teeming with merchants. The vaulted ceilings made it look like a crypt to bury the dead that had never been used. He had heard that the enormous space was actually a series of cellars for the original Roman palace, used to store the vast materials needed for the household. The interconnected chambers were conveniently located next to the harbor, no doubt so that goods could be offloaded directly into the cellars. The walls echoed with the shouts of buyers and sellers negotiating for the wares on offer, from bread and vegetables to leather and wool.

Cristoval guided them to a stand featuring metal tools.

Standing in front of it was a muscular man with a beard who was holding a satchel.

He said something in Croatian to Cristoval.

"This is the first mate, Mutimir," he said in Italian. "He'll take us to the ship."

The mate pointed to the light of an exit at the opposite end of the bazaar and started walking, so they followed him. When they emerged into the sunlight, they were taken to a dinghy. Mutimir pointed at a ship anchored in the harbor. It was aging and in mediocre shape, but Fox supposed it would get the job done.

They climbed into the dinghy, and the mate rowed them over to the ship. Every few moments, Fox caught Mutimir glancing at Nika and then looking away. Fox didn't let on that he noticed, but he would remember to keep an eye on the sailor during the voyage.

Upon reaching the ship, they climbed a rope ladder up to the deck. The captain, a brick of a man with flat face, was waiting for them. Fox gave the ducat that Nika had been playing with to the captain in payment while six of his sailors watched attentively. He bit into it and smiled at the shallow dents left in the surface—it was real gold. Then he put the coin into the purse at his waist and barked something at Mutimir, who strode away and disappeared below deck.

Nika started hopping from foot to foot and whined at Fox, "I have to go."

"Now?" he said. "Why didn't you go back at Cristoval's place?"

"Because I didn't have to go then."

"All right. Away with you."

Nika ran off and went below deck for privacy instead of going off the side of the ship like a boy would have.

"Ask him how long until we get to Trogir," Fox said to Cristoval.

Cristoval spoke his halting Croatian, and the captain answered.

"He says the voyage takes less time than between the bells for none and vespers. We'll be there by nightfall."

The captain spoke again, and Cristoval shook his head. The discussion went back and forth a few times, with both of them looking at Fox, before he interjected. "What are you talking about with him?"

Cristoval frowned. "He said we have to stow our swords while we are on board."

"Why?"

"Because he doesn't know us."

Fox glared at the captain, who stared back at him. "I'll carry my sword on my back, but it will be with me the whole time or we will leave right now."

At that moment, Nika burst onto the deck and came sprinting at him. She bumped into the captain in her frenzy, then rushed over to Fox and pulled him down to hear her whisper in Italian.

"We have to go. Now!"

"Why?"

"I heard Mutimir. He told another sailor that they'll kill you once we're at sea and dump you overboard. Then they'll sell me as a slave in Trogir."

Fox glanced at the captain, who was watching them closely. "How did you hear this?"

"They didn't know I was using a bucket behind a barrel to... you know. The first mate tried to grab me, but I kicked him."

"What about Cristoval? Did the first mate say they were in league?"

Before she could answer, Mutimir lurched onto deck holding his privates and shouting in Croatian. Another sailor followed close behind him. They were both pointing at Nika.

Fox tried to draw his sword, but three sailors who were behind him grabbed his arms. Nika ran toward Cristoval, who seized her by the arm and drew her to him.

"They're going to kill you and sell me!" Nika shouted at him.

Cristoval whipped out his dagger and held it beside Nika's throat. He shouted something in Croatian to the sailors who were coming at him. The captain yelled something, and they stopped.

Fox struggled against his captors, but they held him fast. Mutimir limped over to him and put a long knife up to his face. Two of the sailors let go, while the other kept hold of his hands behind him.

"You slime," Fox spat at Cristoval. "We trusted you."

"And you should," Cristoval said in Italian. "I'm gaining time for us by negotiating with the captain to let me go and keep the two of you. Be ready to drop to your knees when I nod." He spoke in a snarl as if he were insulting Fox to hide his real intent.

At first Fox didn't know what to believe, but then he saw that Cristoval pulled Nika protectively behind him, as if he were shielding her from danger.

Mutimir was grinning as he said something over his shoulder to the captain in Croatian. The captain laughed and answered back.

While they were distracted, Cristoval nodded. Fox tensed and dropped, knocking the man behind him off balance. At the same time, Cristoval flicked the dagger in his hand so that it struck Mutimir in the shoulder, causing him to release the knife.

Fox stood up quickly and threw his head back, slamming it into the forehead of the man behind him. Free of the sailor's grip, Fox rolled toward Cristoval and drew Legend from his back, holding it against the sailors who were advancing on them. Cristoval armed himself as well with his own sword.

"Please accept my apologies," he said to Fox. "Despite the rush, I should have been more careful in whom I hired. I was worried you wouldn't take me to Bogun unless I delivered on the ship passage quickly."

The captain glowered at them while Mutimir howled as he pulled the knife from his shoulder. He threw it at Cristoval, who batted it down easily with his sword. While keeping his eyes on the crew, he carefully picked up the dagger, wiped it off, and replaced it in its scabbard.

"I'm glad to have that back. My father gave it to me."

"They must be smugglers. We'll be more wary with the next crew."

"You'll still let me come to Ston?"

"Of course you can," Nika said.

Fox smiled at him. "How could we turn you down after that display?"

"Can we go now?" Nika pleaded.

Fox nodded at Cristoval. "Take Niko down to the dinghy. I'll hold them back while you climb down the rope ladder."

While they made their way over the bulwark, Fox kept his sword pointed at the crew who were watching him with furious eyes. One of them made the unfortunate decision to charge him with a fish hook and got a bloody leg for his trouble. The quick demonstration of Fox's skill with the blade was enough to deter the rest.

When Cristoval was in the dinghy with Nika, Fox slashed the rope ladder so that it fell into the water. He sheathed Legend and jumped over the side, landing right beside the boat. After surfacing, Cristoval pulled him up and into the dinghy. Fox nodded in appreciation to the Spaniard. Nothing more needed to be said.

As Cristoval rowed away, the sailors cursed at them from the bulwark.

"Smart to cut the rope ladder," he said. "It doesn't seem like any of them wants to go for a swim."

Fox coughed out some water before speaking. "I'm finding myself in the sea far too often lately."

"I'm glad I didn't have to jump in this time," Nika said. She opened her palm to reveal the gold ducat and gave it to Fox.

"Where did you get that?" he asked as he took it.

"From the captain's purse."

Fox laughed. "You remind me of someone I met in Korčula."

"You'd make a good thief," Cristoval said in appreciation.

Nika smiled back at them. "How do you think I made it to Dubrovnik all by myself?"

37

THREE MILES SOUTHEAST OF STON

Bogun paced the deck of his ship as it lay at anchor off a small rocky beach. He still hadn't had word from his main force, which was supposed to be rendezvousing with him at this location. They were already a day late.

"Where are they?" a testy Vitomir asked. He stood against the bulwark with his arms crossed. He was still incensed that Bogun had made him leave his personal guards behind in Dubrovnik, but Bogun knew the cowardly Vitomir still needed his debts paid, so he'd given the treasurer no choice but to agree.

"How should I know that?" Bogun replied. "You were the one who brought that guide who's directing my main force."

"Only after you killed my first choice."

"You'd rather he'd gone to your rector and told him that we're working together?"

Vitomir pursed his lips. "There hasn't been a storm lately. Perhaps they got lost in these islands. We should give them more time."

"I don't want to wait. We need to withdraw the garrison from Ston now."

"I told you I can't go there. They'll know it was me who gave the order to replace the garrison. Word will certainly get back to the rector."

"From whom?"

"The townspeople will talk."

"Not if they're all dead."

Vitomir's eyes widened. "But… we can't kill them all. We need them to harvest the salt."

"Do you think we can't bring Serbians in to do such a menial task?"

"It's a complicated process honed over generations."

Bogun walked over to him. "You told me that this book by Marco Polo could teach anyone this secret method for increasing salt production."

"Well, yes. If we had it."

"It must be in that town somewhere. I don't plan to burn it down. I only plan on making sure no one ever leaves."

Bogun thought back to the Bosnian village he wiped out when taking their flour. The explosion had killed his most valuable men besides Cedozar, but he'd quickly rebuilt his forces by hand-picking soldiers loyal to him. This time, he had recruited enough of them to secure victory.

And it seemed unlikely another natural disaster would spare any witnesses this time.

Vitomir considered the point.

"I suppose if we keep Petar alive long enough, he can teach the methods to anyone new you bring in."

Bogun smiled. "Then it's settled. You'll take Cedozar and twelve of my men to replace the garrison."

"You're not coming?"

"Those two you mentioned, Petar and Jelena, have seen me. If they've returned to Ston and saw me, they'd know for certain it wasn't a replacement garrison."

"Do your men speak Croatian?"

"Cedozar does, as well as a few others."

Vitomir shook his head. "I don't like it. They'll have to keep quiet."

"Only as long as it takes to get the garrison out of the town," Bogun said. "You will lead them back here, where they'll be told a ship is waiting to take them to Dubrovnik. The rest of my men will ambush them. They'll be cut down before they understand what's happening."

"Why didn't my ship anchor in Mali Ston? The commander of the garrison will be curious."

Bogun was getting annoyed by Vitomir's questions. Although he was brilliant with numbers and negotiations, he had no imagination. That was why Bogun had been able to see through that annoying child's pretense so readily and realize she was a girl, while Vitomir remained oblivious.

"Do I have to think of everything?" Bogun said. "Tell the townsfolk that it would have taken too long for the ship to sail around the length of the peninsula."

Vitomir nodded apprehensively.

"What's wrong?" Bogun asked.

"I can't have word of my involvement ever get back to Dubrovnik or the Venetians."

"As long as you follow my plan, I will have no need to tell anyone about what you've done here." Bogun patted him on the shoulder, just enough to make it clear Vitomir was now under his control. "You're much more valuable to me inside Dubrovnik than dead. Don't do anything to reduce your value to me."

Vitomir swallowed hard.

"What do I need to do when I get there?"

"Simply tell them that you've brought the garrison's relief. I'm sure the soldiers stationed there will be glad to be heading back to Dubrovnik, so they won't question the timing."

"And the townspeople? What if Petar objects?"

"Do you really think that the head of the garrison will believe anything Petar says against your orders?"

Vitomir looked out at the shore. "I suppose not." He slammed his hand on the ship's wood railing. "If that foolish Englishman hadn't infiltrated my house, I'd still have that cursed boy and none of this would be necessary."

Bogun crossed his arms. "Don't you mean 'girl'?"

Vitomir turned on him. "What are you saying?"

"When struggling to get free of me during that abortive escape attempt in your house, the child slapped at me instead of punching me. It only occurred to me later—your hostage wasn't a boy, but a girl pretending to be one."

The Croatian treasurer looked dumbfounded. "I... I..."

"Had no idea. I can see that."

"They went to all that trouble to get a *girl* back?"

"Some parents are stupidly sentimental that way," Bogun said.

"Then perhaps Gerard Fox did me a favor. I have trouble believing Petar would have betrayed his town and opened the gates to get a daughter back."

"Which is why Cedozar is going in to open the gates for us instead. But to do that, you will have to ensure a smooth handoff from the existing garrison. Are you up to the task?"

After a brief hesitation, Vitomir nodded, and Bogun believed him. It was a relief because if he didn't think he could do it, Bogun would have had to kill Vitomir right then and there and simply undertake a full-scale assault on Ston no matter how difficult that would be.

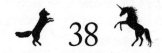

38

TROGIR, DALMATIA

A short, uneventful boat ride to the west took Fox, Nika, and Cristoval to Split's rival city of Trogir the next morning. This time they had found a smaller vessel that would simply take them that distance. They agreed to find a different ship going to Ston once they had found Tino.

Though it was a smaller city, Fox still found it to be a maze of narrow streets that made him lose his sense of direction almost as soon as they were out of sight of the gates. Cristoval had been here once before, so he knew his way around.

When the bells struck for sext, the midday sun wasn't overhead yet, so the timing seemed off. But Fox was more focused on calming his stomach from their sailing. He would attempt to secure some ginger before their next sea voyage to keep the *mal de mer* at bay.

"Are you certain this Tino is still at the fort?" Cristoval asked.

"No," Fox replied, "but Giovanni thought he was taking work there as a man-at-arms. It's the only place I know where to look for him."

"Did this Giovanni say anything more about him?"

"Just that he's been a wandering mercenary for twenty years." Cristoval shook his head. "So he's old."

"We don't have many choices," Nika said. "If he fights well, what does it matter if he's a hundred?"

Cristoval chuckled at that. "You're right, Sir Gerard. He is an unusual boy."

"I'm not an unusual boy!" she protested. "I'm... usual."

That made Fox laugh. "I'm sure Sir Cristoval meant no offense, Niko."

"You are an ardent young fellow," Cristoval said.

"What does that mean?" Nika asked, clearly sensing an insult.

Cristoval smiled at her. "It means I admire your determination to help your town."

That seemed to mollify her, and she stood up a little straighter as they walked.

They arrived at a fortress perched on the edge of a second harbor. The blank sheer walls towered over them, and the top turret must have offered a commanding view of the sea beyond. Cristoval asked the guard at the entrance if he could speak with Tino.

The guard smirked at them. "Tino isn't here anymore."

Nika gave a worried look to Fox.

"Is he still in Trogir?" Cristoval asked.

The guard's smirk got wider. "Oh, yes. Father Davor gave him a job. You can find him at the cathedral in the center of town. It's possible he'll be able to talk at this time of the day." He said it as if there was some hidden meaning, but he didn't elaborate.

As they walked toward the town center, Cristoval asked, "What was that about?"

Fox shrugged. "I don't know."

"Maybe Tino's so dedicated to his job that he can't even take the time to speak with us," Nika said. "That would be a good sign that he's serious."

After winding through the streets again, they came to a stop in front of the Cathedral of Saint Lawrence. An intricately carved stone portal served as the main entrance to the cathedral. Detailed scenes from the life and death of Christ dominated a semi-circular space above the doorway and the two rows of arches over it. The stonework around the door showed the various labors associated with each month of the year along with dozens of fantastical creatures. One beast in particular caught Fox's eye. To the left and right of the doorway, two enormous lions stood watch, and beneath the claws of one was a vicious dragon, which reminded him of the Ston prophecy.

Hellfire rains down when a sacrifice summons a dragon to destroy any enemy refusing to flee.

The line made him think of what the town could face, and Willa might be there right in the middle of it. He thought of what she had to be going through right at this moment, likely convinced that he was dead. He could only hope that she would wait for him to return to Ston. But if he didn't find her there, he would search until he found her, no matter what it took. They had gone through so much together. He wasn't going to lose her now.

"Lorenzo," Cristoval murmured as he looked at the carvings.

"Why did you say that?" Nika asked.

"Lorenzo is Spanish for Lawrence, the saint this cathedral is dedicated to."

"Lorenzo was the name of Cristoval's brother," Fox told her.

"This must be a sign," Cristoval said. "San Lorenzo is telling us that Tino will help me avenge my brother. Let's go find him."

There was a priest inside the church walking toward the altar.

"Father, excuse me," Fox called out as the three of them entered.

The priest stopped and turned, smiling at the newcomers.

"Yes, my son?"

"Are you Father Davor?"

"I am."

Fox introduced himself, Cristoval, and Nika as his page, Niko. "We're looking for a man named Tino."

The priest's expression suddenly clouded at that.

"Tino, yes."

"Is something wrong, Father?" Cristoval asked. "Do you know where he is?"

"I do indeed. Why do you want to see him?"

"We want to ask him to come along on our journey."

Just as quickly, Father Davor's demeanor brightened again. "In that case, I wish you the best of fortune in convincing him.

I owe him a job here as long as he'd like for saving me from being trampled by a team of runaway carthorses, but perhaps a change of circumstances would benefit him."

"Where can we find him?" Fox asked.

"In the bell tower. Let me show you the way."

The priest led them to a stairwell and pointed up. "When you see him, please ask him to come find me when he is able. Of course, if you want to leave with him immediately, I will certainly not be put out by that."

Before they could ask what he meant, Father Davor scurried away.

"He was acting strangely, wasn't he?" Nika said.

"I agree," Cristoval said.

"I have an idea why," Fox said with a sinking feeling in his gut as he thought back to what the guard at the fort told them.

A few turns up the spiral staircase confirmed his fears.

Sprawled on the floor next to the bell was a man with a grizzled beard and bags under his eyes. He was nearly old enough to be Fox's father, and he was snoring loudly, an empty bottle grasped limply in his hand.

"This is not promising," Fox said.

"He's drunk as a toad," Cristoval said with a tsk of his lips. "Perhaps he won't be of use to us."

"At least we know the reason that the bells rang so early."

Nika kicked him in the rear. "Wake up, old man!"

With startling speed, Tino rolled to his side, leaped to his feet, and drew a wicked dagger. He weaved as he struggled to focus on them.

"I'll kill all five of you!" he shouted.

Even from this distance, Fox could smell his foul breath.

"Easy, friend," Cristoval said, his hands raised in a peaceful sign.

"I've sailed with Giovanni," Fox said. "I was on the *Cara Signora* with him."

Tino squinted at him, then smiled and took three tries to put his knife back in its scabbard before launching himself at Fox and giving him a warm embrace.

"Any friend of Giovanni is a friend of mine."

Then he sagged as his energy dissipated, and Fox lowered him back to the floor.

"How is he?" Tino said.

"He's reunited with his mother and back in Florence."

"Truly? That's wonderful."

The situation was suddenly clear to Fox. The priest felt that he couldn't turn out the man who'd saved him, so he came up with what should have been the easiest job in the cathedral. Now Tino was a failure and a drunkard.

Fox was staring at his future if he hadn't met Willa. Although he'd tried to forget his troubles through drink in the past, he'd put that behind him when he'd committed himself to reversing his excommunication. And then, of course, he'd found Willa. But he could see how a life alone with no purpose could lead him back to the bottle.

"Giovanni told me that you're a skilled man-at-arms," Fox said. "You've got some fight left in you. I can see that. Wouldn't you rather go into one last battle than lie here and perform this menial job?"

"I get wine here," Tino answered. "As much as I want."

"We have wine in Ston," Nika said.

Tino stared at her with confused eyes. "Where did you find such a small man?"

She crossed her arms in annoyance. "We'll pay you."

"How much?"

"Enough to keep you suckling at a wine barrel for the rest of your life." If he didn't change his ways, Fox didn't think that would be very long.

Tino considered that. "Who do I get to fight?"

"A very bad man," Cristoval said.

"I don't like bad men. Hate them, in fact."

"Then you will love this job," Fox said. "You want to have some purpose in life, don't you? Something other than drinking yourself to death?"

"Not a bad way to go."

"You are foretold to help us in the prophecy," Nika said. "You are a stranger destined to save us."

"I'm part of a prophecy?" he said incredulously.

"The one told to Ston's priest by Saint Blaise himself. He said that…"

Tino sat upright, his eyes clearing at last. "Saint Blaise?"

"It's a long story," Fox said. "You may not…"

"No, no, no!" Tino objected. "I believe in your prophecy. I have to help you!"

"Why?" Cristoval asked.

"Because I have to make an atonement to Saint Blaise for something I did when I was young."

"Then it's settled," Fox said. He had no idea what the man was talking about, but he wasn't about to turn down his offer to join them.

Fox and Cristoval looked at each other and nodded. They hoisted Tino up between them. He could barely keep himself upright.

"We'll do what we can to help you," Fox said as they guided him to the stairs. "While we walk, stay awake by telling us why you owe a penance to Saint Blaise."

39

Twenty-five years ago—July, 1326

SAN COVELLO, VENETO

As he secured the bag of liquified manure to the tree branch, Tino couldn't help but smile at the embarrassment that was to come for his rival, Baccio. He had spent weeks planning this knavery, retribution for a similar trick played on him. But this time the whole town would be watching when Baccio was covered in filth.

The massive oak tree overhung the town's only bridge, providing the perfect location for the scheme. As he adjusted his position to get a better grip, Tino made sure to hold tight so as not to fall into the swollen creek below.

In the growing early morning dawn, he looked down to see the wiry frame of his best friend, Venzi, tying the thin rope at the base of the bridge. It was festooned with scarlet banners so that it looked like it was part of the upcoming celebration. No matter how many jests the two of them had carried out together, Tino still had to keep an eye out for his simple comrade.

"Not that tight, Venzi," Tino admonished. "You'll drench both of us with this foul concoction before Baccio arrives."

"Sorry, Tino," Venzi replied, loosening the knot. "I'm just eager to see that rooster get what he deserves. When does the wedding procession come through?"

"I heard that they will be called by the bells at terce. By midmorning, the entire town will gather to watch them cross this bridge."

"And you're sure Baccio will be in the lead?"

"He wouldn't let anyone else go first."

Venzi nodded happily. "Maybe Romina won't want to marry him once she sees him covered in filth."

"I think that's hoping for too much," Tino said. "I'll just be happy to see him humiliated in front of everyone."

Of course, the whole rivalry had started over a girl. Tino and Baccio had been in love with Romina, and while Tino was stronger and the better swordsman, wooing the fair maiden came down to money, and Tino had little after his father died. Baccio, on the other hand, was set to inherit the family's fabric trading business, and he spared no expense in convincing Romina's father to give Baccio her hand.

All Tino could do was show her what a good, caring husband and father he would be in their marriage, and his best chance to do that had been standing as godfather for her baby brother. He'd spent the last of his money on a beautiful new tunic and strode toward the church, confident that he would show Romina how bright his future in San Covello could be.

He didn't account for Baccio's devious nature. On the way to the church through the town streets, Baccio had been lying in wait on the second story of one of the houses. As Tino passed, Baccio tipped out the contents of a full chamber pot onto Tino's head.

Stinking to the heavens in his soiled clothes, Tino couldn't very well appear at the church in that condition. He slunk home and frantically cleaned himself, but by the time he got back to the church, the rite had been completed with Baccio as the boy's godfather. Missing the ceremony had been an appalling affront to her family, and Romina never looked at Tino again.

Embarrassing Baccio might not make up for everything, but Tino would certainly enjoy seeing him dripping in dung.

Tino double-checked that everything was in place and then began the long climb down the tree to the riverbank. He dashed over to the wooden bridge and saw that Venzi had finished tying the rope. He looked up at Tino.

"Did I do it right?" Venzi asked like a hunting dog hoping for his master's approval.

After inspecting the job he'd done, Tino smiled at him.

"I don't know how I could do this without you. You're a good man to help me with this."

"Anything for you, Tino. You'd do the same for me."

He wasn't wrong. They'd been thick as thieves since they were boys.

"Do you know what to do now?" Tino asked him.

Venzi nodded hesitantly and held up a length of twine. "I lay this across the bridge and stay underneath until I get your signal. Then I pull the string taut so that Baccio's horse trips on it and opens the bag of manure."

Because there was regular traffic across the bridge, they couldn't activate the snare until Baccio was nearing the bridge.

"Exactly," Tino said. "I'll wave from the hill when I see him coming."

"I just wish I could watch it happen."

"I know. But you'll see him directly after."

Venzi clapped his hands quietly like a little boy. "And what a sight that will be!"

Sometimes Tino envied the enjoyment his friend found in easy pleasures.

After laying the twine across the bridge, Tino waved his hand for Venzi to take the end and hide under the bridge. Then he raced toward the hill and took up a spot behind an oleander shrub. Now all he had to do was wait for the bells to ring at the hour of terce.

He spent his time imagining what he would say to Baccio after he was covered in manure. "Happy wedding day" sounded too mundane. "Have you chosen to wear a new scent that's more rotten than usual?" was definitely a contender. And "What an interesting way that you've decided to begin this celebration" had its appeal.

In the end, though, he thought he would ignore Baccio entirely and address Romina instead.

"I hope you're content with your choice" would be a fitting way to needle both of them.

Finally the mid-morning church bells sounded. Tino peered eagerly through the bush and saw the townsfolk gather at the other end of bridge holding flowers to throw at the bride and groom.

And there the procession was, slowly making its way along the river road from the estate of Romina's family. Just as Tino expected, Baccio was in the lead, sitting high on a white horse in his finest clothes. Romina looked beautiful in her wedding finery as she followed at a respectable distance behind along with the rest of the party so that the groom would not see her before the wedding service at church.

Tino stepped out and waved his hands high over his head three times. Venzi returned the same wave, indicating that he'd received the signal. Tino was too far away to see the string stretched across the path on the bridge, but he trusted his friend with the task.

Tino began walking back toward the bridge. He timed his pace to arrive just as Baccio was crossing.

He chuckled to himself, imagining the embarrassment to come as he made his way down the hill. But the laugh died in his throat when he saw two riders coming along the river road from the opposite direction. His view of them had been blocked by the oleander.

Abbot Lattanzio, head of the town's Benedictine monastery and the most important man in San Covello, had gone to Venice three weeks ago with one of his monks. The abbot had to pick this morning of all days to return with his prior. And it was clear he would reach the bridge before Baccio.

Even worse, the abbot's journey had been to retrieve a relic that had been gifted to the monastery—the jawbone of Saint Blaise, the town's patron saint. It would bring pilgrims from all over Italy to worship and donate money. It seemed that the trek had been successful because when he saw the gathered townspeople, the abbot triumphantly held aloft a precious rock crystal reliquary in a gold and enamel case.

Tino launched himself into a full sprint to intercept Abbot Lattanzio. He had to stop the monastic leader before he got to the bridge.

But as he ran, Tino wondered what he would say to stop the monk. It was one thing for people to suspect that he had sabotaged Baccio's wedding. It was another thing entirely to confirm it. For that same reason, he couldn't yell for Venzi to loosen the string across the bridge.

His only choice was to climb the oak and disable the trap before it could be sprung. He'd lose his best chance to humiliate Baccio, but he couldn't risk showering the abbot with filth.

Tino ducked behind the shrubbery that lined the bank of the creek and ran along behind the riders unseen until he reached the great oak. Abbot Lattanzio was only a few horse lengths from the bridge as he started to climb.

The only way to reach the rope was where it was lashed to the manure bag dangling from the branch. He didn't have time to untie the string that would open the bag. He'd have to cut it with his dagger.

He scrambled up as quickly as he could out of sight of the approaching abbot. He looked down hoping to be able to signal Venzi to cancel their scheme, but his friend was well hidden under the bridge.

Once he was on the large branch, he shimmied his way across. The leaves on the tree gave him some concealment from Abbot Lattanzio and the rest of the crowd below, but he could see enough to know that the abbot's horse was about to step on the bridge.

The urgency Tino felt worked against him. Instead of taking care to crawl securely across to reach the rope, he drew his knife as he moved. Without the proper grip, he slipped.

He dropped the dagger as he frantically grabbed hold of the branch. His feet slid off, and then he was holding on to the bark with just his fingertips. There was no way for him to pull himself back up. The abbot neared the tripwire. Tino was left with no other choice.

"Abbot Lattanzio!" Tino shouted. "Stop right now!"

Instead of halting the coming tragedy, it only made the situation worse.

The abbot looked up in confusion at the strange demand, but

his horse kept walking. As the horse's hoof hit the string, he stared at Tino's dangling body in astonishment.

The trap worked just as Tino had designed it. The string pulled the rope so that it untied the knot around the mouth of the bag. The entire contents of the sack, twenty-five pounds of watery manure, struck Abbot Lattanzio full in the face.

The abbot shrieked in disgust at being doused in filth. And to Tino's horror, the abbot was so surprised that he dropped the relic he was carrying as he clawed at the muck on his upturned face. The priceless reliquary fell to the bridge's wooden boards, bounced twice, and then went over the edge into the rushing creek.

Shrieks of shock and dismay erupted from the gathered residents at seeing their abbot defiled and the relic lost.

Venzi peeked his head out to see the results of their efforts, but when he saw that it was the abbot and not Baccio who'd received the soaking, he immediately ducked back under.

Tino, unable to hold on any longer, released his grip and missed the edge of the bridge, plunging directly into the creek below. He thrashed to the surface and frantically looked to see if he could spot the reliquary, but the precious metals must have made it heavy enough to sink. He eventually reached the riverbank fifty feet downstream. He climbed out of the water and was immediately grabbed by two burly men who held him captive. Several of the townspeople had retrieved buckets of water to clean off the abbot, while others lined the creek hoping to spot the sunken relic.

Abbot Lattanzio, red-faced with fury as he frantically wiped the manure away, pointed at Tino.

"You will pay for this affront."

By this time, Baccio and Romina had reached the bridge. While Tino stood there dripping wet, Baccio looked down on him from his horse with a gleefully smug expression.

"Thank you, Tino, for making our wedding celebration even more memorable."

The abbot dismounted and marched over to Tino. "What do you have to say for yourself, you wretch?"

"I'm very sorry, Abbot Lattanzio. I didn't mean…"

"It doesn't matter what you meant. You have attacked a member of the clergy and made me drop the relic entrusted to me into the water. By God's law, you will be punished. Did someone help you with this plot?"

Tino's eyes flicked to Venzi, who had quietly climbed out from under the bridge and melded with the crowd unnoticed. He could see that his friend was about to step forward.

"I acted alone, Father Abbot," Tino announced loudly. He shook his head, causing Venzi to stop in his tracks. "The fault is mine and no one else's."

The abbot stared at him, but Tino didn't waver. He wouldn't betray his friend.

"Very well," the abbot said at last. "Tino, this will be the final trick you commit in San Covello. You will either be excommunicated for your treachery or you will leave town this day and never return."

"But I…" Tino began, but the white-hot fury of the abbot interrupted him.

"It is your choice. While I am a forgiving man, I'm not sure our bishop will take so kindly to you causing the relic of our holy patron Saint Blaise to be lost. By all rights the saint should strike you down where you stand."

By this time, the crowd was booing and hissing at him as their anger grew. If he delayed his departure, excommunication might not be his only worry.

Venzi looked stricken, but it was clear that there was nothing to be gained by admitting his own guilt and martyring himself, and Tino didn't want him to. With one last look at his friend, Tino said, "I will be gone within the hour."

With his head hanging in shame, he shuffled off to his home to gather his belongings that included little more than a sword given to him by his uncle. He didn't know what kind of life he could make for himself or whether he could ever make amends to Saint Blaise, but one thing he knew for sure was that he could never show his face in San Covello again.

40

November, 1351

MALI STON

When the cry went up that a band of men was approaching the town of Mali Ston from the path to Ston, the garrison soldiers went into full alert, rushing to the walls and preparing to slam the gates closed. Willa rushed to the main gate with Petar and Jelena.

"Can you see who it is?" Willa asked.

Petar and Jelena squinted at the men in the distance and shook their heads. They were still too far away to identify, on foot, fourteen in all.

"Could this be the beginning of the attack?" Jelena wondered.

"That force is too small," Petar replied, sneezing then wiping his nose with a kerchief.

As the men neared, Jelena gasped at the same moment that Willa recognized who was leading them, strutting along in a fur-trimmed mantle over a deep blue tunic.

"It's Lord Vitomir," Petar said, an air of dread in his voice.

Willa frowned at them. "Why would he be here?"

"To take us away, most likely."

"He couldn't do that," Jelena said. "He wouldn't do that. He needs you."

The captain of the garrison, a mountain of a man named Danijel, hurried down from his position atop the wall.

"I'm surprised to see Lord Vitomir here," he said in Italian as he joined them at the gate.

At Willa and Jelena's urging, Petar had warned Danijel of the potential attack on the town, which was why the garrison's soldiers had responded to the potential threat so quickly. But the three of them knew that bringing up Vitomir as one of the instigators of the plan would have been met with derision, so Petar had kept that part to himself.

"Who are those men with him?" Petar asked.

Danijel shrugged. "I don't know. Perhaps they're reinforcements for the garrison."

Willa highly doubted that. "You don't recognize them?" she said.

Danijel looked oddly at the newcomer to the town, as if she were a dog that had spoken aloud. Then he turned back to Petar.

"They could be freshly arrived from Venice."

"You can't trust them," Petar said.

"Why not?"

Petar looked nonplussed for a moment. Willa chimed in to help him. "Didn't you say that you heard tell of Serbian spies while you were on your voyage back to Ston?"

Petar arched an eyebrow at her, then nodded along with her. "That's right. They could be Serbian spies."

Danijel shook his head and stifled a chuckle. "With the treasurer of Dubrovnik?"

"They're very clever."

"I don't know where you got your information, but I find it very unlikely. Besides, I'm bound to do what Lord Vitomir commands."

Petar sniffled and wiped his nose again, then glanced at Willa before speaking to Danijel. "Just promise me that you will keep an eye on them."

Danijel tilted his head in thought. "In all my time posted here, I've never known a smarter man than Lord Vitomir. But if you're concerned, I will be watchful."

"That's all I ask."

Vitomir stopped at the gate, his eyes playing over Willa, Petar, and Jelena before facing Danijel.

"Welcome, Lord Vitomir," Danijel said. "We are pleased that you have visited us again so soon."

"It was not by my choice," Vitomir replied.

"When we first saw you, we were worried that you were the spearhead of an attacking army."

"You were wise to be wary." Vitomir looked at Petar. "What have you heard?"

Danijel waved a hand at Petar. "Word is that the Serbians are planning to invade Ston."

"Anything else?"

Danijel hesitated. "No, my lord. We were hoping you had news for us."

The fact that Danijel didn't act suspicious seemed to put Vitomir at ease.

"There is, in fact, danger of an assault that's imminent."

"And the men you have brought will increase our numbers to repel the attack?"

Vitomir shook his head. "These men are your replacements. You are to accompany me back to my ship. Your skilled soldiers are needed in Dubrovnik in case that is the real target of the Serbians. Gather your men immediately."

Willa's heart raced as she understood Vitomir's plan. These men had to be in league with Bogun. As soon as the garrison was gone, the replacements could do anything they liked, including opening the gates for an invading army. The townspeople would be powerless to stop well-trained men-at-arms.

She leaned over to Petar and whispered, "You can't let them leave."

Petar nodded. "Captain Danijel, you're experienced with the town defenses. Do you think it's wise to switch with another garrison when a potential invasion is imminent?"

"This is not a request," Vitomir said sharply. "The rector personally requested Danijel and his soldiers for the defense of Dubrovnik. Now call your men to order."

Danijel looked at Petar, then at Vitomir. "Of course, my lord. I'll have them gather supplies."

"No need. My ship is at anchor not far from here. We have food and ale aboard for the sailing back to Dubrovnik."

Willa knew this was a death sentence for everyone, but she felt helpless to stop what was about to happen.

After the garrison soldiers had all gathered their personal belongings, Danijel called out and clapped his hands for the men to muster behind him. The garrison rushed down and came to order in front of Vitomir, who gave a sly smile to Petar.

"Very good, captain. I'm glad to see you know how to follow orders."

"It is my duty to serve Dubrovnik."

"Yes, it is."

"May I ask who will be taking my place?"

Vitomir indicated the severe man standing next to him. "This is Cedozar. He will take command."

Danijel bowed his head slightly as he eyed his counterpart. "Are you from Dubrovnik?"

"Yes, from Dubrovnik."

"Your accent is strange. How is it that I don't know you?"

"I have been posted at Korčula for many years."

Danijel peered at the row of replacement soldiers. "And your men?"

"Posted with me."

Danijel paused at that answer, then finally nodded. "There are good people in this town. I trust that you will defend them with your lives."

"We will guard them well."

"Enough of this," Vitomir said impatiently. "They are expecting us back at the ship. With any luck, we can make it to Dubrovnik by nightfall."

"Yes, my lord," Danijel said.

Willa felt compelled to do something. Although the leader of these men spoke Italian, she doubted that all of them spoke Croatian, let alone the Venetian tongue. Even if she could only get them to say a prayer together, the different language might allow the captain a reason to question his replacements.

"Perhaps a prayer is in order," she blurted out.

Vitomir appeared quite annoyed. "It's getting late. We don't have time for that."

"Yes," said Petar, who nodded at Willa. "I think we should pray."

"No. We're leaving now."

Petar looked panicked that they would leave and turned to Danijel. "These men are Serbian."

Vitomir sucked in a breath. "That's absurd."

"I'm telling you…" Petar put his hand to his nose, his breath catching "…they're Serbians!"

As he said it, he let out a huge sneeze.

Cedozar and his men quickly crossed themselves. It looked very strange to Willa. Instead of crossing themselves with a flat hand up, down, left, and right, they pressed together three fingers and crossed themselves up, down, right, and left.

Danijel noticed it, too, because his eyes went wide with shock. "Serbians!" he cried out, and drew his sword. His men were obviously stunned, and some of them were slow to draw their weapons.

But Cedozar was as quick as Danijel. He unsheathed his blade and threw himself at the garrison's captain. With the first impact of their swords slamming into each other, the battle began.

41

Vitomir was knocked to the ground by Cedozar as the Serbian crossed swords with Danijel. The Mali Ston guards took up arms immediately, setting off a pitched battle at the main gate. The defenseless residents of Mali Ston shrank away from the fight.

When one of the soldiers backed his way, Vitomir was kicked in the head, but he didn't know if it was on purpose or by accident. He sat there dazed, with no idea why the fighting had started.

One moment Petar was making his accusations, which should have been dismissed by Danijel. Then he sneezed, and something must have tipped Danijel to the fact that Cedozar's men were Serbs.

Vitomir staggered to his feet and leaned back against the gate's large wooden door as he watched the battle. The count of soldiers on either side was even, but the Serbians had the advantage because they had known they were coming into potential danger. Their reaction time had been faster, and they'd taken down four Croatians the moment the fighting started.

But Danijel's men were proficient. They fought back well, motivated by Danijel's determined duel with Cedozar. Every time Cedozar seemed about to drive him to the ground, Danijel would parry him and push him back.

Vitomir was sick that he'd been so close to leaving with Danijel and his men. The plan was to lead them back to the woods southeast of town, where Bogun and his remaining men were waiting in ambush. Before they even knew they were under attack,

Bogun would decimate them with crossbows and then slice the survivors to ribbons with their swords.

Danijel got the upper hand and slashed at Cedozar's chest. It should have been a lethal blow, but Cedozar dodged the worst of it and went tottering backward.

Blood was flying everywhere, nauseating Vitomir. He was so intent on avoiding looking at the worst of it that he almost missed Petar charging at him with a shovel raised over his head.

"You did this!" the saltman shouted.

Vitomir shrieked and fell back just as the shovel smashed into the door where his head had been. Petar was powerfully built, and Vitomir wasn't a fighter at all. All of his battles were fought with quills, not steel.

He put up his hands as he cowered on his knees. "Don't kill me!"

"It's too late for pleading," Petar growled, his knuckles white as he gripped the shovel's handle.

Vitomir shut his eyes to receive the death blow, but a clang made him open them. Cedozar had come to his rescue and blocked the shovel blade, knocking it out of Petar's hands. Now that he was disarmed and facing an expert swordsman, Petar retreated, perhaps to find another weapon.

Cedozar held out his hand and hauled Vitomir to his feet, wincing and holding his side as he did so.

"We have to go. Now!"

He nodded at the dead body of Danijel on the ground. The battleground was littered with bloody corpses. Almost no soldiers on either side remained standing. Even worse, some of the village men had joined in the fighting. Though they were only laborers, they were hardy souls defending their town with whatever makeshift weapons they could lay their hands on.

The skirmish was lost, and if he and the injured Cedozar stayed, they'd be torn apart by an overwhelming mob.

Cedozar yelled, and the only two Serbians still able to join them ran behind them out of the gate. Not too soon, either, as the doors swung closed when they were less than fifty feet away.

Vitomir looked back and saw villagers gathering on the wall

parapet to watch them flee, jeering at them as they ran. Then he noticed the blonde woman standing slightly apart from them with something in her hands.

It was a bow.

"Who is that woman?" he asked Cedozar, who looked where he was pointing.

"I don't know. She was the one causing all of the trouble for us."

"She has a bow."

"So what?"

"She's drawing an arrow to loose it at us."

Cedozar scoffed. "From this distance? She'll be lucky to have the strength for the arrow to make it halfway here."

Vitomir looked again and saw that she'd already shot not just one arrow, but three. They were arching high into the air in their direction.

"Are you sure that…"

Before he could finish speaking, the first arrow sunk its point into the ground two feet to his right. The second hit one of the trailing men in the upper chest, and the other in the lower back. Both went down with agonized screams.

"Hurry!" Cedozar shouted, speeding up his pace despite his wound. Vitomir shed his mantle to allow him to run faster.

Three more arrows were coming their way, and Vitomir's lungs burned as he sprinted as quickly as his legs would go. He heard the hard thump of the arrows plunging into the ground just behind him and looked to see that the arrows had missed the two of them by mere feet.

He stole a look back, but now she had lowered the bow.

Cedozar noticed the same and reduced his pace.

"We must be out of her range by now."

Vitomir slowed to a walk, trying to suck in his breath. His hands and legs were shaking from the effort and strain of his ordeal. He couldn't believe a woman was able to target them at that distance.

"That woman is a she-devil sent from the gates of Hell."

Cedozar shook his head. "That's what my men will think if they hear you say that, so keep it to yourself."

"They wouldn't fight her?"

"Not if they thought they were up against a demon. As you could see, we Serbians are a superstitious lot."

"What do you mean?"

"Didn't you see what happened?"

Vitomir shook his head. "I saw Petar sneeze, and then all perdition broke loose."

"He accused us of being Serbians at the moment that he sneezed. Serbian tradition says that sneezing is a sign from God that the truth about a falsehood is being told at that very moment, so we all crossed ourselves without thinking about it to ward off the Lord's wrath for lying."

"So? Why did that make Danijel realize you were Serbians?"

Cedozar shook his head in disgust, as if Vitomir should understand such a simple observation.

"Did you see us cross ourselves when Petar sneezed?"

"No, I was looking at him."

"How do you cross yourself?"

Vitomir shrugged. "Like everyone else." Then he crossed with his whole hand top to bottom and left to right.

"Not everyone else. Serbians are Orthodox. This is how we sign."

Cedozar held his thumb to his index and middle fingers with his pinkie and fourth fingers curled down and then crossed himself top to bottom, but right to left.

Vitomir vaguely remembered the difference now that he was reminded.

"It's hard to fathom that was all it took."

"Danijel was a smart man." Cedozar winced as he flexed his torso. "And a good fighter."

"Then how did you kill him?"

"He broke from our duel to help one of his men. The distraction gave me a chance to strike him from behind."

"Were there any of their soldiers left to fight?" Vitomir asked.

"Only one that I saw."

When they reached the appointed ambush point, Bogun emerged from the trees along with twenty men armed with crossbows. His hands in the air punctuated his question. "What is this? Where is the garrison?"

"Dead," Vitomir said.

"I would think that's good except for the way you both look. Where are my men?"

"Also dead," Cedozar said. He relayed what had happened to an increasingly enraged Bogun.

When the story was done, Bogun stomped on the ground and pointed at the two of them.

"This was supposed to be a simple plan, and somehow even it got ruined."

"It wasn't our fault," Vitomir said.

"I know it wasn't Cedozar's fault," Bogun snarled. "It's yours. Again."

"It wasn't mine, either. It was that woman in town."

Cedozar gave Vitomir a warning look as the rest of Bogun's men watched.

"What woman?"

"A blonde," Cedozar said. "A foreign troublemaker with an active tongue and trained with a bow. But the garrison has been virtually wiped out. The only people remaining to defend Ston are the townspeople themselves."

"Do you think we can take the town with the men we have? And what about you?" Bogun nodded at the blood on Cedozar's tunic. "Are you up for another fight?"

"I just need a bandage and poultice and I'll be all right. We can use ladders to get us over the wall and then we'll be able to kill every last man in the town if we want. Without trained swordsmen, the mob won't be able to fight on top of the wall, so we can cut them down one by one."

Bogun squinted at Vitomir, then nodded. "Fine. We regroup

to make our plans, get you taken care of, and then we march on the town."

"When?" Vitomir asked. "You don't have your army yet, do you?"

"If the town is defended by a bunch of untrained laborers, we don't need them," Bogun answered. "We attack at first light. Tomorrow."

THE HELLFIRE

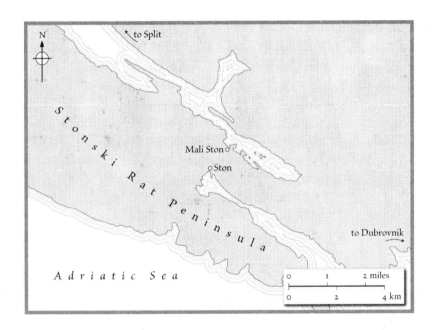

42

Willa had never experienced such an acrid, sour smell. She tried waving the torch to clear out the stench as she entered the cave behind Petar and Jelena, but it was no use. She was even having difficulty seeing because her eyes were watering so much.

"What is that odor?" she asked, holding her nose.

"You asked for bat droppings," Petar said. "You'll find all you ever need in here."

Jelena pointed up. "They only come out at night."

Willa looked at the cave ceiling and recoiled when she saw the entire surface was squirming with bats hanging from the limestone. "How do you know this place?"

"We use the bat leavings to enrich our crops. Works much better than manure, and there's an endless supply. And it's within walking distance of town."

The unexpected battle at Mali Ston earlier in the day only reinforced how important it was to build the rockets that Marco Polo had described in his codex. While the rest of the residents cleared the dead and tended to the wounded, Willa had insisted that they make this excursion outside the walls in the light of the afternoon.

"I still don't understand how bat droppings can help with this new weapon," Petar said, coming to a stop and waving his hand at the cave floor. "But all you have to do is pick it up."

Willa had been studying Polo's instructions for building the rockets. The mysterious people in Cathay had developed an armament powered by flame, a black powder that would explode when touched by fire. She had seen the results of the potential destruction herself not more than a few weeks before in Rhodes. Several barrels of this black powder stowed in the hold of a burning warship blew the entire vessel to scraps when they ignited.

Gerard had noted down the existence of the black powder at the back of the copy of the *Secretum philosophorum* that his mother had given him. That book of riddles, tricks, and arcane knowledge had come in useful on more than one occasion during their travels. Gerard had left the manuscript with her in Dubrovnik and now she would be able to add the recipe for the black powder to it. It was another attempt to convince herself that he really would come back.

"We don't need the dung itself," Willa said. "Polo's book said we need the white powdery remains where the droppings have dried up."

"I know where we can find that. How much?"

"Enough to fill the sacks we've brought." Each of them had one.

In all likelihood, one sack would be more than enough. According to Polo's writings, two other ingredients, measured out in precise proportions, were required to produce the black powder. The first was charcoal, which they had in abundance in Ston.

The second was sulfur, much harder to find.

As Petar led the way deeper into the cave, Willa asked Jelena, "You're certain your mother has some sulfur?"

"I know she has a quantity of it for medicinal purposes, but I don't know how much she keeps on hand. It might not be enough for this secret weapon. What did you call it?"

"A rocket."

"And how does it work?"

"You stuff this black powder in a type of tube described in Marco Polo's book, with one end capped and the other end with a small hole where fire shoots from it. Then you light that end with a flame, and it flies into the sky like a falling star. Apparently, if done correctly, the rocket will explode against whatever it hits."

Jelena shook her head in disbelief. "It sounds fantastical, like dragon's breath. You can make this rocket?"

"If Polo's journal is correct, I believe I can."

"I'd sooner trust the prophecy."

"It does mention hellfire," Petar said. "Perhaps this rocket is what the Lord meant by that."

Willa thought again of the prophecy.

The lure of precious crystals sparks a dire threat to the White Fortress.

My hand guides strangers from across the sea to provide aid in this time of need.

Hellfire rains down when a sacrifice summons a dragon to destroy any enemy refusing to flee.

A miracle inspires a new leader to show the way to liberation.

"The Serbians did seem wary of superstitions," Willa said. "They crossed themselves when you sneezed. Do they know of the prophecy?"

Petar nodded. "It is well known in this region. They would hear of it."

"If we could rain hellfire upon them with these rockets, they might flee."

"But with Bogun as their leader, they wouldn't likely cross him by deserting. He has a reputation as a cruel and demanding commander."

"If only we had a dragon as well," Jelena said idly.

That comment spurred something in Willa's mind, but before she could capture the elusive thought, Petar came to a stop beside a wall bristling with white crystals. They looked exactly as described in the codex.

"Take a knife and scrape off as much as you can," Willa said. "But choose only the whitest crystals. Any dirt or filth will taint the mixture."

Petar began to chip away and said, "I know how to keep my salt pure."

And it did look like salt of another kind as they carefully scraped it into their sacks. Willa shuddered as she thought about the thousands of bats overhead and tried not to look up again. There was such a large quantity lining the walls that it took little time to fill their bags.

Willa fairly sprinted out of the cave and took in a deep breath when they were out in the fresh air.

When they got back to Mali Ston, they found the lone surviving soldier from the garrison saddling Comis for his ride. Willa wasn't happy to give up her horse for this mission, but Zephyr would never accept him as a rider, and Comis was faster than any of the plow horses they had in the town.

Volunteering to go herself wasn't a possibility. Her words would have no weight when she arrived in Dubrovnik to warn the rector of the attack on Ston. It had to be the soldier from the garrison to convey the dire situation and request that ships with an army sail back their way at once.

She patted Comis's muzzle and forced a smile at the man who climbed into the saddle.

"Take good care of her," she said.

The man looked down at her with a grim expression. "I find that horses understand when a situation is urgent, so she'll know that I need to get to Dubrovnik as fast as possible. Those Serbs will pay for killing my friends."

She gave Comis one last rub on her neck, and the soldier wheeled her around and drove her into a gallop, racing through the open gate that closed quickly behind him.

Willa wanted to watch him ride across the plain toward the forest to the south, but she had no time to waste. She had to learn how to mix the concoction that would fire the rockets.

They took the ingredients into Petar's temporary home in Mali Ston and emptied small amounts from the sacks into bowls. Charcoal was already pounded into dust and placed on a platter.

Jelena's mother Marija entered carrying an earthen jar. The top was closed with a circle of waxed linen tied around with string. She removed it and shoved the jar toward Willa. She didn't look very happy about giving up her medicinal remedy, one she used to soothe skin irritations, treat worms, and balance the humors in the body.

"Is this what you need?"

Willa peered into the jar and saw the odorless bright yellow substance. "Yes, thank you."

She tried to take the jar, but Marija wouldn't let it go.

"They said this batch came all the way from Sicily. Do you know how expensive this was and how long I had to wait for it?"

"Mother," Jelena said, prying Marija's fingers from the jar, "this is an important ingredient for Willa's mixture. Once Ston is saved, I'll make sure that we get you more sulfur."

Marija eyed the jar dubiously but said nothing.

Willa poured out the sulfur onto another platter. The mound wasn't very high.

"Is that enough?" Petar asked.

Willa turned to Marija. "Do you have more?"

"That's all of it in Ston."

Willa shrugged as if it weren't a problem. "Then it'll be enough."

It seemed unlikely that the yellow, black, and white powders on the table would produce a deadly weapon, but Marco Polo wrote that he'd seen it himself, and after what Willa had watched it do to a full-sized warship, she had little doubt he was right.

While Willa worked on the mixture using a mortar and pestle, Jelena and her mother set about creating the tubes that Polo had drawn in his book that would form the rockets, rolling thin sheets of sheepskin parchment.

Willa had already created a way to measure out the exact amounts they would need, using wooden cups and spoons she'd scratched with markings to show the correct proportions.

Given her experience in Rhodes, she decided that they should begin with a small amount. She carefully spooned out the charcoal dust, the powdered sulfur, and the bat-salt, as they were calling it, and placed them in the mortar. Then she took a deep breath as she began to grind the mixture as instructed with the pestle. She knew a fire was needed to ignite the powder, but holding such an explosive material in her hands was unnerving.

When she was done, she saw that it was similar to the black powder she'd seen in Rhodes. The amount was no larger than her thumbnail.

"Is that it?" Petar asked.

"I think so."

"How do we know it works?"

She looked around and saw an upended iron kettle. She retrieved it and turned it over. Then she poured the tiny amount of black powder into it.

"Can you hand me a stick from the fire?"

Petar took out a stick that was burning only on one end and handed it to her. Jelena and Marija stopped what they were doing and came over to watch the demonstration. All three of them were crowding around the kettle to peer inside.

"Stand back," Willa said.

They gave her a look as if she were jesting. When she waved her hand for them to step back, they did so.

"Ready?" she asked them. The three of them nodded, but it still seemed like they thought she was silly to be so cautious.

Willa stood back as far as she could and dipped the lit end of the stick into the kettle.

The black powder inside erupted in flame and smoke, shooting up toward the ceiling of the home.

Petar, Jelena, and Marija leaped backward in surprise, with Marija letting out a yelp of fear.

Petar opened the door and waved the smoke out. Thankfully, nothing in the house had been set aflame. Willa was glad she'd first experimented with such a small amount.

Marija looked at the kettle with horror as Jelena comforted her with an arm around her shoulders.

"What is that devil's brew you've brought into our midst?" Marija said.

Petar inspected the scorched kettle, then turned to them with a broad smile on his face.

"It's hellfire."

43

The rider was coming through exactly where Bogun was expecting him to. The most likely route for someone attempting to get to Dubrovnik to request help would be along this narrow trail farther inland.

Of course, the messenger could attempt to take one of their small fishing boats to Dubrovnik, but that would mean sailing from Mali Ston all the way around the Stonski Rat peninsula, which would take far longer.

He and his men were waiting behind an outcropping of rocks, their crossbows cocked and loaded with bolts. Cedozar was a better shot than any of them except Bogun, but his wounds were still being tended to back on the ship. And Vitomir was absolutely no use in a fight.

By the rhythm of the hoofbeats, it sounded like the approaching horse was running at full gallop.

"Wait for my signal," Bogun said to the three men.

The forest encroached on both sides of the path, so they wouldn't be able to see the rider for more than a few moments before he went by. If they shot too early or too late and missed, they wouldn't have time to reload by the time the horse was out of sight. Bogun's own horse was on a ship with his main force or he would have given chase himself.

Bogun peered over the rock face and listened as the pounding hooves got closer with every heartbeat.

Finally, a white horse burst into view. Bogun judged the distance and counted to himself down from five. When he reached one, he called out, "Now!"

The four of them rose as one. The rider yanked back on the reins when he saw the attackers, just as Bogun hoped he would. He turned the horse around as if to flee.

"Loose!" Bogun cried out.

Four bolts launched simultaneously. One missed, one embedded itself into the horse's saddle, and two struck the rider in the back. With a scream, he tumbled off the horse, which startled and ran off back into the woods. Bogun thought that was too bad. He could have used another steed.

They drew their swords and ran around the outcropping, but their haste was unneeded. One of the bolts had plunged into the soldier's heart from the back. Bogun was certain that was his bolt.

He ordered the men to drag the garrison soldier off the trail and toss him into the trees where the scavenging animals would find a meal.

With their deed completed, they headed back to the ship. When they arrived, they found Cedozar up and around, testing his motion.

"How is it?" Bogun asked.

"Nothing that won't heal soon. I can fight. Did they send a rider?"

Bogun nodded. "Dead."

"Should I go back out and wait to see if any more come?"

"No. By the time they decide that he didn't make it to Dubrovnik, Ston and Mali Ston will be securely in our hands."

"Then we march on the town for an attack at dawn?"

"Yes. Get the ladders ready. We'll establish our base just out of view. We'll be over the walls before they realize what's happening."

Vitomir approached with a hopeful look.

"I heard you say you're leaving the ship to prepare for the attack. Does that mean I can take it back to Dubrovnik?"

Bogun exchanged an amused glance with Cedozar.

"You're staying until the town is in my hands. In fact, I think you should come with us."

Vitomir couldn't disguise his fright. "But I'm no use to you in a battle."

"I am well aware of that. We'll let you into Mali Ston through the gates once we've conquered it."

Before Vitomir could answer, a call went out.

"Ship approaching!"

Bogun, Cedozar, and Vitomir went to the seaward bulwark. A large warship was on an intercept course to their anchorage. The banner on the stern displayed a golden lion on a red background.

"Oh, no," said Vitomir. "That's a Venetian watch ship."

"What do they want with us?"

"They stop ships to see if they're smuggling goods. The Venetians are particular about collecting their taxes. They can't discover that we are carrying weapons of war."

"Then you'll tell them to leave us alone," Bogun said.

"They can't know I'm here with a group of Serbians. I can't possibly explain that."

Bogun pointed at the large ship. "They have three times our numbers on that ship. Do you expect us to fight them?"

"If you must, but I can't be seen."

Bogun grimaced at the man's cowering, but he still needed him. "Fine, then. Get below deck. I'll send them off."

"How?"

"You said they like their taxes. I've got an idea. Now, go."

Bogun instructed Cedozar to get all weapons out of sight while the warship heaved to and lowered a skiff into the water. While a phalanx of armed soldiers stood at the ready on the other ship, six men rowed over to them. Three climbed up the rope ladder.

The man obviously in charge strode toward Bogun. He was tall and thin and had an air of haughtiness.

"You speak Italian?" he asked Bogun as he surveyed the vessel with a turned-up nose.

"Yes, my lord," Bogun forced himself to say.

"I am Teodor, a representative of the Doge of Venice. You are the captain of this ship?"

"Yes, sire. I am called Bač."

"Serbian, eh? What is your purpose in these waters?"

"We are cloth traders on our way from Dubrovnik to Trogir."

"What I mean to say is, why are you in these waters specifically? You are far from the normal shipping route."

"We had to stop to make some repairs to a leak in our ship. But it's fixed now and we'll be resuming our route."

"I see. Well, it is routine for us to inspect your cargo and verify that your manifest has the proper seal from Dubrovnik."

"Is that really necessary?" Bogun asked in his most obsequious tone. "We were just about to get under way. We're already going to be late making port."

Teodor gave him a weak smile. "I'm sure you understand that we have to ensure that Venice is given its proper due for the privilege of shipping in the Adriatic."

"Of course, sire. Perhaps it would speed things along for all of us if I paid you our taxes directly."

When Teodor hesitated, Bogun wondered if he'd gotten one of the few incorruptible government officials who was more interested in doing his duty than fattening his accounts.

Finally, the administrator smiled. "That would be kind of you. You know your cargo better than I. What would you think a fair tax would be?"

Bogun had to choose the sum carefully. Offering too much would make Teodor suspicious that they were carrying something so valuable that it should be seized. Too little, and Teodor might be insulted enough to go forward with the inspection, resulting in a bloody mess that none of them might survive.

After sizing him up and deciding that a full gold ducat would be overdoing it, Bogun reached into his purse and removed a generous quantity of silver grossi, saying, "I think this should suffice."

Teodor appraised the offer, then nodded, taking the coins in hand. "I can see you're a shrewd merchant, and I wish you well with your trading."

As Teodor waved his men back to the boat, Bogun said, "And I bid you good travels."

Teodor turned while his men climbed down the rope ladder. "We'll be staying to make sure you sail away safely. After all, given the leak you've had, the least we can do is make sure you have no further troubles."

Bogun chewed the inside of his mouth. "That's very generous of you, my lord, but not necessary. We…"

"I insist," Teodor replied. It was clear that the coins would buy only so much goodwill.

When the skiff was away, Cedozar said, "What shall we do?"

Bogun shook his head. "What choice do we have? We have to sail off."

"They may follow us."

"Then we go as far as we have to." He told the captain of the ship to raise the anchor and make ready to sail.

Vitomir poked his head out from below deck. "Are they gone?"

"Your secret is safe," Bogun said.

Vitomir frowned at the crew preparing the ship for the journey. "Why are we raising sail?"

"We're leaving by order of the Venetian Republic. We may have to sail quite far north before they let us out of their sight."

"Then tomorrow's attack is called off?" Vitomir said it with too much relief.

Bogun stalked over to Vitomir. "Nothing is called off. Tomorrow or the next day, it doesn't matter. We attack the moment we're free of that Venetian scum."

 44

STON

It wasn't quite dark out yet, but Willa yawned widely, exhausted from the day's events. She forged on with putting together the rocket because Jelena hadn't stopped, either. They were alone in the house while Marija had gone to rest for the night. Because they knew an attack must be coming soon, Petar had also reluctantly agreed to try to get some sleep.

They had mixed enough of the black powder to put it into the casing Jelena had built, but it was taking time to figure out the proper method to pack it in so it wouldn't fall out of the tube. The third time that the device collapsed, Willa banged the table in frustration.

Jelena looked up in alarm, putting down her work building another tube and hunching over as if she were ready to run from another fireball.

"What happened?"

Willa sighed. "I'm sorry. Nothing's wrong." Jelena relaxed into her chair at that. Willa added, "Sometimes I think this is just too much for me."

"I'm sure we can learn how to do all of this properly. From the way you described them, Marco Polo's notes and drawings seem very detailed."

Unable to read herself, Jelena depended on Willa's interpretation of the codex.

"It's not that. Even if we make this work, I don't know what I'm going to do."

"After this is all over?"

Willa nodded. She felt her breath hitching and calmed herself to keep the tears at bay.

Jelena scooted closer to Willa and took her hand. "You have a place here."

"You all have been so kind to me," Willa said, facing Jelena. "I couldn't have gotten through the last few days without you. But this isn't my home."

"Where is your home?"

"With Gerard. Wherever he is."

"And if he really is dead?" Jelena said it as gently as possible, but Willa could see the skepticism in her eyes.

Willa couldn't blame her. There was faith and then there was fantasy. She hadn't given up her faith, but it was flagging with every passing day. Was she delusional for believing that her husband was still out there somewhere?

"Then perhaps I will go back to England. But it's such a long way and for a woman traveling by herself, it can be dangerous."

"Is someone waiting for you there?"

"No. I lost all my family, and my dearest friend. But England is the place where I grew up. As beautiful as Ston and Dalmatia are, it's a foreign land to me. Gerard and I had been planning a way to go home someday, and I think the best thing for me is to try to do it on my own." Willa didn't want to give up the hope that Gerard might still be alive, but as the days passed, she had started to look at a future without him, and all she saw was darkness.

"But how will you survive?" Jelena asked. "You have money, but for how long? Will you try to find a new husband?"

"I can't think about that yet. I have skills as a trader. I told a young girl in Korčula that she could build a life for herself from nothing. What kind of woman would I be to tell her that and not believe I could do it for myself?"

"But this world is so difficult for us. You need a man to protect you."

Willa shook her head. "I need a man to love. I don't want a man just because I have to." She thought back to the abbey she'd left outside of Turin, Italy. "If I can't have that—if I can't make it on my own in England—then I will commit myself to becoming a nun. That's what I almost did before marrying Gerard."

Jelena raised her eyebrows in surprised dismay. "Become a nun? I can't imagine you hiding away from the world like that."

"I wouldn't view it as hiding. I love books, and I've always wanted to study and maybe even write something. Have you ever heard of Hildegard of Bingen?" Jelena shook her head. "She was a nun who wrote books, even works to instruct other nuns about medicine and remedies."

Jelena perked up at that prospect. "What a noble life that would be for you. You would be an excellent teacher."

Willa felt the inkling of purpose in Jelena's enthusiasm. She knew that Gerard would want her to make a meaningful life for herself.

"I could start here. There is no reason you shouldn't be able to read."

Jelena let go of Willa's hand and waved at her, chuckling uncomfortably. "Me? No, it's too late for me to learn."

"Why? It's not so difficult. And you just said I would be a good teacher."

"Do you really think I could?"

"If I can, you can."

"I suppose I could try it once we aren't in such a…"

Her words were cut off by the call of someone yelling from the wall.

"Rider! Rider approaching!"

Willa snatched up her bow and arrows, rushing out of the house with Jelena. As they ran toward the wall, the other residents were flooding out of their homes in alarm.

Willa raced up the stairs and looked out over the parapet. In the fading light of dusk, she saw movement near the forest.

Willa saw Comis at the tree line. The call from the watcher on the wall had been incorrect. There was no rider. She was walking back toward Mali Ston, her saddle empty.

"I think that's your horse," Jelena said. "But where's the soldier?"

Willa didn't try to answer, her stomach sinking at the probable reason why. She left Jelena and ran back down the stairs from the wall, calling for the gates to be opened.

Willa whistled, and Comis picked up her plodding pace, trotting the rest of the way to her. Willa ran her hands over her beloved horse, but there weren't any injuries that she could see.

Petar came up huffing behind her, blinking his eyes from his rough awakening.

"How did your horse get back here by itself?"

"Comis is very smart. If she became riderless, I'm not surprised that she would find her way back to me."

"Did the soldier fall off?"

Willa circled around and plucked the crossbow bolt sticking out of the saddle. It hadn't penetrated far enough to pierce Comis's hide. Willa handed the bolt to Petar and pointed to flecks of blood dotting the saddle.

"He was killed?"

Willa nodded. "Or captured. Bogun must have intercepted him."

Jelena joined them. She took in the crossbow bolt in Petar's hand, sucking in breath as she spoke.

"What does that mean?"

"It means that our warning to Dubrovnik will never arrive," Petar said, an air of desperation in his voice. "No help is coming."

45

HVAR, DALMATIA

Nika couldn't help but be amazed by the island town of Hvar and the great fortress that loomed above from its perch on a hilltop. The harbor was enclosed on three sides with a broad promenade leading to a central square where the cathedral and bell tower anchored the town. Unlike Dubrovnik, there was no great wall surrounding the town. But the massive fortress overlooking the buildings that climbed up the hillside must have been enough to deter would-be attackers.

As they sailed toward the harbor with the morning sun dappled on the water, she desperately wanted the ship to move faster. This journey should have been a great adventure for her, one she might never get again in her life, but all she could think about was getting back to her family in Ston.

"How long do we have to be here?" she asked Fox, who was standing next to her at the bulwark. His face was pale, but at least he wasn't emptying his stomach overboard anymore now that they were in the harbor's calm waters.

"Just long enough to find Cristoval's Serbian friend Radoslav." Cristoval was still below deck tending to Tino. Apparently, it took time to recover from so much drink in the Italian's belly.

"This man is Serbian?"

"Yes."

"Aren't the Serbians the ones who are going to attack Ston?"

"Cristoval thinks we can trust him. Besides, not everyone from a country is the same. I'm from England and my mother was French, and I've met good men and bad from both places."

"I miss my home," Nika said, the longing hitting her stomach like a hunger pang.

"So do I."

"Then why are you here?"

"I lost mine."

"How can you lose a home?"

"I suppose you can't. It was actually taken from me. Stolen." She could see a flash of anger in his eyes as he said it.

"I'm sorry. But can't you get it back?"

"Willa thinks we can. We were returning to France to try to do that when we met your parents."

"That's your wife? What's she like?"

"Kind. Brave. Funny. Beautiful. Clever. You'd like her."

"I hope I can meet her. She sounds special."

"She is. She's unlike any other woman I've ever met." He smiled to himself at that statement.

"Do you think she'll be in Ston when we get there?"

"I have to believe she will be. If she isn't, I won't stop until I find her."

Nika liked how Fox talked about her. It reminded her of how her mother and father spoke to each other. The thought made her ache even more.

"Do you think my parents will remember me?"

Fox looked down at her with a disbelieving scowl, as if she were mad.

"Of course, they'll remember you. What a thing to say."

Nika felt her chest heave, but she fought back tears. "How can you know that? I've never been away from them for more than a day before this."

Fox's expression softened, and he leaned down to her. "I'm sorry. You're so capable that I keep forgetting how young you are." He put his hand gently on her shoulder. "Do you remember what your parents look like?"

Nika closed her eyes and imagined them in her mind as if they were standing in front of her. "I can see them smiling."

"That's because they're waiting for you with open arms. You can't imagine the relief and joy they'll feel when they see you again."

"Especially because they probably think I'm dead."

"They'll forget all about that when we return."

"If Willa is still in Ston, what do you think she's doing?"

"If I had to guess, I'd say she's helping them prepare for the attack. Even if she believes I'm dead, she wouldn't give up on your parents." Fox sighed and shook his head. "If our positions were reversed, I don't know if I would have been so strong."

"It sounds like you've already lost a lot."

"More than you can know."

By his tone, she could tell he didn't want to go into that further, so she switched the subject. "Where is this Radoslav?"

"We should ask at the local cooper's first," a voice said behind them.

Nika turned to see Cristoval approaching.

"When I last saw him in Split," he continued, "he said he was coming to Hvar to meet with a cooper, but he wouldn't tell me why. For all I know, he might have gone back to Serbia."

Tino trailed behind, massaging his head and squinting in the sun.

"You look worse than I feel," Fox said as Tino propped himself against the bulwark.

"Nothing that some food won't cure once we dock," Tino said.

"And he needs some," Cristoval said. "He hasn't taken in anything but water since we left Trogir."

"Gerard has been feeding the fish since we left Trogir," Nika said, "so he needs food, too."

The ship was tying up at the dock. They had been told there was a market not far away.

"Then our first order of business is to eat," Fox said.

Fox was ravenous as soon as his feet hit dry land. They found a stand with bread, pickled carrots, and salted fish. The four of them quickly made a meal of it as they sat in the main square, parts of which were decorated with ribbons and flowers.

"What do you think that's for?" Nika asked him.

Fox shrugged. "A celebration of some kind. A wedding, perhaps?"

He was done eating first, so he left them to acquire the ginger that he couldn't find in Trogir. After successfully buying some, he asked around to find the cooper. His accent and clothes got some strange looks, but he finally met a friendly old man who pointed the way.

When he returned to the square, the rest of them were done with their meal. He showed them the path to the barrel maker.

"Are you sure he'll be there?" Tino asked.

"Who is sure of anything these days?" Cristoval said. "But it's our best starting point."

"What makes you think he'd fight against a fellow Serbian?"

"Because I think he might hate Bogun almost as much as I do. When he heard that I was looking for a way to track down Bogun, Radoslav sought me out, much as I sought you out." Cristoval nodded at Fox.

"Why didn't you team up to hunt him?" Fox asked.

"Because neither of us had any idea how to get to him. So we went our separate ways. But we agreed to find each other again if that situation changed, and here we are."

Fox didn't know what to think, but if this Radoslav was fueled by hatred against Bogun, then he might be valuable as an ally.

"I agree," he said. "We should at least hear his story."

"As long as he can fight," Nika said, "it doesn't matter."

"He's a good swordsman?" Tino asked. "We don't want someone who's going to be useless."

"His skills impressed me," Cristoval said. "To keep them up, we practiced with each other for the short time we were together. I'm ashamed to say he disarmed me more than once."

They followed Fox's directions to the local cooper's shop just off the main piazza and spoke to the journeyman at the workshop. He was just closing up and had a bright smile on his face. Nika translated for them.

"I'm going to my wedding," the man said.

"Congratulations," Fox said. "We won't take up much of your time then. We're looking for a man named Radoslav."

The question dampened the journeyman's mood. "You won't find him here. He's being held prisoner at the fortress on top of the hill, along with the master cooper himself."

"Why?"

"For brawling two days ago. I don't know why, but it was very ugly. Knives were drawn. Thankfully, some soldiers were there to stop them before anyone was killed."

Fox thanked the journeyman, and he locked up the shop and walked away whistling.

"That's not encouraging," Cristoval said.

"In one way, it is," Tino said. "Now we know he can handle himself in an actual fight."

"Except he got caught," Fox said.

"At least he's not dead," Nika helpfully added.

It was a slog up the path, which dog-legged back and forth up the steep and rocky slope. When they reached the fortress gates, Fox asked the guard if they could see Radoslav. After a swift refusal, two coins convinced the guard to let one of them in. Cristoval volunteered, but Fox wanted to get the measure of the man himself.

He spoke to Nika. "Stay with Tino and Cristoval. I'll be right back."

"Hopefully with Radoslav," Cristoval said.

"If I can. It depends why he's here."

"Either way," Nika said, "We head to Ston by the evening, yes?"

Fox nodded. "We're not waiting any longer." He'd put off returning to Willa for long enough. He thought his heart would burst if he didn't see her soon.

To get inside, he had to disarm himself. He removed Legend from his back and gave it and his dagger to Cristoval. Leaving the three of them at the gate, he followed the guard into the fortress.

It was an impressive structure that gave an expansive view of the harbor below.

They reached a small doorway and the guard took a torch from a sconce before they descended a narrow stairway. A dank smell rose from below, mingled with the odor of smoke and human waste.

At the bottom of the steps, Fox saw a curving corridor lined with cells fronted by iron bars. The first one held a man who was lying on the stone floor and groaning. In the meager light coming through the tiny window, Fox could see a battered figure curled up like a baby and rocking back and forth.

"Is that him?" Fox asked the guard.

"Fourth cell. You can talk to him while I go piss."

Fox's eyes adjusted to the dimness as the guard retreated with the torch. He crept forward until he stopped in front of the fourth cell.

A young man sat cross-legged on the floor, motionless except for his eyes curiously taking in his visitor. He seemed in much better shape than the man in the first cell. Fox couldn't tell his height, but the muscles in his exposed forearms were appropriately sinewy for a warrior. His curly hair dangled past his shoulders, and his beard was neatly trimmed.

"Are you Radoslav?" Fox said in Italian.

"Who wants to know?" the man answered in a heavy accent.

"My name is Gerard Fox. I'm here with your friend Cristoval."

"I don't have any friends."

"But you know him."

"As well as I know anyone."

"He said you were a good fighter."

"So is he."

"Why are you in here?"

"Assault and brawling in public. Didn't you see the man in the other cell?"

"The cooper? Why were you fighting him?"

He paused before saying, "He wanted to hurt someone I know."

"So you were protecting this person."

"Not that it matters. I'm a Serbian and a stranger. The locals don't care much for either. They wouldn't have believed me if I'd told anyone, so I chose the only path I saw."

Radoslav said this with a matter-of-fact tone. There was no concern in his voice.

"It doesn't sound like you are worried. Are they letting you go soon?"

"I don't care. The wedding will happen today, and that is enough."

"What does a wedding have to do with anything?"

"Why are you asking all of these questions? Who are you really?"

"I have a proposition for you. I can get you out of here, and I'm sure I can pay the guards' price."

Radoslav shook his head. "I deserve this punishment for everything I've done. I don't need anything from you."

"Even if our task is to fight against Bogun?"

That got Radoslav's attention. He got to his feet and grabbed the bars separating them. He gripped them so hard that his knuckles cracked.

"You've found him?"

"Yes, but it's not just about him. He's planning something heinous. It's an impossible errand. Great odds defending a town against an overwhelming force. We might all die."

"Bogun is the one who's leading the attack?"

Fox nodded. "It's against a town called Ston."

"He'll kill everyone there if he succeeds in capturing it."

"How do you know that?"

Radoslav cast his eyes down in embarrassment. "Because I've helped Bogun do it before," he said. "If you knew what I've done, you wouldn't want my help."

"Why don't you let me be the judge?"

Radoslav narrowed his eyes at him. "You wouldn't tell anyone?"

"I'll take it to the grave," Fox said.

"I've never told anyone else this story. How can I trust you?"

"Because if you don't tell me the truth, you'll stay in this cell and never get a chance to face Bogun."

Radoslav paused for a few moments as he considered the options Fox had given him. Then he quietly sat back down, took a deep breath, and in a hushed tone, began his story.

46

BOSNIA

Radoslav was surprised he had been bestowed the honor of riding next to Bogun, given that he was the newest member of the fifteen-man team. Normally, that position would belong to Cedozar, who was on the horse behind him, followed by the rest of the men and two huge oxen carts. The trek up the mountain pass was almost over, as he could see the church steeple of the small town ahead.

"Do you know why I selected you to join us, Radoslav?" Bogun asked as he gazed up at the snowy peak towering over the village.

"Because I pledged to serve you, my lord."

Bogun shook his head. "That's what I *expect* from you. You're riding with me today because of what I saw you do in the battle against the Hungarians."

Radoslav's stomach felt as if he'd swallowed a handful of that mountain snow. He wasn't proud of his actions against the Serbians' enemies, but that army was a threat to the empire and had to be destroyed.

"I only was doing my duty to His Imperial Highness."

"As you are now. How many men did you slay in that battle?"

"I can't remember."

"I saw you kill three, but with the amount of blood on you, the count had to be much higher."

Radoslav swallowed, shame coursing through his veins. "It was a confusing battle."

"Which might be why we won even though we were outnumbered."

"We were outnumbered because of the peasants in their midst." Bogun smiled and looked off, as if he were summoning the memory of a fine meal he'd eaten. "And you dispatched them easily."

Radoslav's bloodlust had been so all-consuming during the fight that he'd waded into a trio of cowering peasants, swinging his sword without thinking until he'd torn through them. It was only after the enemy was defeated that his mind was able to take stock of the atrocities he'd committed.

When Bogun had offered to let him join his soldiers on this special mission, he'd jumped at the opportunity to get away from the main army. He didn't know what the new task entailed, but it couldn't be worse than the slaughter he'd been a part of.

"Yes," Bogun said, looking him up and down with admiration. "You'll do well with us."

They rode into the town across the bridge and past the grain mill next to a swollen stream. The villagers eyed the strangers warily. In addition to the townspeople was a group of ten pilgrims, identifiable by the hats and pins the men wore and the staffs they carried. The sole woman among the pilgrims drew her boy closer to her as Bogun's men passed.

The smiling priest came out of the church with his arms wide in a welcome.

"Why do we have the pleasure of your visit, my lord? Are you simply passing through like these pilgrims from Split?"

Bogun drew his horse to a halt, but he didn't dismount. He surveyed the villagers, who had all stopped what they were doing to watch the proceedings. He nodded at the mill and the granary beside it.

"We require your flour."

The priest's smile faltered. "Of course, we will be happy to sell you as much as we can spare."

"We are not traders. You will give it all to us."

Radoslav was stunned by Bogun's statement. He had no idea

that's why they had come here. The priest looked around at the assembled townspeople, who outnumbered Bogun's men tenfold and were both fearful and angry at this pronouncement.

"But, my lord," the priest said, "we need our grain to last us until the next harvest."

Bogun dismounted and approached the priest. Radoslav felt it his duty to support his captain, so he got down from his horse and stood behind Bogun.

"This grain belongs to Emperor Dušan," Bogun said. "He requires it for his campaigns against our enemies."

Radoslav didn't know why Bogun would say that. The armies at war were far from this town and well fed.

Then he realized what was actually happening. Bogun and his men were thieves. The only possible answer was that they were taking the grain and flour to sell for themselves and collect the profits.

"I can't let you deprive us of our food," the priest said.

"I'll deprive you of your life if you stand in our way."

Radoslav's hand moved slowly to his sword. He could feel the tension crackle through the crowd. A mob was a dangerous thing if provoked.

He kept his focus on Bogun. He didn't know what he'd do if Bogun carried out his threat.

A fast movement caught Radoslav's attention out of the corner of his eye. Sensing the oncoming jeopardy, he drew his sword and whipped around to see one of the townsmen charging at Bogun with a raised dagger. At the same time, the priest shouted, "No!"

It all happened quickly. Before Radoslav knew what he was doing, he instinctively protected his captain. He thrust his sword at the attacker before he could reach Bogun, stabbing him through the chest.

The villagers screamed and began running in all directions. Cedozar shouted for his men to fight. The chaos seemed to give license to the rest of Bogun's gang to begin slaughtering whoever was close by, including the pilgrims who scattered in the commotion.

The priest fell back and called for his parishioners to head to the safety of the church with him. Many answered the call, but dozens of men and women were cut down by the attacking force, even the ones who didn't fight back.

Bogun, his sword drawn and already bright red with blood from one of the villagers, grabbed Radoslav by the shoulder.

"You've done well. Now go secure the mill."

Radoslav nodded dumbly and staggered in that direction as the rampage continued around him. It was as if Bogun's men had been itching for an excuse to start the butchering.

Radoslav flung open the door to the mill and slammed it shut behind him. He stood there with his back to the wall, his eyes clenched shut, his chest heaving. He realized he'd gotten away from the horrors of war only to fall into a situation far worse.

His eyes fluttered open when he heard the sound of a child whimpering. He circled the millstone and saw a boy cowering in the corner. He was about to reach out to him when the noise of feet shuffled behind him on the dusty floor.

He turned just in time to see a man fly at him, a dagger coming down at his face. He reacted as he'd been trained without even thinking. His sword flew up to block the blow, but he used more force than was needed. It not only pushed the knife out of the way, but the edge of his blade caught the attacker across the side of his neck.

The man dropped the dagger and tottered backward holding his neck, blood spurting out between his fingers. He dropped to his knees and then fell against the millstone's brake as he toppled over. The noise of the grinding stone filled the room.

The boy ran to the man and kneeled beside him.

"Papa!" the boy cried out. "Papa!"

"Dmitar," the man said as the life drained from him. "Dmitar, find your mama." He turned his face upward and smiled slightly as he said, "Hicela, my love, protect our boy." Then he went still and silent.

Radoslav recoiled in horror, forcing down the bile that threatened to come up. The pilgrim's hat the man was wearing indicated he was one of the group from Split. This father had only been trying to protect his son.

"I'm sorry," Radoslav said. "I'm so sorry."

"Radoslav!" came a call from outside. It was Bogun. He was coming this way. If he found the boy here, he'd kill him in an instant. Or worse, force Radoslav to do it.

Radoslav dropped his sword and clamped his hand around the boy's mouth as he picked him up and took him over to a large pile of hay against the far wall. He buried the boy in the mound and said, "Dmitar, you must be quiet or they will kill you. Do you understand?"

The boy, tears streaming down his cheeks, nodded. Radoslav took his hand away and hastily tossed the hay over his head. He went back to his sword and picked it up just as the door swung open.

Bogun entered and looked down at the father's dead body. "I see you again did your duty to me as promised."

Radoslav nodded, praying that the boy would stay quiet. "My lord, the rest of the mill is empty."

"Good. Then we can begin loading the flour."

"And the townspeople?"

Bogun grinned and nodded toward the door. "See for yourself."

Radoslav exited while Bogun gathered his men at the granary and gave them instructions about loading the grain and flour into the oxcarts. At least the child was now temporarily safe.

Radoslav circled the mill to be greeted by the horrific sight of the church roof ablaze with three men preventing the doors from opening. Men, women, and children were screaming inside, but there was nothing he could do.

The rest of the village was a battlefield. Townspeople's bodies were strewn about where they'd fallen. This time, Radoslav did get sick, vomiting violently. The three men at the church pointed at him and laughed at his weakness.

Radoslav wiped his mouth on his sleeve and took the reins of his horse, slowly walking it toward the stream as if he were taking it for a drink.

But when he was on the other side of the church and out of view, he mounted the saddle. He couldn't stay and profit from this terror. He was a loyal servant of Serbia and the emperor, but this butchery had no purpose but greed.

Confirming that he was unseen, he spurred his horse across the bridge and out of the doomed town back the way he'd come. Bogun and Cedozar would eventually realize that he'd deserted and might come after him, so he couldn't return to Serbia. He'd be hanged the moment his treachery to Bogun was revealed, no matter that he would be telling the truth about what had happened here, and Bogun would no doubt say that he was just feeding his men.

Once he was out of earshot, he rode hard across the valley, thinking that Dalmatia and the Venetian Republic would be the best place for him to go, although he didn't know what he'd do when he got there except sell his horse to buy food and a roof over his head. Maybe he could find a place as an apprentice cooper—his training before his lord in his hometown had forced him into the army to make the requisite numbers demanded by the emperor.

Radoslav was still considering his plans when he heard a massive explosion. He brought his horse to a stop and turned in his saddle. The mill and granary were completely destroyed and burning. Then came the distant rumble of thunder even though there were no clouds in the sky. In the distance he saw what looked like half the snowy mountain descending on the town like a giant ocean wave. After it came to a stop, the entire town was buried, snuffing out the smoldering fires at the church and mill.

He didn't know if it was right to do so, but he prayed that Bogun and his men were entombed in that snow. If Bogun did somehow survive, hopefully when he discovered that Radoslav was missing, he would think he died in the disaster.

Then Radoslav saw two horses on the other side of the town. It was much too far away to make out the faces of who was on those horses, but he recognized the small shape of a boy and the skirts of a woman. Perhaps Dmitar had found his mother Hicela. He prayed that was true.

Then closer to him, he saw Cedozar approach the river at the edge of the snow's reach. He pulled Bogun out of the water. Bogun held his hand to his ear and yelled something at Radoslav that was unintelligible from this distance.

It was now clear that Radoslav could never return to his homeland. He knew that with certainty. If he did, his life would be over. Instead he would make his way to Split and find some means of atoning for his many sins.

November, 1351

THE RIDGE WALL OF STON

Willa didn't think she'd ever be climbing the wall that snaked over the ridge, but she needed an isolated place to test out the rocket they had finished making this morning. And because they'd be launching it from the walls of Mali Ston, she wanted to be somewhere high to see how far it would fly. Petar and Jelena insisted on accompanying her since they had both helped in the production, Petar with the black powder and Jelena with the tube. Although Marija had assisted too, she declined to make the arduous trek and agreed to stay in the town with Zrinka, who had been watching over Emerik while the others concentrated on the rockets.

They paused two-thirds of the way up to catch their breath. The spectacular view from this dizzying height stretched from the port at Mali Ston in the east to the inlet at Ston to the west, with the mountain rising from the valley below and towering above them. But they weren't yet high enough to see the salt pans or the town of Ston on the other side of the ridge.

"I don't understand why this wall is here," Willa said, dabbing the sweat from her face with a kerchief. "How does this defend against an army when we're so high up?"

The wall was wide enough for them to walk two abreast, with regular crenellations and towers for the soldiers' protection. But from what?

Petar waved his hand at the valley below. "From here you can see the movements of any attacking army. It protects the entire peninsula from a land invasion and discourages an enemy from attempting to scale the mountain and attack Mali Ston from the rear. But I think the real reason is that when we have a wall around Ston, you'd be able to walk all the way from Ston to Mali Ston and back without ever being exposed to anyone besieging us."

"It seems like constructing a wall around Ston would have been a bigger priority."

"The shallow water on the Ston side is ideal for salt pans, but that means there's no deep water for a port. All the shipping happens out of the port at Mali Ston. So that's why Mali Ston has such walls, to discourage attacks from the sea. Anyone would have to attack by land."

"And we should be further along building our walls in Ston," Jelena added, "but Lord Vitomir ceased all work, saying it was too expensive and had no purpose because Venice would protect us. I think we can now see why he did that."

"I refuse to call him *Lord* Vitomir," Petar said.

"I think the rector of Dubrovnik will strip him of that title after learning of his betrayal," Willa said. "What's more important now is making sure we can defend Ston and Mali Ston until they send help to us."

Willa didn't let on that she was doubtful the replacement messenger Petar had sent this morning by sea would convince the rector of an attack. Because the ship would have to sail all the way around the peninsula, even if he could persuade the rector, help wouldn't arrive for days, but she had to put on an encouraging demeanor to keep Petar, Jelena, and the rest of the townspeople from giving up.

With the rocket held lightly in her hand, she continued up the steps one by one. Eventually they reached the flat section at the top that curved around to the other side of the ridge. She stopped there instead of taking the route down to Ston.

Given how a tiny amount of the black powder had nearly burned down Petar and Jelena's home, she wanted to get far from any flammable buildings. But they had to test it out before they built any more of the rockets.

Eventually Willa and Jelena had figured out the best way to make the rocket. The black powder was poured into a tube that was sealed at one end. They used a rod to pack it tightly so that it became almost solid, then added a rolled linen string dangling through the tube that was packed with a tiny amount of the black powder along its length. The tube was lashed to the front of one of Willa's precious arrows, among the ones that were still intact after shooting them at Vitomir and his men as they fled.

According to Marco Polo, when the rolled string was lit, it would burn along its length until it ignited the black powder in the tube, which would cause the arrow to fly all on its own. Supposedly, an arrow's fletching would make it fly straight and true, but she had no idea what would happen when it reached its target. That's why they were now far from both towns.

Petar was carrying a stand they'd built to hold the rocket and arrow in place when she lit the string. He set it down so that it was pointed through one of the crenellations in the wall.

"What are we aiming at?" Jelena said.

"Nothing," Willa said. "I think we should first see how far it can go. We don't want to build more and only when the attack happens discover that they go no farther than the reach of my bow and arrow."

"Or it may simply explode on the stand," Petar said.

"Which is why we're out here."

"Will it set the forest on fire?" Jelena asked.

Petar shook his head. "The recent rains have left the ground and greenery too damp."

"I don't understand at all how this rocket is supposed to work."

"By my reading and the drawings where he showed these weapons being used," Willa said, "Marco Polo describes flames shooting out the rear of the rocket, propelling the arrow to great distances and causing fires wherever it lands."

"It sounds like a ghastly weapon."

"Let's hope the Serbians feel the same way when it is shot at them."

Willa carefully placed the rocket arrow on the stand. It was pointed up at an angle. If Polo's description was correct, it should fly all the way across the valley to the ridge on the opposite side.

"Are we ready?" she asked.

Jelena nodded, fear in her eyes at the hellish demonstration to come.

Standing far from the rocket, Petar took out his flint and steel and lit the cold torch he'd been carrying. None of them had wanted to hold an open flame anywhere near the rocket filled with black powder.

When he had the torch lit, he handed it to Willa. Then he backed away with his arm protectively around Jelena. He seemed to be even warier of it than she was.

Willa held the torch to the linen string with her arm outstretched, ready to collapse to the ground if it burned too quickly.

It caught fire, and Willa scrambled far away with Petar and Jelena, who had her hands over her ears anticipating another explosion.

Willa counted to herself as the powder in the rolled string burned. She wanted to know how long to make a similar one for the coming battle.

At the count of fifteen, the flame reached the tube.

Nothing happened.

"No!" Willa cried in frustration, taking a step toward it. "It didn't work."

But she spoke a moment too soon.

Flames blasted out of the rocket's tail end, which sent the arrow flying forward at an unbelievable speed. The burning of the black powder left a trail of acrid smoke in its wake and made the hissing sound of an angry snake.

The three of them rushed to the battlement to watch it soar into the sky, cheering at the success of their launch.

Again, their elation came a moment too soon.

The arrow began to arc higher and higher, aiming straight up into the sky. Then the rocket rattled within the strings holding it to the arrow's shaft, throwing the assembly into a tumbling course.

Even though she thought she had anchored it as Marco Polo had instructed, the rocket completely detached from the arrow and looped around until it was coming right back at them.

"Down!" Willa yelled.

Petar threw himself on top of Jelena, while Willa dropped to her knees and curled up against the stone wall. Nevertheless, she couldn't take her eyes off the rocket plunging from almost straight above her down toward the ground.

It slammed into the outer side of the wall not thirty feet away, sending a cascade of flame into the air with a deafening crack. A plume of dark smoke billowed into the air and then was carried off by the breeze.

With the danger passed, the three of them stood. Willa went over to the site of the impact to inspect the damage. The stone was scarred by the blast, the surface as black as tar. The wall may have survived, but if the rocket landed in the middle of an army, the effects would be devastating. She was glad she'd insisted on this location for the test shot.

Jelena stared wide-eyed at the impact point.

"We could have been killed."

"That's exactly what we wanted, my dear," Petar said, shaking his head in amazement at the charred stone.

"But if that happened when we shoot it from the town wall, we could set all of Mali Ston on fire."

"We'll keep trying them out until we know why it didn't fly the way it should have," Willa said.

Petar picked up the stand, and they began the walk back down to Mali Ston to make the next rocket. Willa already thought she knew what they could do to attach the rocket to the arrow more securely.

"How many arrows do you have?" Petar asked.

"Between mine and Gerard's, we have enough. I'm more worried about how much black powder we can make. You're sure your mother doesn't have any more sulfur hidden somewhere?"

Jelena shook her head. "You've seen all of it."

"Then by my guess, we have enough ingredients for ten more rockets at most."

"That won't be enough to fight back an entire army, will it?" Petar asked.

"I've been thinking about how the Serbians believe in curses and prophecies," Willa said. "I think the words of the Ston prophecy may be able to guide us. Jelena, you said your mother is an expert seamstress. Do you have canvas for sails in Mali Ston?"

"Of course. We repair the fishing boats all the time."

"Lumber, nails, and hinges?"

"I think so."

"Why would you need all that?" Petar asked.

"If the Serbians are afraid to face a dragon, perhaps we should show them one."

 48

HVAR

A hefty palmful of coins to the fortress guards allowed Radoslav
to walk free from his cell. As Fox had listened to Radoslav's story,
he was shocked to realize that it matched Cristoval's perfectly. Yet
when Fox led him outside, Radoslav embraced Cristoval warmly.
Fox was sure that their shared history in Bosnia was unknown
to either of them or the sparring sessions they had fought before
would have been far deadlier. But Radoslav's guilt no doubt made
him carefully avoid any mention of his experience to anyone, while
Cristoval's pain at losing his brother similarly kept him silent. It
was only because Fox offered them both the chance to confront
their mutual foe that each had told him their story.

The Serb's regret in his role at the town massacre seemed
genuine. A young man following his fighting instincts and the
orders of his superior were hard resist, yet he had refused to
participate in outright murder, which made him a better man than
Bogun. In the end, Fox saw no choice but to accept his help, hide
what he knew from both Cristoval and Radoslav, and hope that
he was making the right decision.

After introducing Radoslav to Tino and to Nika as Niko, the
five of them began the trek back to town. The Serbian had made
only one request before setting off, and Fox had agreed to honor
it since it would only delay their departure until the next ringing
of the church bells. In his shock at hearing Radoslav's story and
realizing the link to Cristoval, Fox had forgotten all about the
wedding Radoslav had mentioned. He couldn't see any harm in

letting Radoslav witness the ceremony, even though Radoslav insisted for some reason that Fox be the only one to know about it.

When they reached the town square, it was already crowded with townspeople there for the wedding, which would take place on the steps of the church at the end of the piazza.

Fox pointed to Tino, Cristoval, and Nika. "You three wait here. I'm going to take Radoslav to get his things. Then we'll head back to the ship."

"Do you want our help?" Cristoval asked.

Radoslav shook his head. "It isn't much. We won't be long."

As they exited the square, Fox said, "Where are we really going?"

"I know a place. I just want to watch. I need to be sure it's done."

Radoslav guided the two of them around the side of a three-story building that abutted the central piazza. He reached under his tunic, withdrawing a key.

"I know this building," Fox said. "This is where we found the journeyman cooper."

"It's the back entrance to his workshop and house. Don't worry. He won't be using it today. And I took the liberty of borrowing the cooper's key."

After closing the door behind them, they went up the stairs to the top floor. The window had an expansive view of the piazza. Fox stood to one side of the opening while Radoslav was opposite him.

Fox could make out Cristoval, Tino, and Nika mingling with the crowd that had gathered to watch the ceremony.

"Looks like a big event," Fox said.

"The bride is wealthy," Radoslav said. "She's an alewife and owns the largest brewery in Hvar."

The wedding procession marched into the square. Leading it was the groom, who was the journeyman Fox had met earlier in the day.

"I've met him, though I didn't catch his name."

"That's Kresimir. He's a good man. He'll make a fine husband."

Behind him was a woman dressed in wedding finery. Next to her was a boy a little younger than Nika.

Radoslav regarded them with a bittersweet expression.

"That's Hicela and Dmitar," he said with a somber tone.

Fox stared at Radoslav in astonishment. "The mother and child pilgrims from the Bosnian massacre?"

Radoslav nodded. "I killed her first husband."

"You didn't mean to."

"Does it matter to a boy who saw me cut down his father?"

Fox couldn't argue with that point.

"Now you see why I can't be down there. I couldn't risk Dmitar seeing me."

Fox suddenly understood. "You came to make amends. How did you find them?"

Radoslav shrugged as if it were a trifle. "I knew their names and that they were from Split, but Split is a big city. I finally found out that her husband was a successful brewer there. When he died, his business was taken over by his brother, leaving her no choice but to return home to Hvar where she was originally from. Her father was a brewer and had arranged her first marriage with Ivanis, whom he knew through the business. Then her father passed on, leaving her as the heir here to his brewing business."

Hicela and Kresimir walked up to the front porch of the church where all weddings were held. The crowd went quiet as the priest began the service, but they were too far to hear his words.

"What brought you here?" Fox asked in a hushed voice.

"When I discovered that she had come to Hvar, I followed her here to see if there was anything I could do for her and Dmitar. It was then that I learned that she had found happiness with Kresimir. But his master wasn't pleased with the prospect. You'd think a barrel maker could hold his wine, but it only took a couple of bottles to get him to admit he was worried that Kresimir, whom he admitted was a talented cooper, would join forces with the biggest brewer in Hvar and drive him out of business."

Fox suddenly noticed that Cristoval was whispering excitedly to Tino next to him and pointing at the bride. He must have recognized Hicela.

"Is that why you fought with him?"

"It was more than that," Radoslav said. "He bragged to me that he was going to cause the wedding to be called off."

"How would he do that?"

"In the cruelest way possible." Radoslav looked as if he'd eaten a rotten apple. "The cooper was planning to force himself on Hicela. After that, she would have no choice but to marry him and be the miserable bride of an unprincipled and greedy man."

Fox nodded. "So you created the brawl to get you both locked in cells."

"It worked. The cooper, whose putrid name I won't use, is unable to watch this joyous occasion from his current accommodations. I wouldn't have been able to, either, until you showed up, but it would have been a worthy tradeoff."

As the priest pronounced the couple husband and wife to the cheers of the crowd, Fox was now certain that Radoslav would be an asset to them.

Below them, Cristoval was angling toward Hicela. Fox couldn't let Radoslav see that Cristoval knew her or the two of them might kill each other before they even left Hvar.

Fox moved to the other side of the window so that Radoslav had to turn away from the scene below to talk to him.

"I admire you for how you've atoned for your previous misdeeds," Fox said. "But I suggest you start clean, and never tell anyone what brought you to Hvar." Fox knew he had to keep Radoslav from mentioning Hicela to Cristoval at all costs.

Radoslav gave him the barest smile. "Thank you, Sir Gerard. But I won't ever be fully whole, certainly not while Bogun draws air. I'm grateful that you're giving me this chance to make things right."

Fox stole a glance at the piazza and saw Cristoval reunite with Hicela. The look on her face was ecstatic, and she kissed his hand numerous times in thanks before introducing her savior to her new husband, who shook his hand with vigor.

"You've done well so far. I'm sure you will be welcomed in Ston."

"You think they'll accept a Serbian's help?"

"If I'm with you, I think they will."

Radoslav turned back to the view outside, but by this time, Cristoval had finished conveying his congratulations to the happy couple, who were now speaking to other friends and family.

"I hope she has a good life and bears him many children."

"She wouldn't have any children right now if it weren't for you," Fox said.

Radoslav didn't answer. The evidence was simply there to see.

"I suppose it's time to go."

"Yes. I'd like to return to my own wife."

"Then we should get to the ship."

As Radoslav walked away, Fox could see that the children of the town had gathered to play games on this celebratory day. Nika frolicked with Dmitar, tapping him on the shoulder and then running from his touch screaming in joy like any child would. Dmitar was giggling with abandon at her antics. Fox reveled in her ability to have a few moments of fun with a boy she'd just met, but it also reminded him that she was just playing at being an adult. It only made him want to reunite Nika with her parents that much more, and perhaps with Radoslav's help, they could give her a chance at her own wedding someday.

 49

THE ADRIATIC SEA, SOUTH OF HVAR

The laughter around the table temporarily made Nika forget about how much she missed her parents, her little brother, and her grandmother. While eating their evening dinner below deck as they sailed from Hvar toward Ston, she, Tino, Cristoval, and Radoslav listened to Gerard telling a story about a thief he'd tried to apprehend in the middle of the night during a rainstorm.

"We were sleeping in a tavern, my wife and I, and I woke to find him pulling on my satchel. Before I was fully awake, he was out the door. I chased him in my bare feet and wearing nothing but my braies. It was pouring rain outside, but I caught up to him."

"Did you get your satchel back?"

"Oh, I caught him, all right, but the ground was so slippery that I fell face first into a puddle. I got the bag, but I was covered head to toe with mud. I must have looked a pig in slop when I got back to the tavern."

"And the thief?" Cristoval asked.

"Escaped into the night. But I'd wager that he wouldn't have sneaked into a tavern if he had known that a nearly naked crazy man was going to give chase!"

They all laughed at that. Even Radoslav, who had been serious ever since they'd gotten him out of prison, let out a chuckle.

Tino held up a finger. "I've got you beat."

Radoslav raised an eyebrow. "Better than a nighttime mud bath in only your braies?"

"How about fully naked outside a brothel?"

"I have to hear this," Cristoval said.

"Niko doesn't need to," Gerard said, who looked troubled about the indecent story. "He should go up on deck."

"Oh, come now," Tino said. "He'll be a man soon enough. He needs to learn these things."

"I do need to learn," Nika said, feigning innocence.

Gerard obviously wanted to protest more, but she knew he couldn't without revealing her true identity. She grinned at his discomfort. Gerard gave up with an amused shrug.

Tino took a swig of his ale. Although he'd been drinking in small but steady amounts since they left Hvar, he wasn't drunk like the first time Nika had met him.

"It was my first time in a brothel." He leaned down to Nika and nudged her arm. "You'll find out what those are soon enough, little man. I was just about to bed my very first woman when someone outside the door yells at the top of their voice, 'Fire! Fire!' Well, I'd almost died in a fire when I was a boy, which my friend Venzi knew very well."

"So you ran out of the room without any clothes on?" Nika asked, wondering what her mother would think of this conversation.

"Worse," Tino said. "We were on the second floor. I jumped out the window. Landed in the street just as my mother was walking by."

"What did you say to her?" Gerard asked, holding on to his belly as he guffawed.

"What do you think I said? When I saw there was no smoke and realized Venzi was laughing his guts out from the front door of the brothel, I kissed her on the cheek, told her I had unfinished business, and went right back up to the room to become a man."

"And how long did that take?" Cristoval said.

"Oh, I was done, clothed, and walking my mamma home before she reached the end of the street."

Nika didn't understand why the men went into uproarious laughter at that, but the effect was contagious, and she joined in.

When it died down, Gerard nodded at Cristoval. "What about our Spanish friend? Are things different in Spain?"

Cristoval shook his head. "I wasn't the one who got in trouble back home. It was my younger brother Lorenzo. I remember one time our older sister beat his naked backside with a stick to find out where he'd put the honey cakes that he'd stolen from her. And that man became a priest."

They all laughed again, but Nika noticed a sadness in Cristoval's eyes when he didn't join in.

"Now you, Radoslav," Gerard said.

The Serbian shook his head. "I'm not a storyteller like you all are."

"There must be something," Tino prompted. "You can't have been clothed your whole life."

Radoslav paused, then said, "There *was* one time with a pig."

"That's always a good way to start."

"Like Sir Gerard in the mud?" Nika said with a giggle.

"It was a piglet, really," Radoslav said. "I was supposed to be looking after it, but it got away from me on the summer feast day. I finally found it somewhere it wasn't supposed to be."

"Where was that?" Gerard asked.

"In the giant pot holding the stew that was to be served to the town leaders."

"Oh, no!" Nika exclaimed. "Did it drown? Or get boiled?"

Radoslav shook his head. "It was fine. It had fallen in and eaten its fill, but it couldn't get out. I pulled him out just before the cook could see what happened."

"So the feast was ruined," Cristoval said.

"Not at all. The mayor of our town proclaimed that that stew was the best meal the cook had ever made. I told him we used tender young pork!"

Cristoval's mirth returned as they all fell on the floor in hilarity. Radoslav seemed bemused that the others found it so funny.

Gerard got to his feet and said, "I've got to go send some of this ale overboard."

"You're going to be sick again?" Nika asked.

He shook his head. "My stomach is surprisingly well. I got plenty of ginger in Hvar."

When he left, the conversation stalled, with the three mercenaries eyeing each other quietly. The silence felt awkward to Nika.

"How long until we reach Ston?" she asked the group.

"Shouldn't take too long," Tino said. "You're ready to get back home, eh?"

Nika nodded solemnly.

"I know how that feels. I wish I could return to my home."

"Why don't you?"

"I can't. Never again. I guess I'll just keep moving these old bones from place to place. Or maybe this will be my last battle."

"From the sound of what we're up against," Radoslav said, "this might be the last battle for all of us."

"As long as I get to kill Bogun," Cristoval said, "I don't care."

"You might have competition for that honor, my friend," Radoslav replied.

"What's important is that he doesn't take my town," Nika said. "Ston is where my parents are. You're all coming to save them, aren't you?"

Cristoval nodded but wouldn't look her in the eye. Tino smiled at her but said nothing. Radoslav tilted his head at her.

"We'll do our best. You know, you remind me of a boy I once met. Dmitar. He thought he'd lost his mother once, but he found her again, just like you'll find your parents."

Nika smiled, which was the only way she could keep from crying. Cristoval had an odd look on his face as he studied Radoslav.

"Dmitar," Cristoval said. "That boy Niko was playing with was named Dmitar."

"He was?" Nika said. He was fun to play with, but she'd never heard his name.

"His mother was Hicela," Cristoval continued, staring at Radoslav. "I met them in a town in Bosnia."

Radoslav glanced at Cristoval with a horrified look and something passed between them, but Nika didn't know what it meant. Tino seemed to notice as well.

"What's going on?" he asked.

"You were there," Cristoval snarled. "You were with him. Bogun."

Radoslav hesitated, a pained expression on his face, before he finally spoke. "I didn't know what he was going to do."

"Liar! You were with that monster when he killed my brother!" Cristoval launched himself at Radoslav, but Tino put himself between them and held him back. Nika could see rage flare in Cristoval's eyes.

Just then, Gerard returned and rushed over to help Tino push Cristoval back.

"What's happening here? We were all laughing, and then I leave for a few moments, and I come back to find you at each other's throats?"

"He was riding with Bogun," Cristoval said, jabbing his finger at Radoslav. "He was there in Bosnia when my brother died."

Gerard grimaced at Radoslav. "I thought you weren't going to tell them."

Cristoval rounded on Gerard. "You knew?"

"Yes, but it's not what you think. He didn't realize what Bogun intended to do to those villagers. He fled when it was clear what was happening."

"That's even worse. He could have protected them."

"He would have been killed like the rest of them."

"I have no idea what's going on here," Tino said, "but it doesn't sound good."

"He's right," Radoslav said. "I'm a coward. I should have done more."

"He's not much older than this one," Tino said to Cristoval while pointing at Nika. "We all make mistakes when we're young."

"So you're defending him?" Cristoval yelled.

Accusations went back and forth, and it seemed to Nika like their band was falling apart, which meant death for Ston and her parents. She had to do something to put a stop to it. She could think of only one thing.

"I'm a girl!" she cried out.

The four men went silent.

Tino squinted at her. "What did you say?"

"I'm a girl. You all call me Niko, but really I'm Nika. I'm pretending to be a boy. Gerard said it would be easier."

The eyes of the three mercenaries turned to Gerard.

"She's telling the truth," he said. "I thought it was better to keep it to ourselves."

Cristoval appraised her. "You fooled me. That's not easy to do."

"Now that you've stopped shouting at each other," Nika said, "maybe you can see we are all on the same side. I need you to fight for Ston, not with each other."

"Cristoval," Gerard said gently, "before he knew your story, Radoslav told me that he saved Dmitar from Bogun. That's why I believe him. He's the reason the boy could get back to his mother."

Radoslav looked at Cristoval. "You said you met them."

Cristoval clenched his jaw before speaking. "I got them out of that slaughter and took them back to their family in Split. After my brother was killed by Bogun."

Radoslav nodded. "I will help you get your revenge on him. I owe you a life debt, and I'll repay it."

That seemed to mollify Cristoval enough so that he was no longer ready to kill Radoslav, even if just barely.

"That's all well and good," Gerard said. "I'm glad we can have some peace in here for now. But I was coming down here to say that we may need your fighting skills sooner than we thought."

"Why is that?" Tino asked.

"Because when I was up on deck, the captain told me that a ship is pursuing us. Apparently, he recognized them as a notorious group from a town called Omiš. Pirates."

 50

Despite the captain's best efforts, the swift pirate ship from Omiš was steadily gaining. Fox wished he had his bow and arrows, but Legend would have to do. The sailors were ready to repel boarders, but they weren't trained fighters like Cristoval, Tino, and Radoslav. The four of them would have to make a stand against what looked like twenty pirates ready to take whatever they could.

That bounty might include Nika if they figured out she was a girl.

He watched the pirates that were only a few ship's lengths away. At least they didn't have bows or crossbows. They would have used them by now. They held a mixture of swords and pikes in their hands.

"Go below deck," he ordered Nika.

"Why?" Nika said. "I can help out here."

"No, you can't. These men will kill you without a second thought if they find you."

She grabbed on to his hand and looked scared for the first time. "Will they kill *you*?"

Fox didn't like to make any promises that he couldn't keep, but her pleading eyes convinced him that honesty wasn't going to help in this situation.

"I'm not going to let anything happen to you or to me. Now go below before I carry you down."

She gently squeezed his hand, and the small gesture gave him an unexpected feeling of warmth. He hadn't ever been fond of children before, but he had to admire her will and resourcefulness. Her affection for him made him feel a surprising sense of protectiveness.

He would keep his promise to her. He would make it through this, both for Nika's sake and so that he would see Willa again.

Fox went over to Cristoval and Tino, who were conferring with each other. Radoslav stood slightly away from them, studiously ignoring Cristoval.

"We're going to have to fight together, you know," Fox said to Cristoval.

"That's what I told him," Tino said, "but apparently Spaniards hold grudges."

"Anyone would in my place," Cristoval growled. "He was a party to my brother's death."

"No, Bogun was," Fox said. "I believe Radoslav."

"Serbians can't be trusted."

"You can see the guilt he carries for what he's done. He came all the way to Hvar to help Hicela and Dmitar build a new life, and that's what he did. I've met Bogun. If Radoslav were of the same ilk, he'd still be riding with him."

"I'll fight for you if it gets me to Bogun. Just keep him away from me."

Cristoval stalked off, but he had his hand on his sword, ready to draw it when the pirates attacked.

"I remember when I was that young," Tino said. "You feel the weight of the world pressing on your shoulders, and all you want to do is push back."

Fox took in the aging mercenary, his beard graying, wrinkles creasing his eyes and cheeks. Although Tino had kept his sense of humor all these years as a vagabond, Fox could tell from their conversations that he longed for somewhere to put down roots. It was easy for Fox to imagine himself in the same position at his age if he hadn't found Willa.

"What keeps you going now?"

"Besides wine?" Tino said with a chuckle. "The chance to do something worthwhile with whatever time I have left. That's why I decided to come with you. One last grand adventure."

"You sound as if you plan to die."

Tino nodded at the pirates, who weren't far behind them. "I'm not saying I won't fight tooth and claw for my life. I'll take at least some of these wretches with me, but it very well may happen today."

"It won't."

"How can you be so sure?"

"Because I have to get back to my wife." Fox took off his wedding ring and held it up so that Tino could see the Latin words inscribed on the inside, *UBI AMOR IBI FIDES*. "Where there is love, there is faith."

Tino became uncharacteristically melancholy. "It must be nice to have love. Hold on to it."

"That's what keeps *me* going."

"It's worth fighting for." Tino looked up at the ropes dangling from the mast. "And I have an idea for the fight."

Before Fox could ask him what that idea was, Tino was belying his age and clambering up the mast with the agility of a cat.

They didn't have much time before the pirates caught up to them, so Fox went over to the brooding Radoslav to see if he was going to be of use in the coming battle.

"Are you well?"

"Cristoval hates me," Radoslav said. "As he should."

Fox nodded. "I was in the English army when we invaded France. Fifteen thousand soldiers marching through the Normandy countryside. I was witness to the most horrific behavior as the army wiped out entire towns on our advance toward battle with the French." Shame gripped him as he recounted the tale. "I couldn't have stopped it. Even if the king had given the order to cease the pillaging, the soldiers were too bloodthirsty to heed the command. I couldn't even save my mother's estate. The best I could do was save our servants."

Radoslav shook his head. "At least you accomplished that."

"You saved a Croatian boy you didn't even know. You did what you could. If you had defied Bogun, Dmitar would be dead and you'd be in the ground right now instead of here helping us." Fox tilted his head at the pirates, who were preparing to board the ship. "We're heavily outnumbered, but that doesn't mean we'll lose. If you give up, however, you're handing them an unearned victory."

"I always thought I would be a soldier protecting the Serbian Empire. I'm proud to be from Serbia. Proud of where I come from. I was taught that winning a battle against a worthy enemy is something to be admired."

"It is."

"But what Bogun had us doing wasn't a battle." Radoslav's eyes reflected the same shame that Fox had felt. "It was a slaughter. As if those people were animals to be butchered."

"Then help us right that wrong. Help us defeat Bogun once and for all."

"I'll do what I can. That is, if Cristoval doesn't kill me first."

"I don't think he will," Fox said, watching the scowling Spaniard. "But I wouldn't get within reach of his sword during this battle."

Fox had already told the mercenaries his strategy. The pirates would somehow try to latch on to their ship. Then they would swarm over the bulwarks to kill anyone who resisted. They might kill everyone anyway, which was their reputation, whether it was earned or false.

The first defensive tactic would be to cut any lines they threw over. Perhaps if enough of the pirates' devices were disabled, they might give up.

But even if they made it over, a fierce and determined defense could make all the difference. Pirates preferred easy prey, and if Fox and the others made them pay too heavy a price for their prize, they would retreat and look for another target.

The bow of the pirate ship pulled alongside, and Fox now saw how they planned to board. Three of the pirates were twirling ropes with grappling hooks attached to them.

Fox steadied his breathing, then crossed himself—his ritual before a battle—in the way he'd been taught to remember it.

Helmet, bollocks, shield, and sword. He drew Legend, and Cristoval and Radoslav armed themselves as well. Fox looked up to see Tino perched on the yardarm grasping a rope dangling from the top of the mast. The ship's crew were gathered toward the bow, armed with daggers and spears. They were prepared to fight, but Fox told them to stay out of the way unless it looked like the battle was getting out of hand.

"Ready!" Fox shouted, raising Legend over his head.

Cristoval, Tino, and Radoslav let out a bone-chilling war cry in response. Unfortunately, it did nothing to dissuade the pirates from attacking.

As one, the three grappling hooks came sailing over the bulwarks and latched on. The ropes were thick hemp, hard to cut. Nevertheless, Fox began to saw away with his sword's sharp Damascus-steel blade as the pirates hauled on the ropes to close the gap between the ships. Radoslav and Cristoval did the same with their ropes.

Fox severed his rope just as he got within range of the pikes being jabbed at him. Cristoval got through his, but Radoslav wasn't fast enough. The distance between the ships had shrunk enough for men to jump across.

As they did, Tino let out a cry and leaped from the yardarm, holding a rope in one hand and his sword in the other. He swooped directly over the men who were coming over. They weren't able to protect themselves from the attack on high, and Tino was able slice two of the men across the chest while sending a third toppling into the sea. He came to rest behind Fox.

"That's a start at least," he pronounced with a smile.

It still wasn't enough, however, to scare the pirates off. Urged on by their captain, the remainder began to scramble over, the ones with the pikes keeping Fox and the others at bay.

Immediately, the fight became a chaotic melee. Fox parried a pike shoved toward his face, grabbed the haft with his free hand, and pulled the wielder toward him, thrusting his sword through the man's stomach. But as soon as he was done with that one, two more pirates slashed at him with their swords.

Thankfully, they were brutal but unskilled. Fox was able to fight both of them off, disarming one, and slashing through the arm of the other.

With the temporary reprieve, he could see that Cristoval, Radoslav, and Tino were living up to their reputations. They were more than holding their own with their opponents. The problem was that they were outnumbered, and some of the other pirates began attacking the ship's crew.

Worse, he saw two men disappear below deck. Where Nika was hiding.

He took off after them, plunging into the gloom of the ship's bowels. Likely they were more interested in the linen, grain, and leather cargo that was being carried. He saw one of them cornering Nika.

"No!" Fox roared. He charged at one of the pirates, who was armed with an axe. He swung its heavy blade in sweeping turns that Fox couldn't knock aside.

He tried to keep one eye on Nika. The one nearer to her reared back with his sword, but Nika threw a handful of grain dust in his face. Then she kicked the temporarily blinded man in the nethers with her heel. The blow was strong enough to cause him to double over.

Nika didn't wait for him to recover. She ran up the stairs at the other end of the hold and out onto the deck.

Fox knew the danger she'd face up there, so he had to get to her. He waited for the axe to take another swing, and as it came around, he ducked under it and sliced the wielder's legs off at the knees.

The horrific scream got the attention of the second swordsman, but he was still blinking the dust out of his eyes. Fox made quick work of him with one swing and sprinted after Nika.

The battle was still raging up on deck, which was littered with bodies. Only a few of the crew had been hurt. Most of the victims were pirates.

Fox scanned the deck and saw Nika huddled against the bulwark, aghast at the carnage around her.

One of the pirates with a pike spotted her and stalked toward her for an easy kill. Fox raced over and tackled him so that the point of his pike missed Nika's head.

The pirate tried stabbing at Nika again, but Fox dropped Legend so he could hold back the pike with both hands. He was pinned against the bulwark with Nika beside him. If he could just shove it back for a moment, he'd be able to grab his sword to finish off the pirate.

He didn't have to. The pirate lost his head with a single slice of Radoslav's sword. He reached down to help Fox to his feet.

"Thank you," Fox said, grabbing Legend.

"You saved her," Radoslav said, nodding at Nika.

"And you saved me."

Yet another pirate ran toward them with a pike aimed at Radoslav's chest. But before he could get there, he stumbled forward and planted his face on the deck, a dagger embedded in his neck.

"Now I saved both of you," said Cristoval, who had thrown the knife from the other side of the ship. "Can we finish this?"

Tino, standing at the stern, seemed to be having the time of his life, actually grinning as he fought off two of the pirates, with another advancing on him.

Fox, Cristoval, and Radoslav all ran to his aid, each of them slaying one of the pirates.

Tino looked quite displeased at being rescued.

"You spoiled my fun!"

The four of them turned to see seven pirates staring at them. They must have been stunned at how easily their comrades were dispatched because they launched themselves back over to their ship. As soon as they were aboard, the pirate ship turned away.

With them gone, Fox looked around and saw Nika running toward him. She leaped into his arms, and Fox lifted her up. She buried her face in his shoulder, her chest heaving.

"I'm not crying," she said, her tremulous voice muffled by his tunic.

"I know," Fox replied. "You were very brave."

"So were you," Cristoval said, holding out his hand to Radoslav. Radoslav paused for a moment, then grasped the hand in his own. "You're injured," he said, thrusting his chin at a gash in Cristoval's arm.

"We can apply a cloth to it to hold it closed until it heals."

"Well, we're not dead, are we?" Tino said. He surveyed the corpses littering the deck. "I suppose we should start cleaning up this mess."

"Did we lose any of the ship's crew?" Fox asked.

"One dead and one wounded," Cristoval said.

"It would have been all of them if we hadn't been here," Tino said proudly.

Radoslav sheathed his sword. "I have some experience taking care of battle wounds. I'll see if I can do anything for the injured sailor." He looked at Cristoval. "Then I'll take care of you."

He walked toward the bow while Tino and Cristoval began checking the pirates to make sure none of them had survived.

Nika leaned back to look at Fox. Her eyes were red, but resolute. "Are battles always like that?"

Fox nodded. Nika pursed her lips in acknowledgment. "Do you think we have a chance against Bogun?"

Fox looked at the three mercenaries who had just come together to rout an experienced group of fighters. Then he focused on Nika and made himself smile for her benefit.

"An excellent chance."

 51

THE RIDGE WALL OF STON

Willa shook her head as she and Petar trekked down from their rocket-testing site for the third time in two days. The second try at firing it with a more secure connection to the arrow caused it to take off and plunge straight down toward the valley after traveling only fifty feet. And today on this test, something had gone wrong with the construction of the rocket itself. It exploded before it ever left the stand.

"Do you think this will really work?" Petar said. "Maybe we should think of something else."

"You don't believe in the prophecy?" Willa asked with a raised eyebrow.

He shook his head vehemently. "Of course I do. But we may not be understanding God's will."

"Marco Polo left us detailed plans. If we can build a rocket that flies the way he describes, I believe we will be able to drive Bogun back, which will fulfill the prophecy. We just need time."

"Which we may not have."

Willa looked back over her shoulder at the villager pacing along the high point of the wall far above them.

"That's why I think you had a good idea to station that man on the wall. He should be able to warn us of an army arriving on foot from either direction."

"The people of Ston will fight hard if we have to," Petar said, "but I fear that we aren't the soldiers that you're hoping we can be."

"With the gates of Mali Ston closed, Bogun will have to get over the walls somehow. As long as we can keep that from happening, we can hold out."

"But for how long? I've sent out a fishing boat from Mali Ston, but it's a long and treacherous route around the Stonski Rat peninsula to Dubrovnik. It could be some time before they get word to the rector, and who knows if they'll be believed, especially if Vitomir has returned to call them liars."

"Perhaps you should have gone. As the head saltman, you have the strongest voice to make that claim."

Petar shook his head again. "I won't abandon my town in its hour of need. Whatever happens to them happens to me."

"You're a good man, Petar. The people of Ston and Mali Ston are lucky to have you."

They were halfway back to Mali Ston when a surprising sight caught her eye. Sailing into the harbor was a large ship. It had been out of view when they were on the wall facing the valley. A number of men were assembled on the deck, but she couldn't make out who they were.

Willa's heart started pounding. Was the attack already beginning?

"Do you think that's Bogun?" she said.

"It's not the fishing boat I sent out."

The two of them hurried down the steps. They had to get back into town to help raise what defenses they could. If Willa could get to her bow and arrows quickly, she might be able to take down enough of them to make Bogun rethink his attack.

She surprised herself about how casually she now thought of killing men, and it disturbed her. Earlier this very year, she was a simple maid in service to a lady and had never killed anything larger than a rabbit during their childhood hunting ventures in the forests of Kent.

Now she was an experienced slayer, although every single time in defense of herself and others. She wanted to believe it never got easier, but it did. In fact, she was upset with herself for allowing Vitomir and the Serbian with him to get away.

Nevertheless, she girded herself to fight this afternoon if the arriving ship wasn't simply a trader here to exchange goods.

The ship pulled up to the dock as she and Petar descended below view of it. Together they raced for the small door leading from the wall into the town.

They burst through, shutting and barring it behind them. From this position, they could see that the doors of the gate leading to the harbor were wide open.

"Are they mad?" Petar cried out as they ran down the stairs to ground level.

Willa was right behind him. "Perhaps they recognize it as one of your regular trading partners."

"Who Bogun could have paid off."

Willa conceded he had a point. From what she knew about him and Vitomir, that could very well have been a tactic they'd use.

Their concern transformed to panic when a woman screamed.

"That's Jelena!" Petar shouted, taking the last set of steps in a single bound and going into a full sprint, leaving Willa trying to catch up.

She took a few moments to stop in the house where she was staying to pick up both her and Gerard's bows and arrows. Although she'd been training Petar to use the bow, he wasn't very skilled with it yet. Still, it was better than shooting arrows alone.

When she got to the gate, she saw Jelena running out toward the dock with Petar on her heels. Jelena held her hands out as she ran, and it was only when she bent down to sweep a child into her arms that Willa realized why.

Jelena twirled around with pure joy as she held Nika in a tight embrace. Petar, on the other hand, halted in his tracks, as if he couldn't believe what he was seeing. Then he snapped out of it and ran to them. The three of them clung together, Petar repeating Nika's name over and over.

"It's a miracle!" he added.

Willa didn't know how this return was possible. She'd seen Nika fall when Bogun had pushed her and Gerard over the wall.

Perhaps she had survived the fall, and these men had picked her up from the sea?

And if they had, maybe they knew something of Gerard as well. Willa saw three men—a fit older man, a younger man dressed in fine clothes that were marred by blood on one sleeve, and the youngest in more humble clothes—getting off the ship, all of them armed with swords. They didn't look like traders at all, but they didn't look hostile, either. Maybe they could tell her something useful.

Not wanting to interrupt Petar and Jelena's reunion with Nika, she went up to the swordsmen, and all three of them looked at her with interest.

"Excuse me, sirs," she said breathlessly. "This girl was with a man. Perhaps you found him…"

Willa didn't want to suggest the idea of them discovering his corpse, but she had to prepare herself for the worst of answers. If she could even see his body, at least she would know for certain.

The older man spoke first. "My name is Tino," he said in fluent Italian. "You must be Willa."

For a moment, she was flabbergasted at being called by name. "How do you know that?"

"There can't be many golden-haired beauties in this part of Dalmatia," the finely dressed man said with a strange accent. "I am called Cristoval."

"You know what I look like?"

The youngest man nodded and pointed at his own chest. "Radoslav. You are just as Gerard described you."

Her breath caught, and she forced herself to take in air. "Gerard? You know him?"

"He's why we're here," Cristoval said.

Willa looked around frantically. "Where is he?"

"We had to leave him on the ship," Tino said with a shrug. "The pirates made a mess of it."

Willa could hardly breathe. "Pirates." How could this man be so flippant about leaving the body of her husband on the ship? Her soul was shredded at the thought that Gerard had survived falling from a towering wall into the sea only to be killed by pirates.

"I have to see him," she said, and turned to run to the ship, only to freeze at the shocking sight in front of her.

Gerard *wasn't* dead. There he was, very much alive, walking down the gangplank. He spotted her and broke into the widest smile. As soon as his feet hit the dock, he ran toward her.

Up until this moment, she thought she'd been deluding herself that she'd somehow see him again despite the odds. But now her heart threatened to erupt from her chest as she dashed to him, dropping the bows and arrows as she ran.

She launched herself into his arms and pulled him tight to her. The familiar smell of him came back to her in a rush, causing her insides to melt. She badly wanted to kiss him, but she was too aware of the myriad eyes on them.

"I knew you were alive," she whispered into his ear. "I knew you'd come back to me."

"You could go to the ends of the earth," he said, "and I would find you."

Willa didn't want to let go, but she wanted to see him. She pulled back and took in his glorious face. It was just as she pictured in her mind every night before she went to sleep to dream of him.

"How did you get more beautiful in my absence?" he said.

"How did you get more charming?"

Gerard nodded at Cristoval, Tino, and Radoslav, who were watching them with amusement.

"Probably from being around these rogues."

"Who are they?"

"Men-at-arms who've come to defend Ston. I'm glad to see Bogun hasn't attacked yet."

"He tried to, with Vitomir's help. But we've found Marco Polo's book. It might give us an advantage."

"How so?"

"With rockets. What's this I heard about pirates?"

Gerard shrugged. "Just a minor inconvenience on our journey. I'm sorry it took me this long to come off the ship. I'm the only one in this group with any money, so I was paying the captain for getting us here. What's a rocket?"

"It sounds like we have much to tell each other," Willa said. "Such as where you've been for the past week."

"Spending my time with Nika. She's a girl, in case you didn't know already."

"Oh, I learned that long ago."

As he said that, Nika detached herself from her grandmother, brother, and cousin, who had joined in the celebration of her return. She trotted over to Gerard and took his hand.

"Thank you, Sir Gerard, for bringing me back home." She looked up at Willa shyly.

"You're welcome, little one. I'd like to present my wife, Willa, Lady Fox."

"It's nice to meet you, Lady Fox. Gerard talks about you a lot."

"He does? I hope he says nice things."

"I thought he was lying when he said how pretty you are, but he was telling the truth. Are you also as clever as he says?"

Willa bent down on one knee to look her in the eye. "I'm sure you're the clever one for getting away from Vitomir and returning here. And you may call me Willa."

Nika looked up at Gerard. "I like her."

"I do, too," he replied.

Petar and Jelena came over. Petar clapped him on the back. "You are a true knight and gentleman."

Then Jelena threw her arms around him and said, "I can never thank you enough for bringing our Nika back to us."

Gerard pointed to the mercenaries. "Nika is to thank for bringing help back to fight for Ston."

"She's lucky I don't make her rear raw with a switch for following us to Dubrovnik," Petar said.

"I'm sorry, Papa," Nika said. "I'll never leave Ston again."

"Don't be so hard on her, Petar," Jelena said. "She's been through enough."

"I wouldn't be here if it weren't for her," Gerard said. "I was in a bad state when she hailed the ship that picked us up. If not for that, we would have drowned for sure."

"All right," Petar said, mussing her hair. "But don't ever do anything like that again. Now let's go get you back in girls' clothes. Then we'll have a feast to celebrate."

All of them cleaned up before a huge meal was served. Fox, Willa, and the three mercenaries joined Petar's family at the head table. Incredible stories on both sides were related to gasps and appreciation. Tino had Marija, Zrinka, Nika, and Emerik in stitches over stories of his antics with his boyhood friend in Italy, while Fox, Cristoval, and Radoslav listened with wonder as Willa, Petar, and Jelena recounted their adventures with Marco Polo's rockets. Willa enjoyed the camaraderie of the newcomers getting to know the townspeople they'd come to fight for, but what she relished most was simply sitting beside Gerard, even venturing a few times to hold his hand under the table. For a little while, it felt like her normal life had returned.

It was only at the end of the meal that the mood was abruptly dispelled. A man burst into the room where they were eating. She recognized him as the villager who had been posted on top of the ridge wall. He was out of breath and could barely get out the message he'd run all the way to deliver.

"An army is coming!"

THE SACRIFICE

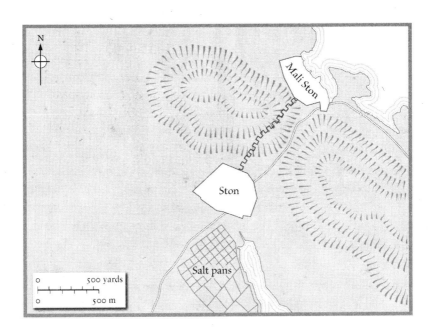

52

The town of Ston was completely empty, as Bogun had expected. All of the villagers had pulled back to safety behind the walls of Mali Ston. It wouldn't help them anyway now that he had rendezvoused with one of his other ships, which had landed at a tiny beach southwest of Ston. He had fifty men to take the town while they waited for the other hundred men to arrive as reinforcements.

As they marched to the valley leading to Mali Ston, Cedozar caught up to him.

"My lord, I've heard rumblings from some of the men about the Ston prophecy."

"What of it?"

"They know of the foreign stranger who was helping Petar and Jelena in Dubrovnik and the woman shooting arrows from the wall at me and Lord Vitomir."

"Vitomir's mouth is too big for his own good."

"Still, they are worried that the prophecy is being fulfilled. They're scared about facing a dragon's hellfire."

"How does the prophecy go again?"

Cedozar recited it from memory.

The lure of precious crystals sparks a dire threat to the White Fortress.
My hand guides strangers from across the sea to provide aid in this time of need.

*Hellfire rains down when a sacrifice summons a dragon to destroy
  any enemy refusing to flee.*
A miracle inspires a new leader to show the way to liberation.

"They think this Gerard Fox was the sacrifice," Cedozar went
on.

Bogun chuckled at that. "That was no sacrifice. He put up a
good fight before I threw him and that girl off the wall."

"Still, we need to make certain the men will fight."

Bogun stopped abruptly, so the entire column of men following
him did so as well. He turned to face them. Apprehension radiated
from many of their eyes.

Raising his voice to reach all of them, he said, "It has come
to my attention that some of you men still fear the prophecy
supposedly protecting Ston. That God is on their side in the
coming battle. That a dragon will rise from the city walls to smite
us with its fiery breath."

His words elicited even more uneasiness. Several of the men
shifted in their stances and glanced nervously at the wall rising
over the ridge.

"God's word is powerful," he continued. "Prophecies shouldn't
be ignored. I understand if some of you may not want to tempt
fate. There's no shame in leaving now and returning to the ship.
Whoever feels they can't face the enemy, step forward now and I'll
relieve you of your duty."

They all looked around, but no one moved. Finally, one soldier
stepped up, emboldening two more to do the same. He could tell
that more wanted to join them, but perhaps they saw the look in
Bogun's eyes.

He nodded like a disappointed father and walked toward the
first one.

"You wish to leave."

"Yes, my lord," he answered in a shaky voice.

"You fear damnation?"

"Yes, my lord."

"Do you fear me?"

"N-no, my lord," he stammered.

With a lightning movement, Bogun drew his sword and slashed the deserter across the throat. He collapsed to the ground in a gush of blood.

"You should." The two other men who had stepped forward were fixated in horror by the sight of the dead man. Bogun raised the tip of his sword toward them, and they rushed back to their places in the formation.

Bogun paced in front of them, his sword still brandished. "Listen to me, men. You *will* carry out my orders to the letter. When you agreed to join me on this quest, you knew the dangers, but you also knew the rewards. I expect all of you to fight to the death to capture this town. There is no going back to Kotor in defeat. And I hope it is clear that you should fear me far more than some century-old prophecy recited by a backwater priest."

He kicked at the man he had just slain.

"This soldier died easily. If I catch anyone trying to desert this assault, either Cedozar or I will cut off your limbs one by one and leave you for the crows. Do you understand?"

The men nodded.

"I said do you understand!"

"Yes, my lord!" they yelled back.

"Are you with me to the end?"

"Yes, my lord!"

Bogun smiled, but his good mood was soured by Vitomir walking toward them at a brisk pace.

"I checked the salt house," he said with a bright tone. "It's all still there."

"You expected them to destroy it?"

"I thought they might have moved it. It's the only way…"

Vitomir lost his voice when he saw the corpse sprawled on the ground.

"What happened?"

"My men were just being reminded that I am their commander," Bogun said. "No prophecy will deter us from our rightful conquest."

Vitomir averted his eyes from the blood, leaned closer, and

lowered his voice. "Do you think it wise to kill your own men? Especially before the assault on Mali Ston? We are not at full strength yet."

"There is no *we*. You are in my employ now."

A flicker of annoyance crossed Vitomir's face. "I am in no one's employ. I am the treasurer of Dubrovnik."

"A treasurer with massive funds missing. Debts that can only be repaid with money I control." Bogun edged closer, his voice a quiet growl. "If you defy me, I will make your life an earthly hell."

Vitomir gulped. "This partnership will benefit us both."

"If that's how you prefer to think of it, so be it. Now, we march on. I want to be sleeping in a Mali Ston bed by nightfall."

They continued into the valley. Bogun was watchful for an ambush, no matter how unlikely it was from the townspeople. Cedozar pointed up to a blackened spot on the ridge wall. Bogun saw that it looked fresh.

"There must have been a fire," Bogun said.

"Up there?" Cedozar replied. "How? None of the surrounding trees are burned."

"Maybe someone dropped a torch. It doesn't matter."

They pressed on and emerged into the narrow plain in front of the city wall. In the fading light of dusk, Bogun could see men gathering on the wall. A few villagers with pitchforks and shovels would be no match for his hardened warriors.

"What is the battle plan?" Vitomir asked.

Bogun was irked by the civilian in their midst, but he enjoyed explaining his tactic for taking the town, a story he would likely recount many times in the future. "We have six ladders. Four men will be hoisting each one up to the wall, spaced out at wide intervals."

Vitomir eyed the wall nervously. "But the woman with the bow and arrows…"

"That's why we have the shields," Cedozar said, pointing to the men holding wide wooden shields faced with steel. "They'll protect the men carrying the ladders."

"And once they're inside," Bogun said, "our men will open the gates so that the balance of our force can enter and subdue the remainder of the citizens."

Vitomir understood what the word "subdued" meant.

"You can't kill Petar. We need him."

"Yes, for the salt production. And if you had this precious book by Marco Polo, we wouldn't need him."

"You need his family, too. He won't help us if they're dead."

Bogun sighed. "All right. I can't promise you, but we'll kill as few of the residents as we can until you tell us who is indispensable."

"That's all I ask."

Cedozar pointed at the wall. "My lord, look."

Bogun saw a blonde woman standing above the gate, bow in hand. "Is that the woman who shot arrows at you and Vitomir?"

"Yes, my lord. But who is that man standing next to her? He was not in the garrison when we were last here."

Bogun had been so focused on the woman that he hadn't registered the tall, bearded man beside her. He squinted to get a better look, then the recognition slammed into him like a runaway horse cart. "No!"

Vitomir stared at the man with his jaw open. "It can't be!"

"It is," Bogun said. "I never forget a face. That's Gerard Fox."

 53

Fox recognized Bogun and gave a mocking wave, but the Serbian leader was too far away for him to make out the reaction. Fifty men were arrayed against Mali Ston with shields and six ladders. It was clear what their strategy would be. They'd attempt to get over the wall at multiple points so that the invaders could open the gates for the remainder of the soldiers to swarm inside.

All of the men of the town were posted on the battlements with whatever weapons they could scrounge. Some wielded swords and pikes left by the garrison. Others held axes and pitchforks.

Most of the wall towered over steep hills that would be difficult for the attackers to climb, so the assault would be concentrated on the relatively flat ground near the sea. Still, it left a good portion of the wall to defend.

Though Fox's side had a slight advantage in numbers, the villagers would be slaughtered by Bogun's experienced fighters if they got inside. Therefore, they had to keep the Serbians from overwhelming them on the walls.

Fox and Willa were the only ones armed with bows and arrows, but the garrison had been supplied with five crossbows. The crossbows' main advantage was that they were easy to shoot, but their drawback was that they were difficult to reload because the cranequin took skill to wind back the string. Each wielder would likely get to launch only one bolt.

Cristoval, Radoslav, Tino, Petar, and Willa were gathered around Fox. The rest of the townsmen had been instructed by

Petar to follow the orders of the mercenaries, while the women and children were gathered together in Mali Ston's tiny church. Fox knew for a fact that a church wouldn't stop Bogun's men from killing them all, but the townspeople didn't, and Fox needed the men to focus on the task at hand. Fox knew the only way to prevent a slaughter was if Mali Ston remained in their hands. Even God couldn't help them if Bogun's invasion was successful.

"I thought they'd have more men," Cristoval mused as he observed the assault force.

"More may be coming," Fox said. "But from the little I know of Bogun, he is an impatient man. He likely thinks that Mali Ston is his for the taking now that the garrison has been wiped out."

"I can confirm that sentiment," Radoslav said, drawing a glance from Cristoval.

"My fellow residents will fight with vigor," said Petar, who was holding an axe.

"I'm sure they will," Fox said. "But Bogun surely has brought battle-hardened soldiers with him. While a man fighting for his home is nothing to be trifled with, most of your men are simple laborers with no experience in fighting except for a few drunken brawls. They'll be no match for trained swordsmen."

"What about this revolutionary new weapon that your wife seems to have concocted?" Tino said. "I'd like to see one of these rockets in action."

Willa shook her head. "We haven't been able to produce a successful weapon yet, although Jelena, her mother, and Zrinka are trying to build the next one as we speak."

"Would it be enough to drive them away even if it doesn't work as well as we'd like? Just from your description of their power, it might scare them out of their braies. Now that would be amusing to watch."

"Not with Bogun there," Radoslav said. "As Lady Fox observed, my people are superstitious and take portents and prophecies seriously, but Bogun is a brutal and uncompromising commander. It was sheer luck that I was able to get away from him, but most of his men wouldn't dare defy him."

Fox noticed Bogun's men beginning to disperse, four men to a ladder. Bogun and the rest held back in reserve.

"Get to your posts," Fox said. "Remember, don't shoot your bolts unless you have a clear view past those shields. Willa and I will do our best to thin their numbers."

The four men trotted out toward each end of the wall, Petar and Tino on one end and Cristoval and Radoslav on the other. Now that the Serb had proven himself trustworthy against the pirates, Cristoval was willing to fight by his side. That left Fox and Willa alone directly above the main gate in the center.

It was no use trying to talk Willa into hiding with the other women. He knew her too well by this point. But his one demand was that she stay beside him. Despite the dire circumstances, now that he had finally returned to her, he didn't want to let her out of his sight.

"I know you're up to this challenge," Fox said.

"It's only because of you."

"Remember to stay low whenever you aren't loosing an arrow. They are armed with crossbows as well. The weapons don't have great range or a proper angle for engaging us, but they could still get lucky."

"It's nice to know you still care for me," Willa said, moving closer to him.

"You don't know how much I longed to be back with you."

"I know it's not as much as I did. Even though I saw you fall, I knew in the marrow of my bones that you were still alive. I never want to be so close to losing you again."

Fox didn't care about decorum now that they were facing down an enemy. He pulled Willa to him and kissed her like he'd never kissed her before. She melted into his embrace, and the two of them were locked together for an eternity that was far too short.

When they pulled apart, Tino whooped from his position along the wall.

"Why don't we all get our own dose of something like that before the battle!" he yelled to them.

"Eyes out!" Fox shouted back in good humor.

Suddenly their attention was directed to enemy movement. The men with the ladders hoisted their shields above their heads and began double-marching toward the wall. The ladders were designed to be extra-long to make it to the top of the thirty-foot walls.

The most perilous part of the attack for them would be climbing. The townsmen were supplied with anything weighty they could find: iron pots, heavy tools, the women had even boiled water in huge iron kettles for the townsmen to dump over the side. Whatever they could drop on the assaulters to knock them off.

As the soldiers got closer to the wall, the townsmen with crossbows were able to land a couple of hits while Fox and Willa launched arrows at them, with Fox covering the western end of the wall and Willa the eastern end. After two of the soldiers were hit, the attackers realized all of the arrows were coming from one central location, so they shifted their large shields to thwart the attack.

Then they did something unexpected. The men carrying three sets of ladders rushed forward together on one side, and the same happened on the other side, so there were now just two sets of ladders. Once each of them was a unit, they charged forward as fast as they could.

Three men broke out on both sides to take aim with their crossbows at Fox and Willa. Their shots were off, but it was enough to make Fox pull Willa down, allowing the men with the ladders to advance.

"They're not attacking at six points," Fox said. "They're trying to outman us at only two locations."

"Would that work?" Willa asked.

Fox took her hand. "It might. I think we have to separate, much as I hate it. You go to Cristoval and Radoslav. I'll help Petar and Tino."

He kissed the back of her hand and reluctantly let her go. He watched her draw another arrow as she hurried along, barely missing the exposed leg of one of the soldiers.

Fox tore his eyes away, knowing that if enough of Bogun's men got up and over to open the gates, they'd all be executed. He took up a position fifty feet from Tino and Petar and the rest of the villagers supporting them. They had linked up as a unit, trying to anticipate where the ladders would go up.

Checking his bag, he saw that he was already running low on arrows. Just three left. The others were allocated for the rockets, although now that seemed like a futile gesture if this attack succeeded.

As soon as the cadre of men reached the wall, they threw the ladders up against the stone, all three side by side. The tops barely reached the spaces between the crenellations. Soldiers began to climb.

Fox took aim at the one closest to him. The soldier was using his shield to fend off pots and pans falling on him, so his body was exposed. Fox had to time it right. The arrow hit him in the stomach, but shockingly the man was so charged from the battle that he didn't seem to feel it. He kept right on climbing.

The second arrow, however, did the job. It struck him in the chest, which killed him instantly. He tumbled sideways, sparing the man climbing up behind him.

Down to his last arrow, Fox shot it at a man nearing the top. It caught him in the buttocks, hindering his climb, but not disabling him.

Fox dropped his bow, drew Legend, and ran to aid the townsmen. Some of them had been trying to slide the ladders aside to make them fall, but the angle was too awkward to shove them off. Pushing them out to tip over backward was impossible because the ladders couldn't be forced out far enough. They simply bounced back against the wall.

By this time, the first soldiers had reached the top, with three of their number lying dead on the ground around the ladders below.

Fox slashed at one of the soldiers at the top, catching him on the shield, which fell away. The soldier drew his own sword, but he couldn't fight back effectively while clinging to the ladder. Fox made quick work of him with another strike. The nearly headless man fell backward, striking the man directly beneath him and sending them both to the ground far below.

Fox stole a moment to see how Willa was faring. She had husbanded her arrows more carefully, so she was still shooting as Cristoval and Radoslav were beating back their attackers.

The defense seemed to be working. The soldiers weren't getting over the top of the wall. But it only took one racing past them to the gate below. If that happened, the town would be lost.

But then Bogun sprang another surprise tactic. He didn't wait for the men on the ladders to open the gates. With the rate of arrows and crossbow bolts from the defenders slowing to a trickle, he led the balance of his forces charging across. They were simply going to try to get everyone over the wall at once.

This time the soldiers weren't slowed down by their shields. Half of them rushed to each set of ladders and began to scramble up. As soon as one man fell, the next would take his place.

At the other end of the wall, Fox could see that one had made it over. He was going after Willa, and she fought back while Cristoval came to her aid, leaving Radoslav as the only trained man fighting off the remaining climbing soldiers. The villagers would do their best, but their makeshift weapons meant they would be quickly overwhelmed.

Then Fox saw that Radoslav was trying an unusual tactic. He was hooking the tines of a long pitchfork sideways under the top rung of the ladder. When the strong base of the fork was braced against the top rung, he thrust the ladder away from him, sending it backward. The weight of the men on it finished the job for him. It smashed into the ground on top of the attackers, shattering when it landed.

Unable to help Willa and trusting Cristoval to protect her, Fox turned his attention back to his own ladders.

One of the townsmen had been using another pitchfork as a weapon. Without a word, Fox sheathed his sword and snatched the pitchfork out of the man's hands. While Tino and Petar fought against men on the other two ladders on Fox's end of the wall, he pushed against the one closest to him as Radoslav had on the opposite end of the wall. With all his might, he heaved it away from the wall. As soon as it was far enough, the ladder kept going, tipping all the way back and slamming into the ground, breaking apart in the process.

As he leaned out to check that the ladder was no longer usable, he saw Bogun below, looking up at him with undisguised fury. Bogun snatched a crossbow from one of the other soldiers and aimed it up, launching the bolt.

Fox ducked, but he realized that Tino was directly behind him. The bolt hit Tino in the shoulder as he was fighting a man threatening to pull him over the wall. He cried out from the hit, his grip tenuous.

Grabbing Tino's legs, Fox yanked backward just as the soldier he was wrestling pulled on his arms. Fox's grip was stronger. Tino and Fox fell to the battlement floor while the soldier cartwheeled down to the ground outside.

Petar had seen Fox's tactic of using the pitchfork and picked it up to continue pushing the ladders away. His first attempt was unsuccessful because his push wasn't hard enough, and it bounced back. But once he got it, only one was left. Tino tore the bolt out of his useless right shoulder, maneuvering his sword to his left hand to keep assisting in the fight.

Suddenly, farther down the wall, Fox saw Willa wrestling with a soldier while Cristoval fought off two more. The remaining townsmen were too distracted with their own fights to help.

"Go to her!" Petar yelled.

Fox leaped to his feet, drew Legend, and sprinted along the wall. Before he could get there, Willa reached for a spent crossbow bolt that was lying on the ground. She shoved its point into the soldier's sword arm, causing him to drop the weapon.

He backhanded her with his fist, catching her in the shoulder, but she didn't make a sound. The action gave enough time for Fox to reach her. With one swipe of his sword, he ended the soldier.

He lifted her to her feet, her bow still in hand.

"Are you all right?"

"Yes. Help Cristoval."

Without a weapon to fight with, she backed away, giving room for Fox to take some pressure off Cristoval who was barely holding his own against the two soldiers.

Fox stabbed one of the soldiers in the chest, and Cristoval regrouped at his side.

"Thank you, Sir Gerard."

"Don't thank me yet."

They kept fighting, but soldiers poured over the wall, despite Radoslav pushing his second ladder over. The battle was going to get out of hand unless they stopped men from coming over. Already several of the townsmen lay dead from the stout defense of Mali Ston.

Cristoval was an excellent swordsman, and the two of them were able to dispatch three soldiers in quick succession. Then one of the men they thought was dead grasped one of Fox's legs and tripped him.

He went down, and the Serbian tried to plunge a dagger into Fox's throat. He grabbed the soldier's wrist, stopping the point of the knife a mere finger's width from his neck.

Then with a slash of a sword, the soldier's hand was separated from his arm by Cristoval, who then put the man out of his misery.

Cristoval reached down and hauled Fox to his feet.

"Make sure they're dead," he said.

Fox was about to answer when he saw Radoslav, standing on the crenellation, pushing against the third ladder with the pitchfork. The ladder was heavily laden with soldiers. It was about to go over when the last remaining Serbian on the wall rushed to stop him.

The next sequence of events seemed to happen in the blink of an eye, far too short a time for either Fox or Cristoval to intervene.

Radoslav parried the man's sword while he held on to the pitchfork, continuing to push the ladder out. Seeing what was about to happen, the soldier latched onto Radoslav, who simply refused to let go of the pitchfork. Radoslav launched himself onto the ladder as it was levered from the wall, taking the enemy with him.

For a moment it teetered completely upright. Radoslav could

have pulled it back to the wall, but he nodded at Fox, accepting his fate as he shifted his weight, causing it to fall away from the wall.

The ladder crashed to the ground. Radoslav landed on the man who'd been fighting with him, but he lay there, dazed.

Bogun had come over from the other set of ladders to reinforce this group. He crowed with delight at recognizing Radoslav.

He said something in Serbian to the unarmed Radoslav, who looked at him from the ground with utter contempt. Bogun grinned up at Fox.

"I told him that he shouldn't have let you bring him back," he called up.

"You've done me an honor bringing me here, Sir Gerard," Radoslav said. "Save them all."

"He won't," Bogun said.

Then without hesitation, he raised his sword with both hands and brought it down without taking his eyes from Fox, stabbing Radoslav through the heart. The young Serbian gasped from the impact. Fox thought he could make out an expression of regret on Radoslav's face before the light left his eyes.

Fox had to restrain himself from crying out, "No!" Radoslav hadn't deserved such a swift end to his quest for redemption. Fox wanted to make Bogun pay for yet another atrocity, but without arrows for his bow, all he could do was watch impotently from above.

It was Cristoval who shouted down. "Do you remember me?"

Bogun squinted up in the fading light before nodding. "You had a brother once."

"You killed him."

"I've killed many."

"I'll make sure you die for your crimes."

"You can try," Bogun said as he gathered his men to retreat after the failed attack. "I'll be sure to give you another chance, because I'll be back with the rest of my army long before any help can arrive from Dubrovnik."

He started to walk away with his men when he called out over his shoulder.

"Oh, and none of these deaths are crimes. This is war."

 54

Vitomir sat uncomfortably in the provost's house in the abandoned town of Ston, wondering when this nightmare would be over. At least they weren't forced to sleep out in the wild, but he worried that Fox would attempt a sneak attack.

"Do you really think it's safe here?" he asked Bogun, who disdainfully chewed on a scant meal of salted fish and bread. "You lost twenty men at Mali Ston for nothing."

"We still have thirty men here," Bogun said, seemingly unconcerned about the setback. "And it wasn't for nothing. We inflicted casualties on them, and now we know the strength of their forces. In addition, they must be nearly out of arrows, which will make our next attack decisive."

Cedozar sat on the floor, leaning back against the wall.

"Now that the Serbian traitor is dead, I counted two real fighters besides Fox," he said. "And that woman, if you include her."

"She killed two men with her bow," Bogun said. "I think she counts."

Vitomir was appalled at how casually they were speaking. "But what if Fox brings his men over here tonight?"

"Let him. The only reason they repelled us was because of that wall. He'd never attempt to attack us head on with two or three mercenaries and some villagers with pitchforks."

"How do you know he doesn't have more on the way?"

"I don't, but I know *I* have more men on the way. Over a hundred, with horses, supplies, and tents."

"Are they bringing siege weapons? Because that might be the only way to take Mali Ston from what I witnessed."

"Given what we saw of their capabilities," Cedozar said, "we'll have an overwhelming advantage. They won't be able to stop us next time."

Vitomir thought about the relative numbers and the rate of losses on each side in this initial skirmish. "You lost twenty men while your count says they only lost five, and four of those were untrained townsmen."

"Don't forget the mercenary shot by the crossbow bolt," Bogun said.

"We don't know if he's still able to fight."

"No, we don't. But it won't matter. I can throw men at them until they're wiped out." Bogun cast his eyes around in thought. "Isn't that true? You're good with numbers."

"If their tactics or numbers don't change," Vitomir said, calculating in his head, "you should be able to defeat them even if you lose half of the reinforcements. But when will they get here?"

"Four more ships will be landing soon," Cedozar said. "Tomorrow is my best guess."

"That's not good enough. I need to go back to Dubrovnik. The rector will be wondering where I am."

Bogun stood and walked over to Vitomir, putting a hand on his shoulder. "You're exactly where you need to be."

"I think we both know I'm no good to you in battle."

"On that, you and I agree. No, I have another task for you."

Vitomir idly inspected the pewter cup that was the best the provost's house had to offer. It was a crude piece, nothing compared to the beautiful engraved silver tableware he had back at his home in Dubrovnik. He longed to get back to his possessions, but his boredom here outside of the battles had become so dreadful that he wouldn't mind having something to do. At least it would keep his mind off the constant gore he was forced to witness.

"I suppose I can coordinate distribution of your incoming supplies."

"Cedozar can take charge of that," Bogun said.

"I do it for an entire city. I think I'm more suited to managing it here."

"It's no trouble at all," Cedozar said, smiling at Bogun.

Now Vitomir realized that something else was going on. "What is this task?" he asked.

Bogun sat on the table and focused on Vitomir with a distressingly intense gaze. "We will be able to conquer the town by brute force, but it's a terrible waste of men, particularly when I might need them to repel a Venetian counterattack once they realize I've taken Ston and Mali Ston."

"We've gone over the counting," Vitomir said. "You'll have at least eighty men left after you've invaded Mali Ston."

"Which means how many men of mine would be dead."

"Fifty more."

Bogun nodded. "I'll sacrifice those fifty men if necessary. But I'd like to have them for any future engagements."

"Then I suggest you change your attack plan."

"What about going through the front gates?" Cedozar prompted.

"We have no leverage over Petar any longer," Vitomir said, exasperated. "I thought you understood that."

"There's another way to open them from the inside," Bogun said. "You mentioned it yourself."

Vitomir shook his head in confusion. "I made no such claim."

"The defect in the wall," Cedozar said, rising to his feet and joining Bogun at the table. "You told us that it was never repaired properly."

Vitomir's throat went dry. They had been planning this conversation all along. "I... Well, they wanted too much money to fix it the way they wanted to."

"So they plugged this hole with rough stones," Bogun said, "instead of limestone and mortar? For once, your greed has provided us an opportunity."

Vitomir got to his feet and backed away. "I don't know what you're proposing, but I can't help you."

"You are the only one here who knows exactly where that defect is. If it was as shoddily repaired as you said, it shouldn't take more than a few hours to excavate those stones to create a hole wide enough to squeeze through."

Cedozar nodded. "No one would suspect someone opening the gates from the inside. If we time it correctly, we can be through before they mount an effective defense. Our casualties would be small."

"But the hole is on the opposite side of Mali Ston," Vitomir protested. "You'd need to approach from the north by ship."

"That's not the only way," Bogun said with a smile.

"Yes, it is. Otherwise, you'd have to go over the mountain…"

He abruptly stopped talking when he realized that's what Bogun meant. The two Serbs stared at him with knowing looks.

"No."

"I have two men who grew up in the peaks of southern Serbia," Cedozar said. "They are as sure-footed as mountain goats."

"They'll guide the way," Bogun said. "And you'll go with them to show them the breach in the wall when they get there. I can't have them wandering back and forth looking for it in the daylight and risk being spotted."

"I can't."

"You will," Bogun said with a decisive grin. "Perhaps you don't think you're capable of such an arduous trek, but I believe in you, Vitomir."

"You'll need to be into the town by dawn the day after tomorrow," Cedozar said. "That's when our forces should be in place for the next attack."

Vitomir wanted to argue more, but Bogun's hand was casually resting on his dagger. If Vitomir refused, he had no doubt there would be no reason to let him live.

Then he suddenly realized he might be able to turn the situation to his advantage. The Marco Polo book must be in Mali Ston. If he could retrieve it and keep it out of Bogun's reach, he would have a powerful negotiating tool. With it, he might even be able to rid himself of Bogun and reap the rewards of the increased salt trade all for himself. Surely he could find a more pliable henchman to do his bidding.

He tried to speak with the right mixture of reluctance and acquiescence.

"All right, Bogun, you've convinced me. When do we leave?"

 55

It took most of the night to gather up the dead and tend to the wounded. Willa helped Marija dress Tino's injury as best she could with a poultice, but he would be severely limited in the battle to come. They asked Zrinka to bandage him when they were finished so they could turn their attention to other tasks. They had a brief ceremony before burying the townsmen who'd died defending Mali Ston, but Willa could tell it was losing Radoslav that had bothered Gerard the most.

Morning arrived before Willa had time alone with him. With Bogun having retreated to Ston, there wasn't an imminent danger of another attack, but men were posted on the ridge wall to look out for any sign of his force returning. She and Gerard were given a small room to get what rest they could, but Willa couldn't sleep despite how exhausted she was.

"When do you think he'll come back?" she asked as she stared at the ceiling.

"How do you know I'm awake?" Gerard replied, even though his eyes were closed.

"You snore when you sleep."

"Loudly?"

"It's not bad. I turn you over when you do it."

"You mumble. It's soothing. Bogun will return when the rest of his men arrive. It could be any time. That's why we should rest now."

"But how can we possibly win?"

"We don't have to win," Gerard said. "We just have to last long enough for Dubrovnik and Venice to drive them away."

"With just you and Cristoval as our fighters?"

"And you. I saw how many soldiers you took down with the bow."

"Not good enough. Besides, we only recovered a third of our arrows after Bogun retreated." The rest had been damaged beyond repair in the battle. "And I can't wield a sword."

Gerard opened his eyes and propped himself on one elbow to look at her. "I know you're not suggesting we surrender."

"I'm not."

"You want us to leave?"

"Even if I wanted that, you wouldn't abandon Nika. I saw how you were with her."

"She grew on me," Gerard said, shaking his head.

"You sound surprised."

"Oh, she was annoying at first. But she impressed me. I didn't know children could be interesting. Turns out, I like them. Well, maybe just some of them. Ours I will, certainly."

Willa caressed his cheek. She wouldn't have thought she could love him more, but he was constantly proving her wrong.

"I can't wait to see you as a father."

"And you as a mother. If I weren't so tired, I'd give it a try with you right now."

"We'll have plenty of time once we save Ston."

"I'm glad to hear you have faith that we can do it."

"It's because of their prophecy."

"You still believe that?"

She nodded. "Listen to it again."

Gerard listened as she recited the lines.

The lure of precious crystals sparks a dire threat to the White Fortress.

My hand guides strangers from across the sea to provide aid in this time of need.

Hellfire rains down when a sacrifice summons a dragon to destroy any enemy refusing to flee.

A miracle inspires a new leader to show the way to liberation.

"I admit," he said, "the first two lines do seem to have come true, but what of the rest of it?"

"Petar thought that the sacrifice had been you and Nika."

"You think we willingly fell off that wall?"

"I didn't say *I* thought so. I knew you were still alive."

"How?"

"My heart told me."

"You do have a good heart. So there was no sacrifice."

"Yes, there was. Radoslav. He saved all of us by pushing that ladder off the wall."

"He was doing what any of us would have." Gerard's face darkened. "Then Bogun killed him."

"That's why it was a sacrifice."

"He was trying to atone for his sins. I only hope helping us fight off Bogun's attack gave him peace in the end."

Gerard said it as if he blamed himself for Radoslav's death. He had told her about Radoslav's role leading up to the killing of Cristoval's brother.

"It's not your fault," Willa said. "Radoslav came here of his own accord despite knowing how dangerous it was. Now we need to make sure his death mattered."

Gerard considered that before speaking. "You said you've made hellfire. I'm looking forward to seeing a demonstration."

"And we have a miracle. That's what everyone in Mali Ston was calling it when you brought Nika back alive."

"It *was* fairly miraculous that we were plucked out of the sea by that ship. I suppose I can see what you mean about the prophecy. Now we just need a dragon."

"I think I've already solved that little problem. What if we create one?"

Gerard laughed. "Are you a sorcerer now?"

"We can make our own," Willa said. "I already had Jelena gather canvas and lumber to build one. We can dye the canvas red with the herbs I have."

"An entire dragon?"

"Well, maybe just the head."

Gerard cocked his head at her in doubt. "And that would scare off an army?"

"You didn't see how superstitious the Serbians are. A simple sneeze by Petar gave them away because they were convinced it was a curse. If they saw a dragon, they would run away screaming."

"Not with Bogun there to stop them. He's a brilliant tactician, and he rules with an iron fist. Unless that dragon was swooping down on them breathing fire, they would stand their ground." He sat up straighter at that. "What if we combine the hellfire with the dragon?"

"What do you mean?"

"These hellfire rockets you've made. What if we shot them from the head you're making. It could be even more than just a head. Tino is an excellent craftsman. He might be able to fashion something more convincing than just a head. If the Serbians saw a dragon breathing fire, it might be enough to convince them it was real."

"They'd run even with Bogun at their backs?" Willa asked.

"No, they likely wouldn't. Which means we need to get rid of Bogun."

"How could you do that?"

She could see wheels turning in Gerard's head, and she usually didn't like what that meant.

"He wants to kill me and Cristoval. We might have to give him the chance to do just that."

"How?"

"By luring him away from Mali Ston."

Willa's heart started racing at that thought. She shook her head vigorously. "I won't let you. I already thought I'd lost you. I can't go through that again."

"What other choice do we have?"

"Could you shoot him with an arrow?"

"I'd never get close enough. A hail of crossbow bolts from his army would stop me before I got into range."

"You want to ride out there and draw him away without getting killed by those crossbows? No. It's too risky."

Gerard took her hands and kissed them. "I don't want to leave you again, either, but this is our best chance. Once the head of *their* dragon is cut off, they will be too scared to keep fighting. They'll turn tail and run all the way back to Serbia. I'll talk to Cristoval and see if he's willing."

"Do you promise to come back?"

He smiled at her, and it sent a shudder of warmth through her.

"I already did. I'll do it again."

His confidence was overpowering.

"All right," Willa said. "Given how much he hates Bogun, I'd wager there's nothing that would keep him from following you."

"The only thing I don't like about the plan is that I have to leave you here."

"I suppose if the plan doesn't work and Bogun attacks again with a larger force, it wouldn't matter whether you were here or not."

Gerard frowned. "I did promise myself that if I ever got back to you, I'd never leave you again."

"Well, that was a silly promise," Willa said with a smile. "You're going to be with me day and night for the rest of our lives?"

"I could think of many worse fates."

"Like not taking advantage of this time alone together?"

He drew her to him and kissed her deeply. She could sense his desire and pressed her body against his. Suddenly, sleeping didn't seem like a priority.

"Are you still tired?" she said between kisses.

He pulled away just long enough to give her a hungry grin.

"Wide awake."

 56

The hundred remaining men of Bogun's army arrived at midday, which meant Vitomir was sent off under protest late in the afternoon on the mission to infiltrate Mali Ston. While he was spending the rest of the day climbing over jagged rocks to get behind the city, Bogun was setting his army in place in front of the city walls. The plan was to attack at first light the next day, and Vitomir was going to be right in the thick of it whether he wanted to or not.

Vitomir's deal with Bogun had steadily been getting worse. He would be tempted to simply walk away and find a ship sailing back to Dubrovnik as soon as he was out of sight of Ston, but he still needed the Marco Polo book. In any event, the two men at his back were surely sent by Bogun to keep him from fleeing.

Only one of them talked, a one-eyed brute named Kohlar. He regularly scratched under the eyepatch at some disgusting affliction that Vitomir could only guess at.

As they approached the top of the mountain, far from the wall that went over the southern ridge, Vitomir was panting hard.

"Stop," he said, sucking in his breath. "We need to rest."

"*You* need to rest," Kohlar replied without stopping. "We don't."

"Do you know who I am?" Vitomir pointed at his clothes, but he looked down and saw that he was filthier than he'd been since he was a child, and his shoes were starting to separate at the toe. They hadn't been designed for an arduous climb.

"You are the Croatian scum who's supposed to show us how to get through the city walls."

"I am the treasurer of Dubrovnik, second in authority only to the rector."

"Like I said, scum."

The nameless Serb, whose scraggly beard only grew in patches, snickered at that.

They obviously weren't going to allow a stop, so Vitomir pressed on. When they reached the peak, Kohlar finally stopped and got to one knee as he peered over the top.

Vitomir took the chance to take a drink of ale from the small bladder he'd brought. The climb down the other side looked even more daunting than the climb up.

Kohlar pointed at Mali Ston, whose walls were visible from this vantage point.

"We can't go down this way," he said. "They'll see us even with the light fading."

The sun would set in just a few hours.

"You can't possibly think we'll be able to climb down in the dark," Vitomir said.

"Did I say that?"

"Then what *are* you saying?"

"We have to descend just behind the ridge to stay out of sight."

That would mean an even longer trip. Vitomir stifled a groan. He wouldn't give them the satisfaction of more complaints.

"Can you see the defect in the wall from here?" Kohlar asked.

Vitomir scanned the wall as if he were searching for it, but he already knew exactly where it was. He wouldn't tell them now and risk them leaving him behind.

"It's too far away. I have to be closer."

Kohlar chuffed in annoyance at that. "You can find it?"

"I'll recognize it when I see it."

"You better not be taking us all this way for nothing."

A deadly stare from Nameless echoed the sentiment.

The two of them started along the ridge, with Vitomir struggling to keep up behind them. At one point, he tripped on a rock, falling on his face and sending a small landslide down. Kohlar and Nameless went sliding, and they went still when they came to rest.

Vitomir pushed himself up and patted his face frantically. "Is there any blood?"

Kohlar stood and wiped the dust from his clothes, ignoring Vitomir's cry of panic.

"Is there any blood on me!" Vitomir shouted.

"Keep your voice down," Kohlar scolded. "The only mark on your face is that ugly splotch on your forehead."

Vitomir calmed down but was incensed at being called ugly by the likes of a surly Serbian. "It's the mark of nobility."

"It's the mark of the Devil for all I care," Kohlar said. "I'm more worried about the dust you've sprayed into the air. Hopefully, they're not watching this direction closely now that Bogun is massing his army on the other side of the mountain."

Vitomir wanted to argue further, but he knew his points would fall on deaf ears.

By the time they reached the bottom of the ridge, dusk was consuming the light. They were only a few hundred yards from the city wall. They crouched to watch Mali Ston, giving Vitomir a chance to take off his shoes, empty them of pebbles, and massage his sore feet.

Nameless pointed at a villager on watch along the top of the wall.

"It looks like there's just one man walking the wall on this side," Kohlar said. "And even then he comes through only so often. Now can you tell where we should go?"

Vitomir nodded. "I think it's on the right side near where the wall abuts the mountain. A storm caused a channel to undermine the wall."

"Will it be big enough for us to crawl through once it's dug out?"

"I think so."

Kohlar exchanged an irritated glance with Nameless. "We came all this way because you *think* so?"

"I only saw it from the inside of the city. They were filling it with rocks but no mortar. If it's the same size on the outside, we should be able to fit."

That seemed to satisfy Kohlar, but Vitomir was worried about what would happen to him if he were wrong. He just prayed that the patch work had been shoddy enough for them to take advantage of. He thanked the Lord that he hadn't supplied them with funds to fix it properly.

When night fell, a full moon lit their way as they found a route to the wall, stopping only when the guard on the wall walked by.

Vitomir kept telling himself that this ordeal would all be worth it if he could find the Marco Polo book once he was inside. Let these two fools take the riskier task of trying to open the gates unseen.

When they finally reached the wall, they picked their way along it until Vitomir found the rough spot where rocks were stuffed into the opening that had been scoured under the wall.

"Here," he whispered.

Kohlar and Nameless bent down to run their hands over it. In the moonlight, Vitomir could see that it would be wide enough for his shoulders once it was emptied of stones.

Kohlar nodded and kept his voice low. "We can remove these, but it will take time because we have to be quiet." He regarded Vitomir with a derisive expression. "You're useless as a laborer, so you keep a watch on the wall. Let us know whenever that watchman comes by."

Far from insulted, Vitomir was relieved. He took a few steps back and sat on the ground. Finally he could rest while Kohlar and his comrade went to work excavating the rubble so they could sneak into Mali Ston. With one eye looking out for the wall walker, Vitomir contemplated how he was going to find the Marco Polo codex to save his own life.

 57

Fox focused on each step as he climbed the ridge wall lit only by moonlight, Zephyr's reins in his hand as the horse trailed him. Their reunion had been a celebration for both of them. They'd been through many ordeals together, but walking up this narrow stone pathway in the dark of night was one of their most difficult trials.

Cristoval followed behind, leading Comis. Fox could see the firelight from Bogun's large encampment and saw a few wandering guards, but the rest of the men were asleep, no doubt getting rest before an attack at dawn. Fox had no reason to think Bogun would wait any longer than that.

"The blankets seem to have worked," Cristoval said in a low voice once they reached the crest of the ridge. They'd covered the light-colored horses with dark blankets to make them less visible. Both of them were going slowly so that Comis and Zephyr's footfalls were as quiet as possible, minimized by cloth coverings over their shoes.

"It doesn't look like they've noticed us," Fox agreed. "And even if they did see us, I don't think they'd have an idea about what we're doing."

"I said I'd come with you on this misadventure because I wanted a chance at killing Bogun. It doesn't mean I think it's likely to succeed."

"Bogun won't let us get away. He's too proud to allow me to escape him again."

"You know him that well?"

"Would you let *him* get away again?"

"I'd prefer to ride right into their camp and behead him."

"We wouldn't get within a hundred feet of him. They'd stick us with a dozen crossbow bolts before we ever got close enough."

Zephyr's hoof slipped on a slick stone and lurched sideways. Fox put his hand on the horse's neck to steady him, and he didn't let out a sound. They were on a flat section now for a while, but the real test was to come when they were walking down the wall on the opposite side of the mountain.

"He's well trained," Cristoval said. "Most horses would have balked at this difficult terrain."

"My brother trained him."

"He's not your horse?"

Fox didn't like to talk about it, but Cristoval had lost a brother as well, so he was a kindred spirit. He might be the only one who would understand the loss he'd suffered.

"Zephyr belonged to my brother. My horse was named Velox."

Cristoval interpreted his tone correctly. "How did you lose them?"

"At the Battle of Crécy. Velox died while I was trying to save my older brother. I couldn't. Other than my memories, Zephyr is the only connection I have left with James."

"You don't have his lands? I thought you were a knight."

Fox was glad Cristoval couldn't see his face as they talked. He was sure his expression of anger and sadness was undisguised, but he could temper his voice.

"My lands were taken from me," he said, leaving out that he'd been excommunicated in the process, a fact that would have repelled Cristoval. "Willa and I hope that I will be able to regain them someday."

"How?"

"By finding evidence that they were seized unjustly. That's why we're planning to go back to France when this is over. We believe that we can find someone there who will testify to the truth on my behalf."

Thankfully, Cristoval didn't inquire as to whom this witness would have to testify. Only the pope himself would be able to reverse the ruling against Fox.

"I'm sorry for your troubles," Cristoval said. "I wish you Godspeed on righting these wrongs."

They had reached the descending portion of the trek, so Fox slowed his pace even further, taking each step down carefully and guiding Zephyr so that his footing was sure before taking the next stair.

The town of Ston was pitch-black before them. Not a single fire burned inside a house, indicating that Bogun had positioned every single one of his men in the encampment outside Mali Ston.

"What of your lands?" Fox asked, as he took a moment to stop on a flat section for a short rest.

"My home in Córdoba is with my sister Madelena. She is managing it while Lorenzo and I went on pilgrimage. Now I have to return without him. But I couldn't imagine telling her about his death, so I wrote it all down in a letter trying to explain." He pulled a folded piece of parchment from his cotte.

He paused for a long while after putting it away, but Fox sensed he had more to say, so he stayed quiet. Finally Cristoval continued. "Lorenzo died before he could tell me what he wanted me to say to Madelena."

"What do you think he'd want to tell her?"

"That I was reckless and didn't protect him as I should have."

"You don't really think that, do you?"

"No. That's me speaking, not Lorenzo. He'd likely have told her to take care of me. He was that kind of brother, never thinking of himself."

"Except for when he stole those honey cakes."

That got a rueful laugh out of Cristoval. "I suppose 'never' is a strong word. I wrote her the truth. Lorenzo died in service to others."

"He sounds like a great brother."

"He was. Like yours must have been."

They remained silent the rest of the way down. When they got safely to the bottom, they found a water trough for the horses and took time to rest as they went over their plan.

They had to kill Bogun so that the Serbians would flee in terror at the sight of the fire-breathing dragon. But they had to separate the Serbian commander from his men to do that. They'd spotted Bogun and four other men on horseback when his army assembled on the field. That seemed to be the extent of mounted soldiers. If they could get Bogun to give chase, Fox and Cristoval would have an opportunity to decapitate the Serbian leadership, even though they'd be outnumbered. The attack might continue even without him, but Fox didn't think the second-in-command would be as resolute.

"I'll take the lead," he said. "Comis likes to follow Zephyr."

"And we just ride past the encampment as though we're heading for Dubrovnik?"

"We know that Bogun killed the garrison soldier to stop him from doing so. He's likely to want to do the same to us."

"How can we be sure Bogun himself will follow?"

"We have to make sure he sees that it's us."

"Are you sure we can get to the ambush location before they arrive?"

"Zephyr and Comis are fast."

Cristoval shook his head. "Fast enough to outrun crossbows?"

"That's the whole reason we've made this trip. They would have spotted us the moment we opened the gate. We would have been riding right past their encampment toward Dubrovnik. But there's enough open land behind them to get out of crossbow range if we start from Ston."

"I wish I had a better plan. But I don't. How many arrows do you have?"

"Three. Willa needed the rest for the rockets."

"There could be up to five of them following us."

"Then I'll have to aim carefully."

"As long as we agree that I kill Bogun," Cristoval said.

"But he's the one we need to kill first. I can take him with one arrow to the neck. You said yourself you're not an experienced archer."

"My sword deserves his blood. Either you swear that I am the one to kill him or I stay right here."

Fox grimaced at the requirement. The ambush would allow him to launch an arrow at Bogun before he realized that he'd ridden into a trap. He could stop this assault with one pull of his bowstring.

But Cristoval knew his advantage. Even if he had made this demand back in Mali Ston, Fox would have had no choice. Cristoval was the only healthy swordsman available to fight. Tino, too injured to fight effectively but still on his feet, was back in town helping to prepare the defenses for the final attack while Willa and Jelena built the rockets and crafted their deception.

Fox nodded. "All right. I'll reduce their numbers to give us a better chance."

Cristoval held his hand out. "You swear to me on your brother's grave that you won't kill Bogun before I have a chance to?"

Fox wouldn't go back on his word even without swearing, but Cristoval didn't know him well enough to be sure of that. Fox took his hand in a firm grip.

"I swear on my brother's grave that I will not kill Bogun without giving you that chance first. But if we are in the thick of a fight, I won't hesitate to finish him."

Cristoval nodded. "I accept your terms. When do we go?"

"Just as dawn is coming. They'll be massed for the attack at that point, but we'll be able to make sure Bogun recognizes us."

"Then it's set," Cristoval said, sitting and leaning against the trough, seemingly through with talking.

Fox stood by Zephyr, stroking his neck and looking at the sky.

At the first hint of light, they would ride. Only providence would determine whether it would be their last. As always, his thoughts turned to Willa as he tried to hold on to her faith that God was on their side.

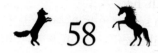 58

Nika wanted to help build rockets, but her mother wouldn't allow it. She said it was too dangerous. Nika had never seen an explosion, although she'd heard the latest versions being tested before Bogun's army arrived. It had sounded like a clap of distant thunder. She couldn't imagine a manmade device making such a noise, and she wanted to see it for herself.

However, no matter how much she begged, Jelena wouldn't let her take part in the process. Instead, Nika was given the task of running for supplies when they needed them in the construction of the dragon. She didn't understand how it would scare off the enemy, but she knew it had to do with the prophecy.

In between errands, she lingered in the house where the rockets were being made, watching from a safe distance. She stood far back as Willa tamped down black powder into a hollow tube. Nika had never seen such a blonde woman before, and her golden hair was mesmerizing.

Still, Nika preferred her own brown hair. It must have been a chore to keep that hair so clean. Jelena would have had Nika dunking her head in a rain barrel every time she went to play in the fields. Though she was now back to wearing a girl's skirts instead of a boy's hose, she had no intention of behaving like a girl again.

Willa referred to the book that Marco Polo had written and given to her grandfather. Then she made an adjustment and pushed the book aside. When this was all over, Willa had promised to read some of the book to Nika. In a whisper, she'd also told Nika that she would teach her to read, a prospect that had excited Nika even more than seeing an explosion.

"I hope I can be like you when I grow up and be able to fight alongside the men. But they'll probably stick me in the church as soon as we see the army."

"That will be the safest place during the battle," Willa said.

"Are you worried about Gerard?"

Willa's hands stopped for a moment, and she took a deep breath. "Of course I am. But I have faith that he will be protected, just as he was when he was with you."

"He saved me."

"I heard it was the other way around."

"Maybe it was both."

"You two make a good pair," Willa said, finally looking Nika in the eye. "You say you want to be like me when you're older. I hope someday that I have a daughter who is just as strong and capable as you are."

"Nika," said her father in a stern voice, startling her.

She turned to see Petar standing in the doorway with his arms crossed.

"Come out here and help us. And stay away from that infernal concoction."

"Yes, Papa."

Ever since she had miraculously returned, her father was more protective of her than ever.

She exited the house to see her mother, grandmother, and cousin with a group of other townswomen dyeing huge swaths of canvas bright red while men cut lumber and nailed the boards into shapes that she had never seen before. Another group of women was whitewashing sharpened stakes. Tino was directing the assembly.

"How is all this supposed to be a dragon?" she asked him.

"You'll see, Nika," Tino said, putting a warm hand on her shoulder. His other arm was in a sling. "For example, those white stakes will be its fangs. Up close it may not look real, but from far away, we think it will fool them."

"How big will it be?"

"Well, we're not building the whole thing, just the head and claws. Possibly wings."

He tried to spread his arms, then winced in pain before the sling stopped the motion.

Zrinka rushed over to Tino when she saw him in pain. She lightly scolded him in Croatian. "Don't do that, you brainless Italian. You'll start bleeding again." Although she was pursing her lips, her eyes were smiling as she rearranged the sling.

Tino smiled at her. Nika had seen that look before. It was the kind of grin a man made when he fancied a woman. Nika knew Zrinka's first husband had died in the Great Mortality, which was why she had gone to Dubrovnik in the first place. Maybe she could find happiness again with someone new.

"She has been babying me ever since I was injured," Tino said. "Of course, I don't mind at all."

Nika noticed that Zrinka took far longer to adjust his sling than she needed to, running her hands down his arm as she checked on him. Nika made a face at this display.

"Nika," her father said sharply, "I want you to go to the house where we're staying and get another kettle. The dyeing isn't going fast enough, so we need to mix more."

"Yes, Papa."

Before she could run off, her father grabbed her by the arm and pulled her into a tight embrace. He gently ran his fingers over her cropped hair.

"I keep forgetting how big you're growing."

"Unless you're getting smaller."

Petar laughed, his heaving chest like a warm blanket against her face. Nika wanted to stay this way all night, but he held her away and swatted her playfully on the rear. "Now go."

Nika took off running. When she got to her temporary house in Mali Ston, she ran inside to grab the pot. But what she saw made her insides freeze and she skidded to a stop.

Lord Vitomir was holding her little brother Emerik by the shoulder in front of him, one hand clamped over his mouth.

The treasurer's hair was dusty, and his clothes were filthy and torn. The contents of the room were strewn about as if he'd been searching for something.

"If you scream," he said quietly, "I will wring his neck before anyone can get here."

Nika flashed back to the brutal death of her uncle. She had no doubt that Vitomir's threat wasn't idle. Nika's heart was racing, and she held back tears that threatened to burst out. She had any number of questions, particularly how he had gotten inside the city walls, but she knew he wouldn't answer them.

"I won't scream," she said as calmly as she could. "Please let my brother go."

"Not until you tell me where the book by Marco Polo is. If you give it to me, I'll leave, and your brother will be safe."

In addition to the book Willa was consulting to build the rockets, Gerard had told her about stealing the second copy from Korčula. Nika was so dismayed that she blurted out her response. "Which one?"

The surprised look on Vitomir's face told her immediately that she had made a mistake. He didn't know there were two.

"Which one?" he said with a satisfied smile. "I want both. Where are they? Tell me and your brother will live."

When she hesitated, he added, "Do you really think I won't do it?"

He would. She was sure of it. He had the crazy eyes of a desperate man willing to do anything to get what he wanted.

Nika slowly walked over to her bed. She had been studying the strange drawings in the Korčula book without her father knowing, and he'd been so busy preparing for the battle that he hadn't noticed it was missing. She'd tucked it into an old cloth so he wouldn't see it.

She unwrapped the book and handed it to Vitomir. He opened it to the first page and nodded.

"I've seen this one before. Where is the other one?"

"Willa has it."

"Willa? Is that the blonde woman?"

"Yes."

"Then I want you to get it from her and bring it back here."

"I can't. She's using it." Nika wasn't about to say for what.

"It doesn't matter if she's using it," Vitomir said, tightening his grip on her brother, whose eyes bulged in terror at this strange man holding him hostage. "Go get it. Now. If I hear anyone but you coming, I will kill him."

"His name is Emerik."

"I don't care. Are you going to do what I say, girl? Oh yes, I discovered your little deception long before you put your skirts back on."

Reluctantly, she nodded. She went to get the kettle she'd been told to fetch.

"What are you doing?"

"My father asked me to bring this to him."

Vitomir squinted at her. "All right, take it. We'll be waiting right here."

Nika hoisted the heavy iron kettle in her trembling arms. She considered swinging it at his head, but it was heavy and she wasn't sure she had the strength. She might misjudge and hit her brother instead. Then Vitomir might kill them both in a rage. She would have to think of something else.

She went back to her father, who looked at her curiously when she arrived.

"That took you longer than I thought it would," he said, taking the pot from her. "Time is getting short."

Nika wanted desperately to tell her father about Vitomir holding Emerik, but she knew that her father rushing in to help would probably only make things worse.

He took the kettle to Zrinka, who poured in water and put it over a fire. Her father was immediately distracted by another task, so she took the chance to sneak back into the house where Willa was at work. A row of three finished rockets attached to arrows were already lined up beside her, and she was now completing the final one.

"Can I help you?" Nika asked, sidling up behind her. She hated the thought of deceiving Gerard's wife, especially when she'd been so nice, but Nika couldn't think of a way of helping her brother other than doing what Vitomir wanted.

Willa didn't take her eyes off her task as she poured more powder into the tube she was holding. "I'm sorry, dear. Your mother said you're not allowed. In any event, I'm almost done. But I appreciate the offer."

Nika needed to think of an excuse to get closer to Willa so she could get her hands on the book without her noticing.

"What's that?" she said as she walked forward then pretended to trip, steadying herself with her hand on the Marco Polo book.

"Careful, sweetie," Willa said. "This powder is very dangerous. Are you all right?"

Her warm smile made Nika regret what she had to do.

"Yes, I'm sorry. I should go."

Willa went back to work, saying, "Your mother might need help outside."

"I think I'll check on my brother first. He's alone at home."

"You're a thoughtful girl."

As she withdrew, Nika casually pulled the Marco Polo book with her. She tucked it into the breast of her kirtle as she walked outside.

Before her father could see her, she disappeared around the corner and went back to the house. When she went inside, she saw that Vitomir had tied a thin rope around his wrist that was also attached to Emerik's wrist.

She handed Vitomir the book, and he took it with glee.

"Now you have them both. Let us go."

"Not yet, my pretty young thing," he said, tucking them into a satchel that he slung over his shoulder. "You're coming with me."

Nika's breath caught at him going back on his word. "But... you said you would leave."

Vitomir let out a sinister cackle. "I didn't say I'd be leaving alone."

 59

Four rockets weren't much, but they would have to do. When Willa was finished making them, she pondered testing at least one of them, but at this point they would either work properly or they wouldn't. Perhaps just seeing the flames would be enough to scare off the Serbians, but she thought it would take an effective demonstration for them to accept the fakery as real.

She went outside to see that the dyeing work and framing was done. Now all they had to do was attach the skin of the dragon to the frame, and it looked like Jelena and Marija were already supervising that job. With Zrinka's help, Tino was showing the townspeople who'd be manning the dragon skeleton how it should be operated.

Petar was holding a huge wooden horn that was long and straight, with an end that flared out. He noticed her looking at it.

"This is based on a local instrument called a sopila, but this one is far larger. We wanted to have a way to communicate between Ston and Mali Ston to alert each other about the danger of invasion without sending a runner, so we constructed this and its twin that's still in Ston. It sounds like nothing I've ever heard before, so the Serbians likely haven't, either."

Willa appreciated his cleverness. "The roar of the dragon."

"We never had to use it until now. Are the rockets ready?"

"As well as I can make them. I just hope they don't set our dragon on fire."

"It won't be long now until sunup. We have to start moving

all of this into place to be ready for their advance. I just hope Sir
Gerard's plan works. No one is coming to save us."

She could see the worry etched on Petar's face.

"Then we'll have to save ourselves."

He regarded her curiously. "You didn't have to do any of
this. You and Sir Gerard could have left as soon as you were
reunited."

"Leaving you to fend for yourselves."

"This isn't your town."

"One of the reasons Gerard and I came together was because
of our shared loathing of those who would use their position of
power to take from those who have none."

"That sounds very high-minded."

"Maybe so, but it's the truth. More than that, we recognize that
there is a shortage of kindness and honor in this terrible world.
It's worth protecting people with those qualities when we find
them." She didn't mention that it was also partly their fault that
Petar and Jelena hadn't been able to obtain help from the Knights
Hospitaller.

Her guilt only increased when Petar next said, "I know our
people are worthy of your kindness and honor. But my actions
are what have led us to this point. I'm just happy that you have
overlooked my faults when you offered your aid."

Willa quickly seized on an authority that would give Petar
the heart he needed. "Petar, don't you see? You are the one the
prophecy has foretold."

He shook his head in confusion. "I don't understand."

"*A miracle inspires a new leader to show the way to liberation.* You
said yourself that Nika's return was a miracle. I've seen how her
sudden appearance has given you hope. You are the leader this
town needs. And didn't you mention that people in Dubrovnik
have spoken about independence from Venice for a long time?"

"I've always hoped that was a possibility in the future. To be
free of their taxes and dominion would be the greatest blessing
for our town."

"With men like you to lead the way, anything is possible. That's why Gerard and I are still here. Without that kind of hope, the world is lost."

Petar nodded. "I will do my best to make myself worthy." He looked as if he might say more, but he was distracted by something over Willa's shoulder. "Why aren't those men on the wall?"

She turned and saw two hooded men disappear around the corner of a house heading toward the front gate. Something about their movements seemed off, furtive and stealthy.

Petar must have felt it, too, and spoke to Tino. "Would you come with me?" He picked up the axe he'd used as a weapon during the first assault.

"What's wrong?" Tino said, his good hand instinctively touching his sword at Petar's concerned tone.

"I don't know."

They walked after the men. Jelena came up to Willa and said, "What's going on?"

"I'm sure it's all right," Willa said, although she had the same tickle of worry as Petar. "I'll follow them and make sure it's nothing. You just keep working."

"We're almost ready thanks to Tino's guidance."

"Good. I'll be back shortly."

Willa went in the same direction she'd seen Petar and Tino go. When she turned the corner, she was astonished to see Petar and Tino holding the two men at the points of their weapons. The men in hoods stood their ground, defiantly refusing to back down. Although Willa hadn't been in Mali Ston long, she thought she'd seen everyone in town. These men were strangers.

"Who are they?" she asked, edging closer to the captive men.

"Serbians," Petar answered.

"They crept into town somehow," Tino said. "I'd wager they're here to open the gates for Bogun's forces."

"But how did they get over the wall?"

"We'll have to see if there's a ladder on—"

While Tino was speaking, one of the Serbians went for the sword on his hip, causing his comrade to do the same. Willa called out for help, but the fight would be over one way or another before any aid arrived.

The first Serbian was still drawing his weapon as Tino lunged forward and stabbed his own blade into the man's chest, killing him instantly.

Petar was a bit slower, but he swung his axe while the second Serb had his sword held aloft for a strike. Petar's powerful swipe struck him down.

Petar was breathing hard as he looked at the results of the fight. Willa well remembered her shock the first time she had ever killed a man, so she wasn't surprised at the look of dismay on Petar's face. Tino meanwhile calmly wiped his blade on the dead man's clothes and resheathed his sword.

"That's disappointing," he said, looking down at the dead Serb. "Now we don't have either of them to question about Bogun's battle plan."

A half-dozen townsmen burst into view, weapons at the ready. Jelena and Zrinka were among them. Zrinka went up to Tino and shook her head as she saw a new spot of blood on Tino's shoulder. She clucked her tongue then spoke to him in Croatian.

"Yes, I know I've opened the wound," Tino replied in Italian. "It's better than being dead."

Petar pointed to the two dead men. "We have to find out how they got in. Search carefully along the wall for any ladders and pull them up if you find any. But I can't imagine how we could have missed such a thing."

"We should throw these men over the wall," Tino said. "To show Bogun that his plan failed."

Petar shook his head as he peered at the corpses. "No. Better to leave them unaware of what's happened."

Tino nodded in appreciation for Petar's tactical acumen. "I suppose that will keep Bogun off balance."

"You see?" Willa said to Petar as the men he'd commanded ran off to carry out his orders. "You are the leader this town needs."

His eyes crinkled as he considered her words.

"Who are these men?" Jelena asked, wide-eyed at the carnage.

"Serbians," Petar answered. "They've failed in their mission."

Suddenly, Jelena swirled around in a panic. "Where is Nika?"

"She wasn't with you?"

"The last I saw her," Willa said, "she was going back to your house here in Mali Ston."

"That's the direction these men were walking from," Petar said ominously.

He and Jelena took off at a sprint. Willa gave chase, looking up as she followed them. She could see that they were quickly running out of time.

The first hint of light was visible in the distance. Dawn would come far too soon.

THE DRAGON

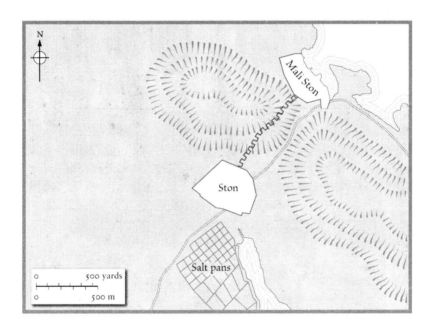

N

500 yards

500 m

Mali Ston

Ston

Salt pans

60

With the sun getting ready to rise over the coastal mountain range, Bogun ordered his men to mass for the attack against Mali Ston. He had no way of knowing if the mission to infiltrate the town had been a success. The two men inside were ordered to open the gates as the soldiers charged the wall. If they had succeeded, the army would storm into the town and take it easily. If not, his men had double the number of ladders as during the previous assault. In either event, Mali Ston, and by extension the entire Stonski Rat peninsula, would be in Bogun's hands by the end of the day.

Cedozar would be leading the army, while Bogun and four of his most loyal men on horseback would patrol the back of the formation with crossbows, both to catch any townspeople who attempted to escape Mali Ston and to deter any potential deserters who were still scared by the prophecy.

The army was arrayed into six groups. This time, they really would climb the wall at six different locations, overwhelming any defense that Gerard Fox could concoct. If the gate didn't open as planned, he'd lose more men, but he would still have plenty of soldiers to repel the inevitable Venetian counterattack.

As the one hundred and twenty-five men got into position, Bogun rode over to Cedozar. They were out of earshot of the soldiers, who were being guided into place by the men on horseback.

"Have you heard any more chatter about the prophecy?" Bogun asked.

Cedozar shook his head. "I think your demonstration had the desired effect."

"I've instructed the horsemen to cut down anyone who runs in the wrong direction."

"And I've reminded them that there will be no turning back. Either we take the town or we die."

The breeze increased, and Bogun looked up. Clouds were rolling in, but they didn't seem laden with rain. However, in just moments, they would darken the sky, mask the early signs of dawn, and plunge the field back into night.

"We'll have to wait for true sunup before we can attack."

"We'll be ready," Cedozar said.

Bogun peered at the top of the wall. The number of men upon it was steadily rising, but he didn't see the man who he thought would be leading the makeshift defense.

"Any sign of Fox?"

"None. Nor has the blonde woman been spotted."

"I don't see that Spaniard, either. If you can, leave both of them for me." Bogun ran his fingers down the burn scar on his ear and neck that he'd received from the exploding mill in Bosnia. "I owe them a payment."

Cedozar smiled. "I'll do my best not to kill them, but I can't promise anything in the heat of battle. And Lord Vitomir?"

Bogun thought about it and realized the Croatian could still be of use as a spy in Dubrovnik's government.

"He lives as long as he's useful. If he doesn't report to me with everything I want to know, I'll simply reveal that he was behind all of this, and the Venetians will hang him for me."

The thump of distant hoofbeats pounded toward them. Bogun looked around and counted all four of his horsemen. Then he realized the sound was coming from the valley that led to Ston.

"The Venetians?" Cedozar asked with alarm, his hand going to his sword.

Bogun shook his head. "I hear only two horses and no footfalls."

"They're riding fast."

"Ready the men to defend themselves."

Cedozar cried out for the army to turn toward the approaching danger and bring their weapons to bear. Bogun called for his horsemen to come to him.

Two horses emerged from the valley at full gallop. Instead of charging at the invasion force in a pointless attack, they angled as far away from the army as they could. The horse in the lead was a mottled silver, the other pure white, the same color as the horse that had carried the now-slain garrison soldier. Both were riding as fast as he'd ever seen horses run.

As they came to a point close to the army, but still out of effective crossbow range, Bogun could just make out the faces of the riders by the light of the moon. The one bringing up the rear was the Spaniard Cristoval. The one in the lead was Gerard Fox.

"How did they sneak out of the town? They must be going for help in Dubrovnik," Cedozar said.

Bogun considered what he was seeing. Fox and Cristoval running from a fight? It didn't fit the men that he knew. They would die to defend the town.

"That's what they want us to think," Bogun said.

"But if they get to Dubrovnik before we have the town in our hands, the rector could send an army to stop us."

"Fox would know that help can't come in time. He's trying to bait me."

"You're not going to follow them?"

"No."

As he said that, Fox abruptly pulled his horse to a stop. He turned to face the army, who were all watching the events in silence.

"Bogun!" Fox yelled. "I see you're too cowardly to take us!"

"You're the ones running!" Bogun shouted back. He was acutely aware of the eyes of his men upon him.

"Only to meet with the Venetians who've come to reinforce Mali Ston."

Cedozar frowned at Bogun. "Can it be?"

Bogun ignored him and yelled at Fox, "You're bluffing!"

"I'm happy to hear that you can take that chance."

"Leave now," Cristoval shouted, "and your army won't be destroyed!"

"This is your only warning!" Fox yelled, then he turned and galloped away with Cristoval close behind.

Bogun turned to see his men staring at him with concern. Then the clouds cut off the moon, and darkness fell again.

If he didn't give chase, it was clear Bogun would be seen as a failed leader to his men. This whole venture would be for naught if they no longer feared him.

He leaned down to Cedozar. "At first light coming through those clouds, begin your attack."

"Even if you haven't returned?"

"I don't believe Fox for a moment that the Venetians have arrived, but the men might. We have to get them into action before their doubts can creep in. I'm trusting you to lead them."

Cedozar straightened up and nodded. "We will take it. I promise you."

Bogun pointed at the horsemen. "You four, come with me." Then he raised his fist and addressed the army. "I will kill these lying foreigners, and we will take this town for our glory, our emperor, and our empire!"

In the dimness, he could see the men throw up their hands in solidarity and cheer.

Bogun kicked his horse into a gallop and charged in the direction Fox and Cristoval had gone, down the land route back to Dubrovnik. If he understood the English knight as well as he thought he did, he had an idea what Fox was up to. And it wasn't a ride to meet any Venetian army.

Fox wanted to get Bogun away from his men in order to kill him.

If Bogun were in the same position, he knew exactly where along the path he'd set the trap. After all, he'd sprung his own there before.

61

Fox crouched behind the rock outcropping along the narrow path to Dubrovnik, the thick forest rising into the hill behind them. It was exactly where Petar had told them it would be, the perfect location for an ambush. His bow was at the ready, three arrows prepared for his pull hand. He crossed himself for the upcoming battle. *Helmet, bollocks, shield, and sword.*

Cristoval sat to Fox's side, his sword already drawn. Zephyr and Comis were tied up nearby, hidden by the trees but accessible in case Bogun tried to escape. Everything about their plan hinged on killing him.

Even though he didn't think Bogun would flee, Fox was ruing his promise to Cristoval. Putting arrows in three of the Serbians would leave just two opponents including Bogun, but it did carry the risk of him getting away.

Cristoval didn't seem to share his misgivings. "We have to carry his body back to Mali Ston," the Spaniard said, keeping his voice low. "We have to show them that he's dead."

Fox pointed at the leaden sky. It was starting to brighten despite the cloud cover. "It has to be soon. The army will be attacking at any time."

"Your wife has those rocket weapons she built."

"Even if they work," Fox said, "she doesn't have enough of them to repel the entire army. And we can't get back into the town to help. The soldiers need to believe the prophecy, and Bogun can't be there to push them forward in spite of their fears."

Cristoval peered around the rock and shook his head impatiently. "It's been too long. He should have been here by now if he was giving chase."

He was right. Bogun had had ample time to follow them. Fox had been expecting the Serbians to be charging through by this time. He was sure Bogun would follow. He didn't want to have to ride back to taunt Bogun a second time.

Then he heard horses galloping toward them at full speed. Four or five horses by the sound. Bogun had taken the bait after all.

Fox nodded at Cristoval. "It's an honor to have you with me."

"For my brother," Cristoval replied. "Justice will be served."

The horses were getting close. Fox lifted his bow and nocked the first arrow, pulling back on the string. He was prepared to loose an arrow at each of the first three riders after Bogun, assuming he'd be in the lead.

But Fox was shocked to see the horses come into view around the corner. There were five horses, but only one rider leading them. He had the reins of his horse in one hand and a loaded crossbow in the other.

Fox had to act quickly or the rider would race past and be free to come back to attack them. He loosed an arrow at the man, hitting him in the chest. The Serbian fell from his saddle, but the horses kept running.

Cristoval saw the riderless horses and said, "Where's Bogun?"

Suddenly, Fox got a sick feeling in his stomach. He turned to see Bogun and three of his men tearing through the forest behind them, swords raised to strike.

Just as Bogun had been hoping, Fox had picked the same place for his ambush that he had used to kill the garrison soldier. He had ordered one man to wait for a count of three hundred and then ride ahead, not telling him that he would likely be a fatal distraction, while Bogun and the rest of his men stole up on Fox and Cristoval from behind. The thunderous noise of the galloping horses masked the sound of their footfalls in the forest as they outflanked the two men.

Fox was fast, though. He was able to loose a single arrow, taking down one soldier with a hit to the chest, before another just barely missed cutting Fox down, instead slicing through his bowstring with the sword and nicking his outstretched arm.

While the two surviving soldiers took on Fox, Bogun went at Cristoval. Since he was coming from higher ground, he had the advantage in position. He swung down with a mighty strike in an attempt to cleave the Spaniard in half, but Cristoval knocked aside the blade.

"You're going to die for killing my brother," he snarled.

"Not if you are as pitiful as he was."

The jeer enraged the Spaniard, just as Bogun wanted. Cristoval charged forward, swinging wildly, his emotions overtaking his obvious skill with a sword.

Bogun parried each blow, maneuvering to get Cristoval off balance. He glanced to the side for a moment and saw that Fox was no threat. He was barely able to stay on his feet as Bogun's best swordsmen hacked at him from two directions.

Bogun finally found the opening he was looking for, stepping up onto a log. He was about to strike what he thought would be a killing blow when his foot plunged into the decaying wood, trapping it within.

Cristoval smiled at his predicament. The Spaniard pressed his advantage, slashing back and forth while Bogun tried to keep from falling over, all the while attempting to wrench his foot free.

Now Bogun feared that he would actually lose. Every slice of Cristoval's sword threatened to cast his own from his hand. Then he would be a dead man.

Providence smiled on him, however. A scream came from one of his men as a thrust from Fox's sword slashed his neck. He teetered over, but the other Serbian was able to take advantage of the situation and deliver a kick to Fox's side, causing him to topple onto his back. The Serbian fell on him, pressing the blade of his sword toward Fox's throat. Fox was valiantly holding it back with his own sword, but he was clearly a few heartbeats away from death.

Cristoval shot Bogun a look of disgust, then raced over to help Fox. As he did that, Bogun was finally able to pull his foot out of the log.

With a single swing, Cristoval plunged his sword into the soldier's back, causing the rest of his body to collapse on top of Fox. Bogun ran at him while he was distracted. Cristoval turned just in time for Bogun to run him through.

That still wasn't enough to kill the Spaniard, though. With the sword still embedded in his stomach, Cristoval grabbed Bogun's arm so he couldn't retreat, raising his own blade to strike a killing blow.

Bogun had only one chance. He kept pushing forward, the two of them twisting in an awkward dance as he did so, and Cristoval stumbled backward. Finally, he lost his footing and fell, landing on his back atop the rotting log with Bogun's full weight on top of him, the sword plunging into the wood and pinning him there. Cristoval let go of his own sword, which slid down the slope behind him.

Fox pushed the dead man off himself and staggered to his feet, sucking in his breath. Bogun tried removing his sword from Cristoval's chest, but it was stuck in the log. No matter how hard he pulled, the sword wouldn't move.

He backed away as Fox advanced, the dagger he drew no match for the deadly sword in Fox's hand.

"You brought a knife to a sword fight," Fox said.

"Give me a sword so we can have a fair duel."

Fox glanced at Cristoval, who was coughing up blood. He looked back at Bogun with pure revulsion. "What makes you think I want a fair fight?"

Bogun could see he was about to die, so he did the only thing he could.

He turned and ran. Living to fight another time was a better choice.

A glance back over his shoulder revealed that Fox wasn't giving chase just yet, but he would. Bogun had spotted Fox's horses when they were sneaking up, so he made a run for them.

When he got there, he tried untying the mottled silver stallion, but it snapped at him and reared up to kick him. Taming him wasn't worth the bother, so he took the white mare instead.

He mounted the saddle and kicked it back toward Mali Ston. She kept fighting him, but a few strong blows from his fist between the ears got her running in the right direction.

As he rode back the way they'd come, he saw the dead soldier and his crossbow. He bent down to pick up the weapon as he rode by, hoping to have one more shot at Fox, but the bolt was missing.

Before he rounded the corner, he looked back once more to see Fox still leaning over Cristoval.

Fox frantically tried to yank the sword out of the wood and release Cristoval, but it wouldn't budge. Cristoval grimaced in pain and put his hand on Fox to get him to stop.

"It's too late," he said. "Go."

"I'm not leaving you here," Fox said to the dying man. The wound was obviously mortal.

Blood gurgled from Cristoval's mouth as he tried to speak. Fox bent down to him as his words came out in a stuttering whisper. "You have… to do it… for me."

He meant "kill Bogun."

"You'll get your justice," Fox said.

Cristoval nodded and began to smile as his eyes seemed to focus on something in the distance. "Lorenzo… Madelena…"

Then Cristoval's stare went blank, and he heaved out a final breath, his siblings' names the last words to leave his lips.

Fox stood, fury flowing through him. He would fulfill his promise to Cristoval. Bogun had to be stopped from destroying any more lives.

Fox sheathed Legend, took his bow with its dangling strings and his last arrow, and ran to Zephyr.

62

With the firm grasp that Vitomir had on her brother's neck, Nika didn't dare scream for help as they hid in an empty house near the northern wall of Mali Ston. By the time anyone came to her rescue, the two of them would be dead. If they were going to get away, she would have to do something herself.

She looked around the house as Vitomir peered through a crack in the door. Townspeople were combing the streets in packs yelling her and her brother's names.

"Where are you taking us?" she asked, holding on to Emerik's hand to give him strength.

"Out of Mali Ston," Vitomir replied. "You'll be safe with me in Dubrovnik."

"I don't want to leave," Emerik whined, the first words he'd spoken.

Vitomir sneered at him, then spoke to Nika. "You'd better keep him quiet or I'll knock him over the head and carry him out of here senseless."

Nika knew he'd do it, too. She bent down to her little brother. "Emerik, you need to be silent. Remember that game of hiding we've played?" He nodded. "You have to stay that quiet, just like you do when you don't want me to find you." He nodded again.

"Good," Vitomir said. "You be quiet, too, girl."

"How are we going to get to Dubrovnik?"

"We just have to find a boat to hire. We might have to walk to find one."

"My parents will come for us."

Vitomir laughed joylessly. "Just like they did the last time. And yet, here I have you again."

"I don't understand. You have what you want."

"You don't have to understand."

Then it occurred to Nika. What if he just wanted to keep them until he escaped Mali Ston safely. He could get rid of them after that. And it wouldn't be by letting them go.

She had to get Emerik untied somehow before they left the town. A blade would be best, but anything sharp would do.

Vitomir had a dagger on his hip. If she could snatch it from him, she could cut her brother loose. But should Vitomir catch her, he might just stab her or both of them with it instead. Her timing had to be right.

Four townsmen went by calling for her. Vitomir shut the door. When they were gone, he opened it again a crack and looked out.

"Now. Come."

He pulled Emerik by the rope in one hand and held Nika's wrist tightly with the other.

"This way."

He led them toward the city wall on the north side, stopping at each corner to see if anyone was coming. When they reached it, he sped up his pace and crept along it until they reached an old piece of broken wood that was leaning against the stone.

Vitomir pushed it aside to reveal a hole in the wall just big enough for an adult to crawl through.

"Go in there," Vitomir said. "Wait for me on the other side."

The hole was dark and foreboding in the dim morning light. Nika could imagine the kinds of creatures that might be lurking inside, but she wasn't afraid of them. Instead, she saw it as an opportunity for trickery.

She started crying. "I can't go in there."

"You can and you will. Now go."

She went to him, grasping his tunic to plead with him. "Don't make me. Please."

Vitomir grabbed her shoulders and shook her as he growled at her. "Do what I tell you, girl."

He didn't notice that her crying drew no tears or that she had slipped his dagger from its sheath.

She spun around and sliced down on the thin rope, cutting Emerik free. "Run!"

No longer frozen with fright, Emerik dashed away. Vitomir, his face contorted in fury, snatched at her brother's shoulder in an attempt to catch him. Nika thrust the knife trying to stab Vitomir, but she just slashed him across the back of the wrist.

Still, it was enough to make Vitomir lose his tenuous hold. Her brother ran around the corner screaming.

Vitomir howled and stared at his arm in abject horror. "Blood!"

He pushed Nika in the chest, sending her flying and the knife skittering away. She landed hard on the ground, knocking the breath from her.

Vitomir furiously wrapped a kerchief around his arm as if he couldn't stand the sight of his own wound.

Once it was covered, he turned his anger upon Nika, stalking toward her. "I'll kill you!"

Nika finally was able to take a deep breath and shrieked at the top of her lungs, not because she was frightened, which she was, but because Emerik was no longer in danger and she could call for help.

Vitomir reached out to her with his uninjured hand. He was going to strangle her for sure.

"Nika!" came a shout behind her. She looked up, as did Vitomir, and she saw her father running toward them holding an axe. Her mother was right behind him, calling her name as well.

Now Vitomir truly panicked. He squealed and ran for the hole in the wall, diving into it just as Petar reached him.

Petar grasped Vitomir's foot and pulled while Jelena kneeled beside Nika and cradled her in her arms. "My baby," she cried. "Are you all right?"

"Yes, Mama," Nika said, collapsing into her embrace. Over

Jelena's shoulder, she could see her grandmother watching from afar with Emerik secured in her arms.

Petar hauled Vitomir out by his legs. The treasurer of Dubrovnik scrabbled to find any handhold to stop himself from being pulled backward, but he was no match for Nika's well-muscled father.

By the time Vitomir was fully out of the hole, a gaggle of fifteen enraged townsmen had gathered. Petar yanked Vitomir to his feet and slammed him against the wall.

"You tried to steal my daughter again?"

"I'm sorry, I'm sorry, I'm sorry," Vitomir repeated, blubbering the whole time.

"He has the Marco Polo books," Nika said.

Petar searched him roughly and extracted the two books from his satchel, giving them to Jelena for safekeeping.

The wound on Vitomir's arm was exposed by his struggle, and blood dripped down his hand and fell off in droplets. When Vitomir saw it, he vomited violently.

"Jelena," Petar said without taking his eyes off Nika's captor, "take the children away. I'll be with you soon."

Jelena nodded and stood, taking Nika by the hand.

"What's Papa going to do?" she asked her mother as she was led away.

"What needs to be done," Jelena replied.

Nika looked back at her father, who was watching them, the axe dangling in his hand. Vitomir, a sniveling mess, was bargaining to the end. "I've got gold. I can pay you! All of you!"

When she turned the corner with her mother and was out of sight, the crowd roared, and that's when the screaming began. It didn't last long.

63

Bogun fought against the horse the whole way back to Mali Ston. It was as if the stupid creature were actively trying to resist him. No matter how much he prodded or whipped it, the horse wouldn't go faster than a canter.

He emerged from the forest to see the army marching forward two hundred yards ahead. It was now light enough for the attack. Then Cedozar ordered the army to halt, passing through the men to see who was coming on the white horse. He raised a crossbow ready to shoot, obviously assuming it was Cristoval.

Bogun waved his hands and shouted for Cedozar to stop. It looked like his second-in-command was about to loose his bolt when he abruptly lowered the weapon.

Less than a hundred yards away from reaching the soldiers, a man's piercing whistle sounded behind him, and the white horse came to a stop so quickly that Bogun had to hold on to keep from falling off. As soon as he was secure in his seat, he looked back to see Fox galloping toward him.

The Englishman whistled again, and this time the white horse began trotting toward Fox. Bogun savagely pulled on the reins to stop it, but the horse insisted on following the sound of the whistle.

With no way to stop from being pulled to Fox, who had his sword in his hand ready to kill, Bogun leaped off the horse with the unloaded crossbow still in his hand. He began to sprint toward the army, then noticed all of his men staring at him. He looked like a coward running from a fight.

Cedozar called out to one of the squads of men, who began to advance to protect Bogun, their crossbows wielded to shoot Fox. It was an even chance that they would get in range to kill the English knight before he could slaughter Bogun, but the Serbian commander knew he would never again have his men's full belief in his leadership if they had to come to his rescue.

He put his hands into the air and shouted, "Stop!" both to Cedozar and Fox.

They both ignored him and kept coming, so he shouted even louder.

"Halt! Now!"

Fox likely could see that he would be killed before reaching Bogun, so he pulled his horse to a stop. The white horse came to a halt beside him and snuffled the other horse.

Seeing that Fox had paused, Cedozar followed his command as well and ordered his men to stop.

"What is this, Bogun?" Fox called out.

"Is your friend dead?"

Fox's jaw clenched. "It's just you and me. Are you afraid to fight me like a man?"

Bogun saw his troops watching expectantly. "I'm always interested in a fair duel, but as you can see, I have no sword."

"Then we're at a draw."

"Not if I have Cedozar bring me a sword."

"And have another soldier at your side to fight me? I don't see that as fair. But I have an alternative."

"What's that?"

"We both have bows. I only have to string mine. We use them for the duel. One arrow for me, one bolt for you."

"The terms?"

"If you kill me, the town is yours. I left word that they should open the gates in the case of my death. If I kill you, your army leaves before the dragon that we have destroys it."

Bogun laughed. "Dragon?"

"You've heard of the Ston prophecy?"

"Everyone has."

"Then you know about the dragon that has been foretold to bring hellfire down on the town's enemies. We haven't unleashed it yet, but we will. It will breathe flames to burn your men alive."

"You jest."

"Attack Mali Ston and see for yourself."

Bogun knew that Fox was probably lying about the town giving up if he died, but he had to accept Fox's terms or suffer humiliation in front of his men at the very moment of attack. He was surprised that Fox agreed to this form of duel. A cranked and loaded crossbow was much quicker to shoot than a bow and arrow. From this distance, he couldn't miss. Once he'd killed the English vermin, he'd be in an even stronger position in the coming battle.

"I agree to your terms. But Cedozar will have to bring me a bolt."

Now that Fox had accepted the duel in plain view, each of them would have to wait for the other to be ready. To act before then would be disastrous for his reputation.

Fox dismounted and detached the broken string from his bow. "Have him shoot it to you from there. It will still be usable when it hits the ground."

He nodded at Cedozar, who raised his crossbow.

Willa watched everything from the battlements of the wall, her heart pounding at the sight of Gerard on the other side of the army. Even at this distance, she could see that he was tensed for a fight.

"Can you hear what they're saying?" Tino asked. A torch was in his good hand, ready to light the rocket fuses.

Willa shook her head. "They're too far away. But it looks like Gerard and Bogun are going to fight."

"With swords?"

"No. Look."

The Serbian who had come into Mali Ston with Vitomir pointed a crossbow into the sky in Bogun's direction. He loosed the bolt, and it rose in an arc and landed next to Bogun, who picked it up and placed it into the crossbow in his hands.

At the same time, Gerard was stringing his bow. He had a single arrow in his hand.

Tino marveled at what he was seeing. "It looks like some kind of duel. What is Fox doing?"

"He must have a reason to fight Bogun this way," Willa answered.

Petar came up to them, a bloody axe in one hand and the horn in the other.

"What happened to you?" Tino asked.

"We found Vitomir," Petar said. "The people of Mali Ston showed him how unwelcome he was."

He looked out at the field. "Who is that?"

"Gerard and Bogun," Willa said. "I wish I could hear them, but we think they're having a duel. Gerard knows what he's doing." She said the last as confidently as her pounding heart would allow.

"With bows?"

"Gerard is a master with a bow."

"I know," Petar said. "I saw for myself back on the ship. But against a crossbow?"

Willa couldn't respond. She felt her insides being pricked by needles as she watched helplessly.

Gerard walked away from Zephyr to give himself room, holding the bow at his side and the arrow in his draw hand.

Bogun set the bolt in his crossbow and held it easily in his hands across his body. All he had to do was raise it and pull the trigger, while Gerard had to nock his arrow and pull the string back in the same amount of time.

Willa knew she had to anticipate the next act that Gerard was setting the stage for. Despite her fears for her husband, she tore herself away from the sight, determined to justify his faith in her. She turned to Petar and Tino, saying, "Help me ready the dragon."

Fox wasn't sure if his suggestion was a good idea, but he was committed to it now. For all he knew, Bogun was an even better shot with a crossbow than Fox was with a bow and arrow.

They stared at each other as Fox tried to get a hint of any movement that Bogun was going to shoot. The decision was *when* to shoot.

If Fox shot first and missed, Bogun would be able to take his leisure to loose his bolt. But if Fox waited to let him go first, Bogun might hit Fox and keep him from shooting his arrow at all.

Better to see him raise the crossbow and shoot at the same time. Bogun would be concentrating on his own shot and less likely to be able to avoid the incoming arrow. As Bogun stood there studying him, he was likely thinking the same thing. The only question was who would make the first move.

Fox thought that Willa must be watching him from the top of the city wall. He wanted to signal her in some way in case this was his last moment, but any movement would distract from his task at hand. He slowed his breathing and focused on Bogun.

The edge of Bogun's lip curled into a smile, as if he were already savoring his victory. He nodded.

Then his arm twitched. This was the moment.

Bogun wasn't going to let Fox get the first move. He snapped the crossbow up to bear, but he was shocked at how lightning fast Fox was.

The Englishman had the arrow nocked and was pulling back on the string as Bogun leveled the crossbow at him and activated the trigger.

Time seemed to slow in that instant. The air stilled, and everything fell silent.

Bogun never took his eyes off the bolt, which flew in a straight line aimed at Fox's heart. As the English knight loosed the arrow, his body turned, but it wasn't enough. The bolt went into his side, and Fox fell to the ground.

Satisfied that he'd won, Bogun tried to sigh with relief. But his breath wouldn't come.

He looked down and what he saw didn't make sense at first. Then he realized Fox's arrow was protruding from his chest.

He tried to suck in air, but his lungs wouldn't respond. He collapsed to his knees, then keeled over on his side. He could see his army and the city wall behind them as the life ebbed from him.

Cedozar stared at him, stunned. Then anger twisted his face. He turned and raised a fist into the sky as he charged through the army, who swung around to follow their new leader. Bogun knew that Cedozar would ignore the bargain his leader had made with the Englishman and use his death to muster the troops for the assault.

Bogun sensed that he didn't have long to live, but at least his name would be known to the entirety of Serbia as the man who'd conquered Ston for His Imperial Highness. Songs would be sung about him throughout the empire.

Then he heard a terrifying sound that sent a chill through his body. It was a maddened cry issued by a demon unleased from the pits of Hell. Was the Devil coming for his soul?

Though his vision was narrowing, he could clearly see the fearsome sight that was appearing at the top of Mali Ston's wall as the hideous call continued to rend the air.

A massive scarlet claw with black talons came over the parapet, followed by a second one a full ten feet away, implying a massive creature hauling itself up.

The army came to a stop at the horrific sight. Could what he was seeing be real or was the pain and fuzzy vision playing tricks on his mind? Bogun willed his soldiers to proceed, but his mouth made no sound.

Then a monstrous head with horns and glowing eyes slowly

rose into view, revealing a huge jaw with white fangs large enough to skewer a man. The hellish mouth opened and closed with each howl.

Finally wings rose behind the head, flapping as if the beast were going to take flight.

As he felt the life draining from him, terror gripped Bogun. This was the last dreadful vision he would have before facing eternity, and he feared it was a sign of the tortures that awaited him.

It seemed that the prophecy was true. The people of Ston really did have a dragon.

64

Willa was still paralyzed by the sight of Gerard going down when he was hit by the crossbow bolt. She couldn't believe she'd had to witness him being killed by Bogun, who was motionless on his side with an arrow jutting from the center of his chest. She watched Gerard for any sign of movement, praying that he'd get up, but he lay still.

Could Gerard have come all this way just to be slain right in front of her? Her face was numb, and her body quaked with horror at the sight of his unmoving figure. It was only Tino's prodding that jolted her out of her shock.

He held up the rocket in his hand. "We have to do it now!"

As frightened as she was about Gerard, she didn't have time to dwell on his condition. Even with Bogun defeated, they were all going to die if they didn't carry out the plan.

Operating the dragon took extensive coordination, directed by Tino, but Willa was relieved to see it was having the desired effect. Even from this distance, she could see how scared the Serbians were of the devilish figure. Their forward movement had stopped, but she knew their hesitation might only be temporary.

"Raise the wings up and down like you're flapping them," Tino said to each duo of men holding up the pieces of lumber controlling the two wing sections. "Not too fast. Just enough to look threatening."

The practice they'd undertaken during the night had paid off. One man was working the jaw in concert with every blow of

Petar's horn. The lanterns behind the eyes glowed red through the cloth in front of them. The whitewashed fangs looked sharp and hungry.

From this angle, the dragon wasn't frightening at all. Just a hollow shell with people maneuvering it from below. But when she had seen the completed combination from the front, it looked impressively real. From farther away in the diminished light of the cloudy early morning, it had to be an unholy sight.

"Why aren't they running away?" Tino said, frustrated at the army's immobility.

Willa pointed at the man leading them. It was Cedozar, the same one who was with Vitomir when the garrison was wiped out.

"He must be keeping them to heel."

"The rockets?"

She nodded. "Let's try it."

As they'd practiced, Tino set the first rocket arrow on the stand inside the dragon's jaw. They'd made it adjustable so it could be aimed, and he angled it so that it was pointing straight down at the arrayed force on the field.

The new Serbian leader cried out and waved his men forward. They started marching anew toward the wall.

"Light the fuse," Willa said. "Petar, sound the horn."

The jaw opened, and Petar blew on his instrument, producing the terrifying otherworldly roar. Tino dipped the torch down and tapped the flame against the string. It began burning, and all of them stepped back. They'd cleared the space behind the rocket of any of the dyed cloth, but even so, if the arrow went awry, it could hit the fabric, setting it afire. The entire ruse would be revealed.

The rocket ignited, and the arrow went shooting out of the dragon's mouth, but the angle was wrong. It flew over the heads of the soldiers and landed between Gerard and Bogun's prone bodies, exploding in a gush of flames.

Even though it had missed hitting anyone, the rocket had done its job. The army came to a halt once again, the soldiers yelling and chattering to themselves about the radical demonstration of power. Cedozar tried to calm them down, but Tino already had the next rocket in place and the rolled linen string lit.

She pointed to Petar to sound his horn again.

As he finished, the rocket leaped out of the dragon's mouth. This time, the aim was true. It landed amidst the army, blowing up among a half dozen men, who were thrown to the ground by the blast.

Now they were in complete disarray, but Willa's eyes kept flicking to Gerard, urging him to stir. Her breath caught when she thought she saw a flicker of movement in his arm but feared that her eyes were creating what she wanted desperately to see.

Then he lifted his head, and she nearly fainted with relief. With careful and deliberate measures, he got to his feet and let out a whistle. Both Zephyr and Comis trotted over to him. He was too far away for her to tell how badly he was hurt, but she saw that it took him much longer than usual to mount the saddle.

Without needing to be told, Tino had the third rocket in the cradle of the stand and ready to fire. This time, it was aimed even lower, at Cedozar, who was trying in vain to rally his troops for the assault.

Flames shot from the rocket's tail, and it launched right at the Serbian leader. He screamed as it shot straight toward him, and when it impacted his torso, it exploded in a shower of fire, setting his clothes ablaze. Howling with an agonized shriek, Cedozar staggered around like a human torch, waving his arms wildly as he tried to extinguish the flames, then finally went silent and collapsed as the fire continued to consume him.

With Bogun felled by an arrow and Cedozar killed by the demonic beast, the prophecy's fulfillment was complete. Any Serbians who stayed to fight would be sent to perdition by the dragon, so they threw down their weapons and retreated in a chaotic panic, heading for the valley whence they came and presumably back to the ships that had brought them to Ston.

For good measure, Tino fired off the final rocket at the

stragglers, causing them to run even faster to get away from their nightmarish tormentor.

The residents of Ston and Mali Ston let out a cheer at seeing the invaders vanquished. The town was saved, just as the prophecy had foretold.

With the army fleeing, Gerard rode toward Mali Ston.

"Open the gates!" Willa called out. She sprinted for the stairs.

By the time she got down to the ground level, Gerard was coming through the gates.

A crossbow bolt had pierced his tunic on his left side. He let out a cry of pain as he climbed down from Zephyr, then collapsed to his knees as he took in shallow breaths from the exertion and pain.

Willa cupped his cheeks with her hands. "Why did you scare me like that?"

"I had to make it look good for the army, didn't I?"

She glanced at the bolt, whose scarlet point stuck out of the back of the tunic. From its position, it likely punctured only flesh, not vital organs.

"Is it bad?"

He shook his head and spoke through gritted teeth. "Nothing you can't mend, I'm sure. But I didn't want to take it out before I had your ministrations."

"We'll have to put a poultice on it right away to keep it from poisoning you."

"Your healing touch is all I need. Then we'll go get Cristoval."

"Where is that Spaniard?" Tino asked with a smile as he joined them along with Petar. "The army is completely gone by the way, so you can tell him the plan worked."

Gerard's grim look told them the truth. "He gave his life to save me."

Tino opened his mouth to say something, then closed it. Zrinka, emerging from the nearby church, overheard the comment and put a comforting hand on Tino's arm.

"I'm sorry, Gerard," Willa said, helping him to his feet now that he'd caught his breath.

"I think he'd consider it a fair trade," Gerard said, looking out at Bogun's body that lay on the field of battle. "He got his justice."

"Thanks to you," Petar said. Nika ran up and hugged her father while Jelena held Emerik in her arms with her mother Marija by her side.

"Is it over, Papa?" Nika asked.

He tousled her hair and smiled. "Yes, my heart. We're safe now."

Nika came up to Gerard and pointed at the bolt still embedded in him.

"Are you going to die?"

"I don't think so, little one," Gerard said, taking the child's small hand in his to give it a squeeze. "Not with Willa as my healer."

Seeing Gerard warmly soothing this child who had come into their lives made Willa's heart ache for him all over again.

"Good," Nika said. "I would be mad at you if you did."

Willa smiled. "So would I."

65

Two weeks later—November, 1351

STON

Fox turned the wax-sealed letter over in his hands as he kneeled in front of Cristoval's grave in the churchyard of Saint Blaise. It was for Madelena, Cristoval's sister back in Spain. Fox didn't know what it said, but it was the last communication Cristoval would have with his family.

The midday sun felt good on Fox's face. Except for the chirping of birds, the town was quiet, all the villagers absent. It was his final chance to pay respects to the people who'd died defending Ston and Mali Ston from Bogun's forces.

Willa walked up behind Fox and put her hands on his shoulders. "They'll be starting soon," she said. "We should go."

Fox stood and stretched his side.

"How is the wound feeling?" Willa asked.

"Just a little tight," he said. Her poultice had helped the injury heal nicely.

She pointed to the letter. "Is that Cristoval's?"

Fox nodded. "He told me about it. I think he wrote it in case he never made it back to Spain."

"I'm sure he didn't think he would be buried in a small seaside town in Croatia."

"He knew the risks and came anyway. He was a true knight. I'll add my own letter as well. His sister deserves to know what he did here."

Willa indicated the grave next to Cristoval's. "What about Radoslav?"

Fox shrugged. "I don't know if he had family or where to find them."

"He was just as much a hero as Cristoval. His sacrifice is the reason we're all here now."

"I know. I hope that gave him the peace he was searching for."

Willa took him by the hand, and they walked back to the horses.

"Liberty is not sold for all the gold in the world," Fox said as he considered the price each of them had paid. When Willa looked at him with curiosity, he added, "Petar said that's the phrase carved into the doorway of the fort that overlooks Dubrovnik. I like it."

"If only that were the motto of every realm."

Zephyr and Comis were tied up beside the church. Fox patted Zephyr on the neck and mounted his saddle. Willa lifted her skirt to get her foot in the stirrups, and the gesture reminded him of the day he'd met Nika when she'd given herself away.

They went off at a trot back toward Mali Ston. Willa peered at the unfinished wall.

"Jelena told me that the townspeople have renewed motivation to complete the wall from Mali Ston to Ston and ensure that Ston is encircled by it. They're also going to build a rampart in Mali Ston to make a fortress that they can retreat to in case of future attacks. She was told it was designed to be virtually impregnable."

"I'm sure Petar will see it through," Fox said. "He's taken to the role of town governor quite well. I'm not surprised the rector gave him the position after hearing how he valiantly saved the town for Dubrovnik."

The trip through the valley didn't take long. The fields in front of Mali Ston had been swept clear of bodies and weapons, and there was no indication that a battle had taken place. The city gates were open and inviting, showing that the threat was gone.

They rode into town to the square where all of the town's citizens had gathered for a feast of thanks before the beginning of Advent. The four weeks before Christmas would be a time of fasting, so this was their chance to celebrate their freedom and honor those to be remembered.

A cheer went up as Fox and Willa came into view. Fox felt a flash of embarrassment at the adulation, but Willa beamed from the welcome.

"I'm going to miss them," she said to him as they dismounted.

"I will, too. Do you want to stay?"

"It wouldn't be the worst life, but I don't think Zephyr and Comis like being hemmed in here. Anyway, there's something more important to do. Cristoval got his justice. I want you to get yours."

Despite how fondly he felt about the people of Ston, he agreed with her. The cloud of his excommunication would always be hanging over them unless they found a way to secure his absolution. Even Petar and Jelena might disavow the two of them if they ever discovered the truth. They were good people, but he'd seen firsthand how superstitious people could be in this part of the world. Another good reason for them to depart.

Tino came over to them with a big smile and pressed tankards of ale into their hands.

"I feared you would miss the party." He waved his hands at the lavish affair. Long tables were set with oysters, fish, bread, and stews, all interspersed with bowls of salt from the Blaise and Lazarus pans filled to overflowing to flavor the food as the feasters saw fit.

Petar and another townsman were playing smaller versions of the horn Petar had blown as the dragon's roar. The instruments sounded sweet and lively, and many of the residents danced to the tune.

Children took turns batting at a hanging clay pot shaped like a fattened pig with sticks while blindfolded. When it was Nika's turn, she gave it a good whack, shattering the bottom. Copper coins, candied fruits, and other treats spilled out, and the children swarmed around to gather them up.

"We wouldn't have missed this for all the gold in the world," Fox said.

"Where is your lovely bride?" Willa asked.

Tino looked around, then pointed at Zrinka, who saw him and winked back coyly.

"She's in charge of the food. I don't know how I got so lucky to find such a good cook for a wife."

"You make a wonderful couple. I'm sure you'll both be happy."

"Oh, we are," Tino said with a sly nod. "We've been making every effort to start a family as soon as possible."

Tino had decided to make Ston his home after his whirlwind romance of Vitomir's former maid. Although the speed of the courtship raised some eyebrows, it was clear that the couple was smitten with each other from first sight, and no one could deny they deserved to find love after the heartaches both had suffered. The wedding had been held as soon as possible after the banns were read.

Tino's injury hadn't healed as well as Fox's, but it didn't matter since his mercenary days were over. He had completed his search for the home he'd been yearning for during the past twenty-five years.

He noticed Zrinka waving to him.

"I have to go. She needs me." He raced to her, as happy as any man Fox had ever seen.

Willa waved Jelena over and opened the satchel that was on her shoulder. She took out the two Marco Polo books and gave them to Jelena.

"Thank you for letting us borrow these," Willa said. She and Fox had spent the previous week copying the most interesting drawings and information into Willa's personal journal and Fox's *Secretum philosophorum*.

"I still think you should keep them," Jelena said as she took them. "You deserve to have them after all you did for us."

Willa shook her head. "They should stay with your family. They'll be safer here. I've been teaching Nika to read and she's picked it up as quickly as you have. Ston's priest has promised to continue your education. Maybe you and Nika can read the journals together."

"Maybe we will. But in the meantime, we're going to keep the journals hidden. They've caused us enough trouble for now."

Petar finished his song to great applause and joined them.

"Are you sure you have to go tomorrow?" he asked them. "You can see how fondly everyone here thinks of you. You're welcome to stay as long as you like."

"And we appreciate that," Fox said. "But we have unfinished business back in France."

"We'll find a ship in Dubrovnik to take us there," Willa said. "But we'll miss all of you terribly."

"If you ever return," Petar said, "and we all hope you do, you might not recognize Dubrovnik if those murmurs about gaining independence from Venice come true. They certainly didn't do us any good. Repelling this attempted invasion without their help shows that only we can protect ourselves."

"Because you've shown us how," Jelena said.

"Spoken like true leaders," Willa said. "I can't wait to come back."

"Come back?" Nika asked as she ran up to them, her mouth full of sugared fruit. "Where are you going?"

Willa and Fox exchanged glances. They hadn't told Nika yet about their departure, but now it was time.

"Tomorrow we're leaving," Willa said.

Nika looked at the two of them, tears swelling in her eyes. "No!" she sobbed. "You have to stay!"

Fox kneeled down to her and wiped her tears away. "We will never be far away. We'll always be here and here." He gently tapped her head and her heart. Then he put his hand on his own chest. "And you'll always be right here. So we're going to be together forever."

She nodded, her lips trembling, and threw herself into his arms.

After a long hug, he stood, taking Nika's hand.

"Now, you were going to show me that wooden dragon you carved."

Her mood immediately brightened. "Yes! It looks just like the one Willa and Tino made to scare off those men."

"Then run and get it. I want to see it."

Nika skipped away, apparently already forgetting that Fox would soon be gone.

"You're good with her," Jelena said.

"We had plenty of time to get to know each other. She's a good child. You should be proud."

"We are," Petar said. "Well, it's time for another song. Then we'll toast and begin the meal."

"I'll make sure it's all ready," Jelena said.

The two of them walked away, leaving Fox and Willa momentarily alone.

Willa put her hand on his arm and looked into his eyes. Her loving and beautiful gaze reminded him how fortunate he was to have her in his life. Being separated from her for so long had only reinforced for him what a remarkable woman she was.

"I'll miss them," he said, "but everything I need is right here."

"I was just thinking the same thing. No matter what happens, no matter how far apart we are, we always find each other again."

"How could I not be drawn to you?" Fox said, fully facing her now, the celebration fading into the background. "Any man would thank the heavens to be with you."

Willa gave him the winsome smile that made him love her so much it hurt.

"I wouldn't want just any man," she said. "I'm so glad it's you."

Afterword

Beth Morrison

For *The White Fortress*, Boyd and I decided to have Fox and Willa journey beyond the confines of Western Europe for the first time, into new territory for us in more senses than one. Neither of us had ever visited Croatia, but we had long heard of its spectacular medieval architecture, stunning coastline, and longstanding reputation for maritime trade. But although I have long studied fourteenth-century France, medieval Croatia remained largely unknown to me. Given the amount of literature published on France in the era, I thought it would simply be a matter of digging into the research and soaking up what was offered. Sadly, medieval Croatia has attracted far less scholarship than Western Europe, and almost all of it is in Croatian, which I unfortunately do not read. Furthermore, few Croatian illuminated manuscripts of the period are available online, so another one of my main research resources was also largely unavailable. The fortunate corollary was that we would have a chance to share what we had learned of the rich medieval history of this region with readers who were likewise wholly unfamiliar with it.

Early on, Boyd and I identified two main themes specifically related to medieval Croatia that we wanted to showcase in the historical setting for the novel: the salt trade and Marco Polo. Because salt is so cheap and readily available today, it is difficult to impress on modern audiences just how important the salt trade was in the Middle Ages. In our time there is a general concern about the over-consumption of salt, but in an era before mass-produced, pre-packaged foods, ensuring there was enough salt available in one's daily diet was an effort. Salt was so necessary to life and such a prime commodity that Roman troops were essentially paid in salt—the word "salary" derives from the Latin *salarium*, which was the monthly allowance paid to soldiers for salt.

In the Middle Ages, salt was either extracted from underground mines or collected through the evaporation of seawater in geographically suitable locations. These natural resources were rare, so the commercial distribution of salt was a prime aspect of medieval trade routes. The location of Ston, Croatia, at the mouth of the narrow isthmus of the Pelješac peninsula provided the ideal conditions for evaporating seawater brine in shallow, open salt pans that occupy an area almost the size of four Olympic-size swimming pools. The vast amounts of money made through the sale of Ston's salt made it prime real estate for in-fighting among the surrounding rulers, and thus a great location for the plot of our novel.

The second historical attraction of the area was the legend associated with Marco Polo (ca. 1254–1324). Most people are familiar with Marco Polo as one of the first European travelers who not only made the trip to Asia and back, but also wrote an account of his journey. What many people don't know is what happened to Marco Polo after his return in 1295. He brought back a fortune from the East in gems, and it is said that his claims that the wealth of Kublai Khan could be measured in the millions earned him the nickname *Milione*. Of course, other legends say that the moniker came from a shortened version of the family name Emilione or even that it was based on the idea he told a million lies in his story. What is more certain historically is that sometime after 1295 Polo went to war on behalf of the Republic of Venice against its Italian rival the Republic of Genoa and was caught during a sea battle as captain of a ship. The Genoans imprisoned him, and while there, he dictated an account of his travels to a fellow inmate and novelist, Rustichello of Pisa.

The resulting book, *The Book of Marvels*, became a bestseller of the late Middle Ages, being translated into numerous languages, and is a rich source of information about European knowledge of Asia. There is some dispute, however, as to what battle Polo fought in before his imprisonment. A sixteenth-century travel writer, Giovanni Battista Ramusio, claimed that Polo was captured at the Battle of Korčula, an island close to the Pelješac peninsula. Today, Korčula takes pride in the idea of Marco Polo having been imprisoned there for a short time, and goes further, asserting that Marco Polo was actually born on the island. Modern scholars, however, feel certain that Polo was born in Venice, and although it is not entirely clear which battle Polo was involved with, most scholars think that he was actually captured in a different sea battle with Genoa, one off the Anatolian coast. Boyd and I were happy to go with the minority and place Polo in Croatia.

Our story centers on the idea that Polo left his own handwritten account behind in Croatia during the frenzy of battle, and although no evidence exists for a journal in his own hand, it is a tantalizing thought (and I just couldn't resist having another medieval manuscript at the heart of the story). Many aspects of Chinese culture were recorded faithfully in Polo's *Book of Marvels*, including the existence of paper money, porcelain, and coal burning. We made good use of two other Chinese innovations mentioned by Polo: salt production and gunpowder. Although Polo didn't record a revolutionary new way to produce salt or the exact recipe for gunpowder in *The Book of Marvels*, he did discuss them, and our fictional journal elaborated on those writings to create the basis for our narrative.

So in April of 2023 Boyd and I set off for Croatia with his wife Randi to explore the Dalmatian coast along the Adriatic Sea and learn as much as we could about the fourteenth-century history of the area. We started in the celebrated city of Dubrovnik (Ragusa in Latin and Italian), the nexus of the region's trading network in the Middle Ages. Even after sixteen hours on planes and in airports, we marveled at seeing the magnificent medieval walls of the city rising out of the sea. The shape of Croatia, with a large bulbous top and then a long, lingering tail, always seemed inexplicable, until we were actually there and saw how closely the towering mountains hugged the coastline for hundreds of miles, with only a narrow strip of land between the water and their base.

In the Middle Ages, due their value, individual sections of the Dalmatian coast were highly contested among numerous competing powers in the region. In the earlier Middle Ages, the area had been under the purview of Byzantium, known at the time as the Eastern Roman Empire, but later, the land along the Dalmatian Coast was constantly being fought over by the Kingdom of Hungary, the Serbian Empire, the Republic of Venice, and the Republic of Genoa, not to mention fights among the Croatian and Bosnian aristocracies, whose nobles were called "bans." In the novel, we have tried to give a taste of all of these rivalries and land grabs by the various factions, but we have had to simplify a great deal to make the story intelligible. By the mid-fourteenth century, the area was dominated by the Venetian Republic, and Dubrovnik served as its capital.

The most powerful person in Dubrovnik was the rector, a formal position appointed by the Venetian Republic, and always occupied by a Venetian citizen. Because of the strong Italian influence in the area, the Venetian dialect served as a common language among traders and the aristocracy, but Croatian and Serbian, mutually comprehensible due to shared linguistic roots, were the local languages. The patron saint of Dubrovnik was Saint Blaise, who saved the city from attack in 971, and Catholic churches dedicated to him dotted the Dalmatian coast.

Prophecies such as the one we cite in the novel were widespread at the time, not only found throughout the Bible, but also in localities across Europe. Prophets like Hildegard von Bingen (ca. 1098–1179) were highly regarded and even revered for their ability to foretell future events. Unlike Venice and Dubrovnik, the nearby Serbian Empire was devoted to the Serbian Orthodox Church. Superstitions (including that if you sneeze while speaking, you are telling the truth) were common, especially in rural parts of the empire. Part of the reason the area under Venetian control resisted Serbian domination was the forced imposition of the Orthodox Church. This tense stand-off between Venetians and Serbians provided a dramatic setting for the events of our novel, which begins in Dubrovnik. Boyd, Randi, and I had a chance to walk the entirety of the city's walls—where we imagined Fox hanging from a laundry line and Willa climbing from level to level in a burned-up house—and hiked up to the fort overlooking the city where the entire plot is set into motion. The city, so steeped in history, was an inspirational beginning to our research trip.

Our second stop was the unassuming small town that would be the centerpiece of the novel, Ston. Although today it serves as a handy break for tourist busses on their way to Dubrovnik, the town was far more important in the Middle Ages. Anchored by the Church of Saint Blaise and the salt flats, the small village has surprisingly robust fortifications. Hardy tourists are tempted to climb the impressive wall that snakes up the hillside. Boyd, Randi, and I made the trek, and it certainly winded us!

In fact, the Ston walls are unique in Europe and at 4.3 miles in length, are among the longest extant fortification structures in the world. The wall actually connects Ston to Mali Ston (Little Ston), where the deep-water port was used to ship the salt harvest. The shallow inlet on the Ston side was ideal for salt production but prevented large ships from finding a harbor. The peninsula is accessible only at that narrow strip of land between Ston and Mali Ston, so blocking a ground assault through that gateway prevented access to the entire peninsula. In addition, because as much as one third of Dubrovnik's income came from Ston, whose salt was distributed throughout the Balkans, it was carefully guarded.

However, the walls weren't built until the fourteenth century when the town changed hands. In 1333, the wealthy city of Dubrovnik decided to buy Ston on behalf of the Venetian Republic. The problem was, it wasn't clear who owned it. This valuable piece of property was so hotly contested that Dubrovnik ended up paying for it twice, just to ensure clear title. It paid both the Bosnians and the Serbians for the rights to control the whole Pelješac peninsula, including salt production in Ston. The Serbian king—and later emperor—Dušan (ca. 1308–1355) was at that time in sore need of money in the hopes of generating enough funds for his army to turn his kingdom into an empire, a feat he accomplished in 1346. When Dubrovnik bought the Pelješac peninsula from Dušan in 1333, perhaps not trusting the sellers, a plan was immediately established to build fortifications completely surrounding Ston and Mali Ston, as well as a strong wall to connect them. Such ambitions take time, but according to Dr. Andrej Žmegač, a leading scholar of the archeological findings at Ston, records indicate that by the end of the 1340s, it had been determined to finish building all the walls, although it remains unclear when they were actually completed (Boyd and I used that imprecision to our advantage in the story).

The entire reason behind the enormous effort of building the walls was to protect the prized Ston salt industry. The salt harvest takes place under the hot sun of the summer, used to gradually intensify the salt brine over a period of months, so although Boyd, Randi, and I visiting in April were too early for the main action, we were able to wander among the fallow salt pans. We admired the sluice gates used to allow the increasingly salinated water to flow into the next salt pan where it would eventually dry into white crystals and be raked into huge piles for transport by cart up to the enormous warehouse for storage, before being transported to the port at Mali Ston. We found the stone markers used to indicate the nine salt pans by name, each inspired by a saint except for *Mundo*, which means "world." Two of the pans furthest from the sea were lined with granite, an expensive and laborious process, and dedicated to Saints Blaise and Lazarus, used to produce the purest salt, which floated to the top for collection. We even bought some Ston salt to take home to the US, and now we, like others far from Ston in the Middle Ages, can appreciate its fine flavor to season our meals.

Next on our itinerary was the beautiful island of Korčula. Like Dubrovnik and Ston, the tiny town has well-fortified walls all the way around it. Inside, stone houses are crowded side by side across such narrow streets that someone could easily jump from the window of one across to the other. The town museum is a font of information, where we learned that the kitchen was placed on the top floor of these city townhouses to limit the damage of inevitable fires. Down one of the charming streets, we found "Marco Polo's house" where local legend claims he was born. We also saw the tower by the harbor where it was said he was imprisoned for a few days before his removal to Genoa. The main square, where the Cathedral of Saint Mark is located, seemed the perfect location for the scene with our All Hallows' Eve celebration.

The tradition of Halloween being celebrated on October 31 comes from the fact that in the Catholic Church, All Saints Day is November 1. The night before was thought to be a time when ghosts and spirits could return to earth to do harm, so people would disguise themselves with costumes to avoid their attentions. We don't know exactly what form these celebrations took, nor in which parts of Europe they developed, but the kinds of revelry with theatrical plays, games, and even costumes are well attested to by depictions of similar celebratory feasts in medieval illuminations.

We next stopped in the tiny coastal town of Omiš. A small inlet connecting with an inland river cuts through steep granite mountains that hover over the town. We climbed up to the small fort that perches on the lower slopes of one of these cliffs. The last section of the ascent through the citadel takes you through a kind of trapdoor that is so small, we had to wriggle through, but the sight from above was worth it, a panoramic view of the town and surrounding coastline below. It was no wonder to us that this town was primarily known as a pirate stronghold in the Middle Ages. The pirates would ravage and plunder along the coast and then swiftly retreat into the estuary of the river, whose opening was guarded by the fortress. One of these infamous Omiš pirate ships would serve as the proving ground for the newly formed team of mercenaries Fox puts together to help Ston.

Split, the former seaside retirement home of Roman Emperor Diocletian (ca. 242/245 – ca. 312), is truly one of the most astonishing places we've ever seen. It is the only World Heritage Site that houses a living modern city inside. On our arrival at the hotel, we found carefully preserved Roman windows forming the actual fabric of our rooms' walls. In the Middle Ages, Diocletian's own mausoleum was converted into a cathedral, complete with a bell tower adjacent. Other remains of the Roman palace are clearly visible throughout the modern town, overlaid by a dense complex of narrow medieval streets. We could easily envision Fox creeping along the confined paths seeking disreputable taverns to find his soldiers for hire. The cellars of the palace now serve as the main marketplace of the town, with souvenirs and local crafts sold under its dim vaults that open directly onto the harbor. We knew we had to feature this incredible city for its deeply steeped history that is embedded in its architecture.

We next visited the idyllic island of Hvar. A ferry dropped us off at the deep water harbor that fronts the town. Unlike many other towns we had visited, this one was not enclosed by protective walls. What it lacked in fortifications in the lower town was well made up for by the immense fortress looming over the town high up on the hill, where it could oversee the island's important role in the Venetian Republic as a naval base. Today, the path up to the citadel is lined by flowers, benches, and lush grass, but at the time, the brutal, thick walls must have lent the entire town a decidedly military flavor. We explored the fortress's interior passages, including the grim cells that served as the garrison's jail, albeit with beautiful views of the serene harbor below. We even found a display of historic coats of arms associated with the fort and found one with a fox on it that we took as a positive omen.

Our final destination in Croatia was Trogir, a town just east of Split along the coastline, with its historic center on a small island nestled between the mainland and the larger island of Čiovo. Although it seems much smaller than Split now, in the Middle Ages its protected harbor made it a rival to the nearby city. We visited its imposing citadel and climbed the late fourteenth-century bell tower. The adjoining cathedral, dedicated to Saint Lawrence, dates from the thirteenth century and contains one of Trogir's main claims to fame: the grand entry portal carved in 1240 by Master Radovan, who signed it "the best of all in this artisanship." Life-size sculptures of Adam and Eve standing on protective lions flank the entryway, while strange animals, holy saints, swooping angels, and an intricate visual narrative devoted to Christ's life are featured on its interlocking arches, tympanum, and columns to form perhaps the most elaborate and complete Croatian sculptural piece of the period.

Although we were leaving Croatia behind, we weren't quite finished yet with our trip. Our last day was reserved for a visit to the striking town of Kotor in modern-day Montenegro. During the period of the novel, Kotor was an important outpost of the Serbian Empire, and the staging area for incursions into Dalmatia. Set well back in a secluded bay off the Adriatic, the setting is naturally protected from all attacks. Like Hvar, the fortress is perched high up above the town, but here, even higher. As echoed in the novel, we climbed 1339 stairs to reach the top where the crumbling remains of the citadel provide a remarkable view of the sparkling blue waters far below. The idea of throwing one of our characters off those towering cliffs was irresistible.

We wanted to come up with a fitting end for our novel, and the approach to Christmas proved to be the perfect festive season. Our characters had much to celebrate, including the idea that perhaps someday Dubrovnik and its dependencies could be free of the crippling taxation and oversight of Venice. In 1358, just a few years after the end of our novel, that's exactly what happened. Dubrovnik broke free from Venice and established the Republic of Ragusa, ruling itself as a free state and eventually rivalling Venice in importance and wealth. It was at this point that the city adopted a motto that was carved above the main entrance to Fort Lovrijenac: "Liberty is not sold for all the gold in the world." We enjoyed the idea that our forward-thinking characters could have helped plant the seed of independence for a free Ragusa.

And for those of you reading this historical afterword, the ending featured another little Easter egg. The characters in the final chapter are situated at a feast where the children are batting at a clay pot filled with treats. No one knows the exact origins of the piñata, but one legend has it that in China Marco Polo saw a game wherein large paper dolls stuffed with seeds were hit until they burst. We do know that by the end of the fourteenth century, Italian nobles were trussing up little pots called *pignatta* that could be smashed with sticks by participants for luck. You never know, maybe Marco Polo brought the idea back to Italy via his yet-to-be-found personal journal.

Boyd and I were thrilled to set *The White Fortress* in a locale completely new not only to our characters, but to us. We hope that some of the magic and beauty, both natural and man-made, that typify this fascinating country are conveyed through the story. As always, there are surely mistakes and mischaracterizations of the setting and the history, but we hope that they won't detract from your reading experience as you are swept along in the adventure with Fox and Willa as they try to save the White Fortress. After all, in the Middle Ages, salt was the spice of life!

Acknowledgments

For this third installment in the *Tales of the Lawless Land* series, we were delighted to continue working with a stellar team including our agent John Talbot and our foreign rights agent, Danny Baror, as well as Nicolas Cheetham and Greg Rees at Head of Zeus. They provide invaluable advice and encouragement throughout the writing process, working seamlessly together. We greatly appreciate the contributions of Richenda Todd, our content editor, who is so skilled at discerning exactly what the story needs to provide balance and strength in both the plot and the characters, while our eagle-eyed copyeditor Helena Newton catches all our infelicitous errors and makes sure everything is consistent. Our cover artist, Maxim Obsidianbone, has built on our brand by creating yet another graphic and colorful design that captures the sense of adventure inside.

Because medieval Croatian and Venetian history is not a specialty of Beth's we both had to spend a great deal of time learning from experts in the field. First and foremost was Beth's colleague Dr. Zrinka Stahuljak, Professor of Comparative Literature and French at the University of California, Los Angeles, who was a constant source of knowledge and support. (Her name makes a special appearance in the story as a thanks!) She suggested Beth meet with her colleague Dr. Tomislav Matić from the Croatian Institute of History in Zagreb during his stay in Los Angeles, and he provided a great deal of bibliography that proved crucial to our understanding of the history of the area. We reached out to Dr. Andrej Žmegač at the Institute of Art History in Zagreb, who kindly met with us on Zoom, and was a generous resource throughout the writing process. The information he provided about medieval Ston was crucial to the construction of our story, including his own research and that of Lukša Beritić.

For information about medieval funerary practices, Beth consulted her colleague Roger Wieck, who is the Melvin R. Seiden Curator and Department Head of Medieval and Renaissance Manuscripts at the Morgan Library & Museum in New York, while Dr. Lisa Fagin Davis, Executive Director of the Medieval Academy of America, suggested medieval maritime scholars. Dr. Renard Gluzman, game designer and a research fellow at the Haifa Center for Mediterranean History, and Dr. John Dotson, Professor Emeritus of History at Southern Illinois University, both generously answered questions about medieval ships in the Venetian Empire. Dr. Davide Gasparotto, Senior Curator of Paintings at the Getty, was our constant source for the Italian language, while in the Department of Manuscripts at the Getty, Orsolya Mednyánszky helped with her knowledge of Hungarian for a key scene in the book. Beth's colleague Laura Hubber at the Getty introduced us to Dr. Josip Belamarić, who invited us to spend a memorable afternoon at the Institute of Art History in Split, learning all about the history of medieval Dalmatia. Boyd's friend Ben Curtis helped us with initial ideas on the area, and introduced us to his colleague Roberto de Lorenzo, with whom we spent a magical day in Dubrovnik studying everything medieval in the city. Afterwards, we reached out to him numerous times to check on details, which he readily supplied.

In Split, we learned much about the city from a local guide named Boris Berović, while in Korčula, we had a wonderful tour tailored to the medieval lore of the island from Tina Andrijić. Many of these specialists were essentially contacted cold, and not one of them failed to respond to our request with good humor and great knowledge. As always, Doug Cavileer was a font of information about medieval warfare, Prof. Anne D. Hedeman was at the ready in suggesting appropriate fourteenth-century illuminations for inspiration, and Margaret Scott provided encyclopedic expertise about medieval fashion. In all, we felt that we had an international team of scholars to rely on for assistance, although we take full responsibility for any mistakes we may have introduced into the historical descriptions found in the novel.

We rely on family for support and advice at every stage of our novel-writing, from first ideas all the way to completion. Boyd's father-in-law Frank Moretti reads every word in draft form and by now is a vital part of the process. Other family members, including siblings, nieces, and nephews are our most enthusiastic cheerleaders, keeping our spirits up along the way. Beth's partner John Espinoza and her dogs Willa and Hope prove an unbeatable team at home, content to sit by her side during long working sessions and making sure that she is well fed and entertained in her free moments. Boyd's wife Randi Morrison serves as our chief logistics officer, trip recorder, and plot adviser. Most of all, we couldn't do this without each other. When people find out we're a brother-sister writing team, they often say they can't imagine undertaking a project like this with a sibling. We simply say we couldn't imagine it any other way, and wouldn't want to!

About the Authors

BOYD MORRISON is the #1 *New York Times* bestselling author of fifteen thrillers, including six with Clive Cussler. His first novel, *The Ark*, was an Indie Next Notable pick and was translated into over a dozen languages. He has a PhD in industrial engineering from Virginia Tech.

Follow Boyd on

Twitter (X.com): @BoydMorrison
Instagram: @BoydMorrisonWriter
www.facebook.com/BoydMorrisonWriter

BETH MORRISON is Senior Curator of Manuscripts at the J. Paul Getty Museum. She has curated major exhibitions including 'Imagining the Past in France, 1250-1500', and 'Book of Beasts: The Bestiary in the Medieval World'. She has a PhD in the History of Art from Cornell University.

Follow Beth on

Twitter (X.com): @BethMorrisonPhd
Instagram: @BethMorrisonWriter
www.facebook.com/BethMorrisonWriter